Blood of Adam

To Aleta
May God Bless
You with His
endless Grace

♡ Rachel
Neal

Deut. 4:39

The Generations of Noah Series:

Blood of Adam

Rachel S. Neal

A Novel
Generations of Noah
Book I

withallmyheART
Printed in the United States

Cover design by Rachel S. Neal
Cover model photo from Dreamstime.com

ISBN: 978-1478393214

Printed in the United States of America

Scripture quotations are from the Holy Bible, paraphrased by the author.

To Michael, my Beloved,

for his love and support,

and

To Ruth, my Mother,

who showed me the path of Truth

The Lord saw how great man's

wickedness on the earth had become

and His heart was filled with pain.

He said, "I will wipe mankind, whom I

have created, from the face of the earth."

But Noah found favor in the

Lord's eyes.

-Genesis 6: 5-8-

They said, "The Lord will do nothing!

The prophets are but wind."

-Jeremiah 5:12,13-

Historical Timeline

4004 BC: Adam is formed

2948 BC: Noah is born

2348 BC: The Flood

1991 BC: Abraham is born

Chapter One

2348 B.C.

Denah hoisted her bridal garments and sidestepped a manure pile. The cows watched her wind through their pasture, solemn and silent, as if they already knew what the day held. The grass was lined with wagons, the sheer number confirming Denah's suspicions. A mob gathered at Noah's homestead, anticipating another scandal.

Puffs of earth exploded around her sandals as she stomped through the gate and onto the roadway to wait for her entourage. Grit settled between her toes and hugged her ankles on its climb up her shins. She let it rest undisturbed. Contending with dirt of this nature was simple. It just washed away. Her betrothal was another matter. An arranged marriage to Japheth, the fallen son of Noah, stained her permanently.

Denah lifted her face to the sun, eyes closed, allowing it to color her cheeks with its familiar touch, its comforting touch. She made herself inhale the scent of cattle and crops and listen to the sounds above the low intonation of the grazing herd. The countryside whispered. There was no clatter of carts on cobblestones, no screaming merchants, no crying children, no bellowing guards. No clamor, no din, no chaos. And no soft spoken words to soothe the churning in her gut.

She opened her eyes and turned in a slow circle. The blue canopy stretching over Noah's fields connected to the land itself rather than city walls. Lines of vegetation marched away from the road until the stripes merged, smudging earthy hues along the horizon. A breeze stirred the wheat. Golden ripples flowed across the landscape, spilling only a gentle rustle before swishing another direction. The land itself seemed to have paused, waiting patiently for the last bride in the house of Noah.

"We're coming, Denah!" The jubilant voice belonged to Beth, her little step-sister. She trailed four older cousins, the five of them lined up, weaving through the pasture with the bridal canopy sagging beneath their arms. They dropped it at Dena's feet.

"I've never seen any sort if wedding with one of these before," the oldest said. "Why do you have to walk beneath it?"

"It represents the earth, the dirt that God used to make First Man. It's the custom of Japheth's ancestors."

"No one practices those old ways anymore. Doesn't Japheth know that?"

Denah ignored the girl's sneer. "His family follows the traditions of his fathers. All the brides arrive hidden, as if they haven't been formed yet."

"Yes, but-"

"It's not like I have a choice."

Her cousin shrugged. "I know. I just feel silly, carrying that old ratty thing. And it's heavy."

Denah took a long, slow breath before she responded. Noah insisted on virgins to form her entourage and carry the canopy.

These whiny cousins were the only willing ones she could find among her family, bribed with gifts of colorful new garments. And Beth, of course. But she wasn't strong enough to be of much assistance. "It's a short walk from here, then you're done and you can join the celebration while I wait."

The cousins exchanged giggles and glances. "Umm, what if Japheth-"

Denah held up her hand. "Don't say it." She had been asked the question over and over. 'What if Japheth rejects you as his bride?' How many times did she have to hear it? Couldn't they at least pretend that her wedding day was a joyful occasion?

"What?" Beth squinted into the sun, searching Denah's face. "What if Japheth what?"

Denah ran her finger along the girl's jaw and smiled. "Nothing, Beth. Nothing."

A low hum of voices rose and fell from the land where the festivities were well underway. Denah turned toward the stone fortress that would be her new home. This wasn't like the wedding celebrations for Noah's other two boys. Shem married Eran, then Ham took Naomi a year later, both in grand style. That was over fifty years ago. This celebration was for Japheth, Noah and Jael's first-born. Noah and Jael's disgrace.

Denah kicked her toe into the linen fabric. There was no reason to dally. The path prepared for her was set and she intended to walk the course in a gracious manner. The final consequences of the ceremony were beyond her control, the unfolding of her life beyond her power to steer. "Raise the canopy, girls. Let's make our arrival before Noah sends a search party."

Her cousins lifted the four long poles and spread the woven canopy. Denah stepped beneath the covering into shade spattered with irregular dots of light, a lacy pattern falling on her skin. Her offer to create a new canopy, one without moth holes, was rejected without discussion. The groom's family preferred this one, the one passed along for many generations.

Tradition. This wouldn't be the only one that she would have to accept. Noah's line was steeped in traditional beliefs. They adhered to the old ways taught by their forefathers, believing solely in the One God, the God of First Man. The words spoken by their God were revered, his commands obeyed, no matter how many generations passed. The monumental ship on the knoll ahead of her was testimony to their loyalty and now she would dwell in its shadow. After today the traditions of her own upbringing would be left to disintegrate on the shelf of her past. Their God would be her God, their ways, her ways.

The linen was unrolled on all four sides. She was hidden, buried with the dreams of her youth, yet as the tent moved forward, so did she. Her destiny would soon be decided within its walls. Running back to her father's home was not an option. At least not yet.

It was her wedding day and Denah could sum up her feelings with one word. Dread.

♦

The bridal canopy stopped moving amid a chorus of cheers, whistles and blasting trumpets. Denah found herself standing on a blanket of flower petals. Her cousins embedded their poles into freshly turned earth mounds, then scurried away to join the festivities. Beth lingered outside the tent, lifting a corner of fabric to peek inside. "Can I stay with you?"

Denah shook her head. "You have to go. Find Father and get something to eat."

Beth frowned. "You'll be alright?"

"Of course. I'll be fine. Now go. I'll be out in a bit."

Beth looked doubtful. Even in her simple mind, the wedding carried a sense of unease.

"Go. I'll find you soon, I promise."

Beth smiled then disappeared. Denah stood alone beneath the roughhewn covering. The air grew still around her. Voices rose and fell a stone's throw away but no one came near the tent. For the moment, Denah didn't exist. She was dirt without form, without spirit or substance to identify her among the living. She was Eve, waiting for God and man to bring her life.

Her stomach roiled. What sort of life? The announced betrothal had been a complete surprise. She didn't know how Japheth felt about the decision for them to marry. Noah and her father, Carmi, struck the deal and she had not seen Japheth to gauge his opinion.

The bond between their families was forged before she was born. Carmi and Noah were raised as brothers by Noah's father, Lamech. He gave Carmi one of his daughters to wed. She died in childbirth with the stillborn babe in her arms. Afterward, Carmi continued regular visits to his foster home, despite his grief. When Lamech died, the visits ceased. Loyalty did not. Her father had noble intentions. Today, he supplied the fallen grandson of Lamech with a respectable bride.

Sweat trickled down the small of her back. Would Japheth shame his father? It wouldn't be the first time. Once before his rebellion surged, and it had cost him dearly. His rights as the firstborn were given to his brother, along with the respect and position he held in the community. He should have been the first to marry, years ago. Did he harbor resentment toward Noah? Refusing the bride purchased for him would humiliate his father, publicly, and at great expense for the day's festivities. It would make the crowd delirious, Noah's downfall their delight.

One thing she knew for certain. The revelry surrounding the day's events had little to do with the betrothed couple's welfare.

◆

Japheth was keenly aware of the many eyes watching him. He stared at the goblet in his hand as long as he dared then turned toward the tent at the edge of the clearing. The walls flapped in the breeze but revealed nothing of the woman standing within. He turned around to face his family and cleared his throat. "I'm rather sleepy," he said. He knew there was little emotion behind the scripted line. He had not chosen to be the center of all this attention.

Methuselah, his great-grandfather laughed. "Speak up, son."

Japheth sucked in a deep breath and said the line again. "I'm feeling rather sleepy. I don't know what's come over me."

The crowd grew still, too few of them remembering the response. Ham and Shem took the lead. "Go take a nap, then. Go. Go. Go."

The crowd joined in, cheering and stomping their feet in rhythm. "Go. Go. Go."

Japheth felt heat crawl up his neck and was glad to be leaving the probing stares. He turned toward the makeshift earth, the tent standing in solitude on the same patch of ground where his mother waited for her groom and his grandmother waited before her. He, Adam, was anything but sleepy as he prepared for the nap his Creator induced. His Eve waited beneath the tarp. His chest beat out a rhythm double that of the chanting crowd.

He took in a deep breath as he entered, dropping the flap, so he and this woman chosen for him were alone. The air smelled of jasmine. Denah stood in the center of the space, dappled by sunlight poking its way through the covering. She stood like a statue, still and straight with her hands clasped together. Her garment draped over her gentle curves in folds that culminated on the ground in a pool of blue green shimmer. It reminded him of the great sea, and she appeared to rise from it, created not from dirt of the earth but from the depths of fathomless waves.

"Denah," he said.

Her brightly stained lips didn't speak, or smile. Japheth looked beyond the paint accentuating her brown eyes and realized they were tinged with apprehension. Was she worried he would reject her? Or that he would accept her?

"Denah," he said again.

"Yes, it's me," she said. "Were you expecting someone else?"

"No. No." He had known Denah all his life yet could recall speaking to her alone on only a few occasions, and that was in regards to goods at her father's business. Really, he knew very little of this woman purchased for him. Their announced betrothal came unexpectedly. He hadn't asked for her, hadn't pressured his father to allow him to marry after so many years. He certainly hadn't expected someone as respectable as Denah to be offered to him. He found himself not knowing what to say. Or to do. Face to face, it was his decision to accept this bride or turn her away.

◆

Denah licked her lips. Her teeth felt dry and her legs wanted to fold. Japheth wasn't talking. Or doing, other than to stare at her, his focus direct and intense. She ran her fingers over the fine woven cloth draping her skin. She created the dye and sewed the garment herself, adding embroidered borders in silver, gold and red threads. Tiny bells tinkled as she shifted her weight, from ones woven into her black plaits and from those around her wrists and ankles. Japheth had no reason to reject her based on appearance.

If he wanted to reject her.

If he did, Denah would return to her father's home like a widow. Though unblemished by a man's touch, she was no longer a desirable prize, considered married already in some respects. The bride price was paid, the wedding festivities in full motion, and no honorable family would make Carmi an adequate offer if Japheth didn't want her. She would wear the curse of being his cast-off, unacceptable, unworthy of even this fallen son's favor. She would live under her father's roof, unwed. She would never hold children of her own.

If he accepted her, the respect she knew as a daughter in the house of Carmi would disintegrate like a bloom of jasmine plucked from its life preserving limb. She would be another unfortunate woman under Noah's roof. Mockery would follow her around the market, ridicule clinging to her garments. Belonging to Japheth, the fallen son of a crazy man, would not be the life she would choose for herself, either.

She waited. Waited for Japheth to determine the course of her existence.

He finally let a shallow smile cross his lips. "Fear is seeping out of your pores. Are you scared of me?" He took her quivering hands and pressed them between his own.

"I'm not scared."

"Scared of my decision perhaps?"

Denah snapped her face from his gaze and held her breath. He released her hands, crossing his own over his chest.

"Better not faint on me, Denah," he said. "I don't intend to carry you out of here like a bag of produce. What would people think?"

Denah looked back into his eyes, finding them more relaxed.

His decision was made, she could tell. She swallowed past the lump in her throat and drew her hand there, finding the necklace placed over her head that morning by her father. The rare, pure black onyx pendant clung to the chain like a drop of water. It was an apology, perhaps, a token to ease the unrest in her thoughts and remind her of his favor. Denah ran her finger over the teardrop's smooth surface. Its presence eased the rapping in her chest. No matter what Japheth decided, she would always have a place to call home.

♦

Denah's finger rubbed the pendant around her throat. He tried to make her smile, but the humor fell off her ears unnoticed. She surveyed every aspect of his face, landing on his eyes, searching for a hint of the disgraceful conduct the waiting crowd envisioned. She finally exhaled and her shoulders dropped. "I won't faint," she said. "Married, or not, I will walk from this tent on my own legs."

Japheth laughed. Their betrothal was a surprise, yes. A disappointment? No. Already he liked the spirit within this woman. But he would not make this decision alone. He would not take this bride without her consent.

The crowd outside the tent grew quiet except for the anxious peep of children. "Where are they, mama?" They waited for Japheth's decision. Some grooms pulled their bride from the tent in seconds as a sign of great delight in their chosen mate while others hesitated to increase anticipation. Japheth did neither. He waited, but not to delight the crowds. He waited for clarification. "Are you willing to marry me, Denah, daughter of Carmi?"

Denah blew out trapped air from pursed lips. "It isn't my decision to make." Her hands gripped the fabric of her garment.

Japheth waited a moment longer for her to speak her mind. If she wanted to be released, now was the time to let him know. His God did not allow brides to be returned. Denah shifted from foot to foot, holding his gaze. She would chew a hole in her bottom lip if he waited much longer. Japheth untied the linen sash from around his waist, then gently tied it around hers, giving Denah his rib. "You are now bone of my bone, flesh of my flesh, Denah," he said.

It was done. He was married.

Chapter Two

I t was done. She was married.

Denah wiped her palms along her thighs before taking the hands of Japheth, the hands of her husband. He chose to act honorably and she let out a sigh, the relief gushing through her emotions then cascading from her eyes. She pulled out of his grasp away and swiped the tears from her cheeks.

Japheth stepped back. "I'm not the man you dreamed of marrying, I know. I'm sorry this day is a disappointment."

There was no mocking in his voice. Denah straightened her spine and reached out to take his hands back into her own. He was right, of course, but it didn't matter. The two were one, her course established. "You didn't reject me, Japheth."

A smile returned to his lips. "No. I didn't."

"Thank you." The words slipped out. She didn't know if marriage to this man was actually a better alternative to returning to her father's home. Her mother would not have approved of him. Had she lived, she would never have permitted to Denah be in this position. It wasn't just Noah's eccentricity or Japheth's reputation, it was the curse. The wives of Noah's sons had wombs sealed shut, empty after five decades.

But curses came and curses went. The right god at the right time and the blanket over Noah's household would lift. Denah intended to bear a cartload of sons since Japheth didn't reject her. Although she couldn't alter her husband's standing, she could cushion the blow to her own respectability. She could find fulfillment in the cries of her own children.

"Are you ready?" Japheth had a hand on the flap.

Denah sucked in a deep breath and let it escape slowly. "Yes."

Her husband threw back the covering and led her by the hand outside. She tried to make her smile appear genuine as they stood before the crowd. Japheth squeezed her hand and she could feel his tension ease. His face was relaxed now, his eyes reflecting the brilliant blue of the sky. He had eyes like his mother, she realized, and the unruly nest of brown curls like his father. Today the locks were pulled behind his head and he was clean shaven. A few escaped ringlets rested on his deep red tunic, the light weight wool she dyed herself at his mother's request.

Denah scanned the faces staring back at her. Eyes wide, mouths dropped. A few of them were honestly happy that her father allowed her to marry, but there was disappointment etched behind the shocked expressions. Japheth didn't provide the spectacle the crowd anticipated and small fortunes would exchange hands throughout the afternoon. Her wedding was not the disaster they desired. This made Denah smile for real.

◆

Japheth threw back the tarp and led his wife outside, lifting their clasped hands high. He didn't want there to be any question that the two were now one.

Cheers erupted from his family, then flowed throughout the

clearing as hundreds of eyes fell on Denah, the unexpected new bride in the house of Noah. Japheth watched her cheeks turn crimson under the scrutiny yet she remained steady, keeping her eyes to the crowd, bearing a hint of a smile. For the first time in many years he felt a contentment reaching far into his soul, like the satisfaction of completing a task, without error, without compromise, without persistent regrets of how this or that should have been managed in a different fashion.

He had no idea why the shackles of his past had been released. The betrothal was announced without explanation, and, like any uncomfortable situation in his family, the matter wasn't discussed. The plans simply proceeded as they would have fifty years ago, as if his foolishness hadn't forever altered his life. It was fortunate the roots between Carmi and Noah ran deep.

The union wouldn't be an easy one for Denah. He couldn't scrub the stigma from his name or his family's. If he read grief or horror on her face, he would not have given her his rib, even though it meant disgracing himself again. It wasn't Denah's choice to be in this situation and he would not lay the burden of this marriage upon her if it wasn't her desire to see it come to pass. She cried, but didn't bolt from the tent, or beg for freedom. She was strong, and she would need to be.

The celebration filled the open territory outside his home. The clearing, once a forest of mighty gopher trees, was a now a field of stumps. The trees had become the skeleton of the great ark that sat on the rise beyond the home. It presided over the festive landscape like the presence of the One God himself. Japheth hoped his God was pleased.

Tables lined the perimeter of the clearing, stacked with fruit-filled pastries and honey-soaked breads, roasted grains and vegetables in rich creamy sauces. Servants dove in and out of the crowd with trays of delicacies and large pitchers of wine that flowed liberally from cup to cup. There were treasure hunts and camel rides for the children and hammocks in the oak trees for their parents, permitting a nap before they indulged in the feast for the second or third time. His father spared no expense. Japheth would have preferred a quiet family ceremony. His mother wouldn't consider it.

Today, the stomping of dancing feet replaced the steady drumming of hammers. Music rose to the sky, not scaffolding full of men and tools. Children jumped on tree stumps, waving colorful ribbons attached to long rods. Plates were emptied and filled, mugs filled and emptied.

Japheth hated the pretense displayed on the faces, smiling as they devoured his father's food, drank his father's wine. Only a handful of people genuinely celebrated his marriage. The lure of scandal drew many faces he had never even seen before, eager to eye witness the event rather than cling to the vines of gossip. Wagers slithered through the crowd, the stakes rising in conjunction with the volume of wine consumed. Most of the bets focused on him, that he would reject his bride in spite. He heard of others, too, some regarding Denah's reaction, some estimating how long it would take before Carmi passed out on the lawn. His own uncles and cousins wagered against the harmonious union. Japheth was happy to squelch their earnings.

He turned to Denah. She was a jewel among the daughters of Eve. And she was his. "You look beautiful," he said.

His father told him long ago he couldn't marry until all his wrongs were made right. He could never make restitution for what he had done to the One God, yet today he stood hand in hand with this wife of his own. He didn't understand it. He didn't need to, not today. It was his wedding and that was enough.

◆

Ham and Shem whisked Japheth away from her side. Denah climbed onto a stump and skimmed the crowd. A bony arm stuck up in the air and waved. Beth sat in a ring with other girls, munching on breads drenched in oils and stuffed with cheese. Denah waved back then returned to her search, eager for one particular reassuring presence.

Her father stood with Noah and Jael under the shade of an old oak. Carmi's hands were animated as he spoke, soon followed by Noah's deep laugh. Jael laughed, too. All three appeared happy, genuinely happy. She hoped it wasn't just because a scandal was avoided.

Carmi wore a beaded tunic, lined with colorful gems and swinging tassels. Noah's simple garment had no such decoration and neither did Jael's. Still, her mother-in-law was striking. Many men glanced at their hostess as they passed, their gaze lingering until her look of disapproval sent them slinking back to the shadows. Jael's eyes then returned to her firstborn son. She watched Japheth as he danced, her eyes dancing with him, she in place, and he in the circle of men.

Denah caught her father's eyes and his smile immediately broadened as he beckoned for her to join them. She jumped from the stump and carved her way into Carmi's open arms, allowing his ornate tunic to press divots into her cheek.

"Well, well, well," he said. "You are just married and already you run back to your father." His breath was laced with the fine wine he drank from a copper goblet. His beard, neatly braided and beaded, wore the same crumbly bits of pastry that dotted his ample tunic. His eyes were bright as he pushed her back to arms length, jeweled hands capping her shoulders. "I have lost a daughter from beneath my roof today, but we will see what I will gain in return, hmm?" Denah blushed at the hint of the children to come.

Carmi looked over her head to her new father-in-law. "Ahh, my old friend, Noah," he said. "This is a joyful moment." Carmi turned Denah around to stand face to face with Noah and Jael. "Behold your son's wife."

Jael's radiant expression turned to stone before a word left her lips.

Denah stopped her arms in midair as they were poised to embrace the mother of her groom. She slowly let them drop, searching Jael's face. The woman's eyes flared. Jael pressed her lips into a tight line, her arms into a tight knot over her chest.

Denah ran a hand over her face then looked down at her clothing. Nothing seemed amiss. She shifted her gaze to Noah, whose ruddy complexion paled, then re-saturated in stain that crept up his neck and spread over his face. He swallowed hard.

"Carmi," Noah said, "Oh, Carmi." Her father-in-laws eyes watered.

"Isn't she a work of beauty?" Her father slid his hands down the fabric over Denah's arms and he chuckled. "We are family again, Noah. What's mine is yours and what's yours is mine, hmm? Just like old times."

Noah pulled Jael close to his side. Her wide eyes flittered between Denah and Carmi and the earth at her feet.

Carmi put his hands back on Denah's shoulders and edged her closer to Noah. "She's a hard worker, this one. My business will be sorry to see her go. For you, my brother, it's worth the cost."

Noah peered into Denah's eyes. She stared back, searching for an explanation, finding nothing but his own need for understanding. After a moment, his intensity softened. He exhaled softly and took her in his arms for a brief embrace. "Welcome. Welcome to the family," he said.

Jael generated a smile whose purpose seemed to stave off a flow of tears. She took Denah's hands. They quivered, Jael's first, then transferring to her own. "Yes, Denah," she said. "Welcome to your new home. You look beautiful, and you'll be a fine wife for my Japheth." The glistening in her eyes intensified. She dropped her hands and turned away.

Denah didn't respond. The joy dancing between her in-laws only moments ago vanished. She had no idea why. Did they regret their decision? They looked at her, bride of Japheth, and decided they made a poor choice?

She turned to Carmi in question, but he didn't notice the abrupt chill in the atmosphere. A smile crossed the width of his face. "We must dance, my daughter. Come, let's celebrate your union to the son of Noah."

Denah followed Carmi to the ring of dancers and joined in the familiar steps with the women as they circled the ring of men. Over her shoulder she saw Noah with his arm wrapped tightly around Jael, her head resting on his shoulder. The two eased from the crowd then disappeared through the doorway of the stone wall surrounding their home.

It was her home now.

Denah shuddered. What had she done to deserve this?

Chapter Three

Japheth's side of the bed was cold. He was already up, calculating the amount of pine required for this or the number of nails needed for something else, all before the sunlight made its way across the fields. His face was beside hers on the bed for the first week after they married, their bodies tangled together, soaking in one another's warmth. He woke up before she did those mornings but he stayed put, delaying his tasks of his day for the comfort of her arms. It didn't last. Japheth was dedicated to the ark of his father and its call was stronger than her own.

Denah exchanged his pillow for hers and lay back down on the cool surface as long as she dared before forcing herself to rise. The freshness of morning rippled the curtains. She peeled them back and leaned out the window. The room faced an open courtyard, formed by the home's four sides. Stone pathways divided the space into neat wedges that intersected at a pool, bubbling and cascading over stony walls. Streams ran from the pool in stone-lined channels, nourishing an array of herb beds. Basil and lavender clung to the morning air. She inhaled deeply and looked beyond the courtyard gate, beyond the clearing, to the ark, cloaked within the mist. Japheth was in its bowels.

Noah's vineyards were to her right, flanked by woods that whispered her name every morning. After three months in this household, she hadn't been beyond the rows of grapes to explore the trees and shrubs, the grasses and ferns, the lichens and flowers that filled the wooded region in a harmony of green hues. She wanted to gather ingredients to make dyes for the drab household linens. She wanted to inhale the wet cedar and feel cool moss on her toes. She wanted time away, alone.

Denah slipped a tunic over her head and found a wide tooth comb to pull through her hair. She couldn't go today. Her time was spoken for. All her time, it seemed. Mornings in the kitchen were followed by afternoon chores. These differed from day to day. One afternoon she was told to grind grain, another to weed, and another to form clay pots. The chores never ended and finishing one meant another was assigned. By early evening the family gathered in the courtyard for a meal but no one left afterward. They sat around the table and discussed progress on the ark or the latest news from the city. Nephilim raids, black locusts, the going price for solid lumber. Denah was expected to remain and listen, knitting or sewing until darkness fell.

It wasn't like she shunned work. She was used to labor, but she managed her own time. She could scour the woods for supplies at will. The weaving of linens, dying of wools and stamping hems with decorative borders were juggled. When fabric was fully stocked, she went to the city market and worked beside her father in his shop. She was productive, at her own initiative.

It was different under Noah's roof. Under Jael's roof. Filling that ark seemed to be all that mattered, and her mother-in-law kept the family workforce under tighter rules than her actual servants. There would be no walk in the woods today.

Chatter mingled with the clang of pots and chop of knives as

Denah stood outside the door to the large open kitchen. Jael, Eran, and Naomi had a comfortable tempo as the meals for the day were prepared. Comfortable until she arrived, anyway. Denah was an intruder in their familiar routine. Since her first morning, even the cooking fires couldn't warm the air once she set foot inside Jael's domain.

Denah inhaled the welcoming aroma of baking bread before stepping into the unwelcoming atmosphere. "Good morning," she said.

The chatter subsided. Jael scrutinized Denah's colorful tunic with a sweeping glance, a glance that said what her mouth did not. Denah bit down on her lip. She dressed no differently than she had before she was married and the woman didn't seem appalled then. Jael's daily inspection left her feeling tawdry.

Her mother-in-law's plain garment tied at the waist with a woven cord. Sleek black hair fell down her back in one neat braid and there was not a hint of face paint or jewelry to be seen. The only fierce color came from her eyes. They were blue like Japheth's but Jael's were daggers, stabbing through Denah's exterior into her spirit, the sharp point cutting away the good dwelling there, leaving her faults raw and exposed. She handed Denah a bowl of avocados without a second glance. "Will you prepare the avocadoes please," she said.

Denah ran the day of her wedding over again in her mind. She still found no explanation for her mother-in-law's sudden displeasure. A displeasure that had not resolved. Jael knew that it was she that had been purchased for Japheth. Carmi had only one other unwed daughter and little Beth was not suitable for marriage. What made her turn to stone when Denah came near? What had she seen? Was her mind irrational, as everyone said?

Carmi demanded a substantial payment for the betrothal. If Jael thought the bride price was too high, she shouldn't have allowed Carmi the upper hand in their negotiations. She and Noah were regular customers and knew how her father liked to negotiate. Jael let him have the force of her tongue more than once at his exaggerated prices, backing her words with a smile and always getting her way. The price for Denah's hand was fair and certainly not beyond Noah's control.

Denah had always liked Jael, and thought the woman felt the same about her. Though rarely purchasing her most beautiful fabrics, she took time to notice the details in Denah's newest creations, details that others missed, like the tiny birds among the vines stamped along an edge or the soft drape of a fine weave. There had never once been tension between them. If she decided Denah was not good enough for her firstborn after all, her animosity was mis-directed. Denah had no say in the betrothal. This flinted Jael she faced each day was nothing like the gracious one she spoke with in the market place.

She took the bowl of fruit and sighed. She had no idea what to do with an avocado. No one expected her to work in the kitchen at home. Carmi's servants managed the meals, not the family. She grabbed a knife and cut a slit into the dark leathery skin, then gently peeled the first bits off the fruit, trying to avoid getting the soft green pulp all over her fingers.

Naomi giggled. "That's an interesting method," she said. Naomi stood across the table, effortlessly transforming lumps of dough into perfectly sized rolls. Her eyes twinkled above an amused grin as she worked. She was a good match for Ham, walking the edge of discipline like he did, never crossing the line. Her voice raised in anger could be heard beyond the complex walls. So could her laughter. One side of her mouth smiled as she monitored Denah's progress.

Denah slopped the peeled avocado in a bowl and picked up the second one. Naomi laughed out loud and rolled her eyes.

"What?" Denah tossed the fruit back in the basket. Eran looked at the mess on Denah's fingers and scrunched up her nose. Denah had no idea if the woman liked her. She was flat tempered, rarely raising her voice. Even her laugh hit a midline tone that didn't sound genuine and didn't sound forced, either. She seemed neither pleased nor displeased with life. Eran just existed without sufficient joy or regret to spike emotional change.

"You have to get the seed out, too," Eran said. "Do you want me to show you?"

"Of course. If I'm not doing it right, speak up." Denah tried to keep irritation from her voice, tried to avoid Jael's expression as she looked at Denah's hands.

Naomi grinned. "It's more fun to watch you," she said. "I can't believe you never cooked before."

"I had other responsibilities." Denah pushed her tongue to the back of her teeth before she said anything more, something less than nice.

Eran's small hands deftly sliced the second fruit in two. She whacked the small knife into the seed, plucked it out then scooped the meat into the bowl with a spoon, leaving empty shells of skin to be thrown away. She handed Denah a towel for her gooey fingers then returned to the herbs she was stripping.

Jael watched without saying a word. Her influence formed a shadow, one that Eran and Naomi stood beneath, not venturing beyond her limits. Both followed Jael's example in simplicity of dress and could easily be mistaken for Noah's employees. It suited Eran. She could wear the brightest garments and cover her head with gold chains and jewels and still disappear in a room full of people. Naomi's expressive personality begged for color rather than the drab shades of raw linen and plain wool, though. Neither of them seemed interested in garments stained in rich hues or sewn with a flattering style. They'd lived in this house for years, away from the city, but still they were young and attractive. Apparently pleasing Jael was of higher importance than pleasing their husbands.

The hum of conversation gradually picked up again around her, without her. The women discussed people she didn't know and situations she wasn't involved in. She let her mind go its own direction until her thoughts were interrupted by the entrance of a servant. Denah looked up then abruptly looked away, as she had been taught by her father, as was expected among decent civilized people. The woman was marked. No one was to look upon her face.

"Good morning Renita," Jael said. "Did you see how well the blueberries are coming along?"

Denah winced. The servant woman betrayed her husband. She was marked so everyone would know what sort of person she was and treat her as she deserved. Jael was oblivious to the hideous mark. She spoke kindly to the woman, with respect and friendship. She was treated no differently than Eran and Naomi.

The woman unloaded baskets of produce from the garden and joined the flow of chatter. She moved about the kitchen with familiarity, no efforts to hide her face. Denah lifted her eyes for brief glances, lowering them when the woman turned her direction. The servant's freckled cheeks were sliced into two regions by a jagged pink scar running from the left side of her forehead to below her chin on the right. Her betrayed husband was merciful. He didn't slice her throat as he could have. As he should have. He marked her face and sent her away to fend for herself.

Noah took her in.

No marked woman deserved the treatment this one received. She should be living on the streets, toiling for scraps to eat instead of pleasantly sorting and scrubbing potatoes. Her hair was clean, her tunic fresh and she slept comfortably in the safety of the servant's quarters. She lacked nothing. How could Noah allow such a shameful presence under his roof? He who followed the rules of his god without deviation permitted the face of sin to eat at his table.

Naomi pointed at the potato the woman held up, one that resembled a human head. "I wonder why God formed man from the dirt instead of just carving a potato," she said. Laughter returned to the room.

Denah focused on her avocadoes. Her acceptance in the home compared to the servant's was ironic. One of them was an adulteress, the other virtuous. One freely gave the child she bore to the temple, one longed for a son. One was a nothing in society, the other the wife of Jael's firstborn. Only one was befriended while the other saw less compassion than the beasts in the pasture.

Denah kept her head down, her back turned to the others.

Nothing in this household made sense.

Chapter Four

"God Almighty, God of Adam, forgive the anger within my spirit."

Noah's voice bore through the early morning fog from the vineyard like the call of the great behemoth, anguished, in search of her missing young. Denah stepped gingerly on the stone path, not wanting her footsteps to invade his sanctuary with the unseen God. She couldn't see her father-in-law but felt him as the fog wrapped around her, covering her with his cries to the Creator of man.

"Where is your hand of justice?"

Denah didn't intend to overhear the conversation. The moment was private and she would have closed her ears if she were able. Instead she listened as she walked toward the ark, not to hear the torment pouring from her father-in-law's lips, but to hear the voice that responded. She listened for the voice of the God of Adam.

It was the voice of the One God that warned Noah of the water that was to come and cover the land. The voice told him to build his ark to lift the people above the waters so they would not drown. It was the One God's voice that Noah continued to obey after twenty years of construction. Her father-in-law walked daily among his grape vines, talking to his God, so Denah listened for the voice that demanded so much from him. She heard nothing.

Noah's God was unkind. The ark made him look like a fool. Noah was faithfully trying to please the Creator, given nothing in return. His fields and flocks flourished, perhaps, but what did that matter in a house void of new life, empty of new heirs?

He and Jael were childless more than four hundred years. There should have been many sons and grandsons and great grandsons in that time. Noah let his wife suffer the shame of an empty womb rather than seek blessings from a god other than that of his grandfathers. He could have added wives to bear the children for her. He didn't. That wasn't the way of the One God. Noah was five hundred years old before Jael brought Japheth into being. Shem came two years later, then Ham soon after. Her season for bearing offspring was complete by then and there were no more sons, no daughters. One hundred years later, the number of Noah's heirs remained unchanged. His God was cold.

Denah heard many tales regarding Noah and his unswerving devotion to the God of his fathers. Carmi was an expert on the peculiar man, having lived side by side as brothers. If houseguests didn't broach the topic, her father was sure to work the name of Noah into the conversation himself. He enjoyed embellishing their history together to add to his guest's amusement. Carmi reveled in the astonished attention despite the fact that many of the tales were simply not true.

One fact remained unquestionably true. Twenty years ago Noah's fervency for his God intensified and the flame had not extinguished. He had been speaking publicly of his God's displeasure for a hundred years, before the revelation regarding judgment by the great waters turned his words into a consuming fire. She heard him herself from time to time as he stood on the platform in the city, pleading for repentance, repeating the message from his God. She didn't laugh with the crowds that gathered, no matter how absurd his words. There was no doubt in her mind that he truly believed the message he delivered.

Noah went from farmer to master builder in short order. The expenses he incurred were staggering. The initial purchase of canvas alone was worth a season of barley yet Carmi was paid for the fabric in full. Noah's grape harvest exceeded expectations that season, providing the funds for the tent materials. His olive grove replenished its fruit time after time and covered the wages of the first hired hands living in his new tents. Thistles stopped spreading in his fields and thorn bushes didn't return once pulled and burned. Noah prospered under his God's approval and the construction began its growth beyond the city walls.

Denah approached the great ark resting on a rise in the cemetery of tree stumps. The vessel created a wall, separating her from the village of tents and the construction crew sleeping on the far side. The fog skirt enveloping its sides shimmered in the rays of morning light, revealing the ark's magnitude in segments as the fading clouds grew thinner and broke apart.

The immensity never ceased to take her breath. It measured three hundred cubits from the smooth, rounded front to the tapered skeg at the far end. Not even the temple grounds in the city were that long. Its three tall stories towered above Noah's house and reached higher into the sky than Zakua's temple spires themselves. The structure was massive. Row after row after row of horizontal planking secured to a frame of solid beams that she could not even begin to put her arms around. It was no wonder Noah's family was an enigma. The enormous structure was visible from a great distance and every wandering clan, every band of merchants, every weary traveler inquired about its purpose.

Denah stood at the base of the ark and looked up at the wall of wood. From her position she couldn't see the roof extension with its long row of windows. It was the only place on the ark she found inviting. The rest of the hollow interior was ominous, with only shifting shafts of sunshine penetrating the stillness and never quite filling with light. One could go into a sleeping room, close the door and be in total darkness in the middle of the day. She didn't know how her husband could stand to be in there alone every morning with only a lamp or two.

A worn wooden ramp paralleled the length of the ark. It leveled out into a platform in front of the door where the aroma of freshly hewn timber seeped into the air. Denah stopped at the top to catch her wind. She remembered the forest of gopher trees that once dominated this land. The tall straight trunks, said to be as old as the first man himself, were all gone now, leaving the landscape stripped and the ark its own island in the sea of remains.

She turned and faced the open cavity. Morning light pierced its way through the door in a wide sheath. She stepped into the interior and stood, listening for sounds reverberating in the corridors to indicate where Japheth was working. Her husband liked this quiet stillness, preferring to get a start on his tasks long before the workmen arrived.

Denah's morning task was to speak to her husband, alone, before the pressures of the day wore down her resolve, his patience. Their days of intentionally finding time together had passed. He seemed tired of her company already. She tried to find common ground for them, discovering very little there to explore. He feigned interest in her previous work but she could see that his mind drifted when she described the fabrics and processes required to create them. And she tried to grasp the complexities of all his calculations when it came to the family business but in the end it was all numbers that didn't concern her at all. She wanted him to understand her difficulty with the transition from her father's home, how she missed little Beth, missed the smell of the vinegar fixative, and missed the easy chaos of the city streets. These he shrugged off and found urgent business elsewhere.

Denah ran her hands down her tunic, a striped one reflecting the many hues in the forest. Japheth said once that he liked it. Perhaps it would bring her favor. Denah gathered her resolve and sent his name reverberating down a dark corridor.

◆

"Japheth?"

His wife's voice echoed down the long central corridor of the ark. Japheth stopped his inspection and stepped out of the room into the hall with a lantern. "I'm here, Denah." he said.

Her footsteps made a crisp staccato beat on the hardwood floors.

"Is everything alright?" It was early for her to be up and about and Japheth felt his pulse quicken.

"Yes. Everything is fine. I just came to see what you were doing."

Denah did not look him in the eye as she spoke and she fidgeted with the pendant at her throat, the one her father gave to her on their wedding day. She wore a simple tunic striped with various green shades and tied at the waist with a leather cord. It was the tunic he said he liked once and now it seemed she wore it whenever she wanted something. Three months together and her pattern was predictable. She wasn't especially selfish, never asking for anything extravagant, and most were requests he should have thought of himself, like the extra shelving in their room and the privacy curtains on the window and wash rags that were soft on her skin. He exhaled slowly. It would be nice for her to find him simply because she wanted to see him and that was all.

"I was making sure the newest timbers had been properly treated," he said, guiding her into a small room. A sleeping pallet occupied a corner of the space, set up off the floor by wooden legs. He ran his hand over the wooden surface. "It has to be smooth," he explained, "if one is to sleep on it."

Denah followed his lead and ran her hand over the newly sanded surface. "It's nice. I don't feel any splinters. Why is it so high off the floor?"

"To maximize storage space. Baskets can be stored beneath the bed. One space with two functions." Japheth waited for his wife to respond. She took her time examining the bed but he knew she wasn't there to see his work.

"What is it Denah? What really brings you to the ark so early?" Japheth didn't want to be irritated. He felt it growing anyhow, the seed of vexation.

Denah sat on the edge of the pallet and pulled him down beside her. She folded her hands in her lap and squared her shoulders. "Do you think, would you be willing, I mean-"

"Would I be willing to what?"

Denah took in a short breath then allowed her words to spill. "The full moon is nearly here. The time is here again and I really think we should consider it an opportunity."

"For what?"

"It's our opportunity to, you know, to be blessed."

"Blessed? In what way?"

"Blessed. At the full of the moon by the priestess. At the temple of Zakua."

Japheth felt his face go rigid. Denah looked him the eye and took his hands in hers. "For a baby, Japheth. A son. "

Japheth shook off her hands and stood abruptly. He turned and faced her with his hands on his hips. "You know that will never happen, Denah. Why would you even suggest it?"

"I know it isn't your family way. I know Noah preaches against it. You believe the God of First Man would be displeased, but if that god is angry and we need to find another to open my womb and-"

"Another god? There is but one God, the God of Adam, He Who Sees. It is he who decides to let you have offspring."

"Is that really what you believe, Japheth? No one else relies on only one of the gods. There are many to choose from besides the God of Adam. We can find one that is willing to bless us with children. Your ancestors chose just one but we don't have to choose as your father did. You should question-"

Japheth felt his anger surge, automatically clenching his hands into fists, his muscles to stone. Who was she to tell him that he should question the ways of his fathers? "I should question? I should question the ways of Noah? And of his father Lamech? And his father Methuselah? What about Enoch and Adam himself? You think that is best, Denah? Do you know where my questioning got me once before? Do you really think I would choose that path again?" Japheth bent down and dug his fingers into the soft flesh of her shoulders, peering into her eyes, only inches from his own. "I lost everything."

Japheth pushed Denah's shoulders away from him, throwing her onto the wooden platform. There were tears in his wife's eyes but he walked away from them, retreating to the hall where he paced, a tiger in a cage. Her life here was good, yet she was always pining for the life she left behind. How could she even think of suggesting they enter the temple of a false god? Her words would crush his father. She mocked the ways of his grandfathers and the position of God himself. Japheth slammed his fist into a wooden beam before returning to the doorway. He would not allow her to make the destructive choices that cursed his own life.

Denah remained on the bed with her face in her hands. Japheth kept his voice low and even. "Never mention a desire to go to that temple again. Do you understand?"

Denah stood slowly and stared at the floor. Her hands were balled into tight fists and he knew her own anger broiled in her gut. He caught her wrist and yanked her to a stop as she tried to push past him. She refused to turn and look him in the eye.

"Do you understand?" he said.

"Yes, husband," she whispered, pulling her arm free of his grip and running down the long hall.

Japheth watched her escape the belly of the ark, his sanctuary. He knew he should go after her. But he didn't.

Chapter Five

Denah wiped tears off her cheeks as she stomped down the ramp. Japheth didn't follow her or call after her to apologize. It was his future, his sons she was trying to create. Why couldn't he see that?

Half a dozen men parted to let her pass at the end of the ramp. Bare skinned above the waist, they were already glistening with sweat beneath the tools they carried. Denah stared past them and ignored their questioning glances. Their eyes bore into her back as she headed down the path toward the house. For once she didn't care. Let them stare all they wanted. Let them think whatever they wanted. She was tired of playing the blissful bride.

"Up with the sun gets the labor done."

Methuselah's voice startled her. Japheth's great-grandfather sat on a stump by the stream, where the water trickled over a cascade of small stones. "Come. Sit for a moment young one," he said.

The old man was barefoot and dangled his feet in the current. Even under the water Denah couldn't help but notice the thick yellow nails capping his toes. It wasn't unlike the color of his teeth, at least those that remained. His tunic hung loosely over his knobby figure while the skin on his head stretched tight like a cap, wisps of fluffy white hair poking through just above his ears. Freckles dotted the buckles of skin that rose and fell on his face, traveling up onto the shiny head, getting larger and connecting in brown patches like an old stained garment.

His eyes crinkled. "Sit," he said again. Denah dodged the piece of onion that flew from his lips and she sat on a stone beside him.

"You've been to the ark early. Japheth is there isn't he?"

"Yes. He's working."

"And you've been crying, I see. Is it the men? They've been warned not to bother you women and Ham will punish them if they've been inappropriate."

"Oh. No. Not the men. It, it's nothing." Denah kicked off a sandal and let her foot skim the surface of the water.

"Ahh. Nothing. The great creator of problems. He gets blamed for many things."

Denah smiled at the old man. He didn't pry and there was no judgment in his eyes. He simply offered a listening ear so Denah let the turmoil pour out in one piece. "I just don't understand my husband."

"And he doesn't understand you. Not yet." The half eaten onion in his hand danced through the air as Methuselah talked.

"Has he spoken to you about me?"

Methuselah shook his head. "No. I know because that's how we are, men and women. I have lived a long time and it is always the same. But rest assured, time will connect your spirits." He took another bite from his breakfast.

How much time? Denah wanted to spit out her true thoughts, that Japheth was unreasonable and his ways old fashioned, but didn't as she felt the sting of tears forming again. She turned her gaze to the towering ark and changed the topic. "Does God talk to you?"

The old man whistled through a gap between his teeth. "Yes,

yes. He Who Sees speaks to me. He speaks to everyone who chooses to listen." Methuselah's gaze was directed toward the ark yet Denah sensed he looked right through it, as if he were looking at God himself standing beyond the planking.

"Does his voice come from the sky or is it from close by, as if he is beside you?"

Methuselah laughed and a sliver of onion flew out onto the water and was carried off by the current. "I have never heard the voice of the One God in my ear, like one man speaking to another. I hear the voice of God like a whisper on my heart."

"Not a voice?"

"No, it is not the voice like a man's. More of an impression that what I am about to do is right or what I am about to say is wrong. When I seek answers, the correct path is the one on which I find peace." Methuselah thumped his chest with a crooked finger. "In here, my internal guide to keep me in the ways of my Creator."

"How do you know it's your God? What if it's Zakua or one of the others?"

Methuselah looked into the sky. "In the beginning, God created the heavens and the earth. The One God, Denah. There is but one God, that is how I know it is not another."

"And Noah? How does he hear God?"

"Noah hears with his heart, mostly, but the first prophesy, that was more than a whisper. It was a thought laid heavily on his mind while he was in the vineyard. Pruning the branches, he fell to earth, knowing. Knowing mankind lost God's favor, knowing judgment was coming. A century passed before God spoke man to man in my grandson's ear."

"About the waters of destruction."

"Yes, and the construction plans, the plan for salvation These God spoke to my grandson and Noah recorded them so he wouldn't forget." Methuselah chuckled. "As if a man could forgot the words of God in his own ear."

Methuselah watched her for a moment then cupped his ear with his hand. "Few hear God from the ears he created, but he will speak if you choose to listen for his voice in other ways."

Denah nodded as if she understood. She liked the way he talked to her, even if the words didn't entirely make sense. The old man didn't isolate her, didn't condemn her for being who she was. She had a friend in this prison-home.

"Another question?" He was searching her face.

"Do you believe what Noah says? Do you believe great waters will rise and cover everything?"

Methuselah looked intently in her eyes as he nodded. "Yes, young one. What God has said, he has said. What God has said, he will do. His ways will not be thwarted. His plan will not deviate to the right or to the left, despite the will of man."

"Does Japheth believe it? I mean, really believe it?"

"He knows the truth. Despite his struggles to make sense of God, he knows."

"He questioned God, though, didn't he? He told his father he didn't believe in the God of his grandfathers."

Methuselah released a tired sigh. "He rejected the God of his family, the God of First Man."

Denah nodded. This is what she had been told when the scandal broke and Noah rescinded Japheth's status as firstborn. He would have inherited all that was his father's and held the position of family honor. He lost it all. He was a disgrace in the line of Noah. Shem was now heir to the family wealth and had all the rights of leadership. Her husband had no claim of his own and would work for his younger brother all his life, if Shem would allow. If Shem chose to banish him from the family, he would be banished. If Shem chose to kill him, he would be killed.

Methuselah turned his gaze back to the ark. "He is a thinker, that Japheth, but who can know the mind of God?"

"The fallen son. That's how Japheth is still referred to in town. The fallen son of Noah."

"Yes. He traded his favor as firstborn for a mind struggling to reconcile faith and reason. But that was a long time ago."

Denah picked at loose bark on the edge of the stump. His mind may have struggled but he didn't have to speak his opinions to his father. He would still be the heir if only he let the battle rage and the victor emerge before he stepped out in rebellion. Noah's punishment was harsh but Japheth obviously learned the value of conformance. As she just witnessed on the ark, he followed the rigid line drawn by the One God. He was certainly not the rebellious, trouble making man she thought she was marrying. Much the opposite.

"And you, young one? What do you believe of the ark of Noah?"

Denah caught her tongue before she spoke. She didn't want to offend him, didn't want to tell him that no one she knew believed in the story of the great waters to come. There were plenty who feigned belief in Noah's tale simply to gain his favor. Merchants coveted his business, encouraged the construction, all the while calling him a fool behind his back. They wanted the vessel to be completed. It had a purpose, according to street gossip. A new temple for one of the many gods would be housed within its hallowed walls.

"I don't know what to think. I don't really understand it all."

Methuselah's eyes read hr face. She knew he saw the doubts stamped there. She looked away from him toward a noisy cart loaded with large clay pots of pitch. The elephant pair was driven by a group of rowdy men whose language made her blush.

The old man took her hand in his bony one with the fingers

that bent sideways. "The iniquities of the wicked heap woe on the innocent." The soft choking in his voice made her turn to him again. His moist eyes locked onto her necklace. "A costly gift from your father. It should not be seen, young one. There are many you think you can trust who prove to be most untrustworthy."

Methuselah paused then looked down the path after the rowdy men. "Only He Who Sees sees the true heart of each man."

Denah slipped the onyx stone under her tunic. Methuselah nodded in approval. "Listen with your heart then heed what you hear. When you are quiet, when your heart is listening, you will recognize God's voice."

Chapter Six

Naomi and Eran sat in the clearing with their backs against stumps, bare feet in the grass with a heap of willow branches in arm's reach. Their graceful hands wove the flexible cords in and out of stays, transforming the sticks into sturdy baskets to store seeds on the ark. Dozens of them lined the storage rooms already. Some contained edible seeds, like sunflower and pumpkin while others were reserved for planting. Denah recognized apple seeds and mustard seeds, and the pits from olives and apricots but there were baskets of nuts and baskets of dried beans that she couldn't begin to identify.

Jael didn't assign her the task of weaving the baskets. She knew how, although her hands would require practice to create the tight designs her sisters-in-law formed. Her weave wouldn't be as symmetrical as theirs on the first attempt but she would be able to keep pace after a few trial pieces. She was assigned other afternoon chores. Today she was sent to assist Methuselah with a bath. He refused, comfortable on his mat and not wanting to get cold. Denah stoked the fire and waited until he fell asleep before she left his room.

Eran handed her a basket that she started as Denah sat cross legged beside them. She turned it over in her hands and examined the fine work.

"You do know how to weave, don't you?" Naomi asked.

"Yes, of course. It's been awhile, though."

"I wish I grew up like you."

Denah bit down on her lip, not responding until she could control the snappy response lurking in her throat. "I wasn't pampered. I just worked at other things besides cooking and baskets and such. You know that. You know I worked for my father's business."

"Are you going to make fabrics again?" Eran asked.

"I hope so. I don't know when. It seems my time is assigned rather closely."

Naomi shook her head. "Jael wants baskets, not fancy clothes. You'll never hear her ask you to make something that isn't practical."

"Like these dozens and dozens of baskets? Every last crevice in that ark will be filled. I think she just wants us to keep busy. If we had babies we wouldn't have time to make an endless supply of provisions to store away. We would have real responsibilities."

Eran and Naomi stopped their hands and looked at Denah as if a horn suddenly sprouted from her forehead. She returned their stare. "Why is the curse never discussed? Why does this family just go about their lives as if barren wombs were normal? Don't you care? Don't your husbands care?"

Eran dropped her eyes to monitor at her thin hands. "We care. We've learned to trust that the One God knows best. He will open our wombs when he desires."

Naomi flipped her thick rope of hair over her shoulder and shook her head. "It isn't like we are beyond our years for having babies, Denah" she said.

Denah took in a deep breath and stepped onto forbidden ground. "Have you considered getting a blessing from another god?"

Eran's head snapped up and she slapped her hand over her mouth. "No, don't say such things. There is but one God."

Denah studied Naomi's face in search of a glimmer of interest. She grew up in town, where gods and goddesses were plentiful. Her own relatives didn't adhere to the ways of the One God of Noah. Naomi just shrugged. "Ham would never let me do that. That isn't our way."

"Speak no more of it, Denah." Eran's eyes were wide and for once there was passion behind her words.

"But-"

"No." Eran's eyes focused over Denah's shoulder then dropped to her handiwork as Jael approached.

Denah caught her breath. She had not realized her mother-in-law was near by.

"Are you finished already, Denah?" Jael asked.

"Methuselah refused to take a bath. He promised to do so tomorrow."

"I see. Will you find Renita and help her in the garden then, please?"

Denah didn't respond to her obvious dismissal. She stood and handed her basket to Jael. Eran continued to focus on her handiwork while Naomi looked back and forth between Denah and her mother-in-law. Jael sat and promptly pulled out the little weaving that Denah had completed.

♦

Laughter spilling from the courtyard caught Denah by surprise. It was Japheth's laughter and he was rarely around the house in the middle of the day. She stepped into the shadows of a terebinth tree just beyond the gate. Her husband was on his hands and knees beside the stream, sending showers skyward as he shook his drenched hair. He wasn't alone. Renita, the servant, knelt beside him, filling a clay pot with water. She stood, then poured the water over Japheth's head as he ran his fingers vigorously through his locks.

Denah caught her breath and stayed behind the tree. Her husband stood and whipped the wet curls behind his head. The dripping strands darkened his tunic and sent rivulets down his arms. Renita peeled a tendril from his cheek then handed him a towel. Japheth was gesturing with his hands as he spoke and his words were punctuated with the woman's laughter.

Renita filled her pot again then settled it on her hip, facing Japheth. A scarf held back her hair and she didn't turn her head to hide her marking, looking him full in the face. She didn't show the decency to turn away. Japheth himself didn't turn from the scar, talking to her as if the glaring sign of her unfaithfulness wasn't present.

Renita was a beautiful woman despite the ugly scar. Even in her simple garments she stood with the grace of a carved goddess. Tall and lean, she stood nearly Japheth's height, yet still tipped her chin to look at him from beneath dark lashes. She laughed and Denah's skin prickled. He laughed and her heart ached.

She couldn't recall the last time she and Japheth laughed together. The chasm between them was wide before the fight on the ark but at least the bridge of communication still allowed their mustered emotions to travel back and forth. Anger and disappointment filled the gap between them now, neither venturing far across the hostile territory. They held their ground on opposite banks. Hearing her husband laugh tore into her heart. He didn't need her to find happiness.

Denah leaned against the trunk and watched the man she married walk away with a smile on his lips. She had been blind to miss it. Japheth liked Renita.

The woman wasn't in a position to have another husband, nor should she be anywhere near a married man but the rules under this roof were different. Jael treated her as more a daughter than Denah herself. Without bidding, a possibility presented itself in her mind. Perhaps Jael wanted Renita as her daughter, as the wife of Japheth. Denah dug her fingertips into the tree trunk. Was Noah the one who said no, his son couldn't marry the adulteress? Surely even he wouldn't bend against his God to allow the unholy union. He arranged for his son to marry a respectable woman instead. That didn't mean Denah was the woman of his choice, or Jael's. Or Japheth's. She was a convenience, offered at the right time and by the right man for the right reason.

Denah crept away from the tree and ran into the sanctity of the vineyard, her heart pounding. She wanted to keep running, past the fields and the pastures and the city walls to her own home, her own family, where she found belonging. It wasn't an option. The thought helped her get through the torment of her wedding day, yet deep inside she knew her father sent her here, to the home of Noah, to stay. Unhappiness wasn't sufficient reason to escape her husband. Carmi would make her return. She had no where to flee. Noah paid for her fairly and she was Japheth's wife unless he decided to send her away and that was not permitted by the One God. She needed to succeed here.

Needed, and wanted, she realized. Japheth was the man she was given to, there would be no other. This was her life, and she wanted the union with Japheth to be more than tolerable. She didn't want to be a disappointment, she didn't want that servant to be his joy. She wanted her husband to want the wife he already owned.

She needed to give him a son. Renita might make him laugh now but she couldn't give him a rightful heir. A baby would link

Denah's heart to Japheth's. Perhaps Jael would forget her displeasure with a grandchild bouncing on her knee. Renita would be long forgotten when a baby's cry filled the stillness of night.

The curse could be broken. If Noah's stubborn God wasn't going to allow her to bear children then she had to seek another that would bless her and remove the shameful shroud. Zakua was the goddess of fertility. When the opportunity arose it was Zakua's favor she would seek.

Chapter Seven

Jael strode through the gate into the courtyard with a basket of dirty dishes. Denah waited in the shade for her arrival, knowing she returned from a midday snack with Noah at this time nearly every day. Denah envied their routine. She and Japheth tried to establish a similar pattern after they married but were met with more frustration than quality conversation. Japheth started his day in the ark then went in all directions as the needs of the moment presented themselves. Pinpointing a place and time to meet was futile.

Her husband managed the records for all the family business pursuits: the production of wine, the sheering of sheep, the harvest of grains, as well as the building of the ark. He counted inventory and sealed transactions and bartered for supplies. He could tell Noah exactly how many lambs were born or which tools needed replaced or how much profit they made selling barley on any given day but he could not arrive at a designated location to eat with his wife with any certainty.

He was competent with the figures, competent with his responsibilities. His real interest lay in the work of his own hands, though. He and his brothers were like minded in that respect, the ark as much a product of their sweat and ingenuity as Noah himself.

Japheth performed his work diligently so his hands had time in the day to saw and plane, sand and finish. Denah remembered the feeling of satisfaction in one's labor and that's why she waited for her mother-in-law.

Jael knelt by the pool to tend to her dishes. Denah sucked in a deep breath and joined her. "Did you have a nice meal, mother?" She asked.

Jael glanced up then proceeded to scrub. No smile. No indication Denah was more than a passing stranger in the marketplace. "It was fine. Noah enjoys his biscuits and honey this time of day."

Denah waited for Jael to say something else, anything else to continue the conversation in a socially appropriate manner. She said nothing. Denah plopped down on a stone beside her, the speech she rehearsed washed away like the bread crumbs. "How have I angered you?"

Jael stopped her task and looked at Denah in surprise. She didn't respond immediately and looked away again before she spoke. "You haven't angered me."

Denah waited for her to continue, fidgeting with her hands as the silence grew. "You appear, we seem, we aren't connecting well," she said as Jael reached the last dish.

"I see. I'm sorry you feel that way." Silence again.

Denah licked her lips, pushed her anger aside and forced her voice to sound pleasant. "May I collect supplies to make fabric dye?"

"What are you planning to stain?"

"Some of the household linens perhaps. Garments as well, if Naomi and Eran want me to. It's a skill I can offer. I thought they might enjoy a change."

Jael stood with her basket. "I suppose you may, if that's what they desire."

"I need to collect the supplies in the morning time, when it's still damp and the snails have yet to return to their hiding places. Do I have your permission?"

Jael sighed. Her eyes squinted in the bright light, focusing their intensity on Denah's face. "Is that what this is really concerning, Denah? If you don't wish to be with us in the kitchen then I won't object. I know you don't like to cook."

"It's not that I don't like to cook," she started as Jael turned toward the house.

Jael interrupted. "We have little need of fancy clothing in this family but it is Japheth who must determine if he wants you to continue in that fashion. He's the one you answer to now."

"I realize that, I-"

"Your presence in the kitchen will be missed," she said as strode toward the house. "But do as your husband sees fit."

Denah sat on the stone for a moment before a laugh escaped from her lips. She would be missed? Somehow Denah believed the woman sighed the same sigh of relief that she herself let escape.

♦

The basket emptied as Denah folded and placed clean laundry on the shelving in her room. Beside the towels lay the folded white sash that Japheth tied around her waist on their wedding day. She could wear it for any special occasion. Denah pushed it to the back of the shelf and put clean linens in front of it, knowing she would not ever let it touch her again.

Traditionally the mother of the groom created the wedding sash for her son's bride. It was a show of wealth if there was wealth to show. Many were beaded with fine jewels and precious stones. Others pictured family histories in delicate embroidery, or contained fabric that had been handed down for generations.

Denah made the sashes for her brothers, rather than any of her step-mothers who had no interest in sewing for sons that were not their own. No two of them were dyed with the same colors or stamped with the same patterns. Her father insisted she add gold coins to each one and that was after he allowed her to buy expensive beads and tassels. Her mother would have been pleased with the sashes.

Jael made Denah's sash. Denah hated it. It was the plainest sash she had ever seen. There was no color to it at all. White thread on white fabric and that was all. No added jewels, no golden embroidery or decorative fringe. She paid little attention to it at the wedding, her mind overwhelmed with other concerns. Later she noticed and realized it reflected Jael's opinion of her son's bride. It was not a pleasant reminder of the wedding day.

Lavender rode on the breeze drifting through the window. Denah stopped her task and stood at the opening to inhale the calming fragrance. The hulking frame of the ark was outlined against the fading blue of day. Her husband would be home soon so she lingered in their room and waited for him instead of escaping to the courtyard. She preferred setting out the evening meal for the family like a household servant to being alone in her husband's presence. The tension was too thick. Noah's household never lacked topics to converse as they gathered under the shade of the terebinth trees and no one seemed to notice that Denah rarely spoke as she served. She was invisible in their midst.

Although she didn't want to be at odds with her husband, she couldn't help bristling when he was near, when she saw his face in a perpetual pinch, all softness gone from his eyes. When he did speak to her it was some inane comment about the ark or his work or the food she was serving. Comments you throw out to strangers or merchants or passing caravans of travelers to whom you feel a duty of civility and nothing more. Knowing what she did about Renita, Denah found it difficult to be pleasant. She found herself not even wanting to look at him. His impatience hurt far more than his grip, a vice that left finger sized bruises on her shoulders. The bruises at least were fading. His coldness was not.

◆

"Is the meal nearly ready?" Japheth was surprised to find Denah in their room and said the first neutral comment he could find in an attempt to break her stony silence.

"Yes," she answered, then returned to folding laundry, keeping her distance. He wanted her to greet him with a kiss and ask how his work went, ask how he was, ask or say anything. She didn't anymore. She kept her lips sealed and he hadn't seen her eyes since that day they fought on the ark.

Japheth stripped off his tunic and began washing up in a basin of water. He filled his hands and splashed it over his face, letting the streams carry away the dust in brown rivulets that traveled down his chest. Several days of beard growth scratched his fingers and he could feel the puffiness under his eyes. Lack of sleep made him edgy and he wanted to shake his wife and demand that she remove the wall she erected to keep him away. He needed reconciliation.

The bruises he left on her arm where yellowing and he was grateful the reminders of his anger would be soon gone. He should not have been so rough. Her request to go to the temple was infuriating but she was not raised under Noah's roof and he needed to remember that her ways were not like those of his grandfathers, despite Carmi's upbringing. Her request reflected the common practices in the city and that was all. Japheth exhaled before he spoke.

"Will you never speak to me again, Denah?"

Denah bit down on her lip and refolded the stack of linens she had just folded while he stood and dripped on the floor. Japheth sucked in his irritation and continued.

"Denah, I'm sorry for being so rough with you. I didn't mean to hurt you."

His wife stopped and looked him in the eye. Her eyes glistened with tears. Her coldness was one thing; her sadness made his anger drain onto the floor into the puddle of water that collected at his feet. He wanted to take away the sorrow that crossed her face, like on their wedding day, when he wanted to take away her fear. He wanted his wife to find joy in his presence.

"I'll create my own flood right here if you don't hand me a towel," he said, trying to lighten the mood.

Denah tossed a towel at his feet without speaking. He couldn't stand it any longer and crossed the room, wrapping his wet arms around her and pulling her into his chest. "I can't stand your unhappiness."

Denah's stiff shoulders relaxed against him and he laid his cheek on her waves of black hair, tied in a loose knot behind her head. Jasmine rose from her skin, fresh, pure, beautiful.

"It's behind us. No grudges," he said. "Please."

"No grudges," she said after a few moments. Her voice was soft, without any trace of the venom that had been brewing since the argument.

Japheth released his hold and retrieved his towel. Denah faced him with a cautious smile.

"Your mother said it was alright for me to make fabric dyes, if it was alright with you of course," she said.

Japheth pulled a clean garment over his head. This request was much simpler than her last one, the horrific suggestion that they enter one of those temples to ask a piece of wood to give them a child. Draped in gold, crusted in jewels, even as tall as a house, they were still just firewood beneath the finery. And his God did not approve. Nor did his father. Thankfully, his wife did not enter that realm of requests again.

He could see no harm in granting permission to her current request. And why not? Coloring linens brought his wife a measure of joy that she couldn't seem to find anywhere else. "Yes Denah, that would be fine," he said. What harm could there be?

Chapter Eight

Moisture seeped from the earthen floor, nourishing ferns and mosses, plumping toadstools and saturating the trail beneath her feet. It sucked onto her sandals and held on until Denah pulled them away, leaving peaks of moist earth in her wake. Her outer tunic was soggy, collecting water from the air and holding it like a sponge. She shivered, and tucked dampened strands of hair behind her ears. The coolness woke her senses, encouraging her to keep moving rather than return to the warmth of the cooking fires. It was only a matter of time before the earth dried beneath the sun rays of day. Damp clothing would be refreshing then, and the mud would fall from her shoes in clumps.

A wet cedar fragrance clung to the heavy air, topped by eucalyptus. It traveled with the mist, rising as soft fog, climbing up darkened tree trunks and disappearing in the blue skies above. Droplets of water sat in pools on top of cupped leaves and dangled like pearls off petals and branches. The dappled light of morning passed through the fog and twinkled in the droplets like jewels on a green garment.

Any remaining fragments of frustration melted into the solitude of the woods. The prior evening she forced herself to make peace with Japheth even though he apologized only for hurting her physically. He didn't rescind his decision concerning the temple but it was good not to be at odds with him. She would never change his mind if they didn't speak. Honey was a more powerful persuader of husbands than a cold blade of iron, her mother once said.

Denah breathed a long sigh and embraced the moment, one she gladly shared with no one. Skittering mice in the brambles and pudgy little sparrows in the brush were her only companions. Mornings like this were her favorite time in the woods. It wasn't at all gloomy as her brothers said. The forest was simply waking up, lifting the blanket of night gradually. It was also the safest time to venture outside the city walls or away from open spaces into the dense skirt of trees. The vagrants traveling these trails preferred the full light of day or the complete cover of night, not the sleepy light of sunrise.

Denah readjusted the wicker basket strapped to her back and checked her right hip for the dagger she kept for the rare beast that did pose a threat to her safety. The horned mother lizards were wary when Denah stumbled across a nest of eggs, though none had ever actually harmed her, just stomped and hissed to hasten her departure. It was the footsteps of the behemoth herd that was her greatest danger but she knew the sound of their incessant leaf chewing and could avoid being caught unsuspecting in the path of their mighty feet. Few dangerous predators remained in these woods. Most were eliminated by hunters as the demand for sacrifices to the gods of the city grew.

The gurgling rumble she followed was the call of an old friend. Noah's stream was a spur off the same brook outlining the city, running just outside the city walls. She could follow the main stream around the city and end up near her father's home. There she knew every twist and turn of the trails leading into the dense foliage. She knew where the water cascaded off the rocks into a pool deep enough to swim and she knew the best trees for climbing. She could find the bat filled caves without a second thought, or the berry brambles and jasmine shrubs. Nearly every length of fabric she ever dyed came from something that thrived in this lush expanse of trees. This end of the woods was new territory, yet it was familiar, too. The aroma, the barrage of verdant hues, the chit-chit of birds brought the comfort of a life she once knew.

A green flash and whirl of wings caught her attention above the creek bed. The dragonfly was nearly as long as her arm and hovered over the water for only a moment before it left in a flash of color. Denah carefully made her way to the place the creature had been. Where the green dragonflies hovered lay a cache of snails.

A rocky outcropping held the band of treasure that Denah sought. Barely larger than an acorn each, the little snail troop was making its way from one earthy campground to another. They were the same color as the rock itself but they held a secret. Their bodies contained a pigment that stained whatever it touched the most intriguing blue hue. Denah discovered their secret by accident, playing in the creek and unknowingly crushing the tiny creatures beneath her feet. It wasn't until she got home that she realized her feet were an odd color and she thought for sure she had the rot of death climbing up her legs.

She approached her father in the midst of a business transaction to inform him of her impending demise. The two men with Carmi put down their pipes and leaned as far back into the soft cushions as they could, staring at her feet and hardly daring to breathe lest they catch the contagion. Her father laughed and told her to scrub her legs with barley husks. It was at the bathing pool, scrubbing and scrubbing that Denah unknowingly discovered her first dye, although it wasn't until later she found a way to make it adhere to the woven linen and not leach out onto the skin at the first sign of the sun's heat.

Denah collected a third of the little troop and let the others go their way. Eran might like the blue color if it wasn't too bright. She wanted green for Naomi, the green of boiled sumac bark. She hoped to find some before she returned.

Bushes laden with berries begged to be picked around every turn in the trail. Beth would be thrilled with the bounty. Her young step-sister helped collect the array of berries, leaves and fungi that stained with pleasing hues. Beth chopped ingredients and mixed them over a fire until it was time to add the fabric. She stirred the linens in the pulpy concoctions to render the even coloring then ran them through the wringers to remove the excess liquids. She helped Denah apply the stamps to form intricate patterns and fix the stains in vinegar so they wouldn't fade away. Remembering the processes from start to finish, despite repeated step by step instructions, was something Beth couldn't do.

Beth was the child of her father's newest wife, the youngest of the five supplying Carmi with heirs. The girl seemed normal for the first few years of her life and by the time it became obvious that she wasn't, it was too late for her to be given to the temple. Even the priestesses had standards against the cursed ones. Denah took the sweet natured girl as an assistant and was blessed with a hard worker at her disposal. Beth wanted to please. She was overly needy for attention and threatened Denah's patience. Still, Denah missed her. Her sincere laughter would be a welcomed intrusion in the routine of life under Jael's rule.

The trail wound along the stream and Denah kept a brisk pace. The aroma of grilled meat filtered into the air as the path veered near the city wall. Three of the city temples backed up to the wall near diversion tunnels that provided the inflow of fresh water. Denah realized she was by the temple to the great goddess herself, her mother's god, Zakua. She had walked a greater distance than she planned.

A forbidden world lay beyond the wall. The fertility goddess was not meant for unwed girls. Fathers didn't allow their daughters to venture anywhere near this temple. It was her mother's favorite, however, the lure was irresistible, as were Denah's pleas to peek inside the structure. Her mother relented a few times and brought Denah along as she paid homage to the goddess with coins and sacrifices that she purchased from the tent vendors hovering outside. Carmi stopped the practice before people started talking.

She found another way to enter the courtyard surrounding the temple by accident. Two of her brothers snuck out of the house one afternoon and she followed them, out the diversion tunnel, down the path outside the city wall. They shinnied up a tree and jumped onto the wall before disappearing down the other side. Denah followed as far as the tree, climbing the limbs, allowing her eyes to enter the clamor below without violating her father's will.

Denah waded across the stream and stood beneath the old sycamore, listening to the sounds crossing the wall. Donkeys brayed and vendors yelled. Babies cried and dogs barked. Pots clanged and altars hissed.

The tree had grown; so had Denah, so the climb wasn't difficult. She made her way to a fork splitting the tree into two opposite halves. By pulling back a branch, the temple courtyard was in view.

To her right the back of the great white stone building ran close to the city wall. It was two stories tall and perfectly square. On its flat roof were bronze altars where meat dedicated to Zakua was butchered and grilled by young men given into temple service. The men wore short skirted garments and already she could see blood spattered on their smooth chests and legs from the dedicated animals. Younger boys filled bags with refuse and drug them off to be burned elsewhere while the littlest ones carried the cooked meat to the tent vendors below.

Denah turned away from the slaughter to observe the vendors as they lined up their tent stalls in neat rows. Half the spaces were occupied already as the merchants arrived for the business day. A few vendors peddled only themselves. Men and women alike glimmered in adornments of gold and silver and talked with loud voices above the cages of birds and animals. Perfumes and trinkets, face paints and potions, were sold along side the grilled meat and the vats of cheap wine.

Denah's gaze wandered over the tents then lingered on the small tent closest to the temple where unwanted infants were crying in their baskets. Most were left during the night. She saw a woman bring her baby once, when she was spying on her brothers. It was in the daylight and there were people milling around paying no attention to the woman with the wailing baby. She caught Denah's eye because she headed for the baby tent with purpose in her step. She knew where she going and there was no hesitation in her actions, no second thoughts. She came out of the tent alone and left in a hurry. The baby continued to cry but no one came for it. Denah waited and waited until she saw a priestess chase her brothers away from the veiled women with a broom, back toward the wall. The baby was still crying as she scurried down the tree.

The chosen babies were raised by the priestesses and served in the temple. Those deemed unsuitable simply disappeared. Denah asked her father where those babies went. He wouldn't tell her, saying she would find out when she was older. She never asked again.

Renita, the marked servant, left her infant here. Denah wondered what became of the helpless babe, abandoned by the woman who gave him life. Perhaps he was one of the children on the roof mopping up blood or shuttling meat to the vendors below.

A young couple bartered for a rabbit near the baby tent and it occurred to Denah that she would require a sacrifice to receive her own blessing. There was a price for everything. And a time, and this was not the time for lifting the curse. She made a quick descent, grabbed her basket of snails and headed back the direction she had come.

The mist was long gone and the sun was warm on her skin as she retraced the path back to Noah's land. She had been gone longer that she intended and started a slow run along the trail. It wasn't safe here in the full light of day. Nephilim still roamed this area and women disappeared more often than she cared to think about.

Sunlight streamed through breaks in the foliage and illuminated the dirt in a spotted pattern. It was solid beneath her feet now. She slowed her pace to catch her wind and noticed the signs of life she had missed in the fog walking the other direction. Not just any life, human life. Brush on either side was trampled flat and remnants of food were scattered along the way. She passed several fire rings and a small clearing with sleeping hammocks strung between the trees.

Denah slowed her pace to a brisk walk, trying to keep her feet from making any noise. Every sound turned her head to determine its source and its direction. Each rustle of leaves and snapping twig increased the flow of sweat down the small of her back. She couldn't tell how far she was from the edge of Noah's vineyard.

A loud snap stopped Denah completely. She listened above her pounding heart to the movement somewhere in front of her. The woods were quiet for a moment then laughter. Men, more than one, in the woods.

Denah quickly scanned the area for a hiding place. The trees were too difficult to climb and the creek too exposed. She had no choice but to force her way through the brush into the dense foliage and wait for the men to pass by.

Briars nipped at her skin and grabbed her tunic as she pushed through, using her hands as a shield to guard her face. Branches snapped back at her and smacked with a sting as the undergrowth tore away at her clothing. Denah collapsed on the ground, surrounded by branches and decayed leaves. She pursed her lips to control the loud breathing and listened.

The whistling of a sparrow to its mate pierced the air above her. A small rodent rustled in the twigs, and the stream gurgled over the rocky creek bed. That was all. Denah allowed the trickle of sweat to burn her eyes unchecked. She dared not move, holding herself still, waiting for the sounds of the men as they passed. There were none. If they had been coming toward her, they should have passed by this time. If they were heading in the same direction as she, they were now a good distance ahead. She waited as long a she dared then pushed the branches in front of her out of the way.

A dog barked, followed by the coarse laughter of men, no longer waiting in silence for their prey to reveal her position

Chapter Nine

A pair of rough hands grabbed Denah by the arms and pulled her from the bushes, then dropped her on the ground against a tree trunk. Denah's eyes ran the length of the man's legs and torso to the snarling grin on the face peering down on her. Her captor towered above her, arms as big around as her waist, wearing a sleeveless tunic of crudely stitched buckskins, reeking evil from his pores.

A nephil.

A scream caught in her throat, too frightened to escape. His prickled square jaw opened and emitted a coarse laugh. Denah gagged. He smelled of refuse and sweat. A sickle shaped scar replaced his left eyebrow and the dagger at his side was four or five times the size of Denah's. She had no doubt he knew how to use it.

His younger companion wore a thick braided belt. Items of women's jewelry dangled from it, jingling as he moved. One hand kept his snarling dog under restraint while the other toyed with the belted keepsakes. Both leered, and laughed.

Denah felt for her dagger only to have the older man snatch it away. "What a surprise of good fortune we've found this morning," he said. "Who do you belong to woman?"

Denah pinched her lips together and stared at the quivering hands in her lap. How could anyone ever revere these vile men? They were unruly, mean, using their strength alone as a force that stole and killed and destroyed. Entire herds of livestock disappeared in a night and homes were looted then burned at the hands of the nephilim. Anything they wanted, they took, but it was the abduction of women that was most reviled. The mothers of many sons had disappeared from the fields along with young girls and the occasional young boy. Most were never found but the used, broken bodies that were discovered created an enmity that surpassed the legendary tales of heroism and valor.

Hunts were organized from time to time and men came home with trophies to show off their victory. The large, heavy weapons were only a secondary prize to the real reward, the ears of a nephil. One of Denah's brothers was the proud owner of a one and kept it pinned to a fence pole until it rotted away.

Denah had seen only a few nephilim in her lifetime and they were hanging by their broken necks in the city. They were unmistakable. Several heads taller than her brothers and wearing the clothing of wild men, even dead they reeked of unbridled restraint. She kept her distance from their corpses, frightening and gruesome under death's control, and was glad when the putrid remains were finally removed.

The two men paced back and forth, never taking their eyes from her. The younger one ran a hand through his red hair over and over as if he intended to comb the tangled locks and look presentable. His strong right arm held tight to the rope around the dog's throat. The black eyed beast kept his own vigilant watch on her as it followed its master's steps.

The oldest man leaned over her and ran his dirty hand over her hair. "It's a pretty one," he said. Denah flinched at the touch and the garlic laden breath that washed over her face.

She closed her eyes, a groan filling her ears, her own she realized.

"Touch her again and the next thing you touch will be your grave."

Denah's eyes flew open. She had not seen the group of men arrive. Japheth, Ham, and a half dozen other men stood on the path with daggers drawn. The fury in their eyes was enough for the nephilim to back away without reaching for weapons of their own. The dog strained against the rope leash, his yellow fangs hungry for the taste of violence.

"The woman belongs to you, then. She hasn't been harmed."

Japheth shifted his gaze to Denah for a moment then back to the older nephil. "Her garment is torn. There's blood on her face."

The nephil shrugged his shoulders. "That's her own doing. We found her in the bushes, hiding like a run away. We kept the dog from getting at her. You should be thankful we stopped him from ripping her heart out."

Japheth shifted his gaze back to her. "Have they hurt you?"

Denah shook her head.

By this time Ham's men had the nephilim surrounded. Four to one, not including the dog, were not high enough odds for Denah's liking. Each nephil counted as at least two men and they would fight to the death.

Denah held her breath as the circle of men closed in on the back to back nephilim. Ham's men wore the grins of mad men, dedicated to destruction, shifting their weight in readiness for the slaughter. No one initiated contact, however. It was Japheth's woman, Japheth's fight to initiate. The older nephil faced Japheth, leader to leader. His features were calm but his tall body was tensed, rigid and solid. Japheth's face was crimson, veins on his neck bulging, surging with wrath.

No one spoke. Ham's men let their eyes dart from their targets for brief moments to look at Japheth. Even the dog sat back on his haunches, turning his gaze back to his master, unsure what his command would be.

Japheth cursed the nephilim, then stepped back, lowering his weapon, never taking his eyes from the older nephil's. "Drop your weapons and get out of this region," he said.

Ham and his men looked at Japheth, utter disbelief etched unmistakably in their expressions. The nephil did not move.

"Brother, we must do what we must to protect our property." Ham waved a knife in the air in front of his brother's face. He was ready to draw blood.

Japheth maintained his position. "No. The God Who Sees will not be pleased. He alone creates and destroys the life of man."

"They are not men! They are animals." Ham spat on the ground next to the nephil's feet.

Japheth considered his brother's words, looking at him briefly, then back to the nephil. Ham's jaw was hard and set. He was used to getting his way, sometimes with his charm and other times with his strength. He was a natural leader. But her husband was not a follower. His little brother's thirst would not sway his decision. Denah read the resolve in his eyes.

"What I have decided, I have decided." Japheth's face burned as he stood his ground in a barrage of cursing. "Drop the weapons," he said to the nephilim.

A grin crossed the older one's face, the scar never moving. "And then you destroy us?"

Japheth shifted the dagger in his hand, drew it away from his side and tossed it into the earth point first. "No. Drop your weapons and go. Now. Before I change my mind."

The younger nephil looked at the older who nodded and both threw their daggers at Japheth's feet. Japheth grabbed Denah's arm and pulled her to her feet. The eyes of both nephil traveled over her body and she shivered. Japheth thrust her behind him.

Ham's men cautiously broke the circle while the nephilim took a few hesitant steps backward. Ham stepped forward and held out his left hand to the young nephil. "Give me the dog," he said.

The man's eyes squinted and he cursed Ham until the older man intervened. "Do it." he commanded.

The nephil pulled up on the rope and the dog jumped to his feet and bared his teeth. The nephil's lip curled as he tossed the rope toward Ham's feet and said "Git!' The beast followed the command, lunging toward his enemy's throat. Ham was prepared. In one twisting motion, he maneuvered clear of the beast and ran his dagger across its throat. The dog was silenced, convulsing on the ground in a pool of blood.

The nephilim watched without expression then turned abruptly, disappearing into the woods. Denah heaved the contents in her stomach to the earth beside her feet.

♦

Japheth paced, back and forth, back and forth in the room, rubbing his hands over his face as Denah washed her wounds in the basin of water. Her tattered tunic lay in a heap on the floor beside the basket of snails that had been squashed and now oozed their prized pigment onto the floorboards.

He had been unable to speak to her on the way home as he retraced her footprints in the mud, now solid tracks of dried earth. The fury surging through his veins didn't diminish after the threat was gone and she had to run to keep up with his relentless pace.

Ham and the other men kept a respectable distance between them but their disappointment at the lack of nephil bloodshed reached his ears. He heard the names they called him. If the nephil had any sense at all they would travel far from this region. Once word got out there would be a demand for their lives.

What could have, would have, happened to Denah caused his stomach to churn and he was glad for the silence. He hated the nephilim. They were vile and worthless. Evil reigned in their midst and violence was their god. He would gladly slice them to bits and rid the region of two more of their clan so they could not be a threat to anyone. He would have done so if they actually harmed Denah.

But they had not.

Japheth slammed his fist into the wall. Denah uttered a startled cry. She was pale and still had the wide eyed look of fear carved into her face. Her wavy hair was full of leaves and bits of twigs. It was half out of the knot she tied it in and it fell around her face in an unkempt array. She looked like a crazed woman, like the marked women who roamed the city at night, slowly starving to death.

She wore nothing but a thin vest that she donned as she bathed, her smooth skin untouched and unseen by any other man. The thought of men touching her made the fury resurface and he had to make himself breathe slowly. She was safe. The scratches and skin tears on her arms and lower legs would heal. She was fortunate.

"What were you doing out there?"

Denah slipped a clean garment over her tender skin. "Collecting supplies for the dyes. I, it got late. I didn't realize it was so late."

"You were foolish. I didn't expect that of you."

Denah exhaled before she responded. "I realize that. I've never had trouble in the woods before. The trails at home were safe."

"This is your home, Denah. This is your home."

"I know. I just wanted to get supplies."

"You can't have your old life back. Accept your new one."

"I'm trying. I wanted to make something nice for Eran and Naomi."

Japheth shook his head. "No one in this household has need of the fabrics you make. I thought you could see that by now."

Denah faced the window. Japheth stood behind her and began plucking debris from her hair. "Mother was beside herself. When she realized you left the grounds, she said it was her fault. Why is that, Denah? Why does she think you running off was her fault? "

"I didn't run off. I asked her if I could go and she said it was alright."

"She said you could go into the woods?"

"Well, not specifically, but that is where the snails are, and-"

Japheth sucked in his breath. "You asked me if you could make dye. You said nothing about scampering off into the woods. Did you think I would allow you to go out there alone? Did you really think I would approve?"

Denah rubbed aloe ointment into to the ripped flesh on her arm and said nothing.

Japheth continued. "No, of course not. You weren't up front with me, were you? You intended to deceive me."

Denah's tears spilled down her cheeks. "No, I didn't. I go to the woods all the time at ho-, at my father's house. I thought you understood. I've told you about it, I've explained it all to you."

Japheth ran their discussions through his mind, sorting out key words and stringing the dye making process together. He had not paid close attention. Now he understood. He rested his hands on her shoulders. "You are never to go off the property alone. And there is no need for you to go into the woods, Denah," he said softly. "Forget about your fabrics. Mother will find suitable work for you if that's what you need."

Japheth picked up her ruined tunic and walked out of the room, leaving his wife to cry alone, in the safety of home. He could not comfort her now. He needed to find peace in his own mind first.

Chapter Ten

The cinnamon, myrrh, and hyssop aroma of the market reached Denah's nose long before the cart passed the guards at the gate in the city wall. Eran and Naomi sat opposite her on the wooden benches, talking non-stop on the way. The unexpected venture into the city was a treat for them and they reminded her of children, given an allowance then sent off into the shops alone to barter for sweets.

Jael, too, seemed lighter in mood this morning. Her face was relaxed and strands of silky hair escaped their braid to dance in the air about her face. Her tunic was a soft blue, like the eggshells of the red breasted birds that nested in the courtyard. It accentuated her eyes and brought softness to her impenetrable wall of criticism. Except for the shimmer of gray emerging at her temples, she could easily be mistaken for a woman many years younger.

Denah rubbed the last bits of scab from her arm where the branches scraped her in the woods. Her incident with the nephilim was spoken of only on the day that it occurred, when the stew of anger was brewing hot between Ham and Japheth. Denah had not attended the family meal that day, yet didn't miss a word of the ensuing conversation in the courtyard. The words carried through her window, fearful ones, angry ones. It started with questions about why she was in the woods alone and if she was injured, then moved on to deeper concerns: would the nephilim return anytime soon and what had been their intentions outside the walls? The bulk of the conversation concerned the handling of the men whose intentions were anything but civil.

Japheth's decision not to kill them generated great emotion. Ham insisted they should have been slaughtered on the spot to prevent them from killing someone else's wife. Shem agreed with Noah, that they should have been bound and taken to the city judges even though they had not harmed Denah. They would have, if she had not been rescued, and were no doubt responsible for other crimes. Japheth maintained a continuous thread of defense throughout the banter. Neither nephil actually harmed Denah. He had no right to kill them for a crime they did not commit, whatever their suspected intentions. Methuselah agreed and when it became obvious none could persuade the others, he suggested they speak no more of the divisive issue. What was done, was done. Denah had not heard anyone speak of it again. Even Japheth seemed to let it pass and their routine continued as it had before the incident.

It was different in the kitchen, though. There was an obvious attempt to include her in the conversations rather than simply ignore her presence. The change was initiated by Jael. Denah could read the guilt on her mother-in-law. She wore it like a chain about her neck, tugging her conscience, forcing her into directions she didn't wish to go. She knew Denah wanted to avoid the unpleasant conditions of the kitchen and shouldered the responsibility for the escapade into the woods. Jael felt responsible for the incident with the nephilim.

The forced congeniality was almost worse than being ignored. Their interactions were thick with a sense of duty, the air in the kitchen no longer frigid, but stale. She wasn't the only one to notice apparently and the unexpected shopping expedition was a welcome change in the routine for all of them.

The driver steered the cart into the lot of evenly spaced trees to which other beasts and carts had been tied. The four servants accompanying them were already alert to the movements of people in the area, their hands ready to draw weapons as their eyes searched for trouble. Bodyguards had become a necessity. Anyone with the smallest purse took along a brother or cousin or servant to protect their property from thieves roaming the markets. Denah wiped road dust off her bright tunic as they started toward the center of town, her own allowance of bartering coins securely tied beneath her belt.

Four wide streets in the city center lined a grassy square containing a stone platform. The Meeting Stone was occupied by a trio of men juggling oranges to the delight of several dozen children. Mothers stood patiently nearby, pausing from their chores before dragging the young ones back among the merchants. It was on this stone that Denah first heard the thundering voice of Noah. The deep gentle voice she knew was filled with passion as he spoke and at first she was frightened. Once she got close to Noah and saw the kind eyes, crinkling at the corners, she wanted to stay and listen to all his words. Her mother pulled her away. Noah's head was filled with confused tales, her mother said. Denah better not listen and get confused herself. Besides, she had fabrics to fold.

It wasn't the only time Noah spoke from atop the platform. He was there often with his message regarding the ways of his One God. People listened politely for many years, or simply ignored him and went about their business as he spoke about judgment and rebellion and the need to abandon all gods but his. The response changed when Noah's words became fiery darts, when he spoke of the great flood. They mocked him openly then and threats of stoning brought guards to the scene.

Noah hadn't been back on the platform since his father was

killed, nearly five years ago. The city authorities told him to stay off, permanently, to prevent a riot or his own untimely death. Their tolerance had grown old and the townspeople who bothered to stop and listen only sought a public beating. The platform was for entertainment, not for condemnation, not for threats of destruction, not for absurd talk of water from the sky.

Jael stopped their troupe to barter for saffron and mustard. They would shop here, around the main square and not down the street at the temple stands. Jael would not be purchasing cooked meats, face paints or carved gods. Denah waited patiently while her mother-in-law sniffed pots and sampled bits of spice from the tip of her little finger. Carmi's business was on the other side of the square and she hoped to see him as they made the circuit. Married more than three months, she had not seen her family in all that time.

"You came here every day?" Eran's finger followed her eyes as she examined the colorful array of dried herbs displayed in bowls under the vendor's awning.

Denah smiled. "Not every day. I had to work in the barn at my father's home when the fabrics dwindled. But I was here often. Often enough to actually miss this noise and all the people and the smells and choices of merchandise."

Eran sniffed a vial of fragrance the merchant put in front of her then immediately sneezed. "Too many choices. I don't think I could ever make up my mind on what to buy."

A passing woman caught Eran's arm and gave her a smile containing only a few teeth. "My dear, I know what you need." She opened her bulky vest and revealed tiny clay pots sealed with cork, tucked into neat rows of pockets. She pulled one out and placed it in Eran's palm then wrapped both her hands around Eran's, sealing the bottle within. "The oil of the mandrake, blessed by Zakua," she said. "To make you ripe for the bearing of children."

Eran pushed her hand toward the woman. "Oh, no. Take it back. Please. Thank you, but no."

The woman kept hold of Eran's hand, her jowls oscilling as she shook her head. "You shame your husband with your empty womb. How soon will he tire of you and take another wife to bring him heirs?"

Eran dropped her flushed face to the ground and tried to free her hand. The old woman kept her grip.

Naomi touched Jael on the shoulder and nodded in Eran's direction. One look from Jael and the woman released Eran. With a sneer she shoved the pot back into her vest.

"Move along," Jael said. "We don't want your worthless potions."

A vendor of incense shouted over the crowd towards them. "Perhaps the wife of Noah requires some essence of cedar to freshen the air of that ark?"

Jael ignored the comment and turned to the servants. They seemed anxious to fade into the background, snapping to attention when her direct glance reminded them of their duties. The one near Denah was breathing deeply through his nose and his eyes began darting over the faces and bodies surrounding the family of his employer. His hand rested over the knife tucked into his belt.

The crowd around them grew quiet and Jael's shoulders stiffened. Then someone snickered. Then another. "Have the great waters begun to rise out at your place, Jael?"

"Has Noah's God told him to dig a great well on which to float his boat or will you rely on the morning mist to flood the hills?"

"Noah's God is impotent, Jael. Either that or dead. That's why your sons have no sons of their own."

"He's not dead! He sleeps from all that wine Noah gives him!"

The laughter and sarcasm shot through the crowd from all

directions. Eran pressed her face into her hands while Naomi hung her head in embarrassment, clenching the fabric of her garment in tight fists. Denah's heart pummeled against her ribs. She didn't fear physical harm, though it might have been preferable to the taunts stinging her flesh, ripping away her self respect in ragged chunks. These were her neighbors, men who bartered with her father, women who dined with her step-mothers. She refused to lower her face. Her eyes stung with tears but Denah held them back and watched her mother-in-law.

Jael stood tall and had her jaw set in a firm line. "Seventeen copper pieces. That's all I offer. Do you want it or shall I take my business elsewhere?"

The red faced merchant turned his attention from the jeering crowd to his customer. "Yes. It is good, I'll take it," he said. Jael took the merchandise and turned to her daughters-in-law. Denah alone still held her head up so she was handed the packed spices to carry in her basket.

"There. That's done," Jael said. "Now come, we have many more stops."

Jael turned and walked away from the merchant with the family falling in behind her, flanked by the servants. The crowd melted back and allowed them to pass, a fury of hurtful words following in their wake. Denah knew the words had not simply bounced off Jael's time thickened heart. Her glistening eyes bore witness to the piercing of her soul.

Chapter Eleven

Naomi asked Jael if she could look at the fabrics in Carmi's shop. Denah tried not to appear too eager.

"We have no need for his fabrics," Jael said. A frown crept onto her face.

"Please, just for a moment." Naomi had not regained her vitality, although the mocking had subsided to sidelong glances and hushed comments as the family of Noah made their way around the marketplace.

Jael studied her downcast expression and relented. "Very well. You and Denah may go. We'll be at the Meeting Stone after we purchase the remainder of supplies."

Naomi stepped briskly toward the large tent awning shading the front of Carmi's store and the tables of rich fabrics. Denah stayed on her heels as they and two servants maneuvered through the crowd. Inside the stone building lay shelves of ordinary burlap and woolen fabrics alongside plain linen rolls with not so much as a stripe to give it character. Outside, below the awning was the magnificent array of fabrics the house of Carmi created and sold for a healthy profit. Tidy stacks of folded pieces sat among fabrics that lay open, draped over the table to reveal intricate designs and subtle changes in hue. Bold colors were wrapped around dowels and stood in large bins. Rolls of braid and rolls of cording and rolls of tassels in seven sizes were suspended from the awning, a dangling display of texture at eye level.

Naomi's interest surprised her. Her sister-in-law went immediately to a pile of solid hued linens that had a smooth hand. Denah followed her and retrieved a dark green from the bottom of a stack, one whose color came from smashing the elder berry tree root into a fine paste, then boiling it quickly with fresh cypress leaves. She held it up to Naomi. "You would look lovely in this," Denah said. "It matches your eyes."

Naomi examined the fabric briefly before tossing it unfolded back onto the table. "I prefer yellows and golds," she said. "Not that it matters."

Denah retrieved the piece and carefully folded it, returning it to the pile. "Because of Jael?"

Naomi snorted. "Because of Ham. My husband wants his coins for himself. He pays no interest in my clothing. Japheth won't be any different. He'll see nothing wrong with you dressing as a beggar like the rest of us." Naomi's eyes traveled up and down Denah's bright tunic that was a sharp contrast to her plain one. "You best take care of the pretty things you own, Denah, because you won't get any more."

"Is that why Jael dresses so commonly? Because of Noah?"

Naomi shrugged. "She thinks immoral woman are the only ones who get to wear pretty things. I think Noah would buy her anything she wanted. She just doesn't want anything nice."

"And Eran?"

"Eran would hang gold coins off her nose if that's what Jael did."

Denah looked at her own colorful attire. "Jael hasn't said anything to me about my clothes, but I see displeasure in her eyes."

"She won't say anything. But when those wear out don't expect Japheth to buy you more." Naomi turned from her and ran her hand along the thick fabrics that made elegant coverings for beds and chairs.

Denah didn't need to pay the high prices her father required. She could make her own. She didn't require much. Except time. And that was hard to come by.

Denah poked her head inside the shop and watched Carmi haggle with a man half his age and not remotely aware of the fact that her father was selling him goods at double their value. She smiled at the familiar interaction. His right hand fiddled absently with the gold bead that held his beard in a tight braid. That gesture was as familiar to Denah as her father's easy smile. It meant he was not presenting an accurate picture of the fabric in question.

Carmi possessed the image of a man who didn't toil for his food. There was no earth beneath his nails or on the woven sandals tied around his ankles. The tunic surrounding his girth was delicate of weave, light in color with braided cord along the hems. His left hand flashed in bursts of gold as ornate rings moved through the air, animating his speech. The physical labors of his business were in the hands of his heirs but there was no question who maintained control.

The deal was made with a hearty hug and slaps on the back. Both men smiled as they separated, both sure that they had made an excellent bargain.

Carmi took his daughter in his arms. Frankincense lingered on his clothing and Denah inhaled deeply of her father's familiar scent. It reminded her of the woods in the moist air and of the citrus orchards at their peak of flavor.

"Have you brought me any blue snails, my daughter? No one can find them like you," he said.

Denah pulled back and looked him in the eye. "Greetings to

you, too, father."

Carmi laughed and tugged at the knot of hair on the back of her head. "Oh, hello Denah. Hello," he said. "I'm in business mode, you know."

"Of course, as always. And yes, I did try to collect supplies, then the nephil-"

"I heard. I'm glad you weren't harmed. You will take men with you next time, hmm?"

"I'm certain there will never be a next time. I'm not allowed to go back."

"Ahh, the rules under the roof of Noah. Just like Lamech. Rules and restrictions. So, life on the great ark of Noah is a challenge for you?"

Denah groaned. "Not you, too, father. Talk of that ark has followed us clear around the city today. People are so unkind."

"And your mother-in-law, she stands her ground, does she not? She is a good teacher for you. They are just words."

Carmi's loyalty to Noah's father, Lamech ran deep and Denah knew to guard her own words about her new family. He was thrilled at the marital arrangement and would not welcome any words of unhappiness in the situation.

"Yes, Jael holds her head high in spite of the insults. And I am treated well enough. I do miss you, though, and Beth."

"Your husband treats you with respect? Is he satisfied with you?"

Denah's hand went instinctively to her abdomen, followed by her father's eyes. "Yes, father. Japheth is a good man. I test his patience, but I think he is satisfied."

"But there is no successor in the line of the great Noah, yet?"

"It's only been a handful of months. I am afraid though, afraid that I'll be as the others."

Carmi was quiet for a moment, searching her eyes. He squeezed her hand in his. "There is a way to affect the curse. There are goddesses with the power to help you."

Denah nodded. "I know. I tried to convince Japheth but it is against the will of God Who Sees, the God of Noah. He will definitely not take me to the temple."

"He doesn't need to take you. You can go alone. You can be blessed so that your womb will overflow with sons."

Denah shook her head. "He won't allow it."

Carmi wagged a pudgy finger in her face. "Your father knows what his daughter needs. Think about it," he said. "Zakua blessed your mother with five sons before her young death. Had she lived, you would be the sister of twenty brothers, no doubt."

Naomi stepped into the shop. "We better go. Jael will be waiting."

Denah scanned the shop once more. "Where's Beth?"

"She's useless here without you hovering over her every move. She's heckling the flax."

Denah couldn't imagine the spindly girl dragging bundles of flax though the comb of sharp nails.

"She is-"

"Jael will be waiting, Denah."

Denah nodded and hugged her father before running after her sister-in-law. Naomi held her arms tightly around her waist as they wove toward the Meeting Stone. "Are you ill, Naomi?" Denah asked when her sister stopped suddenly.

Naomi didn't answer. She stared at the Meeting Stone which no longer held the merry jugglers. In their place stood four men, daggers drawn. At their feet was a large form that wasn't moving. The men kicked at the form and spat on it while the crowd closest to the platform cheered.

Denah stepped up onto a crate and saw that the fallen form was a man, dressed in crudely sewn skins, covered with dirt. A nephil. Denah tasted bile rising up her throat.

It was said that the ancestors of the nephilim came from the sky itself. They were companions of the gods, as beautiful and strong as they were arrogant. They hungered for the praise of man for themselves until the gods tossed them to the earth to toil for the honor they craved. At first the men of the earth revered the men of the sky and presented their daughters in homage. The nephilim were born of these unions, not without great sorrow. The offspring were a full hand length longer and wider than a normal newborn. The delivering mothers were torn in two, hemorrhaging to their deaths before the mother cord was severed. The nephilim became the enemy of common man. Their own females were barren so they stole women to carry their sons and to nurse the nephilim infants ripped from the wombs of their dead mothers.

Denah shivered, instinctively wrapping her arms around her chest.

One of the men on the platform took a fist full of the nephil's red hair and lifted his face to the onlookers. Denah gasped and her hand flew to her mouth. It was the younger nephil that tracked her in the woods. His nose was sideways and one eye was swollen closed but she knew it was him.

Another man stepped in and the two of them lifted the nephil onto his knees. He was nearly the same height as his captors in this position although he wobbled and would have crashed to the stone if the men weren't intent on keeping him upright. His left leg had a bend between the hip and knee and Denah heard a cracking sound as he was forced on to it. He winced but did not give the men the pleasure of a scream.

The children who had enjoyed the jugglers now clapped at the new entertainment. The mothers stopped pulling them away and stood to watch and cheer the deliverance of justice alongside their sons and daughters.

The captors roared and taunted their prey until the man seemed to pass out. The sudden limp weight nearly pulled the captors off balance so the third joined in to haul him erect. His hair was jerked back and the nephil's eyes were once again open. A long sharp blade was passed in front of his face from man to man, each taking a sharp cut into the nephil's dirty flesh until the blood and dirt ran in unison into a pool on the stone below.

The knife was passed to the fourth man who stood behind the nephil. He was young and seemed unsure what was expected, so he just stood there and soaked in the praises of the onlookers until the other captors gave him direction. The young man didn't hesitate. In one bold swipe he removed the nephil's right ear. The nephil groaned this time. The man waved his prize, holding it high over the crowd in triumph. The left ear went to another man. The crowd was jubilant.

Denah glanced at Naomi whose wide-eyed stare had not changed. Her grip on her waist had loosened and Denah could see the glimmer of dark green fabric hidden beneath her vest.

The roar of the crowd drew Denah's attention back to the stone, only for a moment as Jael's hands on her arm redirected her attention from the last moment of justice. Her mother-in-law was pale and didn't speak as she gently pulled Denah down from the crate and motioned for the bodyguards to get them all out of the crowd. Eran was in the arms of a servant, chewing on her knuckles and rocking her head into the man's chest. Naomi was unable to stop watching, craning her neck to see the action occurring behind them as they made inroads through the thick mass. Denah looked straight ahead and didn't waver until the sickening thunk of the nephil's decapitated head hit the stone. She didn't remember anything after that.

Chapter Twelve

Denah settled onto the floorboards and leaned against the bench. The servant who caught her when she fainted set her down gently, then stood, peering back toward the square and the excitement of the nephil capture, the nephil kill. The roar had diminished little, ebbing and flowing above the cart, carrying the squeals of delight and the screams of triumph. Denah let her head loll on the wooden boards. It felt light and a sour taste burned her throat.

Violence was nothing new. Men pummeled one another in the streets on a regular basis, drawing crowds and spontaneous wagering. Boys stabbed other boys in dark alleys and women were raped in the night, children stolen from their beds. Evil intent lurked behind smiles that promised peace and justice was awarded to the highest bidder.

This was different.

Mothers, round with new life, turned from sampling jams and whiffing incense to watch the spectacle. Fathers hoisted children onto their shoulders for a better view. Grandmothers cheered as the life blood poured from the red haired man. The intensity of animosity poured out by the nephil's captors spilled over into the crowd, returned as affirmation for the hideous, public pronouncement of judgment. The man's violent end was entertainment.

No one spoke as the cart pulled out of the lot and headed toward Noah's land. Eran sat on the floorboards opposite Denah between baskets of supplies, forehead resting on bent knees. Her gentle weeping brought a lump to Denah's throat. Eran was raised in the hill country, many miles away, and had never even seen a city until her father brought her to the market in search of a suitable employer, one willing take her into his household as a servant. Shem was with Noah that day and according to Noah, Shem couldn't take his eyes off of the whisper of a girl who stood mutely in her father's shadow, eyes frozen wide in both fear and wonder. He had never paid much attention to any particular girl and Noah knew this was the one meant to be his second son's bride.

Noah left Shem with Lamech and approached Eran's father. Rather than bargain for her employment, the man was interrogated as to his daughter's purity and disposition. Eran stood motionless and stared at her feet the entire time. Noah paid the man a handsome bride price, probably more than the farmer made in an entire harvest. Noah took home his supplies and much to Jael's surprise, a wife for Shem.

Eran's bridal march wasn't a feat of endurance. She walked from the servants' quarters to the clearing in less than a hundred paces. She wouldn't have lasted much further than that. Denah remembered seeing her for the first time at the wedding and thinking that the girl was sickly, she was so thin boned and she barely spoke. She had to be taught the familiar dances and was exhausted long before the celebration was completed. She didn't know a single soul at her own wedding festivities and as far as Denah knew, she had never seen her blood family again.

Eran rocked back and forth, long brown hair falling over her

face, hiding her from the harshness of the earth, the hatred of man.
She was still thin but her face was not gaunt nor did her ribs
protrude like on her wedding day. She was much stronger and
healthier now that she had plenty to eat. Denah liked her calm ways
and simple, unpretentious manners. Out of Jael's influence, Eran
may have become a friend. As it was, she kept her distance,
expressing loyalty to her mother-in-law by loving as Jael loved,
loathing as Jael loathed. And in Denah's case, tolerating what Jael
tolerated.

Eran was fortunate that Jael liked her. She would wilt under the
woman's burning gaze of displeasure. Even Naomi cowered under
their mother-in-law's ever watching, ever judging eyes. The free
spirited, bold Naomi Denah remembered from years ago was
suppressed, pressed down and molded into the conformity of the
household. In the market, she laughed loudly, always the center of
attention, surrounded by friends and bubbling her way through life
with teasing glances that drew men to her side as quickly as her fire
could drive them away. Then she got married and melted into the
home of Noah. Denah rarely heard her laughter around the city after
that.

Denah stole a glance in Naomi's direction. She alone seemed
disappointed that they left the scene of the nephil's judgment. She
and Ham were indeed well suited for each other. Her arms continued
to wrap around her waist, hiding the stolen fabric. Denah felt anger
heating up her skin. It was her father's money that Naomi stole. She
let out a heavy sigh and decidedly let the matter pass. It wasn't worth
a confrontation.

"Are you feeling better, Denah?" Jael's voice was soft. No
longer under scrutiny her shoulders sagged forward and there was
heaviness in her eyes. Denah felt a twinge of sadness. The day had
not gone as her mother-in-law-intended.

"I'm better, yes." Denah leaned back on the seat and examined her mother-in-law's profile as Jael returned her gaze off into the distance. There was so much Japheth there in her features, even in the tiny lines creeping from the corners of their eyes. She and Noah waited a long time for him, for their firstborn. Her shame had not been lifted until her middle age years. Denah wondered if Noah ever considered taking another wife once it became evident that the young Jael wasn't going to provide him with heirs. It wasn't as if she put her foot down and refused to let him. Noah's strength exceeded hers in great measure. His strength was kinder than his wife's, though, and Jael's sharp dominance evaporated under his warm demeanor. Even she would have had no say in whether there were additional women under their roof. Noah would have a house full of them if he so chose. But he took no other wives, choosing Jael alone.

The cord binding Noah and Jael together was strengthened by their loyalty to the ways of the One God, a strength evident in Jael's dignity under the barrage of insults that she deflected in the market. Denah had to admire her mother-in-law's stamina. She didn't flinch when stones were hurled at her husband. She stood firm when stones were hurled at her god. Denah didn't know if she would bear so well under the years of ridicule, the years of humiliation. She didn't know if she believed in anything, or anyone, so fervently. Although she considered herself strong, she knew she couldn't stand in Jael's sandals.

The thud of the wagon wheels on the road made Denah's head bob forward, bringing the city scene back into her mind, the horrific death of the young nephil. He would no longer be a threat to the women of the region and that was good. The older nephil would retaliate, no doubt, and the horror would continue until he too was brought to justice at the hands of whomever had the fortune of finding him.

Still, she had not cheered with the crowd. Japheth spared the lives of the nephilim. He put down his weapon and let them just walk away. Her husband's judgment, his sense of justice, was foolish perhaps, but she preferred it to the bravado she just witnessed. He followed his mother in that way, too. He stood strong in the face of adversity, choosing right over reason, mind over heart. Denah hoped his god honored the decision. The One God needed to be pleased so her womb would be opened.

Denah glanced around the solemn cart and longed for the laughter of innocent children to ease the darkness settling in their midst.

♦

Japheth let his hand glide over the exterior of the ark as he walked around its hull in the moonlight. These were some of the first planks to be hammered in place, nearly twenty years ago. They were still as smooth and tight fitting as the ones he helped install on the roof just last year. The mortise and tenon jointed planks were labor intensive to construct, precision a must, with no leniency in the dimensions of each tooled piece. His father had shown great wisdom in that decision. There would be no shearing between the planks, no leakage of flood waters into the interior.

He remembered vividly when the site was chosen and the dimensions marked off. Noah's elbow to fingertip length was used as the cubit measure for the ark, three hundred long, fifty wide and thirty tall. God gave Noah the dimensions and he followed them precisely. He followed all of God's instructions for the ark to the most finite detail. The ancient gopher stand was the first casualty in the line of commands. The hard wood was difficult to form, resisting the saw blades and preferring rigid lines over the gentle curve required for the hull, but God said 'gopher wood' so God got gopher. His father made only three decks instead of the four or five that would easily fit in the prescribed height, and put the long horizontal windows along the top extension for light and air rather than staggered around the perimeter.

Japheth looked up at the massive wooden door laying face down on the top of the ramp.

Iron hinges clung to the base of the door from the deck threshold like bird talons grasping prey. It seemed to be the one flaw in the construction. As of yet, there was no simple way to lift the heavy door into place.

A pulley mechanism was constructed after much discussion with his father, even though the plan wasn't ideal. The system still required the strength of at least ten men. The leverage was all wrong. Japheth adjusted the angles of the pulleys and cables but there simply wasn't sufficient space to get the necessary lift. Even if pushed into position from the outside, there still was no method to secure the door in place. There was no mechanism for tying off the heavy cables required to withstand the weight of the door.

A pocket door made more sense. The massive door set into the wall of the ark could run on rollers side to side, pulled by handles by only a man or two. A simple latch would keep it in place. It could still be constructed. He and Ham had the plans ready, even had the wood in reserve to build the structure. They waited on their father to realize his error. Perhaps Noah misunderstood God on this one point.

Japheth frowned even as the thought traipsed through his mind. His father heard the voice of God, the very voice of The Creator. God of First Man spoke to Noah among his grape vines, not on his knees before a sacrifice, not bellowing out from the platform or when traveling from town to town to speak about repentance. He spoke to Noah while the man toiled in the dirt. And Noah stood firmly on the voice that spoke to him from the heavens. He didn't waver, as crazy as the commands were that he was given. He informed his family of his new vocation and felled the first tree.

As far as Japheth knew, God had not spoken to Noah since then. At least not audibly. The two still communed in the vineyard daily. Noah poured out his thoughts as he traversed the long rows and listened for God to speak to his heart.

Japheth felt familiar pangs of resentment churn in his head. Why did the Creator choose only Noah to let his voice be heard? Where was God when Japheth doubted his very existence? Why did God not intervene and speak, proving himself real? Had God said one word, one word, Japheth never would have questioned the wisdom of his forefathers. He never would've questioned the One God at all. He never would've lost everything as the firstborn heir.

God was silent.

And yet, Japheth knew he was real. He envied his father, actually hearing God's voice, but the knowledge of the One God was still within him. He tried to reason God away, believing the tales of Adam to be just that, tales. It wasn't sensible that everything in existence was created in six days by only one god. Maybe there was no god at all. Maybe there were many gods. That's what he told his father. Even as the words spilled from his lips, he knew what he said wasn't what his heart believed. The knowledge was there, the truth was there, all along, despite his efforts to prove and believe otherwise.

He longed for the actual, audible voice of God to direct him sometimes. Like the day he faced the nephilim. The women came home from town today mere vapors of life after witnessing the brutal execution of the man he set free. Should he have done the killing himself? What did it matter that the nephilim were freed then killed later? Dead is dead. He wanted God to say 'kill' or 'don't kill' but there were no words from the heavens. He relied only on the feeling that he should not shed nephilim blood, and not only he, but Ham and the other men as well. Of what use is a feeling if it is wrong and not from God? The act of mercy seemed foolish now. He couldn't deny being glad that the nephil was dead, however. The hunger in the man's eyes as he watched Denah was enough for any husband to shed blood.

Japheth walked up the ramp and leaned against the rail over looking the house. There was light coming from his window and he knew Denah would still be awake even after her emotionally exhausting day. She would need his comfort in the darkness of the night.

Japheth didn't move although he knew he should. He was frustrated with his beautiful wife and there were times he simply didn't want to be near her. He had never known her to scowl until they were married. She worked diligently at her tasks but there was no joy in her steps, no merriment in her countenance. He heard the other women laughing as they wove baskets beside the stream, finding joy together. Denah was rarely with them, off in the garden or somewhere, avoiding their company. It was rare for her to even speak when the family gathered. The only way he could keep from snapping at her was to avoid her presence.

She married a fallen son. He was no prize, he knew, yet he believed she was a woman who would see beyond his downfall and accept him. This didn't seem to be the case. She was miserable in her married life. He couldn't give her the life she had before with her father and that was the only way he knew to make her happy. And he did want her to be happy. He wanted his wife to find happiness in the life she had here. He prayed that God would grant her a child and satisfy her longings.

Japheth sighed and headed his steps toward home, following the tug at his heart that was constantly in turmoil where his wife was concerned. He would go to her and see to her safety, alleviate her fears and hold her in the night. He did not require a voice from the heavens to know these actions were pleasing in his God's eyes.

Chapter Thirteen

The potato peelings formed a heap on the floor before Denah noticed that her bowl was filled beyond capacity. Her mind was elsewhere, although she couldn't say with any specificity where, exactly. Eran, Jael and Naomi were under the same fog, each one tending to her task reflexively, no interest, no focus. It had been a fitful night and Denah longed to lie down and sleep without the blood drenched face of the nephil startling her into an uneasy wakefulness. The puffy eyes and long faces on the others reflected her own.

No one had to say it. The women wouldn't be allowed to enter the city again anytime soon. The thought occurred to her in the middle of the night as she sat, wide awake, on the bed, trying not to disturb her husband who had finally fallen asleep himself. Nephilim in the woods and growing hostilities in town would restrict them to the confines of Noah's land.

Denah glanced at the women working beside her in rare silence. They were under a blanket of weariness that had nothing to do with the toil of their hands. Did they feel as she did? That there was nothing in their future to look forward to, nothing tomorrow that would differ from today. There were no weddings to plan, no babies to birth, no children to raise. There was no cascade of life with its new beginnings and fresh dreams. This was their life. The ark made sense to her now. It provided the family with a common purpose, not only to fill their days but to quench other aspirations. What would they do when the ark was complete?

The steady shuffle of Methuselah's footsteps and thud of his cane echoed in the hall long before the old man arrived in the kitchen. He leaned heavily onto a carved leviathan rib that had washed onto the shore of the great sea. The cane itself was yellowed and its carvings dulled by wear but the great sea creature that wrapped itself around and around up to a gnarled head with fire in its breath was still evident. It reminded Denah of Methuselah himself, who still spoke the fervency of his God's words while he himself was bending and yellowing to the course of time.

"Merry is the work of the hands to still the maiden from mischief plans." Methuselah spit out the words with a great smile while he planted himself on a stool by the stone oven that glowed with the coals of the morning cooking fire. The four women laughed, as they did every morning now, as if they had not ever before heard the words that the old man repeated each day.

Jael handed Methuselah a small onion, peeled of its skin and slit in such a way that he could peel off triangular bits to chew in the parts of his mouth that still had teeth. The crooked fingers took the treasure and began to work.

"She's nearly done now. Nearly done."

"What's that, grandfather," Jael asked. "What's nearly done?"

"The ark of Noah. The ark is almost done. God Who Sees told my grandson to build that vessel three hundred cubits long and fifty cubits wide." Methuselah held out his left arm and marked off the cubit with the onion in his right, from his finger tip to the crook of his elbow. "With three floors he was to build the ark and with a window all around the top, and a door. This is done. The construction is nearly finished."

"Noah says all the living quarters inside are nearly complete as well. He made plenty of rooms for those who will come with us."

"When the waters come, the people will come. They will listen to my grandson when the waters come. The truth will pierce their hearts."

Denah looked at her sisters. Eran no longer chopped the carrots at her table, listening to Methuselah with the knife held still, poised in mid-air. Her face held a longing for the words of Methuselah to come true. She looked forward to the time of the great waters and the redemption of the family of Shem, of Noah, Lamech and Methuselah. Especially after the mocking yesterday, Eran was anxious for God to show himself as real, as the One God who would come as Judge.

Naomi continued to knead dough on a floured work board. She smiled at Methuselah and asked, "When do you think the flood will come, grandfather?"

"The time is soon, that I know. God said he would send the waters and the waters he will send." A tidbit of onion sailed through the air and landed in the black pot hanging above the burning embers.

Naomi giggled, missing the piercing glance from Jael in her direction.

"Yes, Old Man, the waters will indeed come as God told my husband and God told Adam the First One many generations ago. Judgment by waters and judgment by fires. We shall witness the first and we'll be ready, will we not?" Jael handed Methuselah a rag which he wrapped around the onion.

"We will. We will." Jael helped him as he struggled to rise from the stool. Methuselah's eyes traveled the room, resting on Denah.

"Have you seen it, young one? Have you walked the halls of my grandson's vessel?"

Denah nodded. He forgot again that she had been with the family nearly four months now and his eagerness to show her the ark was as intense as the first day she arrived. "Yes, grandfather. I have seen it."

A bony finger lifted from the onion and gestured to her. "Come and see it again. Be my eyes and tell me what Ham's men are up to today."

Denah looked at Jael. "Go with him, Denah. Take him to his room and see that he's comfortable."

Denah stuck out her elbow for the old man to hold, but he pushed it aside and put his out for her to hold instead, taking his cane in the other hand. She wrapped her fingers around his arm which was little more than bone with a thin covering of blue lined flesh. Every knob of his spine was visible through his tunic as it curled forward, a shepherd's crook, holding his head above the ground. His right foot shuffled forward without actually leaving the floor, then his left slid in beside it. Then the cane went forward. Then the right foot again. It was a short distance from the kitchen to his room but the pace was wonderfully slow and Denah welcomed the chance to be with him. Methuselah spoke little, using his breath for the effort of walking

The old man guided her into his room on the corner of the house. His bed was simply a wool stuffed mattress that lay on the floor. Japheth tried to convince him to use a frame for the mattress but he refused, saying he could never get used to sleeping up off the ground. Several buffalo hides were piled on the mattress as well as soft feather pillows, brown tinged with age. A copper bell swung on a cord beside the mattress so Methuselah could ring for assistance to rise in the morning.

The fireplace on the opposite wall was glowing, as it did throughout the day and most of the night at Methuselah's request. Pegs nearby held a row of clean garments that still appeared new. The layered tunics he wore into the kitchen each day did not appear, or smell, new. He preferred wearing the old ones, all at one time, saving the newer ones for when the current selection wore out. Denah was sure he slept in them as well.

The rest of the room was an odd mix of belongings. The tools he was repairing occupied one corner. A table in the opposite corner was piled with relics: a bleached unicorn skull, a variety of rocks with inclusions that glimmered in the light, a pitcher of water with a chip on the rim, and of course, the wooden chest. The chest contained the clay tablets inscribed by the First Man. Methuselah could read the inscriptions, as could his father Enoch and his father Jared before him. God taught Adam how to mark the wet clay with the symbols telling the histories of the beginnings. Methuselah taught Lamech how to interpret the marks, and Lamech taught Noah. Japheth knew some of the markings from his childhood but it was Shem who was trained to read the tablets when Japheth fell from honor.

The tablets in the chest were sacred. They belonged to the high priest of the One God, a position given to Seth from his father, Adam, then passed though the generations to the firstborn or to the son most aligned with the ways of God. The position would have been Japheth's if he hadn't rejected Noah's beliefs. Instead, Shem inherited the tablets, Shem was considered his god's priest, not Japheth. The title was respected in years past. It was powerless now that Adam's God was no longer favored by the people

Shem carried the blood of Adam, it was said. Not just the sinful inclination of man, it was more than that. His heart was devoted to his God, and he honored the ways of his ancestors, believing in the beginnings, as stamped into the tablets. Shem, as keeper of the tablets, wore the responsibility for man's allegiance to their Creator.

Methuselah eased himself onto a chair facing the window and beckoned for Denah to join him. She carefully stepped up behind him, mindful of the dried yellow spots on the floor surrounding the old man's chamber pot.

"There she is, child," he said, squinting at the structure in the distance. "Tell me what is happening to her today."

Denah took in the image framed by Methuselah's window. She described the morning light and how it bathed the side of the enormous structure, making the newly pitched areas shimmer in long horizontal bands. She told him how the steam rose from cauldrons around the workmen as they stirred the resin into a workable consistency and how the men on scaffolding used long poles topped with hyssop to mop the mixture onto every board and into every crevice. The clear coating made the vessel look new, she told him, drawing out a deep golden glow from the wood.

Methuselah leaned out the window and inhaled through his nose. The odor, like crushed pine needles, was pleasant and he smiled. "The interior lost that nice smell once it dried. It's unfortunate. I like it." He leaned back and seemed satisfied with the descriptions. "Yes, she is nearly complete."

Denah watched the process as board by board the ark was sealed. From the outside, it did appear complete and now it would be unquestionably water tight as well.

"Methuselah, what will happen when the ark is finished? Completely finished I mean, on the inside and out?"

The old man rested his arms on the smooth sill, eyes still looking toward the construction that was just a blur to him now.

"It will be time to move into the ark. Noah will know when to leave this home and find rest within her hull. God will tell him. God will be his guide."

"We'll move in, to live?"

Methuselah thought for a moment. "Yes, I believe that's the plan. When all is prepared you'll wait for the waters in safety."

Denah pictured the myriad of storage rooms gradually filling with supplies. "Are we to live off the food stores in the ark then, or save those for when the waters actually arrive?"

"You will rely on the ark, I imagine."

"So once we move in, we just stay there and wait? How long, grandfather? How long will we just wait?"

Methuselah shook his head. "I don't have that answer, child."

"What if the waters never come, grandfather?"

Methuselah patted her hand. "The waters will come. That is the one answer I know above all others. The waters will come. Soon."

Chapter Fourteen

The three brothers worked in unison to unload bags of grain from the large wagon to the smaller more maneuverable hand carts. Shem stood on the wagon and heaved a bag to his shoulder then dropped it over the side into Japheth's arms. Japheth lugged it over to Ham who loaded the cart with the bags standing upright and packed tightly together. There was a brown haze surrounding the brothers as the fine grain dust escaped captivity and poufed its way into the air. Denah watched them from a distance as she attended to a basket of mending.

Noah's boys were muscular and dark from years of labor on their father's project. Japheth made his calculations, Ham supervised the construction crew and Shem managed the fields, but as soon as they could break away from their individual duties their hands and minds joined in labor. As they ate the evening meal, the fact that the hired men had been paid or the barley was sold or the cows that wandered off were all accounted for was never more than a passing bit of information before the number of beds they built in one day or the indoor garden they designed became the topic of interest. Earlier in the evening the discussion turned to the water trough system they constructed, meant to minimize unnecessary trudging back and forth from the roof top cisterns to the bottom level. Completing the ark pushed them into diligence that united them as brothers.

"It will be too dark for them to see what they're doing soon but they won't stop will they?" Noah sat down on a stump beside her and watched his boys hustle to unload the carts. Crows would feast off the grain stores if left out overnight. A tarp secured over the bags would have been sufficient but Shem challenged his brothers to store them properly.

"They're like my brothers," Denah said. "No one wants to be the first to say 'it's too dark' or 'I'm tired' or 'that's enough for one day'."

Noah smiled and nodded. "Yes. It's like that with most boys, I suppose."

"Was it that way with my father?" Denah was curious what Noah would say. Her father portrayed Noah as selfish and spoiled as a boy, overly indulged by Lamech. It was difficult to imagine. Her father-in-law was always preoccupied with his building project but when he actually stopped doing and thinking and planning, he was still the kind man that she remembered as a little girl. His resources went into the ark as well as his time, yet no one in the family did without the basic essentials of life. He was prudent for sure. Selfish didn't describe him at all in her eyes.

Noah drew his lips into a line and stared into the distance as he thought about her question. "Yes. Everything was a competition to your father. We were close in age, so he and I were raised together, side by side as if we had emerged from the same womb at the same time. We had difficulties, as all brothers do. Your father struggled to find himself, struggled to make himself into his own person after his parents died. He needed to prove himself even though my father treated him as a son, no differently than me. It was as if he had to excel at everything to consider himself worthy as a man."

Denah was well aware of the competitive nature in her father. He used it for good, making himself a prosperous business. "He used to come here to visit quite often, I remember, until your father was killed. He wasn't the same after that. I suppose he felt as if he lost his father for a second time. It's still painful for him to come here I think, even with me living here."

Noah didn't respond. His eyes were still staring at the place where his sons had been even though they had moved from that spot, disappearing in the vessel with a cartload.

"He was glad that you agreed to his offer, though. I know he was delighted with this marriage. Perhaps his heart will heal yet."

Noah nodded. "We shall see what will become of Carmi."

Her father-in-law had a sudden weariness to his voice. Carmi didn't follow in the ways of the One God and no doubt this was painful for Noah. When Carmi left Lamech's care, he abandoned the beliefs and embraced whatever god brought him the best business. His first wife, Noah's sister, followed the lead of her husband and forsook the God of her fathers. Rejection of the God of Adam was not a trifle matter in this family and Denah was sure there were unspoken hurts all around.

"Was he a good father to you, Denah?" Noah asked.

"Yes. I miss him, and Beth. I worry about her. She's vulnerable. Father tries, but she is difficult to manage sometimes."

"Ask Japheth to take you to see her."

Denah looked at her hands. "I'm afraid I try his patience too much with my requests."

Noah let a thin smile creep across his face. "He needs you more than you realize. More than he realizes. Be his friend and you'll see that you can meet in the middle. He isn't the unreasonable man he's made out to be. He's a very good son. He has always been a very good son."

♦

Japheth scratched the growth of hair on his chin, sending a cloud of dust into the air. He washed his face countless times during the day but couldn't rid himself of the persistent film coating his skin and clothing. The dust in the ark was worse today than ever as the grain was unloaded and thrown into their storage bins. Several of the workers had been forced to leave when their coughing and sneezing was more abundant than the actual labor they performed.

"Good evening, Japheth." Denah startled him as he entered their room quietly so as not to wake her. He was used to her being in bed when he came home. She stood by the window in the long plain gown she slept in, brushing her hair, allowing the black waves to fall down across her chest.

Japheth peeled off his tunic along with the bits of wheat that drifted to the floor in a dusty shower. "Denah. You're up late."

Denah gathered his garment and took it to the window where she gave it a vigorous shake, followed by a sneeze as the dust formed a veil around her before drifting into the night sky. "I wanted to see how your day went."

Japheth tried not to show the surprise he felt. She hadn't asked about his work for weeks. "It was fine. I catalogued all the first floor rooms, and we loaded a good deal of grain."

"It appears to have been a dusty job."

"It's from the grain bags. You can shovel the dust out of the bins."

"Are you sure there's still grain left in the bags?" Denah picked the yellow bits from his hair.

Japheth took a cloth and soaked it in a basin then began

stripping his skin of its dusty coating. "We can't keep the place clean. The bags leak fine particles with every movement. There's a haze inside the ark."

"Perhaps it's the fabric. The weave is too loose. Did you buy it from my father?"

"No." Japheth gave her an apologetic grimace. "I didn't. I found it for a better price than Carmi would allow."

Denah put her hands on her hips. "A better price for an inferior product."

Japheth smiled and revealed teeth that felt crusted with dust. "Yes. I believe that may be the case. That's what he said, too."

Denah grabbed another cloth and scrubbed between his shoulder blades. "You know, husband. I can get the weave you need from my father for a good price."

Japheth picked at the grit lodged under his finger nails. "He might just do that for his daughter, although I'm sure there will still be a profit to be made."

"Of course, he'll make sure of it. But an ark that isn't coated in this will be worth any price, don't you think?" Denah rang out the cloth again, in water that was as brown as the layer on her husband's feet.

Japheth didn't answer right away. Surprisingly, Denah held her tongue instead of letting loose her usual banter to get what she wanted. She was right. Even though he saved resources purchasing the burlap, it was inferior and it made sense to start again with a higher quality product. The weeks of work already spent sewing and bagging the various grains would be wasted but the dust was intolerable.

"Yes. Alright. We should speak with your father."

Denah paused in her scrubbing. "He'll give me a better deal if he doesn't have to prove himself in front of you, in front of another man. He has nothing to gain by trying to bluff his way past me to save face."

Japheth turned his head and looked at her over his shoulder. "You don't want me to go?"

"Oh it isn't that, but…"

"What, Denah?"

"I could go see Beth as well as visit my father and I know you're busy. It seems more practical for me to go while you work."

Japheth felt his shoulders stiffen as her motives were prioritized. Her conversations rarely followed a direct line. She found winding little paths to drag him along until she reached her destination. He felt manipulated. He wanted to tell her no, he would go to Carmi, alone, but it was wrong of him to keep her from the man she adored.

Japheth sighed and wrung out the dirty rag. "Take two of the servants, then, and go visit your family. Don't be gone long and stay away from the market other than Carmi's shop. You know how my mother will worry until you return."

Denah returned to the window and faced the moon. It was just shy of presenting itself as a full circle, its light glancing off her smile after he snuffed out the lantern. Her request was simple and Japheth pushed the resentment over her motives aside. It would be helpful for her to make the deal with Carmi and she was right, she would get a better deal without him there.

Chapter Fifteen

The servants were directed to the large barn where Carmi's men napped and tapped into a little wine while their master was at the shop. Denah's father had been eager to make a deal with her on behalf of Japheth, knowing the quantity of grain sacks Noah intended to store on the ark and because she let her father get the best end of the bargain. She didn't want to stay and haggle.

Denah waited until the two men disappeared into the barn. As far as they knew she was in her father's house where they wouldn't be required to monitor her safety. They could relax and consider themselves fortunate to get paid for such a simple task. But Denah had no intention of visiting Beth just yet. There were more important matters to attend to first.

She pulled a long loose scarf up over her head to hide her face and began walking briskly down the street toward her mother's temple. The streets were not yet busy and it was easy to stay hidden in the shadows of the homes and shops along the way. The small pouch of coins tied to her waist jingled in rhythm to her sandals as she clacked over the worn cobbles, stepping clear of puddles that accumulated from last night's mist. She stopped occasionally and pretended to browse while looking over her shoulder. No one followed her.

Denah stopped at the entrance to the courtyard and took in the wonder of the magnificent structure. The Temple of Zakua gleamed in the morning sunlight, as if lit up on its own. Sparkly bits of sediment confined in the bleached white stones reflected light and sent it bouncing in all directions. Off the golden moons adorning the seven tall pillars that lined the front of the building. Off the brazen altars flanking each side of the entrance, sending aromatic smoke swirling into the sky. Off the jeweled women dancing in their stalls, beckoning, waiting for customers.

Vendors with colorful tent coverings were already lining up along the side of the temple with shouts of greeting to one another and shouts of disapproval to their servants and shouts of encouragement to the dancers. Today would be a busy one for Zakua. The fertility rituals performed around the full moon had the greatest benefit and tonight it would rise in fullness of form. The plight of the grain sacks had been a blessing of most fortuitous timing.

Denah paused at the steps and turned toward the merchants, purposefully avoiding the tent of dedicated infants. Simple wooden cages held animals for sacrifice. She didn't want to purchase anything yet, not until she observed the ritual and saw what others offered in payment first. If chickens were offered, she would offer a chicken. If coins were preferred, she was prepared. Her hand rested on the allowance hidden within her belt. Japheth gave it to her the day of the shopping expedition with Jael. She was glad she didn't waste it on some worthless trinket.

The double doors to the sacred interior were open. Denah climbed the seven steps then stopped at the threshold. A familiar aroma hovered in the space and she recognized it as frankincense. It reminded her of her father and she felt her heart quickening in response. She stood on forbidden grounds. He would be angry. With an inward sigh she made her mind relax. No, he wouldn't. She was no longer his unwed daughter. There was no shame in entering now.

Still, she couldn't convince her legs to step forward. Japheth's face pressed into her mind. He would not approve. His God would not approve.

Denah stepped aside to let a young couple pass and enter the temple. She didn't have to ask to know their hearts' desire, to know why they came, together, hand in hand as one. As it should be. Part of her screamed, angry that her husband refused to be blessed, angry that she had to do this alone, angry that she couldn't suppress the anxiety welling in her gut. Another part of her wanted to turn and walk away, without the blessing. But this might be her only chance. If she didn't go now, the blessing, a child, might never be obtained.

The balsam and lemon aroma intensified as Denah purposefully took a step though the door and into the temple hall. The great room was lit from ceiling vents and windows high above her head. Pillars inside the rectangular space held torches that burned and glowed and made shadows move in chaotic patterns on the smooth stone floor. Beyond the pillars was a hall following the perimeter of the back and sides of the building, leading to rooms where priests and priestesses lived. The temple children lived somewhere in those rooms, too.

A melodic chant echoed in the enclosed space, coming from a back room. It could have been one voice as easily as a hundred, she couldn't tell, but the chords sent tingles up her spine. The handful of patrons in the sanctuary spoke in hushed tones to permit the chant to fill the space within the temple walls. Denah walked slowly toward the end of the room where the carved image of Zakua rose from a pedestal. The golden goddess was surrounded by an altar glowing with bronze bowls of burning frankincense. Small animal sacrifices and coins were placed among the bowls to be purified by the fragrant smoke, collected by girls in short rose colored tunics. Each girl had a heavy gold ring piercing her left ear, the symbol of her status as a priestess to Zakua.

The goddess herself sat cross legged on the back of a turtle. The shell of the turtle was covered with tiny stars and it held the sun in his mouth. Two of his feet stood on land and two on the great sea. Zakua's long arms were wrapped around her seven sons, six of whom seemed ready to wriggle free and one who was fast asleep against her shoulder. The goddess had friendly eyes and a gentle smile. She didn't condemn Denah for standing in her presence.

The statue's motionless features held Denah's gaze while the imageless god of Noah captivated her thoughts. Why did the One God have no image? A god who sees, a god who speaks, a god who hears, yet has no face? More people would respect Noah's god if he had his own temple for worship, a place for them to offer their sacrifices and seek his favor. He was an invisible god and that made him unknowable and unapproachable. Zakua offered all that the One God did not.

Several couples stood in line for the fertility ritual under the motherly gaze of Zakua. Denah stood nearby and observed, captivated, like she was the first time she watched, with her mother, years ago. A young couple knelt on a purple cloth, facing each other. The priestess stood between them and waved a smoking vessel over their heads while calling on Zakua to open the womb of the woman and strengthen the man's seed. She then placed an ornate golden bowl before the man. It contained dirt. Denah's mind flashed back to her childhood, hidden in the tree, watching the temple boys gather dirt from the garden to fill the golden bowls. The young couple viewed the sacred bowl with awe while the priestess held it in her long fingers. The man spit in the bowl as directed then handed the bowl to his wife, who took a pinch of earth between her fingers and ate it.

The priestess began to chant and sway, her eyes closed, holding the bowl above the heads of the couple. Her groans developed into only a few sentences that Denah could understand. "From the earth man is formed, from the earth we form man," she said. "Blessed be the woman whose womb gives life. Blessed be the man whose seed is preserved."

When she was finished, the bowl was handed to a young boy who disappeared as quickly as he had arrived. The young couple stood and handed the priestess the payment in coins. "Be fruitful and multiply," the woman said while motioning for the next couple to kneel before her.

Denah had forgotten about the dirt. How did it go from garden soil to holy ground? And how could she receive this blessing without Japheth? She backed away from the scene, unsure what to do.

A gentle hand on her shoulder led to a crimson smile. A priestess stood at her side, the golden band dangling from her ear. Blue paint covered her eyelids, converging with green and sweeping up to her temples in a flourish that connected to her thin black brows. She wore a long rose colored garment that was trimmed in the same purple braid woven through her hair. Stacks of bracelets clinked together as she moved.

"Are you new to the temple of Zakua?"

"No, but it's been a long while since I was here, with my mother."

"Are you here to be blessed?"

"Yes. Well, maybe. I thought so, but my husband isn't here and now I'm not sure."

The priestess placed a red nailed hand on Denah's abdomen and closed her eyes for a moment. Denah caught her breath and stood still. "Yes, you want your womb to spring with life," the woman said.

Denah nodded. "I do. I want sons, children of my own."

They stood together and watched another couple kneeling on the purple cloth.

The priestess smiled and linked her arm in Denah's. "Perhaps you would like to receive a blessing without your husband?"

"I wasn't sure that I could. That's why I came and I don't know when I'll have another chance."

The woman guided her away from the couples, into the hall beyond the pillars. The long corridor was empty except for the resonating chant and the heavy scent of incense, rolling through the narrow space, consuming the walls in a fragrant vapor. They walked down the line of rooms with closed doors until they came to one that was open just a crack. Inside the room a pot of incense burned, filling the air its fragrant haze. The only furnishings were a small table and a mat on the floor covered with brightly hued pillows. "Wait here," the priestess said as she closed the door behind her.

Denah felt her pulse quicken in the unfamiliar room. There was a vulnerability hovering over her, launched by the uncertainty of what was to come and what would be expected of her. She pressed her hand against the coins in her belt and made sure the pendant from her father was hidden beneath her clothing.

There were no chairs in the room so Denah leaned against the wall beneath a window high above her head. Broken conversations trickled in from the temple courtyard, muted by the chants echoing in the corridor. The tones were deep and rhythmic, haunting in a way that made her hair stand on end. Denah fiddled with her belt. She wanted to leave and wanted to stay at the same time.

When the door opened it wasn't the priestess who entered, but a man. Denah stiffened against the wall. It wasn't appropriate for her to be in a room alone with a man she didn't know. The man closed the door and leaned against it. His bare chest was clean shaven and had a shine as if he had rubbed it with oil. The loose trousers he wore were linen of a fine weave and of the same color worn by the priestesses. He too had bracelets around his wrists and ankles and a golden ring in his ear. Denah stared at his feet, at toes capped in red paint.

The priest smiled. "Why are you afraid?" he asked.

Denah exhaled, unable to relax her spine. "I'm not afraid. I didn't know what to expect."

"I was told you desired a blessing. Would you prefer a priestess?"

"No. No. It isn't that." Denah felt heat climb up her face, his meaning too clear.

"You aren't here against your will. You may leave anytime you wish." He bowed from the waist then opened the door and stepped to the side.

Denah hesitated.

The man watched her, then closed the door again when she didn't bolt. He floated down onto the cushions and leaned on his elbow. "You aren't sure, then, that you truly desire sons for your husband. It's your decision. Be blessed or don't be blessed."

Denah licked her dry lips and stayed pressed against the wall, fighting the battle in her mind. This is for Japheth, she told herself. This is for Noah, for heirs. The curse must be broken.

A bead of sweat trickled down her temple. Denah pulled the scarf from her head and wiped it away.

Chapter Sixteen

Denah didn't stop running until she arrived at her father's property. She avoided the house and went instead to the fields where an overgrown hedge provided the privacy she sought. Hot tears washed down her cheeks, doing nothing to cleanse the shame of what she had just done.

Her hand found the raw stripe on her neck where the priest ripped off the onyx pendant in payment for his blessing. He demanded more coins than she had to offer. The kind smile and gentle touch became a sneer and a painful grasp when he saw the pitiful amount that fell from her belt. It wasn't enough. But he had seen the pendant. He claimed it for himself before pushing her out of the smoky room.

Denah sat motionless in the shadows, hugging her knees, willing herself to melt into the earth. Once she fully understood the nature of the blessing, she should have run. She didn't. She stayed, convincing herself that it was necessary. Now she fought the sickening awareness forming in her heart, that what she had done was no more a blessing than eating from the golden bowl where husbands placed their saliva. The temple of Zakua was a lie. It was all dirt, just plain dirt.

The cool of morning crept away as the rising sun invaded her hiding place. Denah followed the shade as the light advanced, piece by piece stripping away her cover until she sat drenched by the light. She wiped her face and forced herself to breath evenly. What was done was done. There was no going back. She tied the scarf from her head around her throat to cover the wound. If Japheth or her father asked about the pendant she would say she lost it or stored it away for safety or something, anything but the truth, that it was payment for her act of betrayal.

◆

Beth held a handful of long yellow flax stems. She pulled the bundle through the heckling comb in short jerky motions as the sharp teeth stripped off the remaining straw, leaving only the polished fibers. Her shoulders drooped and her pace was much slower than that of the hired employees working around her. She stopped after each pull to inspect her work instead of maintaining a steady rhythm. The meticulous scrutiny made her as asset when it came to stamping patterns onto the woven linen. It wasn't desirable in the heckling barn.

"Stop that, Beth. How many times do I have to tell you? Keep working or I'll tell your father what a sluggard you are." The servant woman smacked the edge of the table with a scutching stick near Beth's hand.

Denah crossed the room in long strides to be a barrier between the woman and her sister. "Don't talk to her that way or you'll be the one reported to my father."

The woman held her ground with her hands on her hips. "Carmi wants me to keep her working, Denah. She can't even do this correctly without me to watch her lazy hands every moment."

Denah grabbed the flax from Beth and tossed the bundle onto the floor at the woman's feet. "Then do the work without her." She took her step-sister's hand and led her out into the sunshine.

"Denah, Denah, Denah," Beth repeated as she hugged her sister tightly around the waist. "I'm so happy to see you. No one told me you were coming."

Denah flopped down on a patch of grass and watched Beth dance, spindly arms to the heavens, spinning until she could stand no longer, splattering herself on the ground beside Denah. It was good to be in the radiance of her sister's delight. The girl was born with a smile and considered everything in her world a source of pleasure. She beamed at Denah with eyes set too far apart on her face above a broad flat nose. The smile revealed several gaps and a thick tongue that poked out from between her lips when she concentrated.

"Why are you sad?" The smile changed to a look of concern.

"I'm not sad, Beth."

"You've been crying." Beth gently traced the tear lines on Denah's cheek with a stubby finger.

"I have happy tears. I'm so happy to see you, that's all."

Satisfied, the smile returned. "How is the great boat of Noah? Will you take me to see it? I can't wait to see it. Have you been on it?"

Denah ruffled her sister's straw colored hair. "It's nearly finished, Beth. I'll ask father if you can come see it soon."

"Can I ride it with you when the waters come? I don't like it deep, you know."

Denah knew. Beth rarely ventured into water above her knees. She avoided even the shallowest ponds, associating them with the pools where their father's flax was placed after it was harvested. It was the smelly, slimy bundles of retting flax that Beth really disliked.

"Why are you thinking about the waters of Noah, Beth?"

"I was thinking about you. That makes me think about the boat, then I think about all the water. I'd like to ride with you, when the water gets deep."

"Yes, Beth dear, you can certainly ride on the great ark of Noah with me."

"There you are." Carmi's voice came from behind them. Both girls stood and greeted him. A shroud of shame hugged her soul but Denah pushed it aside and presented him the face of one with no ugly marks to hide. The faint aroma of frankincense clung to his garment and Denah's insides recoiled. The smell of the temple. The smell of deception. The smell of passion, fully legal, yet leaving the sentence of guilt slashed across her mind.

"You need to get back to work," he said to Beth. "Your sister spoils you with her presence. You've had a long break."

Beth looked confused. Carmi didn't know about the trip to the temple or that Denah spent a long time in the shadows alone. He assumed she had been here with Beth since their burlap negotiations earlier that morning. Denah was grateful the girl didn't object.

Denah pointed at the barn. "Is this the right place for her, father? Can't she work in the house?"

Carmi patted Beth in the head. "She doesn't mind the work, do you Beth?"

Beth giggled. "I don't mind."

"Your men are waiting for you. I found them asleep in the barn." Carmi looked into her eyes. Denah feared they were still red rimmed so she looked away. What else would he see there?

"Yes, father. You're right. I should go." She pecked his cheek with a kiss before he turned for the house, squelching images of crimson lips and peacock painted eyes and rose robed women doing the same thing. Beth, she drew in close, squeezing her goodness, hoping it would spill over and bleach the stain of sin.

"You smell like father," Beth said.

Chapter Seventeen

The bubbling stream coursing through Noah's property diverted into a shallow pool that filled and emptied with the adjustment of two wooden gates. Denah allowed the water to fill the pool for the second time, then adjusted the gates so the water continued to flow in and escape at the same rate. She sat on a flat stone in the middle of the clear flow and allowed the cold liquid to numb her body.

The water flowing out of the pool looked the same as the water flowing in. It would not have surprised her if the pure water touched her skin then turned murky, black and tainted, as it made its way through the courtyard and out into the gardens. It wouldn't have surprised her if the herbs and vegetables curled on their stems, yellowed and diseased, as they drank the water flowing past their roots. If the stream carried death in its wake, beyond the home of Noah, to the lands beyond the ark and into the great sea itself, it would not have been a surprise.

The water remained clear.

The old cloth she took from her room was rough, meant for cleaning anything but human skin. It was the only one that would suffice. Bit by bit Denah scrubbed herself. When she finished, she started again until her cold fingers could barely hold onto the cloth. Still she felt dirty.

She examined herself all over. There were no signs indicating what she had done or where she had been except the red welt along her neck. The scrape was superficial, it would hide and it would heal. She expected something else, a mark stamped on her forehead by Adam's God perhaps, or etched into her skin by the priest. There was nothing. No one would know. The guilt would blacken her heart from the inside but no one would look at her and see that she was a fool. A fool for believing in the blessings by Zakua.

Her disgrace was hidden.

Denah tossed the washrag aside and climbed out of the pool. Her skin, red and raw from the scrubbing, her limbs heavy and stiff from the cold water. She pulled a clean tunic over her head then sat on a stone in the sunlight. The screens surrounding the pool were covered in honeysuckle and she breathed in and out deeply, willing her mind to find a peaceful place of rest.

Her solitude was interrupted by the marked woman. "Oh, I'm sorry," Renita said as she came into the enclosure. I didn't expect any one in here this time of day."

Denah turned her head away from the woman and focused on getting her hair into a coil behind her head. Her numb fingers burned with the effort. "It's alright. I'm nearly finished."

The woman stood and watched her.

Denah felt a flush rise to her cheeks.

"Do you know my name?" the woman asked.

Denah looked up at her then immediately turned away. She heard the woman called by name, of course, but she was marked. A no one. Why would Denah call her by name as if she deserved recognition? If she were in the city she wouldn't care if anyone knew her name as she begged for scraps to eat and hid in refuse piles for safety in the dark terrors of night.

The woman laughed at Denah's silence. "I didn't think so." She sat down on a bench near Denah. "Why do you think you're so much better than I?"

Denah whirled around to face the servant and put her in her place. "You are marked-"

She stopped and bit down on her lip, feeling the rise of shame she wasn't able to wash away. She didn't want to admit the truth, truth sitting before her, watching her with questioning eyes. The only difference between Denah and the servant was the visible scar left by the woman's husband.

Denah forced herself to look into the woman's face. The servant didn't know that Denah fell into shame yet she didn't consider herself a disgrace, unworthy of respect. She sat with Denah as an equal. Where was her guilt?

Heat rose up Denah's neck. "You are called Renita," she said. "And you are marked by your husband because of your unfaithfulness. Why do you not carry that shame?"

Renita looked down at her hands. "Why do assume I don't carry that burden? And what is it to you? My actions were of my own choosing and they don't harm you, so why do you think I'm nothing but a worthless waste of food?"

Denah followed the scar across the woman's face. It was raised above the rest of her skin and pulled her face into a pinch around her mouth, making one side of her lip curl upward. The two sides of her face were uneven in shape and color and texture. How did she not want to cover herself even if she reasoned away her own shame? How could Japheth see past it?

"I'm ugly. I know. There's nothing I can do about it."

"Why does Jael like you? How can Noah permit you in his home? Their God would not approve of you so why do they?"

Renita shrugged. "I don't understand all their ways. I was a beggar on the streets and they brought me here to work. Jael made me stop hiding my face. She said it was good for my shame to be a reminder to others and that I was made by her God, deserving to eat and work and live." She looked up at the sky. "I would not have taken me in."

"He didn't kill you."

"My husband? No, he did not. He should have done so."

"Why didn't he?"

Renita shrugged again. "We were good together as man and wife for many years. I gave him three sons and two daughters. Then one night I was captivated by a man in the square, a traveler with charming words. My husband caught us. He marked me. I don't know why he didn't kill me. Perhaps he remembered the times when we were young and only wanted one another."

"He caught you with the traveler. That's how he found out."

"Yes."

Denah took her time tying on her belt as she sat beside the servant. "You had a child, later."

Renita looked past Denah with eyes that glistened. "A son. He had the long skinny nose and big brown eyes of his father, my husband. Not the coloring of the traveler."

"Have you seen your son? Is he at the temple?"

"I left him there but I have never seen him. I'm no longer welcome there."

"And your firstborn son? And your other children?"

"I am dead to them."

Denah didn't respond. There were no words to fill the woman's void.

Renita stood up abruptly and gathered Denah's abandoned clothing. She started to walk away, then stopped, pivoting around to face Denah, her eyes penetrating the distance between them, holding Denah's in a tight grip. Without blinking Renita raised the tunic to her nose. She inhaled.

Denah jumped to her feet as realization spread across the servant's face. Renita nodded her head. "I see," she said. "We all have secrets best left uncovered, don't we? I'll get these washed."

Chapter Eighteen

Denah ran through the woods. Her breath came in heavy gasps and she was drenched in sweat. Thick vines and branches fell around her and she had to thrash with her arms to get them out of the way. The pounding feet that followed her seemed to be gaining but when she looked over her shoulder, no one was there.

When she came to the clearing, she stopped. No one noticed her arrival. The gathered crowd focused on some commotion within the ring they formed. Denah couldn't see over the sea of heads and began to push her way through the mob. The people cheered for a moment then shouts and accusations began flying. Then cheering again, then cursing.

A woman sat on a tree stump, the epicenter of the verbal assault. Her back was turned so Denah couldn't see her face but she recognized the long rose colored garment and the golden band dangling from her ear. Noah and his three sons marched around the woman, hurtling one question after another into her face, inciting the crowd to cheer and jeer.

Denah got down on her hands and knees and crawled to the front of the crowd where she could see the woman's face. It was Renita. She sat serenely on the stump with a straight back, not responding to the questions flung in her direction. She held a sleeping child in her arms.

The crowd grew quiet when Noah raised his arm, revealing a sharp knife. Then the mob erupted with one loud voice. "Guilty. Guilty. Guilty."

Denah realized the child was in danger. She had to save him!

"Stop!" She yelled as she got onto her feet and tried to run towards the woman. She couldn't move. Someone was holding her back, squeezing her arm and calling her name. "Denah! Denah!"

When she looked back at the stump she realized the child was gone and the woman was cradling a soiled tunic. Denah looked at her face. Renita was gone. Her own face stared back. She was the woman on the stump. Japheth stood before her with outstretched arm, knife raised.

"Guilty! Guilty! Guilty!"

"No!"

"Denah!" Japheth held her by the shoulders, his face inches from her own. "Wake up!"

Japheth's eyes were wide in the moonlight streaming through the window. Denah raised her hands to protect her face before she realized he meant her no harm. He wasn't marking her. Or killing her. She was dreaming. She exhaled and relaxed her tightly clenched shoulders. Her heart was pounding in her chest.

"You were dreaming. You're all right. You're safe." Japheth got out of bed and dipped a cloth into a basin of water then brought it to her. She was soaked in perspiration.

"Was it the nephilim?"

Denah looked at him a moment before realizing what her husband was asking. "Oh. Yes. Chasing me, I think."

He handed her a fresh tunic and helped her to change. "What happened to your neck?"

Denah covered the raw skin with her hand. "I must have, I think, I-"

"It's alright, Denah. Don't worry about it. Try to fall asleep." Japheth stretched out behind her and pulled his body up close to hers. "I'm here," he said. His hand ran gently over her hair until his breathing eased and he was asleep. Denah was wide awake. The moon, full with the promise of new life, mocked her from beyond the window.

◆

The Gathering occurred every seventh day on Noah's land. On this day, the usual labors ceased. There were no thorns stacked for burning, no thistles uprooted, no sheep sheered or grapes harvested. Garments remained unwashed and pottery unfired. Even the great ark stood quiet on God's Day of Rest and Remembrance.

Denah sat on her stump in the clearing with the family and a handful of employees. She shifted her position once again, restless from the night before. The old stump was rigid and unforgiving and she was anxious for the gathering to be over.

Noah continued to recite the familiar words. "And God said, 'Let there be light.' And there was light. And God saw that the light was good..."

Denah focused on her father-in-law. He was handsome in a rugged sort of way. Physically, he was very strong with the broad shoulders and sharp defined tone in his limbs like the construction men, and they were half his age at most. Ham had a similar build, but where Ham had nearly a clean shaven scalp, Noah's head sprouted loose brown curls that cascaded every which way down his head. Japheth had the same nest of unruly locks and Denah liked to run her fingers through it and watch the spirals coil back into position.

The emerging gray strands in Noah's cropped beard curled tightly, like tendrils on a pumpkin vine. He didn't bother to pluck them from his beard as her father did.

Long lashes framed Noah's deep brown eyes. Kind eyes, with crinkled corners. They flirted with Jael who sat across the circle in rapt attention, listening to her husband's words as if they were new each seventh day gathering. She could recite them herself, Denah was sure. The words were the same as when she first heard them spoken by Methuselah, many years ago, after she was acquired by Lamech as a household servant.

The carved wooden box containing the writings of Adam sat on her father-in-laws lap. His left hand held the box, his thumb caressing the almond blossom design while his right hand helped him speak. Denah had never seen Noah read directly from the tablets lying in the box. He knew them by memory and repeated them today with enthusiasm and conviction. Even in her less than alert state it was difficult not to pay attention to him. The words he spoke had life of their own.

"And God said let there be an expanse between the waters to separate water from water."

Noah faced the great ark as he spoke. The seat beside him was empty. It was Lamech's seat. Noah's father was murdered five years ago yet his presence in the family lineup was still upheld. Methuselah sat next to the invisible Lamech on a chair constructed with a back rest and sides so he was less likely to fall to the ground when he dozed off. Already Denah could see his lids beginning to drift downward, then fly up only to drift down again.

"And God said, 'Let the water under the sky be gathered to one place and let dry ground appear.' And it was so."

To Noah's right sat Shem. Shem, the designated firstborn, sat erect and mouthed the words along with his father. His hand clasped a small leather pouch, made from the skin of the first sacrifice. The beast was destroyed and skinned by the One God himself when Adam was disobedient. Its hide became Adam's garment. The leather piece, cut from the hem, was given to Noah's forefather with a stone collected from outside the great Eden itself. First Man gave it to his descendants as a reminder of the consequences of disobedience. The pouch was created from death, the very first death on God's earth.

Shem had his father's kind eyes. His face was serene as he silently recited the words in unison with Noah. He inherited more than the tablets and sacrificial pouch. Shem inherited the blood of Adam. He possessed the same keen awareness of man's sin against the Creator that coursed thorough Noah's veins, the same blood that imposed a self loathing and called for days of remembrance week after week, year after year. Denah had no doubt Shem would preside in the clearing every seventh day even if no one else in the land joined him. He was right with his God in this setting that would one day be his to lead.

"And God said, 'Let the land produce vegetation: seed bearing plants and trees on the land that bear fruit according to their various kinds.' And it was so."

Shem was in charge of the employees working the fields and tending the flocks. He had a reputation for being fair like his father, but he was too kind at times. Shem had a soft heart for any sad tale the workers told and often paid them far more than their work deserved. He was like Noah in many ways, carrying the weight of all the trouble the day could hold yet free of burdens at the same time. His trust rested in the One God.

"And God said, 'Let there be lights in the expanse of the sky to separate day from night, and let them serve as signs to mark seasons and days and years, and let them be lights in the expanse of the sky to give light on the earth."

As far as Denah could tell, Shem didn't hold his position as Noah's successor over Japheth's head. He was not given to that sort of cruelty to his older brother and because of it the two maintained an amiable relationship. It wasn't Shem's fault that Japheth questioned the God Who Sees and was removed from his rightful place as firstborn. Shem would eventually control the family estate, determine the rules and set the boundaries, decide who got married and who would work the fields, as well as lead the sacrifices. It was in Japheth's interest to be his brother's friend, although Shem would be fair to his brother even if the two were at odds. That was Shem.

"And God said, 'Let the water teem with living creatures and let birds fly above the earth across the expanse of the sky.'"

Ham sat on the next seat with his chin supported by his hands, elbows on his knees. His eyes were mirroring Methuselah's this morning, barely registering the proceedings. It wasn't the first time he arrived with bleary eyes and unkempt hair. He was known to work late the night before the Gathering Day, not finishing any real work, Denah suspected. More like a round of wine and games with the men. One night she saw him stagger off one of their wagons into the courtyard, returning from a trip into the city in the wee morning hours.

"And God said, 'Let the land produce living creatures according to their kinds: Livestock, creatures that move along the ground, and wild animals, each according to its kind. And it was so.'"

Her husband sat next to Ham. Noah's firstborn, long awaited son to Jael, sat in a position of lowest honor, at the end of the family line. If anything happened to Shem, Ham would lead the family, not Japheth. Her husband sat on the stump listening to every word that his father spoke. He knew the recitations, too, though he did not follow with his lips as Shem did. It was obvious he adored Noah and still craved his approval. What a joy it would be for her husband to produce the first heir. Wouldn't that restore him in his father's eyes?

Denah couldn't imagine what it was like when Japheth spoke his mind to his father. Noah must have felt as if he had been stabbed in the heart by his firstborn. The very disobedience that he spoke against on the Meeting Stone was present in the mind of his own son. Japheth had to have been wrenched in two by his father's aggressive response. He could not have foreseen the cost. She didn't know that for sure, of course. Japheth didn't speak of the past. No one in the household talked about the times before her arrival to any length, especially if the events were associated with something negative. They knew the very days of the beginnings by heart yet let their own failures slide away unremembered. She received answers to her questions only when she asked one of them directly, and even then the response was limited. Pain in the lives of the house of Noah were not revisited. Each Gathering Day the wounds were split wide open once again, however, as the men took their respective seats.

"Then God said, 'Let us make man in our image...'"

Our image? Who was the God of Noah? Denah felt a flush of shame and looked down at the ground, knowing this God was not one to approve the betrayal of one's husband. Did Noah's God even understand why she did what she did? Could the God Who Sees feel her pain and share in her disappointment? Was it he who closed off the wombs of her sisters and of Jael for so many, many years?

Denah glanced back at the great ark and allowed herself the same question that had been Japheth's undoing. Was this God real?

Chapter Nineteen

Smoke rose to the sky carrying the scent of the Gathering Day sacrifice up to the One God, God of Adam, God of Noah. God of Japheth. Japheth breathed through his mouth as he pushed the hind quarters of the burning gazelle into the center of the flames, causing the gray swirls to dance around him before lifting to the heavens amidst his coughing. The scent of burning beast was pleasing to God. He found the smell repulsive. Removal of the hide made the aroma less offensive but Noah would not alter the practice. The sacrifice was to God's specifications, not their own. An entire clean beast was offered in homage. Nothing added. Nothing removed.

It was his family alone in the clearing, after the recitations. The women placed their simple meal on a grassy patch that used to hold many dozens of people. When he was a boy, people came on Gathering Day to listen to Lamech's recitations, then feasted on the bounty of the land. Over the years they came in smaller and smaller numbers until now even the household servants found excuses to avoid participation. No one wanted to think about the beginnings anymore.

Denah sat down beside him in the circle of family. Naomi was chattering on and on about something Japheth could let slide around his ears. He focused on his father, who was reserved, thinking deeply, eyebrows knitted together over his nose. Japheth let the previous days roll through his mind, finding nothing of consequence to explain Noah's concentration. He would find out soon enough, as the time would soon develop into a family meeting, as they often did on these days. Noah waited patiently for the conversation to diminish before he spoke.

"The exterior construction of the ark is complete and we'll finish the coatings of pitch in a few days." Noah leaned against a stump, linking his hands behind his head. His eyes went back and forth between his sons then came to rest on his project, looming over the landscape, silent and still. "The rooms are nearly completed. We have sleeping quarters for several hundred comfortably, and there are additional mats we can utilize as well. We'll have room for all who come, even if it's tight."

Japheth envisioned the living compartments on the top floor of the ark. The rooms were simple, containing a space for sleeping, a low table, and plenty of storage. They were larger than the compartments Noah built for his own family on the middle deck. The top floor was nearer the ventilation window and further from the livestock that would be housed on the lowest level. His own family would be the servants on the ark, it seemed. Their rooms were located among the storage bins, near the two wide ramps that linked the middle deck with the one above and the one below.

Noah grabbed a handful of pistachios from his pocket and began hulling the shells, tossing them over his shoulder into the stream that carried them away. "And what of the provisions? Where do we stand?"

Japheth shifted to a comfortable position. "We've begun gathering grain but we had a problem with the storage."

"That's putting it mildly, brother," Ham said. "We couldn't breathe in there."

Japheth smiled. "Well, yes. But we have a solution. We've ordered a better weave of burlap, a tighter weave, to store the grain in, so the dust will be contained. Carmi will deliver the order soon. Denah stressed the urgency when she made the arrangements."

His mother snapped her head up and looked at him with an odd expression. Was that anger? His father reached over and took her hand, holding it in his own.

"The order is from Carmi?" Noah asked.

Japheth felt the need to take a defensive stand, working hard to control his irritation. His decision was sound. It did not require scrutiny. He inhaled through his nose and continued. "Yes. I realize the first batch I ordered was insufficient and was a waste of resources and now we must pay again for grain bags. And yes, we will pay more this time, I know, but the quality is better. We'll be glad in the long run. We can't have the ark be one giant dust bowl. It will be unlivable."

Noah nodded. "Yes. Yes, it's a good decision, Japheth."

Methuselah nodded his approval. His eyes rested on Denah for a moment then moved on around the circle. "Sometimes that which we toss carelessly into the wind has greater value than that which we deem most treasured. The number of coins we spend does not determine worth."

Japheth and the others paused to consider the old grandfather's words. It wasn't unusual to miss his meanings at first. It was later, Japheth had learned over the years, that the meaning would become clear, after he thought about it for a time. The last few months however, the words of wisdom seemed less and less applicable to their discussions and Methuselah repeated stories more frequently, sometimes retelling the same story two or three times in one day.

Japheth glanced around the circle and noted the affirming nods at the wisdom Methuselah shared. This one they all understood.

Denah paled slightly after Methuselah spoke. She protected her father, of course, and no doubt had the same perception as Japheth, that his parents considered the deal with Carmi foolish at first. Noah covered his opinion, thankfully. It was a sound decision and Denah didn't need to worry it out of proportion. He looked at her profile. She was subdued today, not angry, not sullen, there was no scowl on her face. She just seemed preoccupied. Her fingers kept a consistent fidget with the soft blue scarf around her neck.

Noah waited until his grandfather leaned back and closed his eyes again before he continued. "Yes, it is a good decision to replace the bags. The price is of no consequence if that is what we need, and it won't take long to replace the old ones. Besides that task, we'll finish applying the pitch this week, then finish the cages on the lower deck. Stocking the ark will be all that remains." Noah looked at his three sons in turn then at the ark. "She is almost finished."

They all turned toward the ark, except Denah, her mind apparently traveling a different direction.

Noah twisted a the hairs in his beard into a coil as he continued. "I'm concerned about the construction crew. What will we do as the end nears? They're already quitting earlier in the day and sleeping in longer." Noah addressed the question to Ham who was tossing grapes in the air for Naomi to catch in her mouth.

"It's too soon to make changes in the work force, father. We still need the men around. Once we lay them off and they find other jobs, we'll have difficulty finding replacements. I haven't found replacements for the last few dozen that quit."

Japheth shook his head. "I disagree. The bulk of the project is complete. We don't need to pay these men for work they aren't doing. They're not working hard any more. Three men are doing what one man should easily accomplish in a day. We should begin letting them go."

Ham sighed with exasperation. "No. Your head is too concerned with the numbers, Japheth. It doesn't work that way. We may need them and then what? We spend more time and resources trying to recruit and train new men. We should not let them go."

"Your head is too concerned with what goes on after hours, Ham. You need to let your playmates go home. We shouldn't pay them to entertain you in the tents after dark." Japheth felt his shoulders rise and tense. He forced his voice to be controlled.

Noah held up his hands, demanding silence between the brothers, then turned to Shem. "What's your opinion, Shem?"

Shem looked at the ark for a moment before speaking. "I believe we should keep the men for now. Once they are gone they'll forget about the waters to come. Here, they're reminded of God and his plans. They'll be ready."

Japheth leaned forward and looked pointedly at Shem. "There is no work for them."

Shem looked at Ham then back at Japheth. "Ham can find work for the men. He can keep them out of trouble."

The men grew silent and only the babbling of the stream broke the pause. Denah's hand reached over and covered his with a tight squeeze. Japheth compressed his lips, avoiding his father's gaze. It was Noah's decision. Two against one made no difference. It was Shem's opinion that mattered and Japheth knew it.

Ham was a fool to think they still needed the twenty men remaining in the tents. Five would be adequate once the pitching was completed. No longer did the workmen go back to their beds exhausted from a long day of work. They piddled the sunlight away, then were anxious for entertainment. The nightly sporting contests already sent several men away with broken limbs and the wine and wagers were only going to flow more freely.

Japheth had a good relationship with Shem but his brother would not take sides based on any loyalty or shared respect for one another. Shem put God first in his decisions and this one would be no different. He would act as he felt God would act and usually that meant compassion. His brother chose not to remember God of First Man, the Judge, who threw Adam from the garden and cursed the land on which he toiled. He remembered God of First Man, the Father, who allowed Adam to live, not immediately dissolving him back into the mound of dust from which he came.

Ultimately it wasn't the blood of Adam pumping through his brother's heart that put Shem's opinion above his own. It was Shem's acquired first born status.

Noah captured Japheth's eyes, holding them gently before he spoke. "It shall be as Shem has decided."

Japheth sucked in his breath and sat back against a stump, even though he knew the outcome all along. Ham threw a half eaten biscuit at him and laughed before Naomi playfully slapped him. Shem turned from the uncomfortable moment and addressed his attention to Eran, The conversation would not be discussed any further.

When Noah stood, indicating that the gathering time was over, Japheth was quick to follow. He walked away from the clearing toward the fields where he could work off his frustration and get his anger under control. His right as Noah's successor was gone by his own doing and he had no one to blame but himself. Every action had consequences.

Denah didn't follow him. He couldn't even bring himself to look at her when the decision was made. He didn't want to see eyes filled with disappointment in the man she wed. He wanted her beside him, all the same. He needed her presence. He needed her support, needed one heart to reach out and lift his own from the maddening pit threatening to swallow it.

♦

Denah didn't follow her husband when he strode towards the field. She wanted to, but Japheth just stood abruptly and walked away without looking in her direction. Had he merely glanced her way she would have known that he needed her, that he wanted her presence as he walked off his pain. She couldn't mend his broken status or remove the hurt but she could walk beside him as a friend, as a wife. Japheth apparently didn't want her consolation, working matters out on his own, as usual.

Her husband was right about the men. She heard them from her room, coarse laughter and rowdy games rising late into the starry night. Japheth's opinions on business matters were sound, carefully examined. It was unfortunate his opinion bore little weight if there was a disagreement with his brothers. She knew it made him angry by the way his shoulders stiffened and his lips compressed. He kept himself under control, admirably so, but his eyes revealed the stab of rejection as his father spoke.

She didn't want him to hurt. His fall in status was his own doing, of course. That was years ago. He didn't persist in wearing the cloak of disobedience. Japheth respected his father. It was obvious how greatly he wanted to live under Noah's approval. He was respected by Noah in return, though she doubted Japheth could see it. Noah felt his firstborn's pain when he made decisions contrary to Japheth's opinion. His eyes spoke of his own ache inside.

Jael's eyes spoke, too. She was angry that Japheth bought burlap from Carmi. She tried to cover her displeasure, too late. Denah had seen it. The family had been buying goods from her father for decades, why was there such an issue now? Of course he charged more, it was for a better weave. What was it Methuselah said? Something about the price not being an issue.

Denah put her hands on the scarf hiding the scrape on her neck. She hadn't liked the way Methuselah looked at her when he made that comment. It was as if he was speaking directly to her when he talked about the price of what we give away, as if he knew what she had done. For a moment she thought he was going to announce her deceit. Denah closed her eyes and took in a slow breath. He didn't. He didn't know. She was just reading more into his words than were there.

Denah made her way to the edge of the wheat field where she could see her husband's head bobbing in rhythm to his fast pace between the rows. Her hand went to her abdomen. She wasn't the only one to need a child.

♦

"Shoo!" Jael waved her apron and chased the young blackbirds from her kitchen. Naomi laughed hard enough to nearly fall off her stool which sent Eran and Denah into giggles as well.

"What is it with these birds?" Jael brushed stray wisps of hair from her eyes and sat back down with the raisin cakes she was forming.

"Ham says they're trying to get to the grain. They're flying in and out of the ark all the time now," Naomi said.

"I saw a bird this morning that was green with an orange beak." Eran said. "It sang the most beautiful little song while it perched on my window, calling to its mate."

Denah had just nailed an extra piece of fabric over her window to keep the winged beasts out. "Pretty or not, they're making quite a mess. I have to clean little droppings from my room several times a day."

"And it isn't just the birds making messes," Jael said. "Noah saw monkeys in the woods beyond the clearing, throwing apples to the ground. I haven't seen monkeys around here in years. I thought we got rid of all those pests. We'll have to start setting the traps again before they become a real nuisance."

"Oh, but I like the monkeys, Jael," Naomi said. "They're so smart, they make me laugh. There was a man in town that kept some in a cage. Do you remember them, Denah? They wore tiny little hats and did tricks."

Denah nodded, continuing her sewing as she spoke. "My mother took me to see them. The owner let me feed them pieces of dried up fruit if I would also clean out the cage. I thought I was getting a great deal."

A cinnamon and butter aroma filtered from the large stone oven. Denah inhaled and let the moment linger, wondering if anyone else noticed they included her in the conversation. More often than not, Jael seemed to forget to be angry with her and the kitchen was actually becoming tolerable. Today Jael asked her to work on the burlap as the others prepared the meal. She was a good seamstress, glad for the opportunity to demonstrate her skill and earn favor.

The marked woman came into the kitchen with a basket of produce and Denah forced herself to look up and acknowledge the woman's presence. It had been two months since she had gone to the temple. Two months of restless sleeping, wondering if the woman fully comprehended where Denah had been. And why. Renita had said nothing about the incident by the bathing pool. Denah didn't want to provoke her and loosen her tongue. So she smiled.

Renita glanced at her and nodded before turning to rinse the garden produce. "There is talk among some of the men who went to town," she said. "The body of a priest was found in his own temple."

Denah's heart thumped at the mention of a temple. She looked up at Renita as casually as she could. The woman wasn't looking her direction.

"Found? Found dead, you mean?" Jael asked.

"Yes. Strangled by a nephil they think. His ears were removed and left beside his body."

"A nephil! They haven't made a practice of entering the city for some time. They're avenging the one that was caught and executed perhaps."

"That's why people are afraid. Entering the temple to take a holy one was bold, even for them. It speaks loudly of their contempt for the gods and for their desire to seek revenge."

"Were women taken? Is anyone missing?" Eran paled at her own words.

Renita shrugged her shoulders. "I don't know. The priestesses were safe but there are so many jeweled women outside the temple with their tents, it's hard to say. No one knows for sure. The hunt is on. If there is a nephil in the woods, he will be found."

Denah pushed the young nephil's bloody face from her mind and focused on the rough cloth in her hands. Her stitches were tiny and only the finest bits of grain would find their way through. She sewed three sides of the large bags then added a drawstring through the top. The strings were colored to indicate what was stored inside each bag. The strings had been her idea and Japheth had been pleased. It made his accounting easier when the bags were filled and stacked in the big storage rooms on the ark.

Denah dyed the strings using whatever she could fine on the property. Grapes made purple, sassafras leaves made orange, beets made red and onion skin made yellow. Morning walks to gather supplies were easily arranged now that Japheth approved of her task. She stayed in the open spaces away from the woods, away from the hands of the nephilim.

"Hard at work I see. Good, good. Busy hands still a maiden's mischief plans."

The women gave their obligatory chuckle while Denah assisted Methuselah to his stool near the cooking fire. His eyes were heavy above dark circles of skin that slouched down on his pale cheeks. Jael handed him the onion which he took in his hands as if it were a precious jewel. He smiled at the women in the room, one by one, revealing pink gaps punctuated by bits of multi-colored teeth. His gaze lingered on Denah and she hugged his bony shoulders, breathing through her mouth for a moment to avoid the smell of his clothing.

"Are you warm enough, grandfather?"

"Yes, yes. By the fire it's nice and warm."

"Is there another hug available?" Carmi stood in the doorway of the kitchen. Denah ran to him, putting her arms as far around his wide belly as she could. "Father! I didn't know you were coming."

"I brought another load of the burlap Japheth ordered," he said. "I thought I would check up on my little girl."

"I'm well. How is Beth? Did she come with you?"

"No, she's working."

"I've been thinking about her. She's a good seamstress. Perhaps she could come here for a while and help me sew the burlap. I hate to think of her in the heckling barn. I could use her help."

Jael turned sharply around and looked at her, eyebrows raised. "Is that what Japheth wants?"

"I don't know. I haven't asked him. I just thought about it and I didn't know father was coming or I would have asked him. And you, of course."

Carmi grinned widely at Jael. "Ahh, Jael. Do you not wish to take on another of my daughters? Do they displease you?"

The room grew quiet.

Jael scowled at Carmi. "No Carmi. Denah does not displease me."

"But you have enough of Carmi in this house, already, eh? Another of my offspring running about to remind you of me is too much?"

Jael's face was turning red and she gripped a potato as if she would launch it as a weapon. "Noah isn't hiring any more help, now. That's all."

Carmi laughed, causing his chins to jiggle beneath his braided beard. "Then Beth shall stay put," he said.

Denah frowned. "I wasn't thinking Noah would hire her. I thought he might let her stay here with me as a guest, earning her keep of course. She's no trouble."

"No, Denah." There was finality in Jael's voice.

Carmi squeezed his daughter's shoulders. "No it is. The beautiful Jael has spoken."

"Japheth is at the ark, Carmi. Please talk to him about the delivery. He'll see that you are paid." Jael turned her back to him and began peeling with quick forceful strokes, sending strips of potato soaring through the air.

"I will take my leave, then." Carmi made a polite bow to Methuselah, pinched Denah's cheek and left the room.

Denah sat back down in the subdued kitchen. Why did Jael dislike Carmi so vehemently? Eran and Naomi were looking between her and Jael with the same questioning expression. Methuselah watched Jael's back for a moment then shifted his gaze to Denah. His eyes shimmered and there was an air of sadness about him. Whatever was amiss between Jael and her father, he understood. He was the one to ask what was happening, why the two were at odds. It had something to do with the betrothal, or the wedding, she was sure.

A gentle thud directed Denah's attention to an onion rolling across the floor. Methuselah's onion. His eyes followed it but he didn't attempt to retrieve it. Denah stood to get it when she realized the old man was breathing rapidly. He put his hand against his chest. His face lost its color and was beaded with sweat. She made it to his side as he collapsed against her with a deep sigh.

Chapter Twenty

Methuselah sipped water from the cup Japheth held to his lips. His grandfather had been in bed for three days and Japheth only left the room for brief periods before feeling the need to return to the old man's side. Even as the women changed his bedding and kept his body clean, Japheth stayed nearby. He knew his presence would not increase the days the old man had left as much as he willed the life to remain. He wanted to absorb as much of Methuselah as he could before he was gone.

Methuselah was 969 years old. His life was a treasury of wisdom that Japheth hoarded in his mind, grasping for nuggets that would soon be lost if left unrevealed. Methuselah was the only man alive who knew Adam, the Adam, First Man. Adam talked with his Creator man to man, walked beside his God in Eden. Methuselah listened to the descriptions and the account of the beginnings from the mouth of Adam himself. Japheth tried to etch the images in his memory as the old man repeated the history so nothing would be lost.

It wasn't just the history drawing him to Methuselah's room. He had never known life without the sustaining presence of the man at his side. The ache in his heart was in part fear, fear that he couldn't stand as a man before God without Methuselah's confident reassurance. He was the worn thread that wove the family together and tied up Japheth's frayed ends into a cord of strength far beyond his own power.

Japheth gently lowered Methuselah back onto his pillows and tucked the buffalo hide beneath his chin. Methuselah held Japheth together when he fell from Noah's grace. Japheth would hold him now as he waited for the call of God.

"He Who Sees sees you, my Japheth." Methuselah patted his hand. "Tell me, son, who is your God?"

Japheth took Methuselah's thin hand between his own. "My God is the creator of the earth and the life there upon it and in its waters. He is the God of First Man. He saw Adam in his disobedience and ejected him from the garden of Eden. My God is the God of Abel. He saw his servant Abel in the fields struck down at the hand of his brother. My God is the God of Seth, the father of Enosh, the father of Kenan, the father of Mahalalel, the father of Jared, the father of Enoch."

Methuselah nodded as Japheth spoke the familiar recitation. His eyes fixed on Japheth for a time then he closed them, but his lips smiled, and his hand kept patting Japheth's as he listened to the teachings that every son of Adam inscribed on his heart and added to as the years fell away.

"God saw Enoch and was pleased with his servant so he took Enoch from the earth when he was 365 years."

Japheth never tired of the history of his forefather Enoch. He was like Noah, a man who preached about God to whom ever would listen and to the dirt of the earth when men closed their ears. He spoke against the building of the temples and pleaded with the jeweled women to find husbands. He was against the eating of any beast with God's breath of life inside and would fast for days on end, feeding only on the communication he had with the Creator.

One day he stood in a field, teaching the people about their origins when he simply disappeared. He was there. Then he wasn't. His son, Methuselah and grandson Lamech witnessed the event alongside a hundred or so others. At first the stories regarding his whereabouts were accurate but witnesses soon revised the truth. One claimed it was the nephilim that stole Enoch away. Another that he abandoned his family. Another that he died in the field and was buried. Japheth knew the truth. God simply took Enoch away.

"My God is the God of Enoch who was the father of Methuselah, who was the father of Lamech. And God saw Lamech when his life was taken away at the hands of a murderer."

Only five years ago, Noah's father was in town on business. He never came back to his cart. The spiritual leader of the One God was found outside the city several days later, his body dumped beneath a tree. He had been strangled and his coin purse stolen. Many local miscreants were accused of the crime but no evidence was sufficient to convict any of them and in the end the crime became just another of many that never saw justice.

"And Lamech was the father of Noah. And God saw Noah and told him to build a great ark to save his family from the waters that would flood the land." Japheth stopped the lineage before the last line, 'And Noah was the father of Shem.'

Methuselah opened his eyes and spoke clearly. "And Noah is the father of Japheth."

Japheth spoke quietly. "And the God of Methuselah is the God of Japheth."

Methuselah took Japheth's hand. "Yes. Yes. I know it is so. It's always been so. The knowing of truth has always been within you even though you questioned and reasoned against it."

Japheth nodded. "I was a fool."

"Only a fool turns from the truth and stays turned even when he knows he's in error. You are no fool, my Japheth. God made you wise and full of reason. Your generations will ponder the stars and will look into the depths of the great sea and God will reveal himself there. Some will hear God speak to their hearts and stand firm in his ways while some will refuse to listen until their hearts are thick with disobedience. This is the way it has been and the way it will continue to be. You, my son, are no fool."

♦

Denah sat in the doorway of Methuselah's room and watched her husband tenderly care for his grandfather. Japheth's rumpled tunic was the same one he was wearing three days ago when she ran to the ark to find him, to tell him Methuselah was ill. He was weary from lack of sleep but he would remain near this room until the end, she was sure.

Methuselah spoke of Japheth's generations and the tears once again welled up in her eyes. She blew her nose on a soft rag and held them in. Methuselah craned his head to the side and looked her way then motioned for her to join them.

He was pale under the stack of blankets. His eyes were clear, however, and his grip strong as he took her hand and placed it in Japheth's. His bony hand covered them both. The tendons on the back of his hand stuck out sharply, forming peaks above hollow valleys of skin with no substance beneath.

"United as one. You are bone of bone, flesh of flesh."

Japheth squeezed her hand as Methuselah continued. "Now swear to me this one thing, Japheth."

"Anything grandfather."

The old man smiled at Denah. "You are my witness," he said.

"I want to board the great ark once more. Take me there before I am just dust. Take me to the ark of my grandson Noah that God himself designed."

Japheth nodded. "I promise," he said.

Methuselah's eyes closed and he inhaled deeply, patting their joined hands once more. "Now you go and change clothes, my son. You smell like the pastures after the oxen eat spoiled grain. I'll sleep for a time."

Japheth and Denah stepped quietly into the hallway as he fell asleep. Shem took a chair by the widow to keep watch on the rise and fall of Methuselah's chest. Nether spoke as they walked, hand in hand, the silence a bridge between them rather than a wall. She slipped her hand from his and put her arm around his waist, holding him close as they went to the room.

'Your generations,' Methuselah said. Denah stood in front of the window and pulled back the cloth that kept the birds out. The brightness of the full moon startled her at first. Another month gone by in Noah's household. It had been two months ago now that she went to the temple to seek a fertility blessing so Japheth would indeed have generations to follow behind him. She rubbed her flat abdomen and sighed.

Two months?

Denah gripped the window ledge and stared at the round moon. The time for her cycle of cleansing had come and gone.

Chapter Twenty-one

"One, two, three, lift." Japheth and his brothers followed Noah's command and stood in unison with the litter. They had no difficulty carrying Methuselah. The furry mammoth skin cocooning him in place weighed more than the man himself. Denah followed Jael on one side of the litter while Eran and Naomi walked on the other side. Their conversation was light in the crisp morning air, the focus on the bright eyed man they attended.

Methuselah's head and shoulders were propped up on pillows and he scanned the landscape as if he had never seen it before. He struggled to lift an arm from beneath the blanket, then pointed to the clearing on either side of the path, dotted with stumps. "These were all mighty trees not so very long ago," he said. "It would take three of you boys plus three more to put your arms around some of them."

Noah smiled back at his grandfather from his position at the front edge of the carrying pole. "And I turned them all into support beams. Do you remember, Grandfather, how angry you were the day I took a saw to the first one?"

Methuselah laughed. "Yes, yes, I do remember. I didn't understand the scope of God's design." His eyes turned to the knoll where the great ark towered over the few scraggly trees that remained, the remnants of the old grove. His skin was embroidered with tiny blue lines, Japheth noted, delicate and worn. His mother tried to tuck the blanket back over his arm but Methuselah shook it off again, needing his fingers to point as his eyes absorbed each detail.

The ark was bathed in morning light with puffs of mist clinging to its hull. It had a shimmer from top to bottom now that it was fully pitched. The hevea tree sap dried clear, highlighting the swirling grain of the gopher wood as it traveled in long rows down the length of the ark. Scaffolding still surrounded the vessel as did the large clay pots that held the leftover pitch. The cedar like smell of the oily substance penetrated the dense air.

The men stopped at the base of the ramp. Methuselah inhaled the fragrant breeze then guided them to the side of the boat. He laid one hand upon the hull, the other he lifted to the sky. "Great God of Adam, you took your servant Enoch from this earth with the breath of life still in his mouth. Now take your servant Methuselah with or without breath, then take your servant Noah and his wife and his sons and his son's wives to a place of safety when the waters rise." Methuselah patted the wood and let tears trickle from his eyes.

The family stood quietly beside Methuselah until his laughter broke the silence. "Will you wait until I am a thousand years to take me inside? I don't think we have that much time."

The wide ramp built to handle beams of wood and carts of grain pulled by elephants creaked little under the troop of Noah's clan. The doorway into the interior glowed with a golden light of sunshine and of the many olive oil lanterns that Shem, Ham and Japheth lit in the early hours that morning, as they prepared for Methuselah's arrival.

Methuselah's directed them to the central floor. He looked down the long hall running in either direction, lined with room after room after room. The walls for the most part weren't solid, but slatted to allow air and light flow. They ended at either end of the ark, where ramps connected the middle floor with the one above and the one below. Soft light diffused down the stairwells punctuating the hall, making a light and shadow pattern the length of the structure.

It was quiet in the great boat. Methuselah sucked in a great gulp of air then let out a loud whoop that echoed down the corridor. The noise startled Japheth and he lost his grip for a moment. The tilting litter was righted as Methuselah breathed heavily under his wheezy laughter.

"Let us walk the halls and see the fine work," Methuselah said as he winked at his grandson. "Before Japheth drops me to the earth."

The procession started down the corridor. Many of the rooms were still empty spaces. Others contained neatly stacked bags of grain and seed. There were tools and cooking supplies, hewn lumber and coils of rope. Yards of fabric, pots of medicinal herbs, blankets, rakes, and wheel hubs were stacked in other spaces. The entrances were covered with gates made of bamboo, nailed in an open cross work design to allow quick viewing of the contents but preventing them from scattering all about the floors when the ark was pitching on the waters.

Down the ramp into the first floor, the spaces were larger, like pens, with straw layers covering the floor and stores of dried hay nearby. Each area had a slight slope toward a gutter that lined both sides of the corridor and ran into a temporary storage trough. Japheth looked proudly at the waste disposal system that he and his brothers devised even though it had yet to be tested. None of them volunteered for that task.

Part of the rooms were subdivided into smaller pens and even smaller cages were stacked on top of each other from floor to ceiling. Bamboo pipes connected the cages to central water reserves and food stores were conveniently placed behind the caged areas. The birds and beasts would be confined to small quarters but they would be fed and watered and hopefully kept from one another's waste.

Methuselah examined each room as they walked by. His hand followed the contours of the enclosures as they passed under his hand. "How many will there be, Noah? How many creatures will you put in here?"

Noah shrugged. "I don't know for certain. As many as I can. I made a list of all the kinds of beasts and birds that I could think of and came up with 1,318. It will be a comfortable fit I think."

"Perhaps you will capture a behemoth to store down here."

"If God wants a behemoth on board, I hope it's a young one otherwise we may not float."

"What would Adam think of all this? I met him you know. I met Adam when I was still a young man. My grandfather took me to see him" Methuselah closed his eyes and repeated the familiar story. "I was eighty seven years and Adam was seven hundred and seventy four years. Many, many decades past. He sent word to all the regions, to come, to come to a gathering of the people near the place of their beginnings. He was getting old in years and he wanted to see his off-spring, to pass along the leadership, and to worship as one."

The men walked slowly with the litter as Methuselah talked. They all knew this story, yet coming from the mouth of the old man, it was still fresh and alive, as if it had just occurred.

"Oh, the generations. Young and old. It was eight days to get there, to the gathering in Havilah, the great plain flanking the garden. Many wanted to continue on to Eden but Adam would not allow it. It was guarded so that no man had entrance. He said it was not the will of God for any man to return, he and his descendants were forever forbidden from the land where God himself walked the soil and ate berries from the vines. Yet the presence of the Creator was in the plain, with First Man and his children and his children's children."

Methuselah stopped to catch his breath. No one spoke as they made their way to the top floor where Noah had prepared living quarters for those who listened, those who chose the safety of the ark.

"He was old then, as I am now. Except I am older than he," Methuselah chuckled at the thought. "He sat upon a great stone in the field where we gathered and we sat in semi-circles before him as he recited his story. He told of his beginning, of the animals that ate from his hand. Of Eve and how he lost his breath at the site of her, of her pain with the birth of their thirty-three sons and twenty-three daughters. Of his anguish at her death and how he buried her back into the earth from which she came, praying that God would bring her back to him again. Mostly he talked about the day of doubt, the day he questioned the word of his Creator God and ate of the forbidden tree."

The group stopped at the window in the roof top extension. The protective cover was folded back on its hinges to let in the light and air. The men placed Methuselah on a ledge where he could see out over the countryside.

"When he finished speaking, Adam chose a memorial stone from the land, the elements of the earth his own elements. The stone, like his blood, was wrapped in the consequence of disobedience – a skin of death. He gave the stone to Enoch, his successor as keeper of the ways of the One God. With the stone, he placed three clay tablets into Enoch's care. The tablets were stamped by Adam's own hand with the history of the earth from the beginning. 'Know the words well,' Adam said. 'From these words are all truths birthed.' "

The old man's eyes glistened as he spoke, as did Shem's. Shem's right hand wrapped around the old piece of brown hide that he tied around his neck with a cord. When Enoch was taken by God, the hide with its stone and the tablets were handed down to Methuselah, then to Lamech, then to Noah.

The preliminary transfer of leadership to Shem had been a private affair. Noah, Lamech, Methuselah and his brother took a journey back to Havilah and it was completed. As with most painful situations in his family, the event was never discussed, at least not in his hearing. Japheth never asked his brother about it, either, although he wanted to at times. He had never even seen the stone that lay wrapped against his brother's heart.

Japheth turned his gaze away from his brother. He had no hard feelings toward Shem, but he felt like an intruder in a moment belonging to the line of leaders of the One God, the men who carried the blood of Adam. Not himself.

Methuselah took hold of his arm. "My children," he said to all of them, his eyes fixing on Japheth. "Do not doubt the words of the Creator. In His words are life and truth."

Methuselah looked out the window again, letting the sun bathe his skin. His breathing was slow, his energy playing out. "Take me to my room, boys," he said.

Noah and his sons carried the litter to the middle deck, to the room that had been specially prepared for his grandfather. It was the largest one on the ark and constructed exactly like his room in the house, without the window.

The old man's ragged smile returned. "Yes, yes. I am home."

His grandsons lifted him from the litter to the mattress on the floor. He motioned for Noah to sit beside him. Noah sat down and took his grandfather's hand.

"You walk in the ways of your father Enoch, grandson. God Who Sees, sees you and he is pleased. He is pleased. Your name and the memory of this ark will never be forgotten."

Noah lowered his head and struggled to keep from crying as Methuselah continued. "You prepared me a fine room, Noah. But you know that I am not to go with you when the waters come. I will go be with my son and all those who have gone before."

Noah simply nodded.

"And when the One God returns with his thousands as my father foretold, I plan to be among them. He who is oldest in years should go first, don't you think?"

Noah wiped a hand across his cheek and choked out a reply. "Yes, I believe God will put you out in front to lead the way, grand-father."

Methuselah placed his hand on Noah's cheek. "The God of First Man is with you. He will not leave you. For forty days your heart will cry out in despair. You will feel alone, but after the forty days you will see that God has not abandoned his servant Noah or his sons. You will see."

Methuselah crossed his arms over the wooly covering and closed his eyes. His breathing gradually slowed, his chest rising and falling to a beat without rhythm. Japheth sat on the floor by the mattress with his family. Denah leaned against Japheth's shoulder and he wrapped his arm around her.

Noah placed his hands over Methuselah's and began to speak in a quiet voice. "In the beginning, God created the heaven and the earth..."

Methuselah's lips curled up for a moment then relaxed with a deep sigh. He was gone.

Jael reached into her apron and pulled out an onion. She gently opened the old man's fingers and placed it in his hand before collapsing in Noah's arms, weeping.

Japheth couldn't contain his sorrow and he wept into his wife's shoulder as she wept into his. Methusclah walked with his God at long last.

Shem spoke first as the tears diminished. "When he is gone, it shall come. His name, Methuselah, that's what Enoch named him and that's what it means. When he is gone, it shall come."

Chapter Twenty-two

The divot on Japheth's side of the bed was still warm. Denah ran her hand over the empty place and peered into the dark room. "Japheth?" No answer.

Slipping out of bed, Denah wrapped a warm woven shawl around her shoulders and went to the window. She couldn't see any light at the ark or in the clearing. The dark night held only a tiny sliver of moon among myriads of stars, spilling out of the sky to the earth below where frogs and the crickets sang lullabies to the sleeping land.

There were thousands and thousands of the tiny spots of light. She tried to count them once as a child, after her brother taught her how to count to ten, like the number of her fingers. Then ten more, like her toes, then ten more, using grapes, and ten more, and ten more. She only counted eighty-six before she gave up. There was no way to mark them, no way to know if one star had been counted already or not.

Adam's God created the stars and placed them in the night sky, according to Noah's recitations from the tablets of Adam, along with the one big moon light. She had never heard him explain why the moon grew and diminished on its regular journey in the sky however.

Her mother said Zakua sat in the heavens, tearing off little bits of moon when it was full and tossing them into the sky, making stars. The she fed the moon with her sacrifices and let it grow big again until it was full and ready to give rise to new life. Sometimes her mother woke her in the night to see the bits of moon streak across the sky. They would wrap up together in a blanket and watch the spectacle on the night canvas, just the two of them. Her mother always took a sacrifice to the temple after the moon showers, when blessings were multiplied.

Japheth didn't believe in Zakua. Many people didn't believe in his God, He Who Sees, the Creator, the One God, God of First Man. Noah's line worshipped a God with many descriptors but no proper name and no image. There was no denying the loyalty of Noah, and Methuselah and their fathers before them to this God of theirs. Denah didn't see it in the dedication to Zakua. If Zakua demanded a great ark or closed the wombs of her worshipers, she would no longer be a chosen god of the people. They would find another. Not Noah.

A bull frog let out a great belching call to his mate, answered moments later in a language only they could interpret. Did they even notice the starry ceiling above them? It was hard to imagine that there really was a time when they did not exist, a time when there was no sky, no earth, no moon, no stars. No life. No death.

Denah placed her hand on her abdomen and smiled.

Life and death.

She was sure there was a child within her. Methuselah lived 969 years then he was gone, replaced by a new life forming beneath her heart. Maybe there was a God Who Sees or a Zakua who blesses.

Denah closed her eyes and pictured the withered old Methuselah with her newborn son on his knee. Two bald heads with no teeth to speak of, each wearing smelly under garments in need of cleaning. The image made her laugh. She could see the old man's arms wrapped around the tiny infant, the baby's perfect fingers tightly grasping a gnarled, onion smelling finger as if already he found strength in Methuselah's presence. Two firstborn sons. Two lives dependant on family, one ending and one only just beginning his place among the living. Denah opened her eyes and peered into the night. She hoped Japheth would name their child after his great-grandfather.

◆

Denah's sandals clicked on the stone pathway, interrupting the rhythmic drone of the frogs and crickets. The moisture of the earth was still rising to the surface, covering the land with a layer of cool dampness. Even on the path, her feet were wet and her shoes slipped on the worn cobbles.

Thinking about Methuselah reminded her where she would find Japheth. The stone memorial was in the clearing near the old man's favorite sitting stump, the stump where he had been sitting for years, monitoring the progress of the building project. The stones surrounding his body were stacked nearly as tall as she and continued to grow as Noah's employees honored the wise old man by adding to the pile as they passed. Japheth was there as she suspected. He sat on a felled log next to Methuselah's stump.

"Denah? Is something wrong?"

"No, except the bed was getting cold." Denah handed her husband a soft hide blanket that he threw over his shoulders. She sat beside him, facing the memorial pile, staring up at the vast pool of twinkling lights.

Japheth looked up too and they were quiet for a little while. "Do you see the behemoth?" His voice was soft and he looked at her in question.

Denah searched the stars for the recognizable pattern, "No. I know it's supposed to be there but I don't see it."

Japheth stretched out his arm and pointed to the place in the sky. "It's there, just over the top of the ark. You see four stars that make a rectangle?"

Denah nodded.

"That's his back and two legs. We're looking at him from the side. Off the top corner of his back there are three more stars that arc."

Denah nodded again. "I see them."

"That's his long neck. Do you see it?"

Denah traced the pattern in the sky with her finger. "I do. I remember it. I haven't looked for it in years. The first behemoth, the grandest beast of all that God placed in the sky after it died, as an honor to its kind."

Japheth looked at her. "Do you believe that?"

"Believe it?" She never thought about it as something to be questioned. "I don't know. It doesn't seem possible to put a lizard in the sky, especially one whose back alone is taller than Noah's home. But if your God can make a man from dust…"

"God made the stars in the beginning and put them into place. That's all. What ever they are made from, they aren't animals from the earth. The great behemoth is just seven lights, seven stars making a picture. They look more like a cooking ladle to me."

"I was taught differently. The ways of your family and your God aren't what I was taught."

"I realize that, and I know it's difficult to sort it all out. My father told me once that the story of the first behemoth is just that, just a story. He said to be careful what I took as truth, to question what men say."

Denah exhaled and placed a hand on her husband's knee. "Except him?"

"What?"

"Noah said to question what men say and you did. You questioned him."

Japheth said nothing and Denah could see his lips tightening in a line but they relaxed after a moment and he placed his hand over hers.

"I'm sorry, Japheth. I shouldn't have said that."

"It's alright. It's true. I went through a season when I doubted everything he and Lamech and Methuselah had ever taught me. My brothers, they never did, or at least they were wise enough not to say anything. I told my father I was no longer going to the Gathering, no longer going to memorize the words of Adam because I had more important studies. I had more important truths to learn than the ones he told of a God that I couldn't see and couldn't hear."

"Noah was not pleased."

Japheth laughed. "No, he wasn't." Japheth squeezed her hand, his thought returning to that time that changed the course of his life. "I've never seen my father so angry. No, not angry. Hurt. I pierced his heart when I questioned his God."

"And he took away your rights as heir, as firstborn."

"I deserved it. I deserved what happened to me. It wasn't the questioning my father couldn't tolerate, it was the doubt behind the questions. He knew I doubted the very existence of the God who spoke to him, the God he lived for."

"But he took it all from you-"

"He knew I didn't have the blood of Adam as Shem did."

"And now, Japheth? What do you believe now?"

"Now? The same that I always did. I've always known the truth. I tried to reason God out of existence but his proof was everywhere.

I wanted to be so wise and instead was a great fool. And not because I lost my inheritance. Because for a time, I wanted nothing to do with the One Who Is."

Japheth shifted on the log closer to Denah, rearranging the hide blanket over both of their shoulders, keeping his arm around her. Denah relaxed against him, snuggling into his musky aroma.

"Did Methuselah get angry?"

Japheth's eyes returned to the stones. "No. He alone stood beside me. He was crushed, of course. He didn't let it affect how he felt about me, or how he treated me."

"He alone? What about your mother?"

"She cried. That's what I remember. I disappointed her. When my father took Shem on the journey to the place where Adam gave his writings to Enoch, she couldn't even look at me. We barely spoke those few weeks."

Denah breathed in a few times then asked the question that had troubled her for some time. "Japheth, does your mother like me?"

He turned to her in surprise. "What kind of question is that? Of course she likes you. She chose you for me."

"She chose me? I thought my father initiated the arrangement. And that's another thing, there's tension between them, between Jael and my father."

"I don't know why that would be, Denah. She's been doing business with Carmi as long as I can remember. He does like to get the most trade for his merchandise. Perhaps he pushed mother too hard and she's holding a grudge. It will pass, I'm sure."

Denah bit her lip and refrained from pursuing the issue. Not even her father could push Jael to pay more for something than it was worth. It wasn't that, but Japheth obviously didn't know. He probably never noticed the chilled air floating between herself and his mother for so many months and he wasn't in the kitchen those days when Carmi arrived, unexpected and unwelcome.

This moment, in her husband's arms, was anything but icy. She looked up at his strong face. He was a hard working man, intelligent and diligent with his responsibilities. He wasn't as unkind as some husbands were. She had only a few bruises to speak of and had never been locked in a room or beaten with a stick. He didn't go to the temple and for this she was grateful now that she knew what really occurred in the hallway beyond the statue with her babies. Fallen son or not, she liked the man who held her in his arms.

Japheth returned his gaze to the stones once again. Denah reached up and placed her hand gently on his chin, turning his face toward her own. "I know you miss him greatly, Japheth, but you have a reason to rejoice." She took her husband's hand and placed it on her abdomen. "Your own child lives within me."

Chapter Twenty-three

The dye for the orange garment was a combination of sassafras leaves and plain old carrots. It was a project Denah and Beth did together on a whim, tired of the same old colors and wanting something new. Beth chopped the carrots and shredded the leaves into the tiniest of bits under Denah's watchful eye. Together they tended the pot on the fire as the mixture simmered in water, then cooled into a murky brown stew. The fabric was a thin woolen weave that took on stain as soon as they added it to the pot but Denah let it soak for a long while, poking it with a stick and churning it around in its bath to get the hue even.

At first, she was disappointed with the results. The fabric turned deep orange with brown overtones, not the color of the sun just as it disappeared over the earth as she had intended. She added the fixative anyway, since the vinegar bath was already prepared and the fabric, even as it was, would still sell easily in Carmi's shop. After it soaked and Beth rinsed out the excess dye, they stretched it over the tall racks in the barn so the fabric dried smooth and was kept off the ground.

Beth bolted into the house to find her hours later. "Denah, come and see!" She was so excited and they ran to the barn where the cloth was hanging. It was hard to believe it was the same piece. All traces of brown were gone on the dry fabric and the yellow-orange that remained was bright and even. Denah took Beth by the hands and they danced in circle until Beth was dizzy and plopped on the stone floor, laughing and clapping.

The stamp Denah chose to decorate the edge of the fabric was one that her brother cut from an alabaster stone. It was only the size of her hand so the stamping required several days to complete. She used a rich, deep blue to make the sunburst design, tediously painting the dye on the stamp then placing it in precisely the right position so the edges matched, forming one continuous pattern.

Denah held up the garment she made for herself out of the fabric. The blue on the bottom edge had smeared a bit. It was unsightly to her father, and he didn't want to sell it since the remainder of the fabric was flawless. Denah didn't find the smear unsightly at all since she committed the error on purpose. Carmi never did seem to notice that the most beautiful fabrics ended up with a blemish on one end and he always cut those ends away. Beth and Denah had the prettiest wardrobes in town.

Now the garment was ruined. It looked like pitch smeared down the front of the tunic. The substance was dry but penetrated the weave, creating a stiff yellowish streak that would never come out. Denah folded the tunic and placed it on a shelf. Renita was careless again. This was the third garment that came back from the washing with a mark of some kind. The other two stains faded enough to allow the garment to be worn but this one would never be wearable.

Denah slipped another tunic over her head and tied it with a simple belt, telling herself to release the anger. She had said nothing to the servant about her carelessness. She couldn't afford to make Renita angry. The woman knew. Denah was certain Renita knew where she had been the day she found her in the bathing pool. Who would Jael believe if it came in to question?

Denah pulled the priest's image into her mind once again. He was lighter in skin tone than she, but darker than Japheth. Her child's skin wouldn't be like light like new linen or ebony colored, but something in between. The priest's head was shaved but his brows were brown so it wasn't likely the baby's hair would be the color of flames, if the man's seed brought this child into being. There would be nothing to point to another father. Denah rubbed her temples at the thought. It was unlikely. Japheth had to be her child's father. She had been with the priest just once and with her husband many times.

♦

The warm kitchen smelled of the spicy bean dish Jael had in the big pot over a low fire. She was up earlier than usual these days, since Methuselah's death. Noah had a long list of tasks for her and everyone else in the household that suddenly seemed pressing. Hay was harvested and grain was ground, nuts gathered and berries dried, seeds of every conceivable herb and garden plant were collected and labeled.

Denah spent two afternoons last week gathering kindling wood, stacked it in bins on the ark, then sewed grain bags the rest of the week. Today she would start ladling the pure green-gold colored olive oil from buckets into earthen jars to be capped and stored alongside the skins of wine. There would be an ample supply of the oil for cooking and burning in the lamps if the number of jars lined up outside the kitchen were an indicator of the number of vessels she would fill. The olive trees themselves were cooperative in supplying the demand, the grove producing an unending harvest.

Japheth was checking the tool situation today. Noah wanted

sharpened knives and blades on shovels and picks and axes. He wanted rakes without missing teeth and a supply of replacement handles. There were crates of nails and boxes of saw blades in different sizes to inventory. It would be a long day for him, yet it was his suggestion that they try to meet for a midday meal together.

Eran and Naomi weren't in the kitchen when Denah arrived. Jael sat on Methuselah's stool, stirring spices into her beans as they simmered. Denah hesitated before putting on an old greasy apron and starting her task. She had not yet told anyone but Japheth about the baby. She considered telling her mother-in-law while they were alone but Jael was preoccupied and the moment didn't feel right. Her wonderful secret would keep for a better time.

"Should we take that stool to ark?" Denah said instead as she tied the stiff apron behind her neck.

Jael smiled as her hand patted the worn wooden sides. "I already reserved a place for it by the oven."

Denah dipped a small ladle into the thick olive oil then held it up until the excess drained off the sides. Carefully she tipped the ladle and let a small trickle of oil slide into the narrow mouth of the storage jar. It would take all day to fill one jar at this rate and Eran wasn't there to give her tips. Denah looked at Jael and sighed. "What am I doing wrong? There has to be a more efficient method."

Jael looked at the jar and the ladle in Denah's hand. "Use the funnels. That way you can fill more than one jar at a time."

Of course, use the funnels. Denah lined up three jars and placed the funnels into the top, then ladled the oil into the wide mouths. By the time the last funnel was filled the first was ready to be filled again. Jael turned back to her beans. No exasperation. No daggers of derision from her eyes. Denah let the moment of frustration pass, glad that she asked before Naomi made her entrance.

Her sisters-in-law arrived as Denah got her task into a smooth rhythm. Naomi's eyes quickly took in Denah's apparel, as they did every morning. She laughed at the old greasy apron. "Nice, Denah. You look especially fine today."

The old garments she wore when making dye at her father's house were elegant compared to the stiff yellowed apron she had on now. Naomi, in contrast, wore a pale garment with a long darker brown vest, both clean and barely wrinkled. They were not new but the edge around the neckline was different today. Denah stopped scooping and looked closely. Naomi had embroidered a fine line of tiny green leaves. Denah smiled at her and pointed to the stitching. "That work is beautiful. Don't let my father see it. He'll want you to work for him."

Jael's' head whipped around to inspect Naomi's garment. Naomi's hand immediately went to her neckline and her eyes looked at the floor. Jael said nothing before turning back to the fire.

Denah mouthed, "I'm sorry," when Naomi looked up. Her sister shrugged her shoulders and rolled her eyes, then turned away from Denah to help Eran roll out the bread dough. It was simple, elegant handiwork, and it cost nothing. Why couldn't Naomi have a tiny bit of finery?

"Good morning ladies of Noah's household." Carmi shuffled into the kitchen with his arms wrapped around a bundle of fabric.

"Father!" Denah didn't dare look in Jael's direction. She brought displeasure to the room already and her father would certainly add to the tension. "I was just thinking about you." Denah pulled the apron off and hugged him, inhaling the waxy aroma of his hair oil then the citrus and balsam that clung to his clothing. The moment she caught the scent of the incense, however, she stepped away. She didn't want that scent to linger on her skin.

"I brought the wool. I didn't want to leave it outside with the burlap. It is of the finest quality." Her father's hand stroked the folded piece of cloth. He locked eyes with Denah and one side of his mouth curled up in a knowing smile.

Denah could feel her face flushing as she took the wool and ran it across her cheek.

Jael placed her hands on her hips. "We didn't order any of this wool, Carmi."

"Ah, Jael, but you did. Japheth placed the order a few days ago and I wanted to deliver it myself."

Jael looked at Denah. "Japheth ordered it?" She reached out and ran her hand on the soft downy piece. "I don't know why."

Carmi arched his eyebrows, creasing his forehead in tiny furrows. He looked from Jael to Denah then back again. "A secret then, hmm? Denah knows the purpose of this fine piece, though."

Jael's eyes bored into her face. Denah hugged the expensive fabric. "Yes. It's for the baby," she said. "Japheth's baby."

The room grew still. Denah looked up at her mother-in-law and tried to smile. Jael's eyes continued to search Denah's face, as if there was an answer stamped there. "Baby?"

Denah nodded and Carmi wrapped his arm around her shoulders and squeezed. "We shall have a grandson, Jael. My blood will be your heir. The house of Noah will live on."

Jael looked at Carmi the same way she stared down the servants she caught helping themselves to the food stores. Her eyes squinted and the lines that forked from the corners became steep hills and dark valleys. She pressed her lips against her teeth and seemed ready to burst with venom. Somehow she managed to hold her tongue. When she turned away from him, her expression altered, less severe and full of question.

"Is this true, Denah? You are with child?"

Denah nodded. "It's true." Her heart thumped loudly in her chest and she wanted to dance around the room. She wanted to laugh and sing and rejoice. She willed her limbs to be still however, waiting for her mother-in-law's response.

The peaks melted around her eyes and Jael laughed a quiet laugh before embracing Denah, then laughing out loud. "A grandson! I shall have a grandson. Thank you, God of Noah, God Who Sees. God who has heard my cries once again."

Carmi patted Denah's shoulder. "Jael, you must let my daughter come to my house and speak with her sister, Beth."

Jael simply nodded at Carmi and dismissed him without a word. He squeezed Denah's hand and gave her a solemn look. "Come as soon as you are able. We have much to discuss."

Denah was wrapped in Eran's arms and didn't follow her father out. He revealed her news but now she was glad. It would not seem as if she were gloating when she told Naomi and Eran. Plus she received permission to visit Beth. To top it off, Jael's delight was real and that was worth the unexpected announcement alone.

Eran hugged her as if she were a fragile egg. Her eyes were bright with tears and she too repeated her thanks to the God Who Sees.

Naomi's eyes were moist as well but there was no joy as she offered a stiff embrace. Resentment was written all over her pinched face and she turned away to her bread without speaking. Denah knew she was holding back tears so she looked away and showed Eran the soft fabric.

It was understandably difficult for them. They had been under the curse of this household much longer than she. Naomi acted as if it was of no consequence but Denah knew her heart ached for offspring as much as Eran's. They felt the barbs in the market. They felt the shame.

Guilt began its rise up Denah's spine. She pushed it away. She wasn't to blame for their closed wombs. Whether her visit to the temple had been right or wrong, the curse was gone. She was with child and that's all that really mattered. Nothing but good had resulted from that decision. Denah hugged the soft folds of fabric against her heart and smiled.

Chapter Twenty-four

Japheth stood in the shadow of an oak tree, watching his wife set out a meal in the cool shade of another of the old trees bordering the vineyard. He couldn't tell that she carried his child yet, at least not in her figure. It was her spirit that testified to the new found source of joy. The discontented frown marking her face since the wedding was gone. She wasn't giddy, and he couldn't say she was buoyant, even. Her emotions ran deeper than that, well rooted in soil of contentment, producing a calm assurance that gave life to her demeanor. She was happy. Even as she spread a blanket and worked beneath the tree, he could see a smile gracing her lips.

People believed his family was cursed. He was no more immune to the malicious talk than the women but he never took it to heart. There was no substance to the accusation. Only the One God had power. The others were fabrications of man. It was his God alone able to open and close the wombs of women. And even though Naomi and Eran remained childless, he couldn't believe his God would refuse to provide his brothers with sons forever. It was God's timing, God's planning, Methuselah assured them. No one was being punished.

Japheth had never considered that his brothers didn't have sons because of him. Now that his own wife was pregnant, the thought churned in his mind, gaining substance. God's timing. God wanted Noah's firstborn to provide the first heir and those plans weren't altered even with his disobedience. Somehow, despite his rebellion, he found forgiveness in the eyes of his God. Somehow, despite his past, his mistakes were buried, and the normal flow of life would continue in the house of Noah. Japheth's redemption would come in a bundle, wrapped in strips of linen. Alive! A child of his own.

The damper was still there, refusing to lift completely from his memory. His disobedience reached far beyond his own prideful spirit and he had done nothing to make his sins right before God, in his mind. He embraced the God of Adam now, of course, followed the teachings as best he could, but how could God forget? How could he forgive? Japheth didn't deserve the favor of his God, nor did his brothers deserve the pain of barren wives. He hoped Naomi and Eran would have offspring of their own, soon. When, and if, God opened and closed the wombs of the women was his alone to determine. He could do nothing to change the situation, other than pray to the heavens on their behalf. In the mean time, Japheth was thrilled that Denah was eating for two.

Rows of grapes made even lines before him, tracing the gentle rolling earth to the horizon beyond. Workmen carried woven baskets on their backs, filling them with the harvest as they stepped along. His father's fields always produced. When the little black beetles came and ate the tender leaves of the young barley in the whole region, Noah's crop alone was spared. When bands of behemoths or other great lizards migrated across the territory on their way to the sea, they sidestepped Noah's property while trampling flat the surrounding lands. When sickness spread and laborers were scarce, Noah's employees developed no fever, no cough. The One God had his hand on the family of Noah.

"What bounty of the fields will we dine on today?" Japheth asked as he greeted Denah with a kiss on the forehead. He brushed metal shavings from his tunic then stretched out on his back beside her, locking his hands behind his head.

"Eran's newest recipe for wheat rolls, plus goat cheese, apples with honey and cinnamon and fresh artichokes."

"A meal for a king. I'm a fortunate man."

"We'll have company."

Japheth turned his head and raised an eyebrow.

Denah smiled. "Your parents."

Japheth chuckled. "Really? I've never known them to share this time with anyone. And you thought my mother disliked you."

"Well, she likes the baby."

"That she does. So do I." Japheth rolled on his side and placed his hand over his child. "So do I."

"Should we come back later?" Noah's voice rose from the vineyard where he emerged with Jael at his heels. His feet were covered in the morning mud, splashed up his shins, now dry and crusty.

Denah sat up and made room for them. Jael pulled a wet rag from a leather pouch and handed it to her husband. Noah started with his face and neck, then wiped his arms and hands. Jael took Denah's basket and laid the food in the center of the small group.

"The bounty from the Creator God. Thank you, my wife, for preparing this meal." Noah leaned back against the tree and waved the others to eat.

"Denah prepared it today, Noah." Jael said.

Noah smiled at her. "Thank you, dear daughter," he said. "You're a fine cook like Jael, I see."

Jael snickered and looked away but there was a smile on her face. "Well, she's teaching me," Denah said.

"There have been a couple of monkeys on the ark, father."

Japheth smothered his bread with cheese then topped it with artichoke.

"Hmm. Have they been in the food stores?"

"Not that I can tell. Just rearranging supplies and leaving droppings all over the place. I set a trap but they are clever."

"Perhaps they intend to go with us when the waters come."

Jael threw her husband a look. "Not a chance. Not on my ark. Those nasty things will have to swim."

Japheth laughed. He understood why his mother hated monkeys. They were loud and elusive and left messes of all sorts wherever they went. Trapped in a cage, they would scream continuously, he was sure.

"How will you choose, father? How will you choose which of the livestock and which of the wild beasts to take on board?"

Noah looked over his shoulder at the ark. "We'll just choose the healthiest of the livestock. God will have to send the chosen wild ones in our direction. He'll let us know where to find them and when to start trapping them as well. Trapping antelope alive will be tricky. And I don't know what we'll do about the skunks."

"We'll require large traps and some strong men to accomplish it all. I've stored up enough rope to get us started but we'll need at least three times as much, I believe."

Noah's cheeks rose, allowing room for his deep smile. "My son, the organizer. Planning ahead is good, but don't be too concerned. God will see that there is enough. Whatever we need, there will be enough."

Japheth nodded. He couldn't help but plan and prepare. He would never get a moments rest at night if he didn't. "When do you plan to enter the ark? Do you have an idea yet, now that Methuselah is gone, so I can be sure we're on schedule?"

Noah turned to his son. "I don't know that answer, son. When the animals are collected and the preparations all completed. When the waters come, it is God's schedule, his plan, not my own."

It was always the same when he talked to his father about plans for the ark. Every "how" and "when" was answered with "God will tell us or God will provide." And he always did. No matter how much Japheth worried about the lack of available pitch, there was a sufficient quantity to cover the ark. Just like there was always enough of a certain wood or kind of rope or the elephants had just enough strength. There was always enough.

He looked at Denah as she nibbled on dried apples. Her eyes were full of questions. She asked very little about the ark and Japheth wondered what she believed. She heard the words repeated from God to Noah, but he didn't know what she took as truth and what she took as fable. It was, even to him, an act of deliberate faith to believe the ark had a purpose.

Eran, he remembered, had not stopped asking questions the first time she heard the words of recitation, the history of her beginnings. The frailty that held her body was no match for the power of her search for understanding. She pressed Shem and Noah for answers then accepted the One God without hesitation once the facts were presented. Naomi was less interested in pursuing God at first, holding to memories of her family idols for several years before they became relics of her past. Japheth knew Denah would learn and accept the truth herself in time.

Denah hesitated before she spoke. "And the waters? Where will the great waters come from?"

"I don't know for sure," Noah answered. "God created the heavens and the earth. What is a little more water to him? I suppose he'll make the water he needs."

"What did Methuselah mean, about the forty days? Do you remember, before he died? He told you there would be forty days of despair?"

"God told him of truth that is to come. I believe it means we'll live on the ark for forty days." Noah stared at the construction site, his fingers twirling the curls on his chin. "I've been building for twenty years then for a mere forty days we'll dwell in the safety of her interior."

"Anyone who wants to go on board will wait out the waters in safety, and everyone else will drown? Every one?" Denah's voice had the tone of incredulity. It was nothing new to Noah.

His father closed his eyes and nodded to Denah's question. "Those who don't come will die. It's God's judgment upon the evil in the heart of mankind."

His father's words were too terrible to comprehend. Japheth wanted to dismiss them as fantasy but he knew God would be true to the words he spoke to Noah. He reached over and took Denah's hand and gave her a reassuring squeeze. He and his wife and child would be safe on the ark.

◆

The servants stopped the cart at Carmi's front door then made their way to the barn out back. Denah stepped through the familiar door into the ornate room. Her mother's presence was everywhere in the large space and she was glad to see that nothing had changed in her absence.

Her mother loved things shiny and bright, gilded and jeweled and the room was a showcase of splendor. Chairs with intricately carved designs, tables inlaid with colorful stones, cushions in bright wools and golden statues of Zakua impressed the household guests frequenting the home.

Denah was nine when her mother died while giving birth.

Carmi's fist wife provided no heirs, while her mother gave him plenty of sons. The last one, Denah's tiny infant brother, lived only a few days before he was dead, too. There was a new mother very shortly after that. She had a loud laugh and liked to throw lavish parties. She was kind. Denah liked her better than the next wife her father added, Beth's mother. That wife miscarried twice before Beth arrived then didn't have other children. She had a wicked temper and Carmi sent her back to her father after five years of turmoil. Anna, the wife after her, had been the last.

Her own mother was pretty and had been her father's favorite. Denah knew by the way he didn't change the home to the liking of the other mothers. She liked fancy things and dressed herself up in ornate garments after coiling her braided hair and painting her lips. She dressed Denah up, too, in clothes that would not last long in the woods. Going out with her mother always started with a serious face scrubbing and ended with a heap of jewelry and clothing, put on, rejected, and tossed on a pile for someone else to put away. She glanced down at the simple red tunic she was wearing. Far too plain for her mother's liking, and far too vibrant for her mother-in-law. Denah's life had certainly changed.

Standing in the quiet space, she was aware of the eyes of Zakua, many eyes, from around the room. Did they really see? Her hand went to her abdomen. She hoped Beth would be in the house today so she could tell her about the baby.

"Hello? Father? Beth?" Denah's voice carried through the stone corridors, drawing Carmi from his office.

"Denah, you've come. Good. Sit." Her father gestured to an overstuffed couch. Denah paused a moment before sinking into the plush cushions. Important guests and business clients were directed to sit on this couch. She sat there with her father only three other times. First, when he told her that her mother was gone, and then again when he traded a piece of her madder dyed fabric for an entire pig. The last time he sat her there was when he told her she was getting married.

Denah sat and licked her lips, waiting for her father to speak. His face was pinched, his waxed eyebrows coming together above his nose. He wasn't making eye contact as he paced the perimeter of the room. "Denah, we have a matter to discuss," he said.

"Is it Beth? Did something happen to Beth?"

"What? No. She's fine." Carmi inhaled deeply. "Why don't you wear the pendant I gave you?" he asked.

Denah's hand immediately went to her throat, her heart thumping all of a sudden beneath her arm. "Oh. Methuselah told me to hide it so it wouldn't tempt the workmen, so it wouldn't get stolen."

"So you have it still?"

Denah stared into her lap. She had never been able to lie to him when he asked her questions directly. But the whole truth was too much. "No. No, father. I lost it."

"Lost it?"

Denah nodded without looking at him. "I'm so sorry. It meant the world to me. I'm so sorry."

Carmi stopped pacing and stood in front of her. "I know better."

Denah snapped her head up at the serious tone in his voice.

Carmi rubbed his hands on his temples. "Someone has it," he said. "I've seen it. I've seen your onyx pendant."

Denah clenched her hands together. "Someone found it? Who?"

Carmi searched her face and she knew that he knew the truth. His low tone was full of disappointment. "Why do you lie to your father?"

Denah stared at his feet, pudgy flesh spilling over the sides of spotless jeweled slippers.

Carmi continued. "It was shown to me by a man. A priest, in the temple. He says it's rightfully his. Says it was given to him. By you."

Denah looked up, feeling the heat climb up her face. "I wasn't supposed to go to the temple. I didn't want anyone to know."

"You gave him my gift as his payment?"

"No, father, it wasn't like that. He took it. I didn't have enough to pay. I didn't know about the blessing, what it was really, then it was too late. I'll find a way to buy it back, I promise."

Carmi inhaled and exhaled loudly several times. His hand twirled the gold bead in his beard as he paced. "It isn't about the pendant anymore, Denah. That priest wants his child. Your child."

Denah bolted to her feet and wrapped her arms around her abdomen. "What? His child? It is not his child. This is my husband's son."

Carmi stopped pacing. "But we can't prove it, can we?"

Denah's knees collapsed, dropping her back down on the plush cushions. She rocked back and forth. Her stomach churned. "I don't even know his name. How does he know who I am? I didn't tell him."

"You were seen by many at the temple, Denah. Everyone recognizes the family of Noah. The fact that you are now with child is prime market place gossip."

"What can we do? I won't give up my child, ever."

"He'll tell your husband."

Denah closed her eyes. Japheth told her not to go to the temple and she disobeyed. Their relationship had improved but it could not bear this news. He would be angry. He would not see that she did what she thought was necessary to break the curse on her womb. He would not understand.

"He can't know, father. He can't."

"This priest has offered another solution. He is willing to make a trade, but I don't think it is any more feasible."

"What father? What?"

Carmi sat beside her and took her hand in his. "He will trade the child for the writings. The tablets of Adam."

Denah let the words sink in. The tablets belonged to Noah, to Shem. Heirlooms of their fathers and their father's fathers. They were not some pretty trifle. "I can't do that."

"I don't know what to say, Denah. I offered him gold and fabrics. He was only interested in the writings."

"Why? Why would he want them? Surely a priest in the temple of Zakua doesn't believe in Adam's God."

"He believes they hold the key to Noah's wealth, to his success in whatever business he sets his mind to."

Denah rested her head on her hands. "He has no proof. I can say I lost the pendant and he found it, that he's making up the story that I, I saw him."

"You are with child in a family that is cursed. I would guess the timing of this child's birth will coincide with his story? At least close enough not to rule him out as the father."

"Yes."

"And he has the pendant. His word against yours, my dear." Carmi leveraged his legs against the couch to propel himself off the couch. He stood and faced the window. "I could tell Noah, and see what he wants to do."

"No, please no, father. He'll tell Japheth. They can't know. They don't understand. I don't know what they would do with me. Or the child."

Carmi nodded. "It will be a great day of disappointment for

Noah and Jael, if they find out."

"What will you tell the priest, father?"

"What should I say?"

What choice did she have? "Tell him that I'll try to do as he asks. I don't see another answer. Tell him please to give me time, and to please not tell anyone. Not anyone."

Carmi ran his eyes over her face. "Yes? This is your decision?"

A lump closed her throat. She nodded.

Her father's lips curled, satisfied. "I'll do as you ask, Denah. The child will be saved, hmm?"

Chapter Twenty-five

The cart slowed to a crawl behind a crowd gathering to watch a
fight. No one paid any attention to Denah as they craned in for
the spectacle. She pushed a linen scarf back from her face, relieved
the attention was elsewhere. The scarf hid her identity somewhat,
not completely. A handful of congratulatory remarks were tossed her
way as the driver wove through the city streets. And they shook her
insides. People knew. Knew she carried a child. Knew where she had
been.

It was a mocking joy hurled in her face, spoken with smiles of
derision. These women with their syrup coated slander had been to
the temple; they received the blessings and no one thought it
shameful. It was her marriage into Noah's household that made the
rumored act such fodder for gossip. It was petty talk from petty
women who thrived on the downfall of others. It was her wedding
day all over again.

From her position in the cart, above the mob of heads, Denah
could see the four men facing off in the center of the circle, two
against two, cursing and threatening the other side along with the
cheers of the crowd. Two of the men appeared young and scared
despite their violent threats. Their pale bodies, stripped down to

undergarments, were half the size of their opponents and they would be beaten to death in short order.

The burly servant steering the cart was wide eyed and obviously ready to enjoy the show from his higher vantage point but Denah had no intention of watching the beating. The other servant was in the back of the cart, placing a wager on the outcome. "No, we have to leave," she said, pointing to a side street. "Go that way around the crowd."

The servants muttered to each other just loud enough for her to hear before turning the horses sharply to the left down an unclogged artery of the city. Just off the main street the businesses turned in to dwellings that were linked together, wall to wall for entire blocks at a time. Each stone building looked like its neighbor for the most part, with only symbols painted above the doors to identify the occupants. The street itself narrowed until the space could hold one cart going one way and one going opposite but little else.

The sun sent shafts of light into the narrow space in stripes where it found passage between the roof lines. Shadows predominated and were filled with life and death in no apparent order. A dead rat on a doorstep beside a pot of fragrant basil. Rotting sacks of vegetables beneath a young kitten, tumbling and rolling as he kept a string in motion. Human refuse in a rusty chamber pot beneath a tenacious vine gripping bricks with tiny tendrils and snaking its way to the roofline.

Some doorways framed women in heavy face paint and gaudy jewels that draped their foreheads and dangled from their noses in cascades of cheap glitter. Their lewd lips left no doubt as to their intentions and the servants were quick to offer their own words of desire as they passed. Denah kept on the alert for the bold ones, the ones who left their posts and tried to block the cart, grabbing at her clothing with claw like nails and voicing shameful suggestions.

There were men, too. Men with painted faces and lusting lips, clustered around small tents attached to the sides of the buildings, not even offering a real bed for the selling of themselves. Noah's servants cursed the gilded men and spat on them. The men only laughed and mocked, peeling off clothing and throwing kisses that chased the cart down the street.

In the midst of these were the street children who ran together in small groups for protection. They were dirty and wore rags and many had never lived indoors. There was a regular group of them that came near her father's shop to beg from the merchant next door. He gave them strips of dried meat if they hauled his garbage outside the city wall. Three of the children in that group were siblings; each had a gap in their upper lip that exposed a misshapen tooth on a pale ridge of gum. Their parents sold goat hair tents and lived in affluence. They wanted nothing to do with their cursed offspring.

Denah closed her eyes to the sights around her and listened to Carmi's words again in her mind. The priest wanted his son. Her son.

No. She would never let her child be one of those that mopped blood and refuse from the rooftop. She would not let her child be a rejected one either, no matter what his appearance or how clear his mind. The baby was hers. Japheth's. And it would live and be loved and protected.

The cart slowed to a halt to allow an elderly woman to move from the center of the street. She carried a small empty basket. A movement in the shadows behind her caught Denah's attention. Huddled against the wall was a woman, squatting with her head down. She wore several layers of clothing but all were thin and her skin showed through in many places. Denah could tell that she was eating, quickly, before anyone took the bread away that the old woman had given her.

As if feeling the invading stare, the woman looked up at Denah. Her yellow skin was crossed with old scars, intersecting where her nose had once been. Her eyes were hollow and she watched Denah without emotion.

She was marked.

Denah snapped her head back around as the cart jumped forward again. Was that to be her fate? If Japheth found out and sent her away, marked and shamed, would she beg in the dark recesses of the city, dependant on compassionate old women with scraps of bread? Daily fighting for her own protection, slowly dying? Alone. Forgotten.

Or would her father take her back? It was he who taught her about the women who shamed their husbands. He had no pity on them. Would he turn his back on tradition and hide her away to work in the barns? Would he do that for her? His love ran deep, but Denah felt a prickle of fear. She did not want to put the depth of his love to the test.

Her secret was known by more than just Renita. There were others who could verify her presence in the temple, others who would not hesitate to inform Japheth. Noah's family accepted a marked servant into their home, but a wife belonging to their son? Jael would see to it that Denah was sent away, she was sure. And she had seen her husband's anger. He might do more than mark her. He might kill her.

◆

The little wagon was loaded with jars of pure, fresh squeezed olive oil. Denah lost count of the number she had filled in the last two weeks. It was certainly more than the lamps on the ark would require for forty days, even burning continuously. There were already jars upon jars of the blended oils used for cooking, too, all stored away on shelves. Noah seemed intent on stocking every last crevice available.

Denah walked slowly over the path, pulling the wagon behind her. She wrapped each jar in soft rags to protect them as they jostled over the bumpy ground. At the ark, the rags would tell her if any of the jars cracked or leaked. She carried two empty jars and a funnel, just in case. It took only one leaking container, one oily mess to clean up, to teach her the extra precautions.

It was only mid-morning, yet there were at least a dozen men in the clearing. Several slept, leaning against the stumps while the others threw rocks at a target in the distance. The sound of their laughter replaced the hammering and thundering of equipment that she had grown accustomed to since marrying Japheth. Birds spewed a chorus of calls above her as they flew to and from the top of the ark, no longer shooed away by the pounding rhythms of men at work.

Denah stopped to catch her breath and watch an elephant drag a load of hay up the ramp to the cavernous door of the ark. A lone man followed the beast and pitched the dropped hay bundles back onto the cart when they tumbled from the stack. Another couple stacked dismantled scaffolding off to the side of the vessel, beneath the unmanned cranes. Storage crates in various stages of completion were heaped nearby, no one interested in their completion, it seemed. Only a few workers trickled up and down the ramp, pushing, pulling, and carrying supplies. There were more men playing games than performing labor.

The mournful wail of a peacock drew Denah's attention. The exquisite bird stood on a stone in the stream, its beady eye watching her as its feet shuffled on the mossy surface, making the blue crown of head feathers bob and dance. It continued to watch her as it lowered its neck and sucked in water then arched his neck high to swallow. She had never seen one so unafraid, so close. Beth would be delighted.

Denah let out a sigh at the thought of Beth. The making of dyes together suddenly seemed like a life time ago. It was a simpler time, when she had no secrets.

"Beautiful creatures in the clearing today. May I help this one with her task?"

Denah stood and faced the man that spoke. He was one of the workmen, a younger one. His smiled in a way that made her heart quicken, as if she needed to flee the poisonous intentions oozing from his lips. "No, thank you. I don't need help."

The man stepped closer and put his hand gently on her elbow. "Please, allow me." He held out his hand for the wagon handle.

Denah felt her face flush and pulled her arm back. "No. I can manage."

The man reached out and placed his hand over hers on the handle, slithering his body against hers. He hissed in her ear. "I'm sure you can, but I insist."

Denah jerked away and bumped the wagon, sending a jar of oil over the edge and crashing onto the path. The man started laughing, then suddenly held it back, crossing his arms over his chest. Ham was running in their direction.

Japheth's youngest brother was red faced as he took the employee by the shoulders. "What are you doing? Why are you speaking to her?"

The young man planted a smile. "I was just offering to help. In her condition, I thought the strain might be too much."

Ham's fist slammed into the man's jaw. The workman stumbled backward and fell in the grass. Ham stood over him with hands on his hips. "You will not speak in that way."

Ham looked at Denah. "Did he touch you?"

Denah nodded affirmatively.

Ham took the man's arm and hauled him onto his feet. "Get your things and leave. Now. I'll have no more of this behavior."

The man stomped off toward the ark and the tents behind it, rubbing his jaw while still managing to curse his employer. Ham turned back to her. "I'm sorry about that. Are you alright?"

Denah didn't answer for a moment. The faint aroma of frankincense clung to her brother-in-law's tunic.

"Denah?"

"Oh. Yes. Thank you, Ham. I am alright." Beyond Ham's shoulder the clearing was quiet, all eyes in their direction.

"You should have no more trouble," he said as he walked away, kicking pottery shards from the path as he went.

Denah continued toward the ark, aware that the silent employees were watching her every step. Ham wasn't the only one quick in temper. Shem and Eran were arguing in the courtyard last night and Naomi had been far more biting than bubbly lately. Noah missed midday meal time with Jael twice in three days and Denah noticed she had not even prepared a meal for him today. Her husband alone seemed oblivious to the increased stress the others were feeling as Noah's demands for the ark surged. He was up early and to bed long after she collapsed in restless slumber, yet his face carried joy. In fact, Japheth seemed happier now than at any other time that she had known him. She knew why. He was having a child, the first grandchild in the house of Noah.

Japheth came out of the ark and down the ramp as she got near. "More oil?" Japheth took the wagon and parked it with the other supplies yet to be hauled on board.

"More oil." Denah hugged her husband's sweaty body despite the workmen that lingered nearby. Ham could fill him in on the incident with the wagon. She didn't want to think about it. She needed his warmth and attention without any ugliness.

Japheth hugged her briefly then let her go and stepped toward the wagon with his parchments of inventory. "Let's see. Lamp oil. Two empties. Nine, not ten?"

"One broke."

"How?"

Denah tried not to be irritated. It was his job. "Does it matter, Japheth?"

Japheth looked at her and smiled. "No. Unless you broke it over some poor servants head."

"It just fell out of the wagon."

Japheth ran his hand over the sides of the wagon. "I suppose these could be taller."

Denah let go of a controlled sigh. "Husband, the wagon is fine. It doesn't need fixing."

"Then why did it fall out?"

"It's just one jar. It was an accident. I bumped it. Please don't make this a crisis."

Japheth stared at her then laughed. "Request granted. No more questions about the oil."

Denah uncrossed her arms from her chest and let them relax. "Thank you."

"Now tell me about your visit yesterday."

"What?" Her arms returned to their position.

"With your father. What did Carmi want to see you about?"

Denah faced the ark. "Oh. The dyes. He wanted to know about some of the recipes."

"Of course. Can't let you go, can he? Maybe I should sell him your time, make a little profit."

"Japheth!"

Japheth looked startled at her reaction. "I'm not serious, Denah."

"Is it wrong for my father to want to spend time with me?"

Japheth pressed her hands between his. "I wasn't serious. Relax. Breathe."

Denah took in a slow breath and smiled at her husband. "I'm sorry. I'm feeling a bit, a bit-"

"Like a fire breathing leviathon?"

"Well, yes."

"This son of mine will breathe fire too, if he takes after you, won't he?"

Denah allowed herself to be swallowed in her husband's arms. The baby had nothing to do with her mood.

And everything to do with it.

Chapter Twenty-six

The lamp flickered in the dark room as Denah pulled back the covering from Methuselah's window. Bats darted about in the clearing, rising and falling and changing direction in an ever moving sequence, the only motion detectable in the stillness of the night. It was cool and quiet beyond the hum of the stream and occasional hoot from an owl. Even the frogs stopped their conversations for the night. It should have been peaceful. Denah's heart was thumping strongly in her chest as if Methuselah was there, and knew why she had come.

The dark mass on the knoll beyond the window blended with the horizon. Denah peered in its direction, the hull defined by the lack of pinprick lights that filled the sky around it. Twenty years ago it was night sky streaked with tree trunks that Methuselah saw from this window, not the great boat. Once his grandson had a visit from the God of Adam and was told to do the impossible, the view from the old man's window changed forever.

Lamech wanted the construction on the north side of the house, where the ground was flat and already less forested but Noah chose the top of the knoll where the elevated ark was visible in the city and from the major roads. He wanted to remind each and every person of the judgment to come. The city had since grown and un-obstructed views were difficult to find. Denah could see it from the rooftop of Carmi's house and she used to go up and look at it from time to time until the image was no longer such an oddity. It became part of the landscape.

Methuselah had a front row view of the project. He listened to the rhythm of the saws and watched as the great trees fell. He watched the timbers as they were stripped of their bark and planed into usable boards. He saw his grandson mark the dimensions of the ark, then re-measure and mark again until the day the first cured boards were set in place. He witnessed the gradual rise of the mortise and tenon planking as it was pounded into place with wooden dowels, row by row veiling the starry backdrop.

Noah mastered the building skills necessary for his project and taught his sons but it was Methuselah who united them as a team. He was proud of his contribution in that respect, though he would never admit it to her outright. He cultivated Shem's ability to motivate and challenge his brothers, Ham's creative conceptualization, and Japheth's ability to plan and calculate. These he linked to Noah's passion. He couldn't supply much manpower in his last years and it didn't matter. His wisdom still permeated every decision.

Denah wished he were still here. Methuselah's wisdom would help her now. He might even give her the tablets of Adam and her whole ugly nightmare could go away. She let out a tired sigh.

"Who is it you fear?"

She spun from the window and held up the lamp that quivered in her hand. The words came from a dark corner of the room. The glow lit the face of a man sitting behind the desk. It was Shem.

Denah walked closer to be sure it was him, then set the lamp down. "You scared me, Shem. Why didn't you tell me you were in here? I thought for a moment-"

"What Denah? Thought I was Methuselah's ghost?"

Denah didn't want to admit it. "No, I just thought I was alone."

Shem leaned back in the chair with his hands behind his head. "I didn't want to disturb you. You looked so lost, lost in yourself there by the window. Just like when you were a little girl, your mind busy sorting through the bundles of thoughts that bombarded you, waiting for you to make peace with some and war with others. You don't appear to have made peace with whatever plagues your mind tonight."

"I was thinking about Methuselah. I wish he was here."

Shem leaned forward and allowed his hand to rest on the acacia wood box that held the writings of Adam.

"Why did you ask me that? About who I fear?"

Shem breathed in and out a few times, tracing the almond blossoms carved into the orange grain with his fingers. "Who is it you fear? What is it that you are running from? These are questions Methuselah asked me many times when I was troubled."

Denah smiled. "You sounded just like him when you spoke."

"And you didn't answer the question."

"You think I'm troubled?"

Shem looked her in the eye. "There is a new darkness that shadows you, that's all I know. Your displeasure over your marriage seems to have been replaced with another concern."

"Displeasure? Why do you say that?"

"Your lips were sewn down to your chin at the corners for the first few months here. I'm not sure how you got any food inside."

Denah wanted to be irritated with Shem for suggesting there was something amiss, some way in which she had not been above reproach, but she couldn't. His honesty was not meant to be hurtful. He was like Methuselah in many ways, speaking frankly without being offensive. She didn't feel angry at his observation of her behavior, she felt caught, and that was uncomfortable. She pushed a defensive chord out of her mind.

"Well, it was a difficult start." Shem wasn't in the kitchen every morning. He had no idea how she had been treated. And this wasn't the time to complain about Jael or troubles with Japheth.

"My brother is a good man, Denah."

Denah went back to the window and stared out. Should she tell Shem about the blackmail? It would be a relief to share it with someone and maybe he would give her the tablets. Surely he would think the baby's life was more important than the writings that he knew by heart anyway. The words could be stamped again into tablets.

But then she would have to tell him about the temple. About the priest. About her betrayal of his brother.

No, she couldn't tell Shem. Her brother-in-law loved his God. Her actions could never be justified in his eyes. Shem loved his brother, too, and he would tell Japheth. Shem's compassionate nature would mean nothing in the face of her husband's fury.

"I know. I'm learning that he's not the man people say he is. The darkness over me isn't about Japheth. It concerns Beth, my sister. My father works her very hard."

She didn't look at Shem's face as she spoke, as if he might be able to read the entire truth if he could look into her face. He was like Methuselah in that way.

"The God Who Sees sees Beth."

"Her thinking is very shallow. She can't remember or reason well. No man will want her so she'll be under my father's roof her entire life, working beyond her strength. I don't want her to struggle. She's too sweet for that. My father can't see it, can't see that he treats her unfairly. Will your God intervene on her behalf?"

"Only he can answer that question, Denah."

Denah nodded and watched the darting bats weave invisible

patterns across the darkness. Shem sat quietly at the desk, not pulling her in or pushing her away. Denah forced the temple from her mind and chose another topic. "Shem, is there a reason your mother would not like my father?"

Shem didn't answer for a moment so Denah pulled a stool next to the desk and waited. Her brother-in-law leaned his elbows on the desk and rested his fingers together at the fingertips while he thought.

"They have a past."

"What do you mean? What sort of past?"

Shem stood up abruptly. "I shouldn't say anything. It was long ago and it no longer matters."

Denah rose to her feet. "Please tell me, Shem. The tension between them is distressing. Perhaps there is something I can do."

Shem shook his head. "No. No, Denah. Let it rest. It's past and it isn't my place to speak of it." His voice was not harsh but the conversation was done.

Shem walked to the door, pausing before he left. "It's Truth, isn't it?"

Denah looked at Shem's calm face as he waited for her to respond. "What's truth, Shem?"

"The answer to my question. Who you fear."

Denah turned away from his eyes and stared out the window until she heard his steps retreating down the hall. "Who I fear, Shem," she said to the bats, "is the man who wants to steal my child. I fear the eyes of those who saw me at the temple. I fear the marked woman and her tongue."

Denah sat behind the desk and rubbed one finger on the worn wooden box. It could not disappear now. Shem would realize who had been in its presence last.

Yes, Shem, there was a darkness hovering over her. She was

tangled in its claws and held captive. It spewed vengeful fear that gnawed on her gut and took her peace, burying it in a pit of shame. Her life could be destroyed, her child taken and raised by men in the temple. She had plenty to fear. Her future was uncertain. "Yes, Shem, I'm terrified of the truth."

Chapter Twenty-seven

"I only saw it for a moment before it ran back into the woods. It was magnificent." The wild horse had been seen several times in the last week, darting playfully in and out of the trees near the clearing. Eran saw it from her window when she got up. "It's colored just like Shem said, with black and white stripes all across its back. I've never seen a horse with markings like that."

"I should ask Ham to trap it for us, "Naomi said. "Can you imagine the looks we would get in town if we could train it to pull a cart?"

The three wives sat around a table and sorted racks of dried fruit into the sacks Denah had sewn the day before. Denah intentionally sat close to Naomi and inhaled deeply but the only fragrance was of cinnamon that she was sprinkling on the thin leathery slices of apple. There were no remnants of incense. She wondered if Naomi remembered the scent and recognized it on her husband's clothing. She doubted Naomi went to the temple but if Ham went, what gossip had he heard and what had he told her?

Denah pushed back from the table, away from the scent of cinnamon that was turning her stomach.

"Are you ill, Denah?" Eran leaned over and put her hand on

Denah's forehead.

"No, I'm alright." It was the pregnancy that made her queasy. She had seen it with her brother's wives.

"You're pale."

"Really, I am alright. It's just the baby." Denah rubbed the tiny bulge beneath her tunic.

Eran sat back. "My mother was the same way when she was carrying my youngest two brothers. It gets better in time."

"Unless there's something wrong with it."

"Naomi! Don't say such things." Eran shook her head and turned to Denah. "There's nothing wrong with the baby. Don't listen to her, Denah."

Naomi sorted the edible raisins from the few that wore a fuzzy green layer. "My cousin had the morning illness, too, and her son was born dead. The mother cord was wrapped around his neck and choked him."

"Well, my brothers were born fine and healthy. The morning illness has nothing to do with how babies are born. Your cousin must have angered God so he took her child."

"And what of us then, Eran? Have we angered God so much that he closed our wombs forever? Why is he angry with us and not her? Why is she carrying a child not even a year after marriage?"

Denah kept her eyes on the apricots before her and did not acknowledge Naomi's accusing finger.

Eran didn't respond right away and the three sat in silence.

"I don't know what I've done that was so displeasing to the Creator." Eran spoke in a hushed tone. "I try to remember but I don't know. I don't know what I've done."

Naomi let out an exasperated sigh. "Oh, it isn't us, Eran," she said. "This family has a curse, remember? It isn't our fault."

"Why Naomi? Why would God be angry with Noah?"

"I have no idea."

"My father didn't know there was a problem when he sold me to Noah. We didn't hear of such things out where I grew up."

Naomi tossed a handful of raisins into a sack, most of which scattered on the floor. "Well we didn't know then. I knew about Jael, of course, but Ham took my breath away and I insisted my father make the arrangement. He was still young and there was no evidence of any curse. This family had its own peculiar ways but I didn't take any talk of sealed wombs to heart."

"Did you know, Denah?" Eran asked.

"Yes, I knew. I've heard all the rumors."

"Was your father angry with you, then?"

"No, he wasn't angry with me, Naomi."

"Then why did he arrange your marriage with Japheth? Not only the curse but he has the status, you know, his reputation."

"Japheth is a good man and my father was just showing his loyalty to this family."

"And a daughter in the family meant a hand in the money pot?"

"Naomi!" Denah bit down on her lip at the jab and glared at her sister-in-law. Naomi smirked and shrugged her shoulders.

"Why is Denah pregnant?" Eran said. "There's no curse more powerful than our God. It is he who brought her this baby. Why not me? Why does God hold me in contempt?"

Both sisters stared at her, waiting for an answer. Denah felt her face burning and turned away from them as she shook her head. "How do I know the ways of the One God? Perhaps the God Who Sees wants the rightful heir of Noah to have the first son."

"Rightful?" Naomi's voice was incredulous. "Your husband-"

Jael entered the kitchen and the conversation dropped coldly from their lips. She examined the pile of completed bags and nodded. "Good work this morning, daughters. Denah, will you and

Naomi take them to the ark? Eran and I will start the bread."

Naomi and Denah ignored each as best they could as they loaded the bags onto the cart that Jael left in the hall. Denah took the handle of the full cart but Naomi snatched it from her hand. "I'll pull it, Denah. I don't want you to get hurt." Jael missed the sarcasm and gave Naomi and approving smile.

Denah followed silently behind the cart, pushing from behind when the wheels fell into ruts and grooves between the stones. This wasn't the relationship she wanted with Naomi. The woman was impossible. It wasn't Denah's fault that her sister-in-law was childless.

Japheth was nowhere near the ramp. The workmen milling around the area glanced their way then turned, ignoring their presence, so Naomi and Denah pulled the cart up the ramp themselves. Several men leaned against wooded supports inside the door, watching the one man who was repairing a broken shelf. They turned their gaze away from the women as well. Obviously, they had been warned by Ham to control their behavior.

Naomi approached the foreman and laid her hand on his arm. "Eli, where do these belong?" The man grinned then pointed down the hall without speaking. Coarse laughter followed them down the corridor.

Naomi stopped the cart when she heard more laughter from one of the enclosed rooms. Denah sucked in a sharp breath, recognizing the deep voice of Renita behind the door. "You are brilliant, Japheth. That's so clever," she said.

Denah held the breath at Japheth's easy laughter in response to the praise. Naomi watched her expression with amusement. She made no effort to continue down the corridor with the loaded cart. When she giggled, Denah shoved the cart into the back of her legs.

"Ouch!"

The door jerked opened and Japheth stood in the space. Renita stood behind him, head held high.

"Denah? Oh, a load to store." Japheth pulled the door close into his body, shielding the woman from view. "Thanks for bringing it up. Take the cart to the far end and I'll help you unload in a moment."

Naomi giggled again and took off for the storage bin. "What was that all about?"

Denah glared at her and didn't respond.

"That was odd, wasn't it? The two of them together."

Denah pressed her lips against her teeth and tossed a bag roughly against the far wall of the bin.

"She is pretty, isn't she? Your husband seems to think so."

"Be quiet, Naomi." Denah wanted to ask her sister about the sweet aroma of incense on Ham's clothing, but held her tongue as Japheth walked up. He heaved the remaining bags from the cart. Denah pushed the handle into Naomi's hand. "Take it back to Jael."

Naomi smiled and tipped her head, lolling down the corridor, humming

♦

Japheth studied Denah's expression. Her arms were crossed over her chest and the scowl had returned.

"What's upsetting you this time?" he asked.

"Why were you in that room with the marked woman?"

"Her name is Renita and I was working."

"And she's your helper now?"

"Denah, what's wrong with you? Do you have reason not to trust me?"

"Do you think she's pretty, even with that hideous scar?"

Japheth ran his hands through his hair and groaned. He hated the label Denah gave Renita, 'the marked woman', as much as he hated his own 'fallen son' designation. His wife was by no means perfect. Who was she to condemn Renita? The woman made a tremendous mistake but there was more to her life than the sin she committed.

Japheth liked Renita. She appreciated the life she had been given at Noah's home and she showed it in her willingness to work hard and in her kindness to Jael. She listened when he talked about his work and showed interest in the projects on the ark. She was gentle and forgiving, never condemning in her attitude. She was pleasant company, a pleasant person and did not deserve Denah's malice.

Nor did he deserve her mistrust. "I have to get back to work," he said and turned from her.

Denah followed him into the room and he knew she expected Renita to be there waiting. She wasn't of course. She had only been there because Jael sent her up with the pieces of soft wool that she had made into tiny blankets and soft pads. He showed her his latest project, that was all.

Japheth watched his wife as she scanned the room. Her eyes found the simple rectangular structure that he built. She hesitated to comment, unsure what it was he constructed. It looked like a cage with an open top, but the rails were carved of maple, and the base sanded smooth. She looked at it for a moment then looked at him in question.

Japheth said nothing as he brushed past her and secured the soft wool pads onto the base and part way up the sides of the enclosure. He placed the folded blankets in one corner then stepped away from his handiwork, a safe haven for a baby in a home that rocked to and fro on the waves. Denah's eyes registered the plan and her hand flew to her mouth before she knelt down and slid her hands over the rails.

It was supposed to be a pleasant surprise.

Japheth walked out of the room before Denah could speak. He was tired of all the apologies. He didn't want to participate in her self-induced misery.

Chapter Twenty-eight

Denah sat on the edge of the bed and watched her husband's chest rise and fall beneath the blanket. She apologized for being so emotional about Renita, blaming her moodiness on her condition once again. Japheth accepted her words but was in no mood, or state of awareness, to discuss anything else. He just sighed, pecked her cheek and collapsed on the bed. He was asleep in moments.

Two weeks had passed since she saw her father. Another restless night stretched out before her, one where answers were as elusive as sleep. Carmi was in a difficult position. He couldn't fulfill the blackmailer's request without her help and she had done nothing. The tablets were safe in their box in Methuselah's room. He would protect her position as an honorable wife as long as he could. How long would he be given the opportunity?

She picked up her comb and began teasing through the lowest third of her hair where the snarls were the worst. She'd become lax in this once daily routine. Many of the routines she learned from her mother had been set aside, not just the daily hair combing then brushing and braiding. She stopped bathing every day, for one. She had to scrub her skin daily when she worked with the dyes and smelly vinegar fixatives. Now that she wasn't coated in strong odors it hardly seemed to matter whether or not she went out to the pools. If Japheth noticed, he hadn't said anything.

There were no drops of perfume on her throat every morning either. The jasmine oil was gone and she knew she wasn't likely to get anymore. None of the other women wore perfumes.

Denah knew how to make her own simpler fragrances from lavender or almond blossoms but it wasn't worth the effort to carve the time out of the required chores.

Her hair resisted the passing comb so she started a bit lower and worked upward again. The tangles didn't form so easily when she kept it coiled and knotted against her neck. Pulling it back and securing the mass like a horse tail was easier, and had been her habit of late. Moments like this when she sought to line the strands out again made her regret her laziness. Her hair style, like her clothes, mattered to no one in Noah's household. She hadn't bothered to put on any garments with color or design in weeks, two to be precise, not since she had gone to town to see her father.

Denah put down the brush and gently stroked Japheth's silky curls, lying across his pillow. She didn't want to marry this man with his shameful past yet she was the true disobedient one. She was the one to be to shunned and rejected. He felt as if he lost everything once and he would again if her secret was exposed. She couldn't let that happen. Japheth was indeed a good man. He deserved this child. He deserved happiness. She couldn't let anyone take them from him.

No one ever looked at the tablets anyway.

Denah tiptoed to the window. A low rumble of voices rose from the clearing. It wasn't late, although the sky was dark enough for the first few stars to be visible. The men were usually on the other side of the ark by now, in the tent village. The ark blocked most of the sounds from there and only the night before Gathering

Day would the singing and fighting spill over to this side. Tonight men were still milling about, near the stream, though Denah couldn't see any form of lantern or bonfire.

Her eyes lifted and peered into the darkness where the ark dominated the skyline. She could make out the outline and a small orange glow, moving slowly at an angle down the side of the ark. Someone was on the ramp. Denah watched the light bob along the face of the vessel then disappear around the end, toward the tents. Japheth wasn't the only one working long hours, it seemed.

A woman's shrill laugh pierced the night air from the clearing, hushed as quickly as it started. Denah recalled the man that touched her hand on the path, in the daylight, and shivered. He had dared to be so bold. She didn't like those men on this side, on her side. With a quick motion she pulled the covering over the window and crept back into the safety of the bed and Japheth's arms. Tomorrow she would tell Ham that his men were in the clearing and he would make sure it didn't happen again.

♦

He ignored the first apple core tossed carelessly on the path, and was annoyed by the second. By the time Japheth saw the third one, he was angry. It was obvious there had been more than owls and frogs at play in the night. The clearing was littered with debris. Grape stems, cups of wine still half full, bones with meat chewed off cast aside in mounds, even a lonely shoe in the creek. It looked as if there had been a celebration in the clearing. The morning light revealed the remnants of a night of decadence, not under Noah's approval.

Japheth chided himself for sleeping through the night without any awareness of the activities beyond his window. He quickened his pace toward the ark. He was relieved when it became visible through the foggy mist. Not that it could be stolen, he just needed to know it was there, and that it was intact.

He stood in the door and lit a lantern. A heavy citrus-like aroma clung to the air. He knew the smell, frankincense, and had always liked it when it came across the breeze in the city. In the confines of the ark, it was stale and nauseating. There was no sound from within the hull except the gentle coo of doves nesting in the rafters. There was no movement, no indication that anything was amiss. Japheth let out a sigh and headed down the corridor. He would inspect each and every crevice. No one was allowed on the ark after work hours. They weren't supposed to be in the clearing either, and they had obviously broken that rule. He would make sure no one in a drunken stupor was still on board. He felt sorry for any man stupid enough to remain.

The first of the rooms he entered sent anger ripping through his gut. A bag of dried fruit from the storage area was ripped open and lay on the table, fruit spilling onto the floor. Dark purple stains surrounded a broken jar of wine. A brass bowl, filled with ashes, still glowed with the last trace of incense, filling the room with a smoky haze. The blankets that had been folded neatly on the shelves were now a wadded mess on the mattress. The pillows bore indentations of heads and a woman's garment lay on the floor, partially stained by the puddle of wine.

Japheth slammed his fist onto the table. He swiped its content with his forearm then turned the table onto the floor. The ark had been defiled by the workmen.

The ark had been defiled.

One by one he entered the rooms on the top deck, those prepared for human habitation. Noah didn't spare expenses in these rooms, making them spacious and comfortable with cushions and soft beds. Yesterday they were tidy and organized. Today most were in disarray. The beds especially bore evidence of activity during the night.

Japheth picked up an open jar of wine and hurled it against the wall where it smashed and fell to the floor in a purple bath. They should have listened to him. His father and brothers were wrong to keep the workers employed when there was so little work to be done. Hard work led to hard sleep. Lazy days left energy to spare and this was the result.

The ark was defiled.

♦

Denah awakened to loud voices in the courtyard. Noah was yelling at one of the foremen. Half a dozen other men stood in a semi circle behind the two, hands raking through hair or planted on hips. Japheth stood to the side with Ham and Shem, three sets of arms crossed over chests.

She threw on her clothes and slipped down the stairs, hurrying into the kitchen. Jael was there, standing in the doorway to the courtyard.

"What's happening? Why is Noah angry?" Denah asked.

"Some of the men were on the ark after hours."

"Working?"

"No. Japheth believes they were there in the night for pleasure."

"Oh, no. I saw someone leave the ark after dark but I thought it was just someone leaving late."

"Apparently they weren't working."

"There were people in the clearing, too. I heard them. I was going to tell Japheth and Ham this morning."

"Now they know."

"I should have said something last night but he was so tired and sleeping so peacefully."

"Don't blame yourself, Denah. It's perhaps better for our men to worry about it now, in the light of day."

The men continued their heated discussion until Noah sent the workmen away. He and his sons left the courtyard and headed toward the ark.

Jael set her bowl down and motioned to Denah. "Let's go see what we can do to help."

They followed the men through the clearing where the ground was trampled flat in places and was littered with remnants of food. She never would have guessed there was more than a person or two in the clearing from what she heard last night.

Denah stopped abruptly as she stepped inside the ark, covering her mouth with one hand, the other securing her gut. The sickly odor of temple incense lingered in the corridor.

"What's wrong, Denah?" Jael asked.

"I, I just wasn't sure what we would find when we got here."

"It's safe. The boys made sure no one was still here."

Denah followed Jael, breathing through her mouth, their footsteps echoing in the still space. They found Noah and his sons on the top level, hovering inside the door of one of the rooms.

"They've defiled her," Noah said. "They've desecrated the ark for their pleasures."

Denah and Jael walked behind the men as they went down the corridor, inspecting each room. There had been widespread use of the ark in the night. Ashes on the floor, beds in disarray, food scraps dropped in messy piles. Gaudy face paint smeared the linens and broken pieces of cheap jewelry glittered on the floor. Above it all lay the covering of smoky incense. Many people had come and gone throughout the night.

When the damage had been assessed, they gathered by the long row of windows on top of the ark, opening each shuttered covering to permit the air to flow. The birds could fly in and out all they wanted, their presence pure and innocent, and far more acceptable that the stench within the vessel walls.

Noah rested his elbows on the ledge, then dropped his head on his hands. "My God. My God. Why?" His shoulders sagged, heaving under the weight of his soul. He wept openly. Jael wrapped him in her arms and the two cried together. Denah stood silently beside her husband, their hands clasped, eager to start, whatever tasks, to make the ark right again.

Her father-in-law's eyes were red and puffy when he turned to them. "No one but family is to enter the ark until we know who is responsible for this. And we must cleanse her," he said. "Every piece from these rooms must go. It must all be destroyed." Noah breathed in deeply a few times. "Ham and I will speak with the men. Japheth and Shem, gather the heavy items and place them in a pile in the clearing, in pieces. Jael, you and the girls gather the linens and whatever else you can carry and add it to the pile. Then scrub and cleanse each space."

Denah started with the first room while Jael went to gather cleaning supplies. She laid the linens open and stacked them on top of each other, threw the trash on top, then wrapped it in a bundle. Walking backwards she dragged the load to the small door that opened out onto the roof.

Birds scattered as the door opened, flying to the nearest perch to watch her activity.

The roof of the ark sloped down, away from the windows, but was not too steep to walk on safely. The height above the ground was intimidating, however, and it took Denah a moment to gain the confidence to walk to the edge, pulling the bundle along and dislodging the newest crusting of bird droppings. Her first armload missed the wagon below entirely. She let out a tired sigh. She would have plenty of opportunities to hit the mark, the day ahead promising to be long and exhausting, both physically and emotionally. The sooner it was completed, the better. Already she felt soiled and in need of a long scrub in the bathing pool.

Voices rising from the far side of the ark were subdued. Denah's interest was piqued. She had been on the far side with her husband only once, just to see what was there. It was Noah's rule that the workers were to remain on their side of the construction after dark except for carts coming and going to town. No one had to tell her not to go there alone.

Denah stepped to the other side and looked down on the tents. The men were gone, working, when she went there with her husband. Today the central square in the middle of the tent rows was filled with men, sitting in groups. It was not a social gathering. Noah and Ham were there among them, looking for answers. Her husband had been right. The men should have been let go when the construction slowed down. One night would now result in at least several months of work to replace the objects that would be destroyed in cleansing fires today.

Eran and Naomi were dragging a mattress down the corridor when Denah returned. Room by room the tables, stools, and beds were hauled out with mattresses and linens. The trash was removed then the scrubbing began. Every surface in the rooms was washed and rinsed, every item removed. The odor diminished, but persisted, clinging to the walls and floors like an unholy claim.

Late in the afternoon, in the last room, Denah found a jade idol shoved in a niche that had been carved crudely into the wall. Barely the length of her little finger, the dark green Zakua smiled at her above her round bellied babies. Denah rubbed her thumb over the smooth surface. Her father's home was filled with similar figures, all smiling with contentment. This goddess wore a mocking smile, satisfied by indulgences offensive to the One God. Denah was glad she found it instead of Noah. He didn't need another reminder that his ark was more than a convenient location for mischief. This goddess, and probably countless others, were worshipped throughout the night. Denah tied the idol in her hem to give to Ham as evidence against its owner.

The last room was scrubbed and the last items hauled outside, leaving the top floor of the ark a hall of empty rooms. Denah and the others gathered in the clearing. Weariness settled on each of them as they sat near the great pile of beds and linens. Noah stood with a torch raised to the darkening sky then set the pile ablaze. He didn't speak as the flames licked up the wood and sent fingers high into the sky. He wasn't grieved at the loss of the furnishings, she knew. Nor was the defiance of the workmen the root of his sorrow. He was grieved over the condition of man's heart. Noah felt the anguish of his God's sorrow.

The moon was high in the sky when Denah pulled a clean garment over head onto skin she washed repeatedly. Incense clung to the air so she couldn't rid herself of the fragrance. It followed her, marking her as one of the disobedient workers who ripped Noah's heart. She tried not to envision what occurred on the ark but the persistent aroma took her back to the room she shared with the priest. She had been so naïve to think any of that was real.

Chapter Twenty-nine

Ham's construction team sat on stumps in the clearing, mouths clamped. There were only twenty of them, and all in one place, the number seemed so small. There were at least twice that many tents on the far side of the ark, and for years they were full. Good wages came with hard work on Noah's land, though, and fewer men wanted the challenge. Their somnolence and the stillness hovering over the ark spread an ominous blanket over the clearing. Japheth stood with Ham, making notes on his books, as Noah reviewed each man's owed wages.

There was no way to pinpoint who was responsible for organizing the mayhem on the ark. One man's idea was put into action by countless others. No one knew anything, of course. Everyone was asleep early. They heard nothing, saw nothing, did nothing but fall into the deep slumber of the night. No fingers were pointed, no guilt confessed. Noah and his sons interviewed each and every man and may have been willing to show mercy if the truth was admitted. It wasn't. Tongues remained defiant, the men united in their version of last night's events. Even those with little hope for employment beyond Noah's generous nature had tight lips, the man with one arm, the man who could barely see, the man who wheezed and coughed his way through the workday.

Denah could see raw disbelief on their faces now as they were one by one being let go from Noah's employment. They believed the united front was their protection. They were wrong. Defiant as one, now all would suffer the same penalty.

Japheth had dark circles under his eyes. He spent many hours in the night calculating the expense of replacing the defiled, now destroyed, items. It wasn't as simple as a shopping spree in the city. The hide coverings alone would take a month to replace. There might be a few dozen available but the rest would have to be ordered or they would have to hunt and tan the skins themselves.

The fabric and wool filling for the mattresses, the timber for the furniture, the ruined food and wine stores were all carefully listed and addressed. Japheth made a grand total of the loss then divided it among each of the hired workmen. Every one of them would pay from their owed wages, leaving them very little to take as they left the land for good.

Denah stood with Eran and Naomi, observing the proceedings from the edge of the clearing. The household servants and field workers were clustered around the perimeter at a safe distance. The normal bustle on Noah's land was at a standstill.

"Ham was up all night," Naomi said. "He kept patrol on the ark. He wasn't sure what the men might do."

Eran nodded. "I don't know when Shem came to bed. He couldn't sleep either. He watched the ark from Methuselah's window for a long time while he prayed for God to protect it. And us."

"Ham found tracks over there," Naomi pointed to the far edge of the vineyard. "On the path that follows the wall to the city. He thinks men came from there in the night. There were cart tracks by the road, too. The field was flattened where they parked. Women, he thinks. Women from the city that were brought in. I can't believe we didn't hear them. They knew what they were doing. It was planned."

Eran shook her head. "It sickens me. Noah treats the men well and this is what they do. I'm glad he's getting rid of them. All of them."

Denah scanned the groups of servants. Her eyes landed on Renita. "I wonder how many others were involved?"

Naomi followed her gaze and shrugged. "Ham doesn't think the household staff was there. Not the women anyway."

"And the field hands?"

"They haven't been questioned yet. Noah wanted the construction men dealt with first."

The three stood and watched as the first few men came from the far side of the ark down the path, weighted beneath their belongings. Shem was in charge of the exit process. Each pack was inspected for items that Noah provided. Kitchenware and tools had a way of disappearing when men left Noah's service. Today the stores of these items would be replenished.

Denah pictured Shem facing the men, one by one. He would give his last tunic to someone claiming to be in need, but no one would get the better of him today. Kindness was one thing, stealing another.

"How is Shem, with all this?" Denah asked.

Eran sighed. "He feels like he's at fault since he wanted the men to stay nearby, near the ark. He wanted them all to be safe when the waters come."

Denah imagined the men on board the ark, not liking the image. She didn't want Beth or her own child in the midst of their coarseness any more than she wanted them near her. If the ark was going to fill with people, there were certainly better choices to occupy the space than the rowdy men fuming in the clearing.

"It isn't his fault, Eran," Denah said. "He meant well. He could not have known they would choose this rebellion against Noah."

Naomi smirked. "In other words, Japheth was right."

Denah rolled her eyes. "That isn't what I was saying."

Naomi kicked at the dirt with her toes and turned away.

Jael approached Denah with a scrap of dense linen. "We can start sewing sleeping pads again if that's Noah's desire. Ask Japheth when he's free. He'll need to go to town and purchase supplies if that's the plan."

Denah took the scrap of common fabric. It could be purchased from any number of vendors for a better price than Carmi's. It would give her an excuse to talk to him, though, if Japheth would take her with him. She stared at the judgment in the clearing, her mind turned to the tablets, sitting unprotected in Methuselah's room.

A few of the men were agitated about their wages and voices began to rise. Eran, Naomi and Jael stood transfixed. The servants were hovering around the scene. Noah, Ham and Japheth were here and Shem was in the tent city. Everyone was focused on the proceedings; no one was in the house.

Denah slowly backed away.

Methuselah's stool sat by the fire pit in the kitchen. Denah sat down on it for a moment, collecting her resolve. If the old man were here, he would look into her face and know what she had in mind. Denah felt the claws of guilt sinking into thoughts. She pried them away. Methuselah was gone, and Noah knew the words of the tablets by heart. So did Shem. The writings of Adam could be written again. The emotional attachment was significant to them of course, but the life of a child was at stake. Her child. Japheth's firstborn. Noah's heir.

Denah didn't move off the stool. The God Who Sees, sees Denah. How many times had Methuselah said that to her? Couldn't the God Who Sees see what was most important? Couldn't he see that she was just trading objects for a life made in his own image? Wouldn't the God of Adam want it that way?

The tiny life living beneath her tunic was too precious to lose.

◆

The box was on the desk. Denah sat down and looked at it. Enoch carved it from acacia wood, a tree with a rough, thorny covering, because he knew the wood beneath the prickled bark was resilient. He provided the tablets with an ark of their own, a haven of safety, and it housed the tablets for hundreds of years.

Denah carefully lifted the lid and set it aside. The tablets were made of pale clay that had been stamped with a stylus, then dried and baked into a firm thin brick. She picked up the top one and ran her finger over the etched symbols. Her brother taught her how to read a few of the symbols but she had long forgotten most of the lessons. In her mind, she started the first line of the recitations. "In the beginning, God created the heaven and the earth." Some of the stamped lines and shapes stood for whole words and some for only parts of the word but still could not follow the pattern.

Denah set the tablet with the others as she realized her hand was shaking. Why the blackmailer wanted them was curious. They had no monetary value. They were relics of the past with words no one believed any more, and few could even decipher. Their owner was regarded as a spiritual leader but it made no difference if no one believed in the God whose words were stamped there. If the writings held the secret to Noah's financial success, she couldn't tell from the scribbled marks. He certainly prospered while they were in his possession, as did Methuselah with his many, many years of life. Denah sighed. The truth really didn't matter. If the priest simply believed they would bring him success, it was reason enough.

The voices outside the window continued to rise and fall and Denah knew it was time to act, while the opportunity was available. When the tablets were discovered to be missing, the angry men or one of the servants would be suspected, not her. She gathered the tablets and wrapped them carefully in her wide linen belt. She replaced the lid on the box, gathered her bundle then retreated to her room.

Her stomach was in knots as she closed the door and emptied a basket, laying the wrapped tablets on the bottom. One by one she folded her most colorful garments and placed them on top. She rarely wore them, trying to preserve the ones that remained. No one would question when she said she was giving them to Beth.

Denah plopped onto the bed and closed her eyes. After she saw her father, it would be finished. Carmi would get her pendant in trade for the tablets and no one would have claim on her child. She had to give him the tablets. She had to.

Chapter Thirty

"There's no reason for you to go with me, Denah." Japheth had the reins in his hand, ready to leave. "I may not barter for supplies from Carmi this time. I'll find reasonable prices in other shops."

Denah held onto the side of the cart and caught her breath. He was ready to leave when he heard her calling him and running in his direction. He planned to go to town tomorrow but after the long ordeal yesterday, firing all the men, he was anxious to get supplies reordered. It was nearly evening and he wanted to get back before dark.

"I have some things to give Beth," she said. Her cheeks were pink and long stands of hair were falling to either side of her face. She looked at him with eyes that pleaded and she reminded him of a little girl learning to get her own way with the tilt of her head and hint of a smile. He couldn't resist. Denah was overwhelmed yesterday. He noticed when she slunk away from the clearing, then found her later on their bed, curled in a ball. She was pale and didn't talk much. Today, there was life in her, and he needed life.

Japheth took her hand and looked down at her. "Maybe you're just what I need to take my mind off the troubles of the past few days." He let go of her hand and patted the seat next to him. "Hop in."

Denah hesitated.

"Beth isn't in need of anything so urgently is she? Come on up. We'll bring it next time."

Denah crawled up next to her husband and leaned against him as the cart and two servants on horseback set out for town. She was quiet as they rode, a soothing quiet. He was glad she was there, attached to his side. The cinnamon like smell of cassia oil tickled his nose, wafting from her skin from soap she was making. He missed the sweet jasmine that used to linger there.

♦

Carmi sat beneath an ivy covered trellis, an oasis of shade from which to view his property. Denah stood in the shadows and watched his head move slowly back and forth, monitoring the progression of employees as they left the fields and the barns and filed up the path toward their own homes. He wasn't at the shop and Japheth didn't have to ask twice if she wanted to come here while he tended to the business.

Most of Carmi's fields were a miniature version of the land where she now lived. His grain and grapes and olives were used in the household, not stored or bartered. The two exceptions were the sheep pen and the flax field, each with a set of barns where the wool was carded and spun, flax was scutched and linen was woven, fabrics were dyed, sewn and stored. Her life was in those barns, after her mother died. Seeing a smile return to her father's face when he saw her creations was worth the pungent odor of the retting flax and vinegar baths. She wished she had the tablets for him, to see that smile again.

"Father."

Carmi startled at the intrusion, then held out his hands for her. "My daughter, I've been thinking about you," he said.

Denah waited as he jiggled his way to one side of the bench, creating waves of wine in his cup that lapped over the edge and dribbled down his fingers. She sat beside him and looped her arm through his. "There will be plenty of workers seeking employment if you're in need," she said.

Carmi looked at her with a smile. "Yes. I'm aware of this. There's much talk in town today of the events which have occurred. Your father-in-law set his employees free without notice or compensation, I hear." His eyes were red tinged and there were droplets of wine in his beard.

"That isn't true. They received what they were owed. You heard why Noah fired them?"

"The men paid homage to their gods and for this they were punished."

"It wasn't that at all, father. They brought women into the ark and desecrated the living quarters. They took food from the supply bins and burned incense."

"Well, they are men being men." Carmi gestured with his hands as he spoke and sloshed wine into the air. He looked into the cup which was now half empty, then picked up a jar from the table beside him. A trickle of liquid drained into his cup. With an awkward toss he threw the jar onto a grassy spot and yelled to his wife. "Anna, bring us more refreshment."

Denah squeezed his arm. "Father, Noah is a fair employer. The men broke his trust."

Carmi squinted his eyes and leaned away from her. "So, you defend my old friend, do you?"

"You would've done the same if it was your ark."

Carmi held her in his gaze for a moment before leaning his head back and laughing. "My ark? My ark. Yes, I suppose it could have been me that the great God of Lamech gave such orders to. But Noah was the chosen one. It is Noah's ark, not mine."

Carmi continued to laugh until Anna came out of the house with a fired pottery jar identical to the one Carmi emptied. Denah stood and greeted her but was glad she didn't stay. Japheth would be gone for a while to gather supplies and she wanted the time with her father alone.

"You don't believe Noah's words, do you?" Denah took the jar from her father's unsteady grasp and poured the wine into his cup.

Carmi's eyebrows arched onto his forehead. "The great waters will come and all living things will be destroyed." He thought about it, then shook his head." I don't know what happened to him. I don't know why Noah went mad. He wasn't like that when we were young."

"So you don't believe what he says about his God, what the One God of Adam will do to the land?"

"He's a man with dedication to his projects, I give him that. I believe that he believes his cause is divine. But my dear, I do not fear the waters of Noah. No one does."

"When Noah gathers people to live on the ark, you will come won't you? And you'll bring Beth?"

Carmi snorted and slapped her knee. "Will that day actually arrive? Yes, my dear, I want you to let me know when Noah gathers the people for the great ride on his boat. I'll stand on the top and watch the water cover the land while we float away." He maneuvered his hand in the air like the waves of the sea, laughing at his comments, spilling his cup again.

Denah turned her face from him. Too much wine and Carmi spoke unfairly against his friend. She didn't like to hear her husband's family mocked. She was one of them.

Carmi put his cup down and took her face in his hands. "I mean no offense, Denah. Do not be upset with your father."

Denah's irritation melted into his pleading eyes. "I'm not angry. It's difficult to know what to think of it all. My life there is a turn around from my life here."

Carmi heaved himself to his feet then offered her his hand. "What is this you're wearing? Your mother would be ashamed."

Denah ran her hands over the simple brown tunic tied with a matching cord and groaned. "I know, she would never let me out of the house like this. I didn't have time to dress appropriately."

Carmi picked up his jar then staggered before regaining his balance. Denah took a position beside him and linked his arm through hers so he could lean on her arm. "So my daughter, you are here for the reason I believe you are, hmm?"

"I have the tablets, the writings of Adam."

Carmi took slow swallow of his drink and chased it with a deep sigh. "You have them. I knew you would."

Denah looked down the path. The last few workers filed from the fields and barns, taking the fork leading to the street. One lone employee walked toward the house. The small figure weaved back and forth in an indirect line, head down. It was Beth, distracted by bugs and bees and whatever else lay at her feet. There was no bounce to her step, though. She plodded with feet of fatigue.

"Is she ill? Is something wrong with Beth?"

Carmi focused his attention on his youngest child as she approached. "She isn't ill. There's nothing wrong with her."

The girl that came toward them was not the energetic Beth that Denah knew. When she lifted her head, there was no smile. Not until she recognized her father's companion. She ran the last distance into Denah's arms.

Denah held her tightly then put her at arm's length and looked her over. Her arms were firm but pale from working inside the barn all day and there was a dark line of grit beneath her fingernails. She grinned now but her eyes were tired and the scarf holding back her hair didn't disguise the mass of tangles.

"Beth, are you all right?"

"She's fine, Denah. Beth, go clean up and don't get any of that dirt in the house."

Beth looked from her father then back at Denah.

Denah took the girl back in hers arms. "Go ahead. I'll see you before I leave, I promise."

Beth looked up at Denah and smiled, "I want to show you how I learned to weave with the willow branches to make baskets for-"

"Beth. Go. Don't disobey your father." Carmi pointed toward the house and the girl slipped away.

Denah put her hands on her hips. "Father, she looks terrible. Are you working her all day? She needs a good scrubbing and some-one to comb out her hair."

"She's fine. She's a hard worker. You think I should let her laze about the house like a spoiled child?"

"No, but she needs looking after. Her hair is one big tangle. And she's exhausted. She isn't one of your employees."

Carmi downed his cup and poured another. "She isn't your concern anymore, Denah. Now where are the tablets? I'm tired of this business."

"Has he been back? Has he contacted you again?"

"Who?"

"The priest. The man asking for the tablets. Has he approached you again?"

Carmi looked far down the field with a frown, finally nodding. "Yes. He's asking why there's a hold-up, why you tarry so long in bringing me the simple thing he has asked to have in exchange for his rights to your child. He grows impatient."

"I have them hidden. I don't have them with me."

"Why not?"

"I didn't have time to get them. Japheth left in a hurry and I didn't have a chance."

Carmi sighed. "How does that help the situation? You place your father in a difficult position. The man, he makes other demands now."

"It isn't the way I had it planned. I tried to bring them. What other demands?"

Carmi paced around the patio, glancing off the bench to the table and over to a section of wall before answering. He reached for the jar of wine but Denah took it from him and let it rest on her hip. "Why do you think I like my wine?" he asked. "It makes me forget my troubles for a while. Is that too much to ask from your father? Can you allow him to forget the great sacrifices he must face to keep his family from shame?"

"What sacrifices? What does he ask of you?"

"He requires a large sum of gold in addition to the writings. I'll be forced to sell your mother's pretty things and still, it may not be enough."

Denah's hand flew to her mouth. "No, you mustn't sell anything of mothers. He'll get what he wants as soon as I can arrange it. Tell him that."

Carmi lowered his head onto his hands and moaned.

"What's wrong with father?" Denah turned to Beth who stood behind her.

Carmi's head snapped up and turned to his youngest child. "Why are you back? I told you to leave us."

Beth looked at Denah. "But I want to see Denah. Why are you

sad? Why is he upset?"

Carmi pushed away from the wall and grabbed Beth's arm. "Why can't you listen to me?"

Denah put her hand over his. "Let her go, father. You're hurting her."

"She doesn't have enough mind to obey like a simple dog."

"Don't say that! Let her go, she's concerned about you. Can't you see that?"

Carmi thrust Beth to the ground and turned to Denah with his finger pointing in her face. "You stay out of it."

Beth put her head on her knees and clamped her arms tightly around her ears. She rocked in place, tuning out the loud words.

"Look at me, Beth," Carmi said, taking her scarf in his hands and pulling back on her head. Her eyes pinched together, her mouth grimacing above a squeal of fear and pain.

Denah grabbed Carmi's elbow. "Father, stop it!"

Carmi let go of Beth and spun around to face Denah, a fierce smoldering in his expression. With both hands he yanked the jar from her grasp and rammed it into her gut.

The air in Denah's lungs exploded from her mouth in a scream. Pain clamped onto her muscles and twisted, tightening on itself so that she doubled over and fell backward onto the patio. The jar smashed on the stone beside her, hurled at her intentionally.

Carmi staggered back against the wall in a stream of curses. "You're not her mother!" he yelled.

Denah curled into a ball on top of the pottery shards. They stabbed into her flesh but she dared not move, dared not say anything, dared not close her eyes.

Carmi leaned against the wall, huffing, trying to catch his wind. He looked from Denah to Beth, who was still wrapped in her own arms, sobbing loudly.

The stone beneath Denah's head was wet, fragrant with the scent of expensive wine. It soaked into her hair, her clothing and she could feel the stickiness on her skin. Her breathing was jerky, sending spasms down her spine to her gut. She forced herself to inhale through her nose, then exhale. Inhale. Exhale. Her arms wrapped around her baby, holding and protecting.

A glisten of tears collected in Carmi's eyes. He staggered toward the house, leaving his daughters alone on the patio.

"Beth, Beth, it's all right." Denah sat up slowly, waiting until she could move without emptying her sour stomach. She picked pottery from her tunic and skin then crawled to her sister's side and held her as she rocked.

"She needs to come inside now." It was Anna, standing over them. Her voice was soft and she didn't look Denah in the eye as she helped Beth to her feet. "Your father says you are to wait for your husband by the gate."

Anna gathered Beth to her side and the two disappeared in the house. Denah pulled herself to her feet and wrapped one arm around her abdomen, using the other for balance while she worked her way to the front of the house. She collapsed against an oak tree and waited for Japheth.

Chapter Thirty-one

Japheth didn't notice the hunched figure beneath the tree when he first pulled the wagon up to Carmi's gate. When Denah lifted her head, his heart collapsed. Her ashen face put on a smile, as if she were simply sitting under the tree for shade. He ran to her side. "What happened? Why are you out here? Why are you alone?"

Denah uncurled her spine and leaned against the trunk. Her tunic was covered with dark stains and her hair was undone from its usual knot. Little scrapes dotted her arm, smeary remnants of her blood still evident. "I had an accident, I guess. I'm alright."

"Tell me what happened."

Denah avoided his eyes as her smile faded. "My father is, has had too much wine. He didn't mean to hurt me. I fell."

The pieces didn't fit. "You fell? You mean he pushed you?"

Denah nodded, and bit down on her lip to control the swell of tears forming in her eyes. "Please, take me home. I just want to go. Please Japheth."

The two servants stood on either side of him and he knew they would support a confrontation with Carmi. Japheth's wife had been mistreated and no one had the right to touch her like that except him. She didn't belong to Carmi any longer. Japheth stood and paced around the wagon, once, twice, then twice more, allowing the inferno inside his mind to cool. Denah watched his face and read his thoughts.

"He's really drunk. Please don't go in there. Please Japheth. He didn't mean to hurt me."

Japheth was torn between Denah's request and the need to get in Carmi's face with his fist. But he knew no good would come out of the confrontation, despite a moment of pure jaw cracking gratification.

He exhaled loudly then helped Denah onto the seat. The wine she spilled when she fell covered the front of her tunic. He swung himself up and sat beside her. "I want to tear his head off."

Denah flinched. "He had too much wine. He didn't mean to hurt me."

Japheth stared at her in disbelief. "I can't believe you feel the need to defend him. If he can't control his wine he shouldn't drink it."

🌢

Denah leaned back and closed her eyes. It was her fault that her father was so drunk, so upset. It was her fault he might have to sell the precious gold trinkets that her mother loved, her fault he was hounded by the man who wanted the tablets. He was under so much stress trying to protect her, trying to protect his grandchild. Denah felt the weight of guilt and didn't want any more added on with an ugly interaction between him and Japheth.

Japheth squeezed her hand. "Is the baby all right?"

Denah nodded. "I think so." She ran her hands over her trunk. There was no blood on her clothing. The dark stain was just wine from the broken container. "My ribs are tender but I think I'm fine, and the baby, too."

She didn't want her husband to be angry with Carmi. Japheth didn't have the full picture of what transpired. He didn't understand Carmi's position. It was bad enough that her father took his stress out on Beth. She didn't want her husband and her father at odds. She didn't need another difficult relationship to manage.

For now she just wanted to forget what happened. Carmi would be remorseful once he sobered up. When he came to make amends, Denah would give him the basket. Once he had the tablets he could negotiate for her pendant and all would be forgotten, the matter would be settled.

◆

Gathering Day was subdued and even Noah struggled to stay focused on the words of recitation. The family sat alone in the clearing. The household staff and field hands performed their duties quickly and quietly, giving Noah and his sons a wide berth since the day of mass firing.

Denah focused her eyes on her father-in-law but her mind was at Carmi's house. She had seen her father explode in anger, and she had seen him with too much to drink. She had never experienced the combination. As much as she wanted to take responsibility for his behavior she knew it wasn't hers to carry alone. Carmi was cruel to Beth and there was no excuse to cover his intolerance of her simple devotion.

When Noah finished, Denah excused herself and found a private place at the edge of the woods to throw up the fluids in her stomach. She had no desire to eat with the family and could sit still no longer. Her back was stiff from the fall and crept down her legs the longer she remained on the stump. Her ribs remained tender, and movement aggravated the ache as much as remaining still. Otherwise, she didn't seem injured. Not on the outside anyway.

Empty dwellings on the far side of the ark formed three sides of a square. Denah wandered into the compound and examined the remnants left behind. The tents Noah provided were made of a dense weave, striped with various colors. No two identical tents stood side by side and the overall effect was rather cheerful when they were occupied. Now there was an intense stillness among the hollow shells and gooseflesh rose on her arms, an apprehensive prickle, even knowing the men were gone. She stopped in the center of the compound and listened to the tent flaps as they slapped against support poles in the breeze.

There were hastily compiled mounds within the tent village. A pile of plates and cups wriggled beneath a colony of plundering ants. Another stack contained blankets, another tools and another cooking utensils. There were piles of furniture, piles of garbage and piles of sporting equipment. Another was simply an array of broken furnishings and unwanted goods. The men paid dearly for their indiscretion. One night of rebellion changed everything. Denah bit her lip at the thought.

A warm wind ruffled her hair and she looked up to the God Who Sees. His view of the tent city was like hers from on top of the ark only from further away. Could he really see her, sitting there alone, in the midst of the hollow tents?

"Denah?" Eran walked toward her with a cup in her hand. "Jael sent me, to make sure you were all right."

Denah sipped the water and smiled. She asked her husband not to say anything about what really happened. There was already enough tension between her father and her mother-in-law and it was too raw to discuss with the others. Jael watched her though, and knew she wasn't keeping food down. "I'm fine, Eran. I just need to walk a bit. It's different back here now, isn't it? The emptiness is almost overwhelming. It feels so completely abandoned, so lonely."

"Is that how you feel, Denah? Do you feel sometimes as if you were abandoned by your family?"

Her sister-in-laws eyes were soft, holding no condemnation, no evidence she knew about the incident with Carmi. "Abandoned? Yes, at first. And still, sometimes."

Eran nodded. "I did too, when I was brought here. And lonely." She smiled up at the sky. "But we're never really all alone. He Who Sees is there, watching."

"I wish he would have seen the trouble the men were going to cause and stopped them."

"Shem says we can't judge the ways of the Creator. He didn't stop Eve or Cain. And he didn't stop Lamech's murderer. He chooses when and where and why he will allow disobedience for reasons he alone understands. But I agree with you. I wish he would have told Noah, at least. Maybe it could have been prevented."

Eran turned a slow circle and looked at all the tents. "Isn't this beautiful? I would have loved living in one of these as a girl."

"Did you live in tents, your family I mean?"

"Mostly. We did when we traveled with sheep. Not like these, though. Ours were plain old hides sewn together."

"Do you miss it, Eran? Do you miss the life you had before you married Shem?"

"Sometimes. I miss the wide open pasture land. It was peaceful and uncomplicated. Of course, I also had nothing to eat at times and no prospects of marriage living so far from any cities. I wouldn't want to go back, not unless Shem came with me."

"And when Noah's waters come, what will happen to your family? Will they come here?"

Eran turned toward the ark, the great hull dominating the rows of tents. "I don't know, Denah. It frightens me. It's a good four day journey. Shem assures me we'll have time to send word. But what if they aren't in the house, what if they are out with the flocks? I wish they weren't so far away."

Denah knew her own father wouldn't come. Forty days away from his business was too long without watching his profits multiply. Even if the waters were rising, he would wade through to protect his inventory from damage. Would he fight to protect Beth? Denah felt the water churn in her stomach. "I guess we should get back," she said. "I don't want Japheth to worry that the nephilim have come and taken us away."

♦

The dull back ache sharpened in the night, then turned into cramping by morning, and not just in her back but in her belly as well. Denah stayed on the bed as long as she could with her hands pressed against her abdomen. Japheth was already gone. He and his brothers left early to hunt game once Noah decided they would tan their own hides to take on the ark. It was mild at first, the squeezing in her belly, and she thought it was an aching muscle or a stretching to allow the baby room. But the cramping was getting stronger.

Denah eased into a sitting position to try and alleviate the pain. She put her elbows on her knees and rested her sweaty forehead on her hands, trying to breathe slowly. It was then she realized the bed was wet beneath her. She leaned onto her side and saw the first black-red stain.

Chapter Thirty-two

Jael was the first to arrive after Denah screamed. Eran and Naomi were close behind, hovering at the foot of the bed, their faces reflecting the fear Denah knew she projected from her own. She still sat on the side of the bed, too frightened to move.

"What is it Denah?" Jael put the back of her hand on Denah's face, her blue eyes widening as the heat warmed her skin.

Denah shifted her weight and showed her mother-in-law the blood. "There's pain," was all she could say between gasps of breath.

Jael's face drained of all color. She motioned for Eran and Naomi. "Get fresh linens and warm water. And towels, plenty of towels. Then find Noah and tell him to speak to his God on behalf of his grandchild."

Denah stood on shaky limbs while Jael eased her into a clean gown, then had her sit on folded towels, the gown bunched around her waist. She soaked a rag in cool water from the basin and dabbed it on Denah's face. "There's nothing we can do, Denah, but wait, and pray." Her voice was gentle and choked.

The cramps were constant. Denah's insides felt as if they were being wrung like wet garments in the wash, twisted around and around until they coiled back on themselves. She gripped Jael's strong hand and listened as she whispered fervent prayers to the God Who Sees.

Eran and Naomi tiptoed into the room with arms full of linens. They stripped the bed around her then Jael helped her to stand again. Naomi gasped at the sight of the towels, covered in dark splotches. Eran turned white and folded her lips inside to keep from crying out while she arranged the towels according to Jael's instructions.

Jael helped Denah onto the bed when the linens were ready. She leaned back on pillows propped against the wall. Two stacks of towels were positioned under her thighs with a space in between that also held a supply of linens. A warm blanket was placed over her lap and a cool rag on her forehead.

Eran sat on one side and rubbed Denah's arm in even strokes while Naomi folded and refolded the stack of extra towels. Jael stood by the window and mouthed her words silently into the sky.

Denah tried to breathe evenly and slowly, putting her body back in a normal rhythm. Her son would be all right if she could resist the urge to fight the pain. Just let the pain exist, she told herself. Relax and let the pain work its way out and the baby will be fine. The baby will be fine. The baby - will - be.

Jael turned from the window and traced the perimeter of the room, speaking in a hushed voice "In the beginning," she said. "God created the heavens and the earth."

Denah concentrated on the recitations and repeated the words after Jael. "In the beginning, God created the heavens and the earth."

Jael slowed the pace to allow Denah to speak the words. "Now the earth was formless and empty."

Denah licked her lips and repeated. "Now the earth was formless and empty."

"And darkness was over the surface of the deep."

"And darkness…"

♦

It was nearly noon before the pains diminished and the flow of blood was reduced to a trickle.

Her baby was gone.

Denah was cleaned and the linens refreshed once more before Eran and Naomi silently left the room. Denah leaned back on her tear soaked pillow and watched her mother-in-law line a small woven basket with an otter hide. She placed the soiled towels inside, covered by a woven piece of soft fabric, her grandchild's blanket. Denah's son was in the basket, unrecognizable but a life all the same. Jael treated his remains as she treated the body of Methuselah, her tender touch revealing the nature of the spirit within her.

She set the basket beside Denah then sat down on the edge of the bed. Denah fingered the blanket, only half covered with delicate embroidery. Tiny frogs on rocks. Deer jumping over fallen branches. Brightly hued parrots in flight. She ran her hands over the stitching and over the basket. "Thank you," Denah said.

Jael blew her nose in a cotton cloth and wiped her eyes with the back of her hand. "My heart grieves with you, Denah."

Denah nodded. "I know. I hoped he would have your eyes, like his father."

"Your next son will no doubt be strong and smart and blue eyed like Japheth."

"Will there be another son?"

Jael closed her eyes and breathed deeply. "There have to be sons." She opened her eyes and covered Denah's hand with her own. "Otherwise there is no purpose for the ark."

"Sons, but maybe not sons from the house of Noah."

Jael looked out the window and exhaled slowly. "God made a

covenant with my husband that he and his wife and his sons and his son's wives would enter the ark." She turned and looked at Denah. "God did not say there would be others, Denah. After the waters have come and gone, I believe it is my husband's seed that will be blessed, through his sons. Their wives will bring forth a new generation, a generation that is obedient to the Creator, the God of First Man."

"But there are so many rooms on the ark."

Jael nodded. "Yes, I know. Noah's heart won't allow him to believe his words are spoken in vain, that no one will come. He is ever optimistic, my Noah. I hope he's right. I pray I'm the one who's wrong."

"Then why did this son die? If it's to be as you said, why did this son of Noah's son have to die?"

"I don't know. I don't know why this son was not permitted to live."

Denah bit down on her lip and closed her eyes as the tears trickled through. Because my child was not the One God's blessing, she thought.

Jael patted her hand and stood, gently lifting the basket from Denah's hands. "You must rest. We'll put this child to sleep with his grandfather Methuselah."

Denah nodded and made her fingers relax their hold on her child, releasing him to Jael. When her mother-in-law was gone, she turned into the pillow and sobbed from a heart drained of everything that made her life worth the air she breathed.

◆

The chattering wren on the window ledge woke Denah from an exhausted sleep. The sun was shining through her window, bathing her face with warmth. Her hands went to her abdomen, to the place that was empty and cold and no amount of sunshine could warm and bring to life.

Her husband was still gone and she wondered if he knew somehow that his child was dead. Did he have a feeling that he needed to get home? That he needed to cry out to his God? Did he feel the hollowness that she felt, both in body and soul?

Denah eased out of bed and leaned against the window. She could see the small stack of stones beside the large one of Methuselah. When Japheth came home, all that would remain of his son would rest beneath the memorial. Dust returning to dust.

When Beth's mother lost her babies, their remains were taken away by a servant and buried somewhere beyond the garden. There were no stones placed over them to protect them from beasts, no memorial to recognize their existence. They were alone and forgotten. Her son would not be forgotten. He would walk side by side with Methuselah as they returned to the land from which they were formed. Japheth would keep vigil near the stones for both of them now.

She doubted even Japheth knew about the blanket his mother was creating. He would have been the first to hold his cleansed newborn, wrapped among the frogs. Denah envisioned the handiwork so she could describe it to him later, then caught herself thinking about another item of Jael's handiwork that she owned. Her wedding day sash, Japheth's rib. It lay folded on the shelf where she had placed it months ago. Denah retrieved it and sat on the bed in the swath of sunlight.

The symbol of their marital commitment was plain. No jewels or golden thread, no colorful family crest or shimmering beads. She looked at the sash with new eyes.

The long strip of linen was one color from end to end but it wasn't just bleached cloth. There were vertical rows of white embroidery integrated within the weave. Denah looked closely at the pattern, not recognizable at first, then it occurred to her that the intricate stitches were symbols for words, like those on the tablets of Adam. The sash was itself a tablet of words, with a message she couldn't read. Denah ran her fingers over the tiny symbols on their unblemished white background. It was not an item created in haste.

"I knew you didn't like it. I'm sorry it was a disappointment."

Jael stood in the doorway with a tray of food in her hands. She set the tray down and sat beside Denah. "I meant well," she said.

Denah ran her fingers over the lines. "It's beautiful. I never noticed until now. I can tell you worked a long time to make it. Are these the words of the recitation?"

"No, they are Methuselah's words, the blessing he said over me when I married Noah. They say, 'Blessed is she who walks in the wisdom of her Creator. Blessed is she who dances in the delight of her husband. Blessed is she who flies in the freedom of truth.'" Jael's fingers followed the symbols as she spoke. "I wanted simplicity in color, so it wouldn't compete with your bridal garments, and would speak of your purity."

Denah let tears fall on the sash. She had been foolish to despise it. "It's beautiful. Thank you. I didn't know you could read and write."

"I can't do it very well. Noah had to scratch out the shapes in the dirt, one by one, for me to copy."

Denah ran her finger along the words, repeating the message in her mind.

"I chose you for Japheth, you know."

Denah looked into her mother-in-laws eyes. "No, I didn't know. I wasn't sure you even approved that it was me who arrived under the tent on Japheth's wedding day."

Jael dropped her head, watching her hands, wringing them together. "I knew it was you. I chose you in my heart for Japheth many years ago. You suit his temperament. You're wise about business, like he, and you work hard and aren't satisfied until you get something done right. I saw this in you at your father's shop. As you grew, you didn't turn to silliness and frivolity like so many of the young women. But you could stop the busyness of your hands and mind to laugh, and my son needed laughter."

"You chose me years ago?"

"Noah wanted you for Ham but I wouldn't hear of it. Ham needs, well, Naomi. You can't mix a song bird with a hawk and expect a favorable outcome."

"Why did we not marry years ago, then? Because of my father? I know how much I helped his business to prosper. And he loved me, of course. It was difficult for him to let me go."

"It was Carmi's stubbornness for the past five years. He refused to allow you to leave his household. For, for reasons of his own. Before that, it was Noah's. He wouldn't allow Japheth to marry. Not to you, not to anyone."

Denah nodded and looked down at the sash in her hands. "What changed his mind, then?"

Jael swallowed hard. "Lamech was killed. The circumstances softened my husband's heart towards his firstborn. Lamech and Methuselah both tried to ease the tensions between Japheth and Noah, but my husband was blind to their wisdom. His perceptions of Japheth weren't completely founded in truth. With his father's death, Noah's eyes were opened to the true nature of his son. He saw his own folly."

"What happened between them? Why did Japheth turn from his God?"

"My son has always been strong and sure of himself. Noah saw

Japheth's ability to reason and understand and didn't question what his son understood of God. Japheth needed his father's guidance and wisdom in spiritual matters but Noah didn't recognize Japheth's struggle. He left Japheth to figure out the ways of God on his own while he focused on teaching others. While my husband's faith was strengthened, Japheth's was torn down, word by word. I didn't see what was happening until it was too late."

"They have a strong bond now, it seems."

"Yes," Jael said. "God showed Noah how he was hurting Japheth and my husband repented. It took time for your father to give his blessing over the betrothal. There were other unwed girls to consider in that time. None of them were right. I waited and prayed. I wanted you for Japheth. It was a long overdue wedding date for my first born."

Denah fiddled with the corner of the sash.

"What is it, Denah?"

"It's difficult for me to believe you chose me. I felt like you didn't even like me, for a long while, not until I was carrying a child."

Jael stood abruptly with her fingers pressed to her lips. She turned toward the window, and was quiet. Denah waited, nibbling on the cake of figs from the tray. He mother-in-law's shoulders rose and fell with deep sighs as she collected her thoughts.

"I haven't been kind to you. I've treated you poorly. You didn't deserve it."

"Is it because of my father? I can see when he is nearby how you don't like him."

Jael sucked in her breath and Denah knew it was true.

"Your father and I, we go way back. We thought, once, we would be married."

"You and my father?"

"Yes. When I was a servant here, in Lamech's care. Carmi, your father, made it clear he wanted me for his own."

"But you were given to Noah, instead."

"I was a servant with nothing to offer. My status didn't matter to Lamech."

"Who did you prefer? Which one would you have chosen?"

Jael thought for several moments. "Noah was serious in nature, and far more interested in his grape yield than in finding a bride. He was as indifferent to me as Carmi was charming. I responded to your father's flirting at first. Then Lamech asked me about the two of them, and I told him I preferred Noah. It was, in part, out of my gratitude to Lamech. He bought me from traders as a girl and gave me a respectable life. I didn't want to shun his son. But it wasn't all that. Noah wore a cloak of peace that I wanted to share. He found satisfaction in the simple ways of the land, and in the ways of his God."

"My father's first wife was Noah's sister. He should have been pleased that he was thought of him so highly."

Jael nodded. "Yes, he should have."

"But why then is it you who turns to stone when my father enters a room? He doesn't hold a grudge or he wouldn't have sent me to this family."

Jael breathed in slowly and let the air escape through her nose. She looked at Denah and seemed to choose her words carefully. "It's more complicated than I can share with you. There are hurts and unspoken feelings that travel beyond the surface. Carmi and Noah, your father and I, we share remnants of a past that are seeped in-, well, a past that was never meant to be."

Denah sat quietly as her mother-in-law dealt with the words she was speaking. They came from deep within, clamoring to be released and grasping the secure walls of silence at the same time. She closed her eyes after a moment and hung her head as she spoke. "I was wrong to take it out on you."

Denah simply nodded and allowed the past be what it was, gone. She broke the silence with her own truth. "He hit me."

Jael turned to her. "What? Who hit you?"

"My father. At his house, three days ago when Japheth and I went to town. Father was drunk. He hit me with a jar. That's how I fell."

Denah watched the realization cross Jael's face. "The baby."

"I think so."

Jael's eyes filled with tears and she returned to Denah's side. "Does Japheth know?"

"Partly. I didn't tell him that I was struck. I said he pushed me, accidentally. I don't want any trouble between them. Father was drunk and upset. Normally he wouldn't hurt me."

Jael's eyes squeezed tightly shut. "Your husband needs to know the truth, Denah."

Denah nodded. "He'll be filled with anger on top of his grief. Don't let him hurt my father, Jael. He didn't mean for harm to come. I can't bear anymore sadness." She wrapped her arms around her waist and held her empty womb.

Jael nodded. "I'll speak with him."

Denah leaned into her mother-in-law's embrace and wept. The flow tears did nothing to stop the flow of pain filling, and refilling her heart.

Chapter Thirty-three

The hunt was a great success. Twenty-eight hides soaked in wooden barrels of water on the back of the carts: Nine deer, four elk, eleven antelope, three gazelle, and one buffalo. Japheth thanked his God again for the bounty provided. Small herds nearly walked in front of their bows before the arrows were out of the quiver. It was their favorite hunting place, but never had the brothers seen so much wildlife at one time. There were even beasts none of them could identify.

The meat was split evenly between all of them, servants included, and each man kept the proceeds from the sales. Japheth kept close watch on the men as they stopped in the villages on the road to home, Ham in particular. He liked to spread his wealth with flamboyance on whatever suited him at the moment. It was his to spend, of course. Japheth just didn't want excess attention drawn to their hunting party. They were an easy target for thieves on the open road.

Japheth smiled at the sound of laughter coming from the wagon following his. The servants were in high spirits with the unexpected bonus of wealth. Out here, no one knew who they were hired to protect. The sons of Noah were a name to be mocked, not faces that were recognized. There was no embarrassment in their assignment today.

He had to agree. It was nice to stop at a merchant's stall and not be the object of derision. He didn't enjoy going to town to barter for supplies anymore. The insults and sidelong glances had increased over the years and were wearing. Prices were elevated in his presence and getting them back down to reasonable levels took diligence and time that he would have preferred to spend elsewhere. Today the markets were refreshing. He looked like anyone from anywhere and no one tried to take advantage. His pockets were still full of the copper bartering coins.

Japheth patted his jacket and felt the bottle of jasmine oil that he finally found in the last place they stopped. Ham picked up a comb carved from mammoth tusk and Shem found Eran an ebony flute. That was all they needed, though there was still one more town before the final stretch to home. It was tradition for the brothers to stop there after a successful hunt for a hearty plate of rich food and an indulgent mug of beer.

Ham pulled up on his horse beside Japheth and stuck his leg out so his brother could admire his new sandals. The soft leather covered his entire foot and ran part way up his leg, with lacing down the middle. Boots he called them and Japheth just shook his head at the extravagant purchase. They would be another long forgotten item when Ham's feet grew too warm in the restricted covering. Ham jingled the coins in the pouch tied to his belt. "One more stop to go, brothers," Ham said as Shem rode up beside them.

Japheth nodded. "It needs to be a quick stop. We'll eat but need to be on our way so we make it home before nightfall."

"I don't think we should stop at all. Let's keep moving." Shem looked straight ahead. The light mood he wore earlier had worn off.

Japheth peered down the road, seeing no indication of

problems in the waiting. "What is it, Shem? Do you think we're in danger?"

Shem shook his head. "No. It isn't that. I feel like we need to be home. I don't know why."

Ham let out an exasperated groan. "You *feel* it? My brother, the prophet. It won't hurt us to stop for a quick bite. There are plenty of men guarding the ark. It won't float away while we're gone."

Japheth waited for Shem to think. His brother appeared to be avoiding the conversation while Ham prattled on, but he knew Shem was reaching out to God. Shem had intuition that was more often right than not. The issue over the workmen that should have been let go was one of the few times they had been on opposites sides of the battle. They could not have known then how much it would cost to make the wrong decision. As a result, Shem thought about his decisions for a long time. He made a mistake and now he seemed to question his own ability to hear God in his heart.

He would follow Shem's lead. There were issues to contend and issues to let go. Getting fed was not an issue that Japheth would let interfere with the good natured atmosphere they established the past few days. If anyone heard God, it was Shem. If he felt they needed to avoid another stop, then they would not stop. It would be two against one, and even without Noah to back him up, Shem's decisions would stand.

"...and Eran won't even expect you to be home for three more days."

Shem looked at Ham and shook his head. "Sorry brother. We need to get home."

Japheth watched his brothers drift away from the cart, Ham taking the lead and Shem trailing behind. He wondered what they were preventing by keeping the wagons in motion. Ham getting into trouble, or one of the other men perhaps. The dark cover of night brought dangers, too. It was good to keep going. They were getting back several days sooner than anticipated and though the time with his brothers had been enjoyable, he felt a similar urgency rising from within. He felt the need to be home.

♦

Noah's face was etched in sorrow. Ham jumped from his horse and pulled him by the arm to see the contents of the cart but his father's eyes didn't register the prized load. They were steadfast on Japheth as he reigned in and dismounted. Japheth didn't need to hear his father's words. He bolted for his room.

Denah lay on the bed with her arms wrapped around her waist. She was pale, and dark rings circled her eyes. She didn't move as he came in, watching him with the same eyes that his father wore. Gently he scooped her up and pulled her close to his chest, against a heart beating furiously. He gently stroked her hair.

"The baby?"

Denah nodded against him. "Yes."

A lump lodged in his throat. "I shouldn't have gone. I should not have left you," he whispered.

"Don't blame yourself. I'm glad you're here now."

"I wanted this son. I wanted this son so much," he said.

"I know, Japheth."

Denah described the funeral Jael prepared. He didn't speak when she was finished. He couldn't. He held Denah for a long time as if she, too, would be lost to him if he let her go. His mind was spinning, swirling downward to an unthinkable realization.

"It's my fault," he said. "My fault the child is dead."

Denah looked up at him with an anguished expression. "No. Don't say that."

"My punishment. God has taken my son as punishment for my sins."

"Please don't say such things. It isn't your fault."

Denah's eyes filled with tears and Japheth sealed his lips to the truth. He wouldn't add to her burden with his thoughts. He wouldn't force her grief to face reality, force her to unleash a fury at him that was deserved, undeniably deserved. He held his wife until she fell asleep then laid her in the bed as he let his own emotions overflow. She didn't choose to have this life. She didn't deserve to have this life.

♦

His father sat by the memorial stones where the unborn child had been delivered back to the earth. Japheth sat on the smooth log beside him. Neither spoke as the last light of day was replaced by the veil of night. The stars appeared, one by one, surrounding the half moon that dripped light onto the two mounds of stone.

Noah took Japheth's hand. "I'm so sorry, son." Noah's voice was as soft as his hand was rough.

Japheth squeezed the hand holding his own, the hand he clung to as a child. He let go of it once, purposefully unclasping his fingers and pushing it away. He didn't need the guidance anymore. Or so he reasoned. He did, though. He always had. Even as an adult, the hand of Noah was a confirmation, a comfort, a connection to wisdom far beyond his own understanding. He would never let go again.

"This is my punishment. My fault." He could barely speak the words. His father punished him during the time of rebellion. His whole life as the firstborn son, stripped of honor, changed, and not just in his position in the family and status in the community, but inside. He was not the same confident heir of the house of Noah. He had his just punishment, refreshed with each rising sun. But that was from his father's hand. God didn't punish him then. God had not dealt him a blow. Until now. He always knew, someday, someday, it would come.

"Punishment? I don't understand, Japheth."

"For my sin. For my rebellion against the Creator."

Noah inhaled deeply and ran his fingers over his scalp, pushing the graying curls away from his face. "It's not punishment from God, son. I don't know why this child wasn't permitted life, but God-" His father looked to the sky and sighed. "God isn't holding a grudge against you." He put his hands on Japheth's shoulders and turned him so they looked eye to eye. "There's no reason for God to punish you."

"I questioned his very existence."

"You weren't even a man yet."

"I knew better. I rebelled against my God. I rebelled against you."

Noah stood and began a slow pace around the stumps where they sat. "Yes. You did. And where was I? You were young, you were full of questions, and where was I?"

His family never discussed their hurts. Japheth's mind was suddenly flooded with questions, questions that had ruminated for years, belonging in the past, dead, yet refusing to remain there. His father was allowing them to live. "I don't understand."

Noah sat back down and stared up at the moon. "Where was I? Japheth, my long awaited firstborn. You were wise and inquisitive from the start. 'Why, father?' 'How, father?' 'When, father?' I should have realized when you stopped asking that you were still too young to have it all figured out. When you stopped asking me, I should have been asking you the questions. I should have been filling you mind with truth, teaching you, instructing you. But I didn't. I journeyed to this town and that town to tell the people of God's judg-ment. When I got home I tended the vineyard or tended the herds. Not my son. I didn't tend my own son."

Japheth absorbed the words, words lined with guilt. He shook his head. "I don't remember it like that at all. I was at your side while you worked the fields, and you had to speak the words of God, and to travel. I admired that in you, father. I understood why you went away and that you had God's work to do. Even when I tried to reason God away, I respected your devotion to the God of your fathers. My fathers."

"You were my work, as well, Japheth. With your natural inde-pendence, it was easy for me to forget to raise you. I never suspected doubts were brewing in your mind until the day you told me you didn't believe there was a God. By then, you had answered all your own questions and I was too late."

"Father, I knew the truth. Even if we spent every moment of every day together, at some point, I believe I would've rejected your council and gone my own way. It's who I am."

"Who you are is my wise, and disciplined, good son. When you told me you didn't believe in the Creator I thought my heart would crack open and I would die right there. I spent my waking hours telling everyone of our God and my own beloved son thought I was a fool. I was so angry. You're strong willed and too smart sometimes, but you're a very good son. Now and then."

"I was a fool," Japheth said.

Noah patted Japheth on the knee. "You questioned and turned from your, God, yes. But only a fool stays the path he knows is treacherous."

"I hurt you. I'm sorry."

Noah nodded. "As am I. I was wrong to treat you as I did. You were just a boy."

Japheth felt the anchor of his past shift, relocating to a place further away in his mind, this time lighter, the points less intense. He dropped his arm over his father's shoulder and pulled him in close. What was done, was done. His apology to his father was long overdue. And his father's words, a balm that would help soothe the memories.

"Methuselah said that there was a purpose beyond my understanding," Japheth said. "That Shem carried the blood of Adam and was supposed to be keeper of the writings. It's true. My brother hears God when I don't."

Noah shrugged. "Maybe he's right, I don't know. God has his own ways."

Japheth nodded.

"It isn't punishment now, son," Noah said, reading his mind. "I know the God of First Man didn't take your child as retribution. And there will be other sons. And daughters."

"Has he told you that?"

"No. It's the hope of my soul." Noah fixed his eyes on the ark. "We must trust his timing. Man hasn't completed his purpose."

"The serpent."

"Yes. The evil one. He told the serpent that Eve's offspring would crush his head. Perhaps the flood waters will fulfill God's words, burying sin beneath its torrents. But that isn't our doing. And why, then, will God spare my family? If I am alive, sin is not yet dead. Somehow it isn't finished. There have to be sons and daughters. The words of the One God to Eve will not be lost."

Japheth turned his face to the stars. He prayed that the sons and daughters would come from the sons of Noah.

Chapter Thirty-four

Denah watched her husband's eyes smolder. He breathed in and out forcefully, curling his fingers into fists that smacked against each other. She sat on the bed and forced herself to breath smoothly.

"Carmi hit you with the jar and that's why you fell?"

"Japheth, he was drunk and I made him angry. He never meant for this happen."

"I can't believe you defend him." Japheth's jaw was stiff, compressing his lips into a tight line. "How could he treat you that way? He's your father. What did you do to make him that angry?"

"I was interfering with the way he treats Beth. He's too hard on her. He didn't like my interference."

Japheth stared at her. "That was it? He killed my son for that?"

Denah stared at the hands she had tightly knitted together in her lap.

"I hope I never see his face again. He better hope I never see his face again."

Her husband's voice was even and controlled. It was not a statement released purely in anger but one that Japheth spoke with full awareness and sincerity. Denah gasped and closed her eyes.

Japheth sat beside her and took her chin gently in his hand. "I know how you feel about him. You do understand that what he did was wrong, don't you? Drunk or not, angry or not, hurting you, and the baby, was wrong."

Denah nodded. She knew. She also knew it wasn't entirely her father's fault.

The first pink rays of dawn were reaching across the sky and Japheth put on his sandals, kissed her forehead and left the room. She stood at the window and waited until her husband walked through the courtyard then disappeared like an apparition in the early morning mist. His head was down, shoulders slumped, carrying the loss of his child at the hands of his father-in-law.

He blamed himself for the baby's death initially. Now she passed the blame to her father. She didn't want Japheth to despise Carmi, nor could she bear to watch him rip his own worth into tattered shreds, believing he caused the death of his child. "If I had waited until morning to go to town," "if I didn't let you go with me", "if I stayed while you saw your father." If, if, if.

Denah's mind spun its own set of regrets. If I brought more coins to the temple, if I left the pendant at home, if I had the tablets to give to father.

If Japheth had just taken me to the temple in the first place.

Denah shook the last one from her thoughts. No, that wasn't fair. As much as she hated to admit it, he was right about the temple. There was no divine blessing. She tried to believe it was true, to justify her actions, to validate the beliefs of her mother. Those beliefs wouldn't stick any longer, no longer having purchase no matter how hard she tried to apply them. Like a dark secret, she saw the truth hidden beneath a canopy of colorful ware. It was sensual indulgence and profit and false hope. The temple of Zakua held nothing more. Her brothers didn't pay homage to the goddess when they ventured into the courtyard then disappeared through the magnificent doorway. Her father didn't either. He smelled like frankincense because he had been where she had been.

Japheth wasn't to blame.

She betrayed her husband, plain and simple.

Simple? Only if he never found out. And he wouldn't. There was no baby to bargain for any longer. The stakes dropped without the precious incentive for the priest's blackmail. Her pendant and the tablets were all that remained on the table. Carmi had the upper hand. The priest might still demand the tablets of Adam and attempt to trade them in the market, but he'd make a better profit simply selling the necklace back to Carmi. The matter would be over soon enough. The priest gambled and lost.

Denah wrapped her arms around her womb.

So had she.

♦

Denah stayed away from the family for three days after the baby was gone, not leaving the room even for meals. Japheth was in and out all day, torn between providing a comforting presence and needing to work out his own pain in the labor of tanning the hides. Except for Jael, no one bothered her while she slept and cried and slept some more. Jael brought pots of raspberry and black haw tea to cleanse her womb and chamomile to help her sleep but she knew it was time to face life outside her room again.

What she longed for most was a walk in the woods, alone in the trees with the birds and the frogs and the snails that climbed on the rocks in the stream. She wanted to take off her shoes and wade in the cold water and feel the soft moss between her toes. She wanted to pick a basketful of berries to start a new dye. She wanted to fall asleep in the shade of an old oak with no concerns. It would never happen. Those days were gone.

Her basket of colorful clothing sat on a shelf. The multi-green striped tunic lay on top and Denah plucked it from the basket. The vibrant hues didn't match her mood but the colors reminded her of a simpler life, when her hopes and dreams were full of life and potential, not death and guilt. She put it on with a dab of the jasmine oil Japheth brought her as a gift, even before he knew about the baby.

The low chatter in the kitchen stopped as she entered. Eran glanced at her face then looked away as her eyes began to glisten. Naomi stopped mid-sentence and forced a smile. "Are you feeling better?" she said.

Denah felt the stab dig in to heart. How could she answer 'yes'? It wasn't like she had a simple fever. She did feel stronger physically and there was only a mild tenderness remaining, true. But affirming that, out loud, that she felt better was like saying the hurt in her heart was diminishing, too, like her child was already fading into a memory. She couldn't say 'yes.' She couldn't betray her child like that.

A series of painful questions and the onslaught of tears would follow if she said 'no' though, so Denah just nodded and began kneading a pile of leavened dough. She was torn, torn between wanting them to ask her how she really was, on the inside, and not wanting to speak of it at all. The women took her silence as an indicator and Naomi filled the awkward air with Ham's tales of the hunting expedition.

It was different after Methuselah died. They talked about him every morning in the kitchen and again at the family meal. She heard more stories about the beloved grandfather after he died than while he was still among them. The family recounted his expedition to the great sea, and reflected on his wisdom as they grew up under his tutelage. They laughed about the things he said, and still cooked the foods he enjoyed. He was everywhere among them.

There were no memories of her son. No one could say, 'remember when.' Her son was a brief life that no one held but her.

"…and there were so many odd looking deer, Ham put down his bow and the men just watched them. He said there were deer with horns like corkscrews."

"Did he tell you about the big cats that came into their camp-site?" Eran asked. "Shem tried to capture one but it was too swift. It was orange with dark spots and not very old but too smart to come near the trap he made."

Denah tried to focus on the conversation. Japheth said little about the time with his brothers other than it was a good hunt and they saw many beasts that were unfamiliar or that he hadn't seen in a long while. He made sketches to show Noah, to add to his list of animals that would need a place to live on the ark. She started crying at his depiction of the raccoon mother and her five little ones washing their hands in the stream by the campsite and Japheth changed the subject.

Renita entered the kitchen with a basket of figs. When she saw Denah she put it down and came to her, wrapping her up in her arms. Denah was surprised at her actions and even more so when she could see the glimmer of tears in the woman's eyes. "I'm sorry about your child," she said. "No mother should have to endure such a loss."

Like her own loss, Denah thought. She delivered the child she carried and then it was snatched away from her. She heard her baby's first cry then never heard it again. Empty arms shouldn't follow an empty womb.

They were alike, she and this woman. Pain tied a connecting thread around them that the others couldn't comprehend. Renita, at least, understood the depths of her sorrow.

Chapter Thirty-five

The green striped tunic was ripped. It looked like a knife slashed through the fabric, making a clean line across the front. Denah threw it on the bed in disgust and went in search of Renita. She thought they had an understanding, almost a friendship even. Obviously, she was wrong. The servant still destroyed her clothing when it went to the washing.

Renita was in the olive grove, plucking plump green fruit from the trees. She smiled when Denah approached. Denah grabbed a basket of her own and looped the strap over her shoulder so it hung at her side. She stood beside Renita and picked as she sought words not filled with anger.

"Is something on your mind, Denah?"

"My tunic is ruined. The one that just came from the laundry."

Renita stopped picking and turned to her. "The striped one? It was fine when I washed it yesterday."

"It was cut nearly in two with a knife."

"Oh, no. I'm sure I would've noticed a tear like that. It wasn't damaged when it was put on the line to dry."

Denah faced the servant. "So you didn't do it? You didn't cut it on purpose?"

Renita looked incredulous. "Did I cut your clothing on purpose? Are you really asking me that?"

"What am I to think? Nothing of Japheth's gets ruined when you wash them and nothing of mine that's the drab and ordinary either. As soon as I wear something nice, it comes back ruined. This was the third one."

Renita turned back to the olives and plucked ripe and unripe alike. "Why, Denah, why would I ruin your clothing? What makes you even think I would do that?"

"Perhaps you're jealous. If you can't have nice things, why should I?"

Renita stopped working and let out a groan as if she remembered something.

"What?" Denah asked.

Renita shook her head. "Jealous, yes. But not me. You're blind if you can't figure out what's happening. If you would stop making me your enemy, you'd see more clearly."

"My enemy? I thought we, connected somehow, the other day in the kitchen. I thought you understood."

"No one will fully understand your grief, Denah, and that doesn't give you the right to take out your pain on me. I'm not destroying your clothes."

Denah said nothing. Renita sounded sincere.

"And I'm not after your husband."

Her growing irritation sprouted leaves of anger. "What?"

"I see it in your face, when I'm talking to Japheth. I see how you hate it. Be assured he is my friend and nothing more. I would never hurt Noah and Jael by stirring up that kind of trouble in their household. Japheth is stuck with you. Too bad for him. He deserves better."

"You have a wicked tongue."

"You have a wicked mind. How dare you accuse me of intentionally destroying your clothes? And why did you wait until now to tell me if it happened twice before?"

Denah turned back to the tree and clamped her mouth closed.

Renita was silent, too, wrenching fruit from the limbs with both hands. Then she stopped and threw back her head and laughed. "The temple."

Denah flinched at her words, at the tone of derision.

"I should have known. You were afraid to confront me about the clothes because I know your little secret."

Fear suddenly dug its nails into Denah's heart.

"Is that who you think I am? A conniving little snitch? That piece of news wouldn't be received well would it? You're fortunate that I respect your husband and his parents far too much to hurt them. Your dirty secret is your own, as far as I'm concerned."

Denah set her basket down while Renita watched her, the sides of her face uneven, jaggedly fused into a scowl. Her voice was soft, her eyes cold and direct. "You think you're so much better than me. I wear this mark because I got caught. That's the only difference between us. You may not bear the marks of your infidelity on the outside but they scar your heart. You'll wish your husband found out. You'll wish you were dead sometimes, too."

◆

"I never take them out of Enoch's box."

Japheth watched his brother search through the items on Methuselah's desk for the third time. Shem was rarely frustrated enough to show agitation. This evening he reached the threshold and crossed it. They were packing their great-grandfather's treasures in baskets until the simple task was disrupted by the discovery.

The carved wooden box lay open on the desk. It was empty.

"Shem," Japheth said. "They aren't here. We would've found them if they were in this room. Someone has taken the tablets."

Shem sat at the desk and put his head into his hands. "Who? Who would take them?"

Japheth thought about the men they fired. Angry men. Men who had nothing to lose by hurting Noah's family. Any of them had motive. Which ones knew where the tablets were kept? Methuselah showed them to people, even some of the workers that he tried to take under his wing and teach about the One God. Japheth didn't know which ones they were. He didn't know which of the men had been in this room to see the cherished relics and who was bold enough to come steal them.

Shem raised his head and looked at Japheth. "You've heard about the nephilim?"

Japheth shook his head no. He spent his days finishing the hides, alone for the most part.

His brother continued. "They slaughtered a whole herd of goats not far from here a few days ago. And two homes in the city were broken into during the same night and ransacked. The owners were tied up and left on their beds, their wives and all of the children taken. I wonder if they were here."

Japheth shook his head again. "I can't see them sneaking in here to take just the tablets. They are meaningless to those who don't fear the Creator."

Shem sighed. "I know. It doesn't make sense. Ham's men, maybe. I watched them when we let them go. None came this way, but I suppose one may have doubled back, or come in the night."

"Did mother or father take them already? Perhaps they're already packed safely on the ark."

Shem shrugged. "I think they would've told me. I'm responsible for them, even though they stayed in here with Methuselah. He loved to run his fingers along the writing. I didn't have the heart to take them to my room."

Shem looked away from his brother at the last words.

Japheth knew his brother never felt like he deserved to have the tablets.

"They're yours. Rightfully, Shem."

Shem faced his brother and smiled, relaxing the concerned expression. "You know that I struggle with that, don't you?"

"Of course. You're easy to read. But you should accept it. The past is the past and it isn't going to change. You have the blood of Adam, not me."

Shem's hand immediately went to the leather pouch hanging on the cord around his neck and a look of sadness crossed his face. "I never wanted this, Japheth. When you questioned God and father took away your status, it wasn't because I wanted it to happen."

"I know that Shem. I've never resented you for it. You couldn't have foreseen how stupid I would be, how angry our father would become."

"He was too hard on you. I told him I didn't want your first-born rights. But he wouldn't relent. It was me or Ham and I think father knew better than to leave the inheritance to Ham."

Japheth laughed. "Yes, that would have been a disaster."

Shem ran his hand absently over the empty wooden box. "Shem," Japheth said. "Did you ever doubt?"

"God? Yes. I did. Not until you voiced your thoughts, though. Before that I didn't know there were other opinions to seriously consider. How does one question his father and grandfather and great-grandfather? Then you said some things that had never occurred to me and I had to think long and hard about what I really believed, about all that we had been taught."

"I influenced you? I'm sorry. It really could have been Ham set above us."

Shem chuckled. "Of course you influenced me. How could I not want to follow your steps? Our parents idolized you, their perfect son. But my questioning led me in a different direction. It made my faith stronger. I knew, Japheth. I knew in the inner most part of my being that God was real. I questioned just as you did, I just never brought it to father's attention."

"See, you are the wisest of the brothers."

Shem shook his head. "I was wrong about those workmen. You were right, Japheth. My mistake was very costly."

"What's done is done. You had their best interest in mind. I thought only of the income we were losing."

Shem stood and put his arm around Japheth's shoulder. "I really wanted you to have the first son. It would have justified things somewhat. I pray the next one comes soon."

Japheth nodded as he pushed unwelcome thoughts of Denah's father from his mind before his fury stirred. He wanted his children to be raised around Shem and learn his kindness, and humility, while shouldering a great strength in the One God. He would do everything in his power to prevent them from ever knowing their grandfather Carmi.

Chapter Thirty-six

The idols of Zakua came in all materials: gold, jade, ivory, polished wood and painted wood, even one carved from the horn of a great lizard. They were positioned around the room so that wherever you sat, or stood, or which ever direction you looked, the goddess looked back with her armful of babies. Japheth stood in the center of the room and waited, not wanting to even touch the ornate furnishings. Carmi's home was a shrine to the worthless statues. In the spotless setting his skin crawled with a sense of filth. He waited anyway. He needed to face Carmi.

Japheth didn't trust the man. He never did. His parents supported Carmi's business out of an old loyalty, one that Japheth didn't share. He preferred trading elsewhere. Most merchants were deceitful in one way or another, that was no surprise in the man's shop, but negotiations with Carmi came dripping with honey coated affection. Japheth's existence was barely acknowledged until he stood beneath the roof of Carmi's business, then he was the man's beloved relative and Carmi had bargains, just for him. The pretense was sickening.

Noah had never taken him to Carmi's house and he could understand the reason now that he stood among the many pairs of vacant eyes. Carmi changed once he left Lamech's tutelage, never rejecting the One God outright, just adding many other gods to honor. He was a business man from the slick coated hairs on his head to the tender pink soles of his manicured feet. His platform shifted, modeling the ideals of whomever he partnered with that moment in trade.

Carmi brought grief to the heart of his foster father. Japheth remembered, before Lamech was killed, the disappointment in his face when he returned from Carmi's home. He could have taken the orphaned boy on as a field hand but chose instead to give him an education and sound instruction in the ways of God. Carmi embraced one and rejected the other, the one that mattered.

The sudden loss of Lamech was a blow to Carmi, all the same. Japheth's wedding was the first time he stepped foot near his childhood home since the tragedy. Agreeing to give Denah in marriage was a healing balm for his strained relationship with Noah and for his own grief. It was unfortunate his desire for strong drink didn't diminish as well. His lack of discipline cost him dearly. Japheth never wanted to lay eyes on the man again but he needed to be sure his father-in-law knew that it was his drunken tirade that led to the loss of precious life. He killed his own grandson.

He told no one he was coming, especially not his wife. He hadn't even planned on coming but when he awoke to Denah's soft tears on his shoulder, he saddled a horse. He had no intention of striking Carmi and was resolved to keep his anger under control, for Denah's sake alone.

Carmi emerged from the hall in a long silky robe embroidered ornately with colored threads. His face was puffy, his eyes slightly bloodshot. Japheth insisted that the servant wake him up, and by the looks of him, he'd not been in bed all that long. At this hour Japheth counted on the man's sobriety.

"Japheth? What brings you to my home so early? Are the waters rising?"

Japheth ignored the question and the man's smile. "I'm here about Denah."

The smile diminished for a moment then returned. "Sit. It's good that we talk. What will you have to eat?" Carmi clapped his hands and a servant appeared in the doorway.

Japheth shook his head and stood where he was. Carmi dropped onto an overstuffed couch and leaned back against colorful pillows.

"No. No food, Carmi."

"Very well, son. What's on your mind concerning my daughter, hmm?" One flick of his wrist and the servant disappeared.

"You know very well. You pushed her. You hit her."

Japheth watched his expression. Carmi was calm, listening to him like he was listening to a merchant selling his wares. He nodded evenly but showed no evidence of regret. "Yes. I did. It was an unfortunate incident."

"Unfortunate? She lost the child because of it."

Again, no change of expression, just the impatient twitchings of a man who preferred to be elsewhere. Japheth felt irritation stirring his thoughts. He fought to keep them level.

"Yes. I'm aware of that as well. A servant of your household was in the market buying her the black haw tea. Word got back to me."

Japheth stared at his father-in-law, for a moment unable to speak. It had been two weeks and he made no effort to contact Denah.

"Do you care nothing for her?" He spewed the words from his mouth like poisoned berries.

"That's unfair. What am I to do about it now, Japheth? I can't undo what has been done. I assumed my daughter would rather not see me."

"You took my child, my father's grandchild. Don't you feel any sense of loyalty to the home that took you in? Is that how you repay Lamech for all that he did for you? You feel no need to apologize for your foolishness? If not to me, or Denah, then to Noah?"

Carmi's lips pinched together, along with his eyes.

Japheth ran his fingers through his hair. "She didn't even tell me you hit her until after the baby was gone. She protects you. I don't know why."

He watched Japheth for a moment then raised his eyebrows. He responded slowly. "Protects me? Perhaps, she protects herself."

"From what?"

Carmi shifted his round form so he could pull himself into standing. "From what? Or from who?"

"Carmi, what are you talking about?"

Carmi ran his hands down his robe and smoothed out the wrinkles. "Wait here, son," he said and walked down the hall.

Japheth kicked his toe at the tassels on the edge of a woven rug. Frustration churned in the pit of his stomach and he took in several slow breaths to slow it down. Carmi knew about the baby. How could he say nothing? Feel nothing? Japheth assumed he had not heard and would at the very least say he was sorry. It was his grandchild, too.

Carmi ambled back toward him a few moments later and stood beside him at the window. "Japheth, don't be so quick to pass judgment on matters that are not, perhaps, what they seem."

"And what matters are those?"

"Your father-in-law isn't the evil man you've decided he is. I tried to protect my daughter. I tried to protect your family." Carmi sighed deeply.

Japheth studied his face. The man's tired eyes stared out the window at his land, where workers were beginning to gather and head toward the fields and barns. Japheth waited for him to continue.

Carmi reached into the deep pocket of his robe and took out his fisted hand. He hesitated, then looked Japheth squarely in the eyes. "Here," he said.

Japheth held out his hand and Carmi placed the object on his palm.

The object was Denah's pendant, the black onyx teardrop on a golden chain that Carmi gave her as a wedding gift. "I don't understand," Japheth said. "She gave this back to you?"

Carmi shook his head making his jowls quiver. His hand fidgeted with the golden bead that kept his beard in a tight braid. "No, no. I had to buy it back. It came at great cost."

"Buy it back? From whom?"

Carmi pursed his lips and huffed through his nose.

"Who, Carmi? Who had Denah's necklace?"

Carmi sighed. "A priest. A priest at the temple of Zakua."

"And why did a priest at the temple have my wife's possession?"

"I can't say. That you'll have to ask your wife."

"What does this have to do with Denah protecting herself, as you put it?"

"The priest, he didn't want to sell the pendant to me. He wanted something else instead."

"What?"

Carmi paused. Japheth latched his fingers into the man's fleshy shoulder. "What, Carmi?"

"Your son."

Japheth flinched from the slap of an unseen hand. He faced his father-in-law squarely, gripping the pendant. He wanted to close his ears to any more of this conversation, but he couldn't. "Why would he want my son?"

"It is, was, his son, he claims."

"*His* son?" Japheth staggered back and let the pieces come together in a picture he could not imagine was real.

Carmi put his hand on Japheth's shoulder and watched his face closely. "I'm sorry, Japheth. Denah's actions aren't in accordance with the house of Noah, I realize. I tried to prevent anyone from finding out. I thought you should know the truth. I think now it's good the baby is gone. It can be like this whole messy incident never occurred."

Japheth shrugged away from his father-in-law's touch, repulsed by the man, repulsed by his message, repulsed by the images his mind was creating. He didn't trust Carmi but the pendant was burning a hole through his fist.

"At what cost? You said you bought the pendant back at a high price."

Carmi nodded slowly and his hand returned to the bead. "Indeed. Before I knew the baby was gone. Before I knew there was nothing at stake but that necklace."

Japheth sucked in a breath and held it.

Carmi squared his shoulders and faced him. "It was Beth. My daughter. I sold her in exchange for the pendant and the man's claim to the child."

Chapter Thirty-seven

The black stone dangled in the air, spinning on the chain clutched between her husband's fingers.

Denah inhaled sharply. "My pendant. Where..? How…?"

Japheth let the stone drop to the floor. "Your father gave it to me."

Her husband stood with his legs spread, arms crossed over his chest. His jaw was set tightly and his eyes were the piercing daggers that he inherited from his mother. Denah wrapped herself in her arms and closed her eyes. Her heart thumped wildly and already she could feel the cold chill of perspiration accumulating on her skin.

"You didn't tell me you lost it."

Denah didn't respond. She could tell by the tone of his voice that he knew it hadn't been carelessly lost.

"Your father had to buy it back. Do you know who he bought it from, Denah? Do you know who had your precious necklace?"

Denah opened her eyes and focused on the stone where it lay on the floor, her head frozen, her lips sealed. Yes or no? The damning truth or a lie?

Japheth continued. "He bought it from a priest. A priest from the temple. Now why do you suppose a priest in the temple of

Zakua had my wife's jewelry?"

Two strides and her husband towered over her. "Was it payment, Denah?"

The stained core of her soul refused to stay hidden any longer. Denah choked down a sob. "He, he took it from me."

Japheth exhaled loudly and slammed his fist into the wall by the bed. Denah jumped at the thud and waited for the next one to land on her head. When it didn't come she looked up at him.

Her husband stared down at her, the daggers glistening. "Was it his child, then?"

Denah let her own tears fall. "No, Japheth. I know it was yours. It was your son."

"We'll never know that for sure though, will we?" His pacing began in earnest, corner to corner of the room, hands running over and over, through his hair and wiping over his face.

"You betrayed me. I can't believe you betrayed me." His voice was soft and choked.

"I'm so sorry, Japheth. I wanted a child so much."

"You went to the temple, after I told you not to?"

Denah nodded.

"You defiled our marriage."

"For the blessing! I thought it was for a blessing."

"Really? When he kissed your pretty little lips, you thought you were getting a blessing from the great and mighty Zakua?"

"I, no. I did, at first then, I had doubt, then-."

"You had doubt. You had doubt, but you stayed. You defied my wishes and made a mockery of our marriage."

"I never meant harm. I just wanted us to have a son."

Japheth shook his head. "You never meant harm. That justifies your actions?"

"Please believe me, Japheth. I know it was wrong. I was wrong.

I know."

"You think there'll be no consequences for your unfaithfulness?"

Denah squeezed her eyes closed again. Consequences came in all forms.

Japheth crossed the distance between them and took her shoulders. "Look at me! How could you? How could you betray me? I could kill you if I wanted to. Do you understand that?"

His eyes affirmed his desire to put an end to her life. He gripped her for the longest moment, their eyes locked in a bridge of hate and fear, then he shoved her away, turning his back to her. "Your father sold Beth to pay for that thing," he said as he kicked the pendant. "Her life to save yours. It's fortunate you're your father's favorite."

Japheth grabbed a cloth bag and roughly shoved clothes into it. "You're not to leave this room. Is that clear?"

Denah nodded, unable to bring any words to her lips, finding none to justify. None to redeem or repair or restore the infinite damage she created.

Her husband stormed out the door, slamming it, ensuring a wall of separation between them.

♦

Japheth threw his belongings on the pallet and sat in the dark room. The ark was intensely quiet. He left his family in the clearing, where he held the emergency meeting. He told them everything, everything he knew. His wife had been unfaithful and the child she lost may not have been his own flesh and blood. No one spoke except his father, to ask one question: "What happens now?"

Japheth didn't know.

He had the right to slit her throat.

He could mark her face and send her off to fend for herself.

At the moment both these options sounded reasonable. Denah deserved whatever fate befell her. She never wanted to be a part of his family in the first place but he had tried to give her everything, within reason, that she wanted. It was her own fault that her desires were beyond the scope of what he had to offer. Where he waited for God to provide, she took matters into her own hands.

Now what?

His anger burned. He wanted her to feel his pain and the hurt as he did, to feel the rejection all over again and to question why God permitted it to occur. He wanted her to cry and cry and cry. But not from physical pain. That was too easy. That pain went away in time. He tried to picture her face as he held up the knife, feeling her fear and hearing her screams for mercy. But he could not. As much as he wanted her to suffer, he knew he could never lay a hand on her in that way.

She wouldn't scream, anyway, no matter what he decided. She would stand in quiet resignation as she accepted her fate, grateful to be cast away from the family of Noah, even if it meant the shedding of her life blood.

He couldn't see her face at the end of his knife but the nameless man that thought nothing of what he had done in the name of Zakua was there. Japheth knew he could cut out the man's heart without a drop of remorse. Yet that would never happen either. Denah had gone of her own free will. The priest was not the one to blame.

Japheth turned to the safe pen he built for his son. He slammed his fist down on the top rail, hating the painful arrows shooting up his arm, unable to stop. He hit it again, then again and again until it cracked from the pressure. He snapped each rail in two, not stopping until the last piece of carefully planed, cut and sanded wood lay as scrap around his feet.

He wrapped his bloody hands with the soft wool blankets and sat on the floor, his head on his knees. "Why, God," he cried. "Why?"

♦

Denah buried her face in the blankets and cried until the exhaustion left her dry and no more tears came. Either did sleep. There was no escape from what she had done.

Japheth knew. The whole family knew. She heard them in the clearing talking. They were stunned and after her husband left them they still sat silently for some time. Noah was the first to stand and essentially dismiss the wordless meeting. "It is Japheth's decision from here," he said.

Japheth's decision. He had not killed her on the spot and Denah realized she wished that he had. She deserved it. So did he. He would not slit her throat now, even as his anger flared she knew he would not return to take her life. He would be obedient to his God.

She could have walked away from the temple. She didn't. Even when she realized it was all a lie, like the dirt in the golden bowls, she stayed. Japheth did not deserve a wife like her.

Denah forced herself to get off the bed and stand at the window. The ark and the clearing, the woods and the stream, the bounty of the land would soon be replaced by dark alleys and piles of refuse. It was only a matter of time before she would be marked and sent away. She would not put up a fight.

No one would care about her after today. She would be the topic of conversation in town for a few weeks. People would point and stare and laugh as she scrambled to find a crust of bread. Soon she would be a forgotten name, a no one whose only contribution to the world was to add more pain. She was a disgrace to Noah's family and a disgrace to her own. She failed them all. Especially Beth.

Denah took a washrag and scrubbed herself from head to toe then donned a clean, simple garment and her sandals. After she tediously combed out her hair and pulled it back in a simple braid she added a few drops of jasmine to her throat for the last time. She sat on the bed and waited.

Chapter Thirty-eight

The sun fell behind the ark, taking the last traces of green tinged sky and still Japheth did not return. Denah stood at the window and watched for his familiar gait. He had come and gone from the ark several times throughout the day but the last time he went, with a lantern, he had not come back.

Denah left the curtains open and sat down, taking off her shoes. Her stomach growled, as if reminding her of the life that lay in her near future. Hunger. Fear. Loneliness. Even so, her gut wouldn't allow her to eat. The hours had passed since Japheth confronted her, the anxiety had not.

Her pendant was still on the floor, in a tangle after her husband kicked it into the wall. Denah picked it up. Her father gave it to Japheth. Her father told him where it had been. If anyone was going to stand by her side, she thought it would have been Carmi. She betrayed Japheth. Carmi betrayed her. He was angry about the price, no doubt, forced to sell his own daughter to secure the evidence the priest possessed. Still. He was her father.

Carmi had nothing to gain by telling Japheth, unless he thought Noah's family might try to get Beth back. That seemed unlikely. Eran's hands flew to her mouth and Jael groaned when Japheth told them about her in the clearing that morning. They were appalled, but no one mentioned trying to find her or trying to buy her back.

Her father was a dealer, a haggler. A good one. He never let opportunities pass without gaining a favorable exchange. He had reason to tell Japheth. He had reason to betray her. Somehow he secured a benefit for himself. Just what that was, she couldn't figure out. Whatever the reason, Carmi's betrayal slunk its way into her heart, ripping out roots she thought were deep and strong. Denah bit down on her lip and stopped herself from crying. Again.

A gentle tap on her door made Denah sit erect and brace herself before it occurred to her that Japheth wouldn't knock. "Come in," she said.

Shem opened the door and entered, followed by Eran. Denah couldn't look either of them in the face.

"We brought you something to eat." Eran's voice quivered.

Denah stood and took the bowl. "Thank you," she said and set it on the table. Shem took his wife's hand and squeezed it. They didn't leave.

Denah glanced at Eran's troubled expression and Shem's, full of sadness. "I did a terrible thing."

Shem looked out the window. "I was surprised. I didn't think you were like your father." His voice wasn't harsh, not condemning like she expected. He sounded disappointed.

"Believing in Zakua, you mean? I don't. Not anymore."

Shem looked her in the eye. "Not that. I didn't think you were the kind of person to do whatever it took to get what you wanted, no matter who you hurt. No matter if it was right or wrong. You were strong willed growing up, in a good way. You used your strength to help your father and Beth and others. I never thought you were capable of this."

Denah stared at her feet.

"I want a child more that anything in this world, Denah. But it is the One God who gives life." Eran was on the verge of tears.

"Did the One God take my child then? Was I punished for what I did to Japheth?"

Shem shrugged his shoulders. "Perhaps. I can't answer for God."

Denah dropped onto the bed. She rolled the smooth black stone in her hand, running the pads of her fingers over and over the surface. "I don't know what will happen to me."

Eran sat next to her and put her arm around Denah's waist. "God Who Sees sees Denah. He saw Denah in the temple and he sees her now. He will be with her, whatever Japheth decides."

Her words were like Methuselah's. She was glad the old grandfather wasn't here anymore, to see what she had become. She held up the pendant. "Methuselah told me to hide this, once. He told me it would lead to trouble."

Shem sucked in his breath at the sight of the black stone. Eran turned pale and quickly went to her husband's side.

"Denah. Give me the onyx." Shem's voice staggered, barely controlled.

"Are you going to get Beth back? Are you going to trade this for her?"

"No." Shem held out his hand. Denah looked in question to Eran. She looked away. Denah placed the black teardrop in Shem's palm. "It's mine," he said. "It was never truly yours."

Shem held it tightly in his hand for a moment then took the leather cord and pouch from around his neck. He opened the tiny buckskin pouch and let the contents fall into his other hand. Denah watched. A smooth round stone lay on his open palm. "Do you know what this is, Denah?" he asked.

Denah nodded. "The reminder stone, from Adam, from the

plains of Havilah."

"No. It isn't. It's just a rock I took from the creek bed." Shem drew back his arm and hurled the round stone through the window.

Denah said nothing as he took her pendant and yanked the chain off. He held the black drop by the tip in front of her. "This. This is the Blood of Adam," Shem said. "This is where it belongs." He placed the stone in the leather pouch. Eran sank onto a chair and closed her eyes. Denah tried to make sense of it, and couldn't.

"I don't understand. It belonged to my father. How did he get it?"

Shem put the pouch around his neck, his right hand refusing to let go. He watched her without moving except for his thumb as it rubbed against the leather. "You'll have to ask him, Denah. Ask Carmi how he obtained the Blood of Adam stone from the house of Lamech."

Did Lamech give one boy the writings of Adam and one the stone, trying not to show favoritism? Or had her father swindled it from his foster brother? Both items were rightfully Noah's inheritance, regardless. Carmi was loved but he was not a firstborn in the line of Lamech. The stone belonged to Noah, now Shem. She understood that. Why hadn't anyone explained the stone's significance to her?

Denah shook her head and started to ask why Shem hadn't told her but Shem put up his hand and stopped her. "No more questions. We have to leave. We've stayed longer than we should have. Goodbye, Denah." Shem took Eran's hand and led her out of the room, closing the door behind them. Denah couldn't miss the finality in the way Shem told her goodbye, not good night.

She picked up the broken chain from her father and smiled at the irony. She had worn the precious Blood of Adam, the reminder stone, around her throat, like the priest for the One God, carrying his dismay over the sinful heart of man. She, the betrayer of her husband. How had it not burned a hole in through her flesh?

Chapter Thirty-nine

The rooster's crow bounced down the corridor, drawing Japheth from a fitful sleep. A glimmer of filtered light fell beyond the doorway. It was morning.

He sat up and stretched the kinks from his spine, then examined his hands. They ached. He gingerly opened and closed them before peeling off the bits of fabric still adhering to the cuts. The sharp barbs of pain brought him to full awareness, again. He had been up and down throughout the night, his mind too restless to allow any forgetfulness through sleep, contemplating his options over and over. He was still unsure of the actions that needed to be taken this morning.

He would not kill Denah. He could not. That was clear in his mind. For whatever she had done, he could not take the life that God had given her. He tried in the night to generate that kind of anger but it wasn't there. It would be over and done with if he did, as if she had never lived, as if they had never married. He wouldn't have to worry about her then. There would be no one to accidentally run into in the city, no one to call his name from a dark corner, begging for a morsel of food, no one to stir up the torment in his mind. But he could not raise the knife that would release her back into the elements. God restrained his hand.

The logical choice was to mark her and send her away. He couldn't do that either. He couldn't bear the thought of Denah living among the ruthless men haunting the back ways and sun deprived wedges of space where a marked woman is used and tossed away until she dies, alone. Sometimes their bodies were found only days after they were marked. Some lived for years. It was a heinous practice.

Japheth picked up an unopened jar of wine that Ham brought to him in the night. His younger brother surprised him with the suggestion that Denah be allowed to remain in the household. If anyone wanted blood, he thought it would be Ham. His brother wanted nothing of the sort. "Can you forget it happened, Japheth," he said. "Can you look past her mistakes and see the good in the wife you married?"

Japheth didn't think he was able to do so. He wasn't sure he could look at her at all.

Shem appeared in the doorway and looked his brother up and down. "I don't need to ask if you slept well. Did you rest at all?"

"Some," Japheth responded. "Not enough to get me through this morning."

Shem sat on the bed beside him. "You don't have to decide, of course. It's all in your hands how to proceed."

"I know. I need to decide, Shem. I need to make a decision. I can't bear to let this hang on. And it's only fair to Denah."

Shem smiled. "You're a good man, thinking of her. You're also a man who makes up his mind readily when the facts and choices are laid out. What troubles you the most?"

Japheth leaned back on his arms. "I want her to hurt as I do, I want her to suffer greatly. But I don't want her to hurt. I don't want her to suffer."

Shem nodded in complete understanding. "She is bone of your bone, flesh of your flesh. And she suffers already, Japheth. No matter what actions you decide upon, she suffers."

Japheth let a smile creep up at the corner of his mouth. "She's mine and I don't want her to go and yet, I don't think I can look at her again. I don't know what to do, Shem."

Shem exhaled slowly and his hand went to the leather pouch around his neck. "Brother, there is more to this picture than you know." Shem removed the stone and handed it to Japheth.

"Denah gave you that pendant?"

"It's mine, Japheth. It's not just an expensive stone from the market. This stone is the Blood of Adam, carved at the first great gathering of the people. Carmi had it, and he gave it to Denah."

Japheth examined the precious stone that he had tossed onto the floor of his room. A drop of blood, black with the taint of man's rebellion. "Why did Carmi have it? Lamech gave it to him?"

"It wasn't given to Carmi, that I know. I assume he stole it. The Blood was kept in the box with the tablets, in Methuselah's room. Father noticed it missing one day, years ago."

"And Carmi denied taking it?"

"He was never suspected. He was like family and we didn't know how long it had been gone. There was no way to pin down who had been in the house. Methuselah, remember, liked to show people the writings when he talked about the beginnings. I searched the tents and watched the market but it never turned up."

"I never even knew it was missing."

"No. Father told me not to say anything to you, to anyone. He thought the thief would be weighted in guilt and would return it in time."

"That's why Carmi gave it to Denah? To return the Blood to this family, as restitution?"

Shem exhaled and looked his brother in the eye. "No, I don't think so. The buckskin pouch disappeared with the stone. Our parents found the pouch on this cord, around Lamech's neck, when they were preparing him for burial. There was nothing inside."

Japheth let the implication sink into his gut. "You think my father-in-law killed Lamech?"

"I have no proof."

"Why? Why would he kill the man that raised him?"

"I don't know."

Japheth turned the stone in his hand then gave it back to Shem, picturing a nameless priest taking it from his wife's neck, where it had been since the day she stood beneath the earthen canopy, the day Japheth gave her his rib and they became one. "Mother and father," he said. "They're aware of this?"

"Yes. They recognized it on your wedding day. So did I, and Methuselah, and Eran. The connection between the Blood and Lamech's murder and Carmi's possession of the stone, well, it all connected then. Carmi adamantly refuse to give Denah to you for years, then one day he was eager to make the betrothal. I think, I think he wanted to see Noah's pain. I believe Carmi planted the pendant on his daughter on purpose.

"No one said anything. No one told me."

"No. It wasn't fair to you, to start your marriage off with such a burden. It was obvious Denah didn't know anything about it. I may be wrong about all this. Her father may have purchased the stone, someone else stole it and killed our grandfather. But I don't think so, Japheth."

If he had been told this information before he found out about Denah's infidelity, he would have been furious. Now it was another piece of tragedy in the line of others. Carmi lived under Lamech's roof. He knew about the stone. Methuselah probably showed it to him over nad over again. The ugliness in the soul of Carmi wasn't new. Japheth couldn't rule out the possibility of the man's guilt.

"I've never trusted that man," Japheth said.

Shem nodded. "There is great evil in his heart. But it's not in Denah. She knew nothing of Carmi's treachery, I'm sure. She has no idea what kind of man her father really is. I told her about the Blood of Adam. I didn't tell her how I believe her father obtained it."

"Thank you, Shem. For telling me. "

Shem stood to leave. "Do you want to postpone the family meeting this morning or continue as planned?"

Japheth stood to gather his belongings. "It must be done today."

♦

The wingspan of the large bird circling above her head had to be as wide as Denah was tall. She didn't recognize its kind, floating against the blue morning sky. It hovered in a silent dance, soaring effortlessly above the rising mist, waiting. Waiting as she was, for the family to gather, for her fate to be determined.

Denah sat straight on the stump and kept her hands clasped in her lap. Watching the bird was easier than meeting the eyes that collected on the stumps in front of her. No one spoke.

Japheth was the last of the family to arrive. She turned her focus to his feet and the bottom of his crumpled tunic.

The air was heavy under a damp blanket of cold, wrapping itself around the clearing and the mumblings of the stream. Denah shivered, then willed her limbs to be still. She inhaled a deep breath and looked into her husband's face.

Japheth's eyes were weary, his lips were pressed together. His shoulders slumped and he stared at his hands. Both of them were swollen and wrapped in bandages that seeped fluid onto his lap but he didn't seem to notice. If he had the knife, she couldn't see it.

Denah forced her attention to her father-in-law, sitting beside Japheth. Noah looked her in the eye, not with the malice she anticipated. One by one she turned and looked at each of the family members. Jael's eyes brimmed with tears and she allowed Denah a brief smile before turning away. Eran, Shem, Ham, and even Naomi watched her in silence with eyes that spoke of pain, not anger. Not hatred. Not revulsion.

Anger would have been easier. Anger would have been justified.

Noah broke the silence. "Son, have you made a decision?"

Japheth nodded affirmatively, keeping his head down. When he didn't speak, Noah put his arm around his trembling shoulders. Japheth was fighting to maintain his composure long enough to speak his mind.

Denah closed her eyes, allowing her heart to pound, anxiety and anticipation refusing to find a place of comfort despite her husband's tears. His anguish made her want to take the knife herself, to spare Japheth from the necessary task.

Footsteps on the path made her open her eyes again. All eyes turned to the sound, to the marked servant as she made her way toward them.

Renita wiped a stray wisp of hair from her cheek and tucked it behind her ear. She looked at Noah, then Jael. Noah called her to step forward. "What is it Renita? You may speak."

Denah stared at the woman who mirrored her pain. Renita had once been in her position and knew the consequences. She understood. If she spoke in Denah's defense, perhaps Japheth would listen. Perhaps he would not mark her and send her away.

Renita looked at Denah for a brief moment, then pulled her closed fist out of her pocket. "I found this. I hid it for awhile, but I found it, tied in her clothing when it was washed."

The servant's head jerked in Denah's direction at the word 'her' then she handed Noah the tiny jade idol of Zakua that Denah found on the ark the day it was cleaned and purified. She had forgotten all about it.

"No!" Denah let the word escape and started to rise. Noah held up his hand and silenced her, motioning for her to sit. His expression was no longer soft.

Renita stepped back. She paused before leaving, turning bright eyes to Denah, smiling.

Japheth was on his feet. "I can't have you here," he said. "I can't. You will go to your father and stay there. If I see you here again, I'll kill you."

Chapter Forty

The cart rumbled down the lane, through the vineyards, past the fields where the wheat and barley left short stacks of yellowed remains. Denah sat on the cart beside the driver, neither speaking as Noah's land rolled past. She ran her hands along her thighs, on the one garment she now owned. One tunic, one pair of sandals. Naomi could take all the clothes she wanted now. She didn't have to hide her jealousy behind rips and stains. She could have them all.

Denah let a laugh escape when she though about Naomi's reaction to the contents of the basket of colorful clothing. She would discover the writings of Adam buried beneath the crimson and heather and turquoise dyes. It would confirm in everyone's mind that her expulsion from the house of Noah was warranted. They could add 'thief' to her list of sins, pondering why she took the tablets and hid them. It would be one of those little family mysteries that no one would ever uncover. Because no one would ever ask her.

None of them would ever speak to her again.

Japheth wasn't going to kill her. She could tell that when he arrived at the clearing that he hadn't worked up the fury to end her life. He didn't mark her either. Denah ran a hand along her jaw. He should have. He would have felt better, in time. She didn't know what he was going to decide, then Renita showed up.

Renita's scar thrashed smile was etched on her mind. Her timing was well executed, rehearsed. Betrayal was nothing compared to worship of another god under Noah's roof. Denah was accused of the one inconceivable offense, the one abomination that was never tolerated. Only it wasn't true. Denah didn't worship the worthless little idol. No one knew that. No one cared about the truth.

Truth. Who was she to stake any claim on truth?

A passing cart slowed and a man pointed at her as they went by. The family on board held back nothing as they openly gawked. They didn't know she was being sent away. She was still just the wife of Noah's son, a member of the crazy ark building family. The gossip about her status would spread soon enough and the fathers of daughters wouldn't just point and mock, they would be angry, angry that she bore no marks to reveal her shame.

Carmi traded one daughter to protect another. Now he was getting one back, if he chose to take her. She didn't know how far her father's loyalty would stretch after what he did to Beth, and what he did to her by giving Japheth the pendant. He wouldn't take her marked, but if she knew her father at all, his business sense would prevail. Her skill was worth far more to him than the amount of food she consumed. Business might even improve as the gossip mongers flocked to his shop for morsels. Somehow Carmi would benefit. Somehow he always had the upper hand.

The very thought of being near her father brought a wave of unease. She would gladly live in the barns or the servant's quarters rather than in the house with him, especially without Beth.

◆

Carmi's wife Anna led Denah into her old room, the one she

shared with Beth. Little had changed. Her side was in strict order, the way she left it. Chaos ruled the other side. There were tiny collections of berries and leaves and feathers and flowers, piled in mounds on the shelves. Beth was perpetually on the lookout for dye ingredients and without Denah to monitor the hoard, the room was filling with remnants of just about anything the girl found, living or not. One little table was full of fabric scraps containing rudimentary stitches and the uneven embroidery work of her sister's hand. There were clothes on the floor, in the heap where they were removed.

Denah picked up a soiled tunic and pulled bits of flax fiber from the weave, starting a pile of her own beside a fistful of wilting lilies. The bunch of blooms sagged on rubbery stems that had been gripped tightly until they were safely delivered to the room, then placed, and forgotten on the table.

Denah stopped picking at the garment and stared at the drooping flowers. The blossoms still held their color, the leaves only curled on the tips. They couldn't be more than a day old.

♦

Denah ran the distance to the barns and bolted in the first one, where Beth was working the last time she saw her. Carmi's employees stopped their motions and looked at her in surprise. Beth wasn't there and Denah felt her thumping heart drop in disappointment. She turned to leave but a smiling form blocked the doorway.

"Denah!" Beth shouted.

♦

Carmi was barely in the door when Denah approached him.

"Why did you lie about Beth?"

Her father looked surprised to see her. He looked her up and down, settling on her face. Her unmarked face.

Denah put up a hand to her smooth skin. "Why did you tell my husband?"

Carmi let a smile curl up at his lips as he took off his coat and handed it to a servant. He attempted to put his arm around Denah but she stepped away. He exhaled in an exaggerated way and poured himself a cup of wine.

"So, my daughter has come back and won't even greet me with respect in my own home."

Denah crossed her arms over her chest. "I don't understand, father. Why did you betray me to Japheth? Why did you lie about Beth? You knew that would cut my heart to pieces."

"No harm has come to Beth. And no harm has come to you. Other than that rag you wear for clothing, you are none the worse for your experience."

Denah couldn't speak.

Carmi laughed and lifted his wine to a golden Zakua. "Everything turned a full circle, back to the way it was. I have my two daughters again."

"It is not like it was. I have a husband. Or, had, because of you."

"Because of me? I'm not the one who betrayed Japheth."

Denah let the comment sink into her mind then she pushed it aside.

"Why did you tell him?"

Carmi shrugged. "He was here threatening me. I caved under the pressure." Her father twiddled the end of his beard in his fingers. He was lying.

"Why did you lie about Beth?"

Carmi smiled. "You should have seen you husband's face. It was like I told him the great boat of Noah sailed away without him."

"Just a lie, to hurt him. To hurt me."

"You? I knew you would know the truth."

Carmi topped off his cup and sank down into the couch. He was relaxed, unconcerned. Denah watched him as he toyed mindlessly with a bronze pipe and for the first time in her life, realized she didn't know who he was.

"Where did you get my pendant? Shem claims that it's his."

Carmi pursed his lips and smacked them a few times. "That was a gift from Lamech."

"A gift? Lamech gave you the heirloom instead of Noah?"

"It was a gift to myself. Lamech didn't argue. "

Denah sucked in her breath. "You stole it?"

"It should have been given to me. I was a more competent son than Noah. Lamech gave him everything that should have been mine."

"He gave you a good life. What more did you expect?"

Carmi held up his cup as if in a toast to an unseen guest. "Ahhh. What more indeed."

The tension between him and her mother-in-law, their past, flashed in her mind. "Jael."

"The lovely Jael."

Denah caught her breath and waited for him to continue. "I saw her first. I was the one who saw her in the market being sold to the highest bidder. I was the one who asked Lamech to get her. For me. Tall and defiant, head to toe draped in luxurious fabric and golden chains. And those eyes. Eyes with fire, and strength." Carmi set his cup down and let it slosh across his clothing. "I wanted to tame that fire. But Lamech turned her into a servant, made her untouchable in his household, then he gave her to Noah. Lamech knew she was mine. Noah knew she was mine. Jael knew she was mine. But I didn't get her."

"Lamech gave you his own daughter."

"I didn't want that weak willed creature. He was trying to pay me off. I made him pay for that. I made sure he followed his daughter to an early grave."

"You killed her? You killed, you killed Lamech?"

Carmi laughed and had to steady his own hand to keep his cup righted. "Even with the insane ark business he wouldn't admit that I was the better man. The wife he gave me, she was just weak. She killed herself."

Dizziness forced Denah to sit down. "And Lamech paid with his blood."

"Yes, Denah. That he did."

Denah sat back on the chair and turned her face from her father's decadent round form that made the couch sink toward the floor. There was an answer she needed to hear. "Why did you agree to my marriage into Noah's family? What were you to gain?"

A slow half sided grin drew up on Carmi's face as his thoughts went back in time. "How was I to know that Japheth wouldn't recognize the Blood of Adam? I never dreamed of losing you into that family. Why would I get rid of my best source of new merchandise? I lost a mighty wager when you stepped out of that tent. Married. He was supposed to reject you."

"You intended for me to be humiliated?"

Carmi looked at her as if suddenly realizing she was capable of being hurt. "It was never about you, my dear."

Denah allowed the distaste in her mouth to spread. For all the years, side by side with her father, spitting out unwanted truth, this she had to swallow.

"My gambled losses were nothing when Noah saw the pendant

dangling from your neck, though. Seeing that expression, that was worth it all."

"You used me, used me to hurt Noah and Jael."

Carmi shrugged. "I expected to take you home after the whole tent performance. It was unfortunate your child died, however. I liked the thought of my blood and Jael's mingling in a grandson."

Denah didn't respond, sickened at the reality Carmi pushed in her face.

"Oh, of course it may not have been Jael's blood, hmm, Denah?" Carmi chuckled then snapped his head up and looked at her. "Did you bring the tablets?"

"No, of course not. I was sent away with nothing."

"A shame."

"Why? The baby is gone and the pendant is back. Once you traded Beth-." No, he hadn't traded his daughter in payment. Denah scanned the room. None of her mother's gilded trinkets were missing. "How did you get the stone back?"

"The same way I got it the first time."

"You took it."

"A dead man puts up no fight. We had a pleasant evening together first. That priest and I were, let's say, familiar. I saw the stone when he disrobed for me. It wasn't his to keep."

Denah felt the color drain from her face. His death was blamed on the nephilim. She closed her eyes and willed the image of the priest to go away. "The priest didn't threaten you. There was no blackmail. You lied to me. You lied to me just to get those tablets."

Carmi laughed and saluted her with his cup. "Lamech was a fool to choose Noah over me. I was better than him in every way. I should have been the next leader of his One God. Those tablets should be mine. I wish you would have brought them with you, Denah."

Denah was on her feet.

Carmi beckoned her over. She stood still, reeling inside from the flood of madness pouring from her father's lips. "It's over," Carmi said. "All that messy business. My gods have poured out their favor on me. No one is hurt. We're the same as we were before."

No, Denah thought as she fled from the room. Nothing is like it was.

Chapter Forty-one

The damp air prickled Denah's arms. She wrapped a cloak around her shoulders and stepped outside into the still morning. Out of habit, she looked toward the ark, rising from the mist. Of course, it wasn't there. More than six weeks had passed since she left the shadow of the great vessel. It called for her to remember anyway, every new sunrise.

She walked through the fog toward the flax fields that ran the length of her father's property. They were empty now, the stubble turned beneath the earth in long furrows and the thistles pulled in preparation for sowing the tiny seeds. Delicate arms would push to the surface soon and the cycle would continue as it always had, sowing and reaping, sowing and reaping.

The sodden trenches gripped her bare feet, cool ooze slipping between her toes, sucking at her soles as she pulled her legs up and moved them forward. Later, as the soil firmed, the walking was easier, but it was at this break of day she preferred to seek Noah's God, hoping he would respond as the earth slumbered beneath its misty blanket.

She first sought the One God the day she moved home. The day she realized she was nothing more to her father than a tool to extract vengeance on his rival. The man she adored betrayed her, used her. Her father, the man she strove endlessly to please, destroyed the loving hands that raised him. And not only Lamech, but the priest, too. Without remorse. He intended to hurt Noah, and Jael, and the fact that his own daughter was a victim of his evil heart mattered not at all.

She wished at that moment that Japheth had killed her.

She was a fool. For believing in her father. For relying on Zakua. For treating Japheth the way she did. Her husband's wisdom was far beyond hers, she just couldn't see it. Or chose not to see it. Her own desires, her own methods trumped all else. Everything was lost to her and as she ran from Carmi's presence that day, she saw no reason to exist.

But God was there, in the field, where she collapsed on her face. She didn't even realize she had been calling out, but he answered. It wasn't a voice, but a presence, a warmth that wrapped its arms of comfort around and held her tight. It was the voice that Methuselah described, the whisper on her heart. She poured out the hurt and the guilt and the shame, knowing, knowing she wasn't crying into the empty mist. God was there.

She stayed in the field for a long time not knowing what to do. Beth found her eventually and Denah went back to her father's house. She had no where else to go.

She came to the field every morning, now, talking to the God with many names and no image, waiting for a reply. She wanted to hear him like Noah did, clear and direct, but it didn't happen. He spoke in the quiet way, the way that forced her to listen and put her own thoughts aside.

This morning as she traversed the field her focus was on Japheth, as it had been more and more as the days passed. After she was banished, she tried to shut him out of her thoughts completely.

She couldn't bear to see his face or hear his voice. He reappeared, unbidden, footsteps in the morning mist, prodding her to remember. His smile. His focus. His heart. She dealt with the pain as the recent memories scrolled through her mind. She longed for his touch.

♦

Bear cubs wrestled in the grass at the edge of the clearing. Japheth watched the pair, tumbling over each other, rolling over the foliage in one tangled ball, and considered setting a trap. They would be a menace if they discovered the food stores and the ark held room after room of the dried bounty. He only entertained the thought of the trap for a moment, realizing he couldn't do it. They reminded him of his younger years with his brothers, full of life, abiding in simple faith without the cares that follow the years of time. He would not subject them to a cage without sound reason. Not yet.

Japheth turned back to the trap he was finishing. It was sized to contain a boar, and was just one of many he had constructed over the past six weeks. Noah gave him no instructions as to the size and number they would need to capture the creatures for the ark, so he just started with one, then kept working, varying the sizes as he went.

He positioned the door and set the nails before realizing the latch was on the inside of the cage. The hammer landed with a thump on the ground where Japheth tossed it. Another careless mistake. He had a run of mistakes the last several days. His thoughts strayed, away from his work, away from the ark, always landing on Denah. She was ever present lately, the images of her becoming more vivid and intense, demanding more than just his passing thoughts. He was compelled to think about her.

Yesterday he almost ran his cart into a merchant's stand of trinkets when he saw her standing at the perfumers. Or thought he saw her. It wasn't Denah and he realized he was relieved and disappointed at the same time. He saw her face and heard her voice everywhere. He tried to focus on his purchases while his eyes roamed the sea of faces, searching as he bartered.

The brunt of his anger was gone. He was left with a gnawing emptiness, like he'd lost more than his wife, but a part of himself as well. He tried to shake the feeling. He had been generous in his treatment of her, not killing her or even marking her as she expected. Carmi was no good but Denah would survive in the man's home. He would tend the one who made his profits soar.

Japheth intended to let her stay with him, here under his father's roof. Maybe not as man and wife in the same room for a while, he wasn't sure about that. As he watched her on the stump, peaceful almost, following the crane that soared above her, as if she was resolved to letting him slice her throat, resolved to face the punishment she deserved. He resolved right then to forgive and try to forget. Then Renita showed up, and showed them the idol. The fury building in Noah's eyes settled his decision in a different place, not keeping her, not killing her, just sending her away. In retrospect, he knew Denah didn't worship that thing, at least not anymore. She had seen the lies that governed the temple. He didn't know why she had it, it wasn't her god. It didn't matter though. He sent her away. Denah was gone and it had been the right decision. That's what he told himself.

Japheth climbed the ramp and sat at the edge of the landing above the line of stacked cages. For something that dominated the last twenty years of his life, he had spent very little time on board since he sent his wife away. He withdrew from the one as the other withdrew from him. His fervor to complete the mighty vessel was gone. The rest of the family seemed to feel the same way. None of the new furnishing had been built and no one seemed to care that the guest rooms were either empty or filled with more food stores. He used the extra lumber for his traps, building and building, even though there were obviously enough now. The mindless chore kept his hands occupied while his soul stagnated.

He wasn't the only one to miss Denah, though no one ever mentioned her in his presence. The usual routine persisted in Noah's home, with a void, the persistent sense that a part of the family was gone. First Methuselah, then his child, then Denah. Japheth felt a lonely ache deep in his heart.

A flash of motion in the courtyard caught Japheth's eye. His heart quickened at the sight of a woman drawing water from the stream.

It wasn't her. It was only Renita. He watched her as she worked.

"Are you here to visit an old friend?" Noah asked, patting the side of the ark from the doorway before he sat beside his son. "Or are you going to dismantle her to make more traps?"

Japheth smiled. "I don't know why I'm here. I don't know many things at all."

Noah's gaze followed Japheth's. "She's a beautiful woman."

Japheth jerked his eyes away.

"She reminds me of your mother, the way she faces adversity, holding her head high." Noah looked off toward the city. "Carmi wanted to marry her."

"Renita?"

"No, no. Jael. Carmi wanted to marry her and so did I. He admired her beauty and wanted to tame her fire. I admired her tireless spirit. I knew she could make me a stronger man. My father gave her the choice. She chose me." Noah looked at Japheth. "I don't believe Carmi ever forgave me, or her, or my father. I didn't see the full darkness in him. I was blind to his nature."

Japheth nodded. "I'm sorry that he's Denah's father."

"From the start, he was difficult. He always had to compete, always had to win. I thought it was because he lost everything and needed to find himself, but it never ceased. My father and Methuselah poured themselves into him. It was never enough. Carmi was never satisfied with what he had. He always wanted more, expected more."

"Like that stone. I'm glad you didn't tell me at the wedding, that he took it and that he killed my grandfather. I would've reacted badly, I would've sent Denah away right then. Despite all that has happened, I'm grateful you allowed me the chance to have a wife. I don't know how I earned it, how I righted my wrongs, but I don't regret marrying Denah."

Noah turned his face to the sky. "Righting your wrongs. Those are my words to you. Oh, Japheth, I wish that I could take those words from your ears. I was the one who was wrong. I expected you to confess a sin you never committed."

"What sin?"

"Your wrong wasn't the rebellion against God. I was speaking of the Blood, the stone. I thought you took it."

Japheth couldn't suppress the surprise in his voice. "You thought I was the one who stole it? Why?"

"I thought you were laying claim to what you lost, your firstborn rights. I vowed you would never marry until you returned the stone. When I found the pouch on my father's body, I knew I was wrong. Very wrong."

"Why didn't you confront me? Why didn't you ask? I've never lied to you, father. Never."

"I wanted God to convict you of your crime. I wanted you to right your wrong to honor him rather than because you were caught. I didn't want you to return it to please me. I wanted you to want to please your God."

"Shem said something like that. I didn't realize he meant me."

"Your brother swore you had nothing to do with the stone's disappearance, Japheth. He and Methuselah were never convinced that you were involved. Never. They knew you better than your own father."

"So Carmi took it."

"From the tablet box. He's had it for years. I suppose he put the pouch on my father after he killed him to hurt me again, or draw suspicion elsewhere. Maybe so I would know that his hands killed the man I loved. I don't know."

Japheth sifted through his memories, putting the pieces in order. All those years, his father thought he was a thief, yet he never detected mistrust. Noah handed him management of the family finances. He worked so hard to mend his father's disappointment with no way of realizing he couldn't fulfill Noah's expectations. He didn't have the stone to return.

He laughed, the absurdity of it striking him. There was a difference in putting family matters away that were settled and those that weren't. "It's good that I know all this. It's good that it's past."

Noah squeezed Japheth's hand. "Your wrongs were righted long before mine, son. Your marriage long overdue."

Japheth pictured his wife on their wedding day, rising from the pool of fabric. "I'm sure Denah didn't know what her father did."

Noah shook his head. "No, she wasn't aware."

"He had no remorse in killing my, Denah's baby."

"That child wasn't meant to be, Japheth."

"God has closed the wombs of my brothers' wives yet my unfaithful wife was with child. Perhaps it is our seed, father. Perhaps God has placed his hand on us so that the heirs of Noah will be no more."

"There will be sons, Japheth. God will fulfill his promise to

Adam, but his timing will be his timing. Trust him."

Japheth turned his eyes back to the courtyard, where Renita scrubbed his clothing. Was she to be the mother of his sons?

Noah put his hand on Japheth's shoulder. He was watching the servant, too. "Don't make a hasty decision. God didn't destroy First Man and First Woman when they were disobedient. He sent them away from paradise, yet he didn't leave them. He was still their God. They returned to him in their hearts."

His father pulled himself up into standing. "Take your wife and your sons and your son's wives, God told me. I don't believe he meant only Eran and Naomi. He meant all my sons' wives, not just those of your brothers, Japheth."

Japheth watched his father descend the ramp then stood and followed. The falling cloak of evening brought the piney scent of a wood fire wafting around him, drawing him home. The scent was friendly and warm. It wasn't the fragrance he wanted to envelop his senses, though. He longed for night blooming jasmine clinging to Denah's skin.

Chapter Forty-two

The buzz of a hummingbird woke Japheth from the depths of sleep. It took him a moment to realize why he was awake. He wasn't as diligent as Denah about covering the window at night to keep the birds out and this anxious creature seemed determined to whirl around his face until he sat up. Now it paused in the window, framed against the pale sky of morning. Its black eyes watched him as if holding a secret, daring him to follow as it zipped away in a blur of feathers.

Light was just beginning to pierce the shroud hovering over the land and he thought for a moment he might return to the absent realm of sleep. Then he heard the sounds. The air carried a strange combination of noises, noises arising from the clearing. Japheth's mind jolted to full wakefulness and he sprung from the bed, peering into the clearing just long enough to gasp before he threw on clothing and bolted outside.

His father was at the far edge of the courtyard, facing the clearing with its mighty wooden backdrop. He was face down in the dirt. He was sobbing.

Japheth dropped to his knees beside Noah and tried to speak but all he could do was stare into the lifting curtain. Jael and the rest of the family fell beside him and together they watched in wide eyed silence as Noah's heart burst before his God.

Creatures.

Creatures of all shapes, sizes, and colors ambled among the tree stumps.

♦

When Noah stood, his face was smeared with dirt, his eyes on fire with a passion that Japheth felt ripping across his own heart. His father faced the family with an intensity of purpose but before he could muster a word his eyes dropped to the ground, where two prickly balls were scurrying past him, heading for the grand gathering in the clearing. Noah smiled, it broadened to envelop his entire face, then he threw back his head and laughed. And laughed. And laughed. He laughed from deep within, the laugh of fulfillment, of pure delight in the ways of his God.

Ham slapped Japheth on the back. "Good thing you got all those traps ready, brother."

Japheth squeezed his brothers in a tight embrace, still breathless as the prophesy unfolded before their eyes. Beasts roaming the clearing were interested in finding the sweetest grass to nibble or the softest grounds for napping. No animal was intent on devouring another. The only swift motions were of young pairs, chasing one another through the legs of larger animals and jumping hurdles of smaller beasts in playful disregard of danger. A golden lion leaned against a tree stump and licked his paw, paying no attention to the pair of young antelope leaping over him as they darted over and under and through and around the menagerie. A skunk allowed a bear cub to push him over with her nose, again and again, until the cub's attention turned toward a sleeping buffalo that he viewed as a rock to scale.

Eran was the first to leave the human cluster and step up to an ostrich. She caressed its long neck and allowed it to take a gentle tug of her coat before it bounced away, barely missing an armadillo that transformed itself into a ball of plating. Above her, a pink cross in the sky honked and circled until it found a landing strip near another flamingo, that one resting one-legged in the stream beside a dozing crocodile couple. Japheth and the others watched incredulously as she walked fearlessly among the beasts and birds, like First Woman, Eve.

Noah eyes glistened as he called her back and addressed the family. "God has spoken to me. We have seven days before the waters come. We are to gather seven of every clean creature, males and females, and one male and its mate of the unclean ones. Find places for them on the ark." Noah looked out over the clearing. "Use the traps as cages and pens, if you need to. The birds and the beasts that will go on board are here. God sent them."

◆

Denah woke with a start. She sat up in bed, her heart thumping in her chest. She tossed back her covers and tiptoed over to Beth. The girl was asleep, snuggled under a thick layer of soft skins, breathing evenly. It wasn't Beth who woke her up. Denah moved to the doorway of her room, then out in the hall. The house of Carmi was undisturbed in the stillness of the morning.

It was still dark as Denah got dressed and went outside. Something wasn't right, or something needed to be done. Something was not as it should be. She felt anxiety rising in her chest but she didn't know why. She started to head out to the field then stopped, feeling an ominous pressure, like she needed to act. Now. Quickly. But doing what?

She dropped to her knees and lifted her face to the black sky. "I don't know what you're saying. I don't understand."

"Come home," the voice inside her said.

Denah waited in the wet grass for more but God spoke once and that was all. She pulled herself up when the light of day was peeking over the horizon and went back to her room.

Home? She didn't belong under Carmi's roof. Noah's house was no longer her home. Japheth told her to leave, that he would kill her if she went back. Where was she to go?

♦

Japheth looked intently toward the road when he heard the fast clomping of a horse in gallop. He could see his father's old mare from the long ark window, running like a colt as it neared the barn, as if it, too, was spurned by the people in town and wanted to escape the hatred dwelling there. Only one rider dismounted and Japheth let a sigh escape. Denah wasn't with him.

He didn't ask his father to go get her specifically. Noah's focus was on the many lives that still could be saved if only they would listen. Denah included. He came home each evening with the same report. Ridicule. Disbelief. Threats of violence. He came each evening with the same number of believers. None.

Even the animals, filling the clearing three mornings in a row, did nothing to persuade anyone that God's mind was set, that judgment was imminent. They knew Japheth was building traps with the lumber and roping that he purchased and accused Noah of fabricating the story. No one cared to see for themselves. No one cared that the traps were re-purposed as cages for the arrivals that stepped out of the woods and into the shadow of the ark. No one cared that the cages were filling the rooms intended for them.

Noah dismissed all the field hands and household servants and told them to go to their homes and tell everyone about the strange birds and the reptiles as big as the elephants and the tiny crawling and flying creatures that were making new homes on the ark. He told them to gather their families and return quickly. There were only four days left.

So far none had returned.

Japheth hoped Denah would listen, that she would be persuaded to return to his father's land. He said he would kill her if she did. He didn't mean it. She didn't know that he threw the hateful words as a weapon and would do anything to take them back.

He didn't ask his father if he could go to town, either. He and his brothers worked from dawn to nightfall getting birds and beasts situated and he knew that was his priority. There were already far more than they realized even existed and the flow of animals had to end soon. Surely he could get to Denah before the seven days were completed. She was back in her father's home with her dyes and fabrics. It was the life that she longed for. Maybe, just maybe, she would leave it all behind. For him. For God. For her life. He prayed that she believed.

The foul stench of animal waste rose from the collection pile Ham started in the center court of the tent city. Japheth looked out at the refuse heap that Eran, Naomi and Jael were building with their wagon loads. When the waters were gone, the site would flourish from the fertilization and his father mentioned starting the new vineyard there. Everything, they would begin anew when the forty days ended and the ark settled back onto the land. He couldn't wrap his mind around it fully, that everything would be under water, that everything would be destroyed. That everyone would perish. His home and entire cities would lie in ruins, and there would be bodies upon bodies to bury. The carnage was unthinkable.

Japheth knew God's judgment would be thorough.

Denah had to come back.

♦

"I must take Beth. She wants to go with me. She's been asking to see the ark for years. Can't you allow her one pleasure?"

It was the third morning in a row that Denah woke with anxiety and the need to flee. Japheth's home was the only other she had ever known so it was there she would go, but not alone. She faced her father with an easy smile and a calm demeanor she didn't feel. It didn't matter if Japheth killed her when she arrived. The whisper on her heart was too strong, too compelling and for once she listened to a voice greater than her own reasoning. No harm would come to Beth at Noah's home. She wouldn't be punished for Denah's own sins, and she wouldn't wear her father's handprint on cheeks for being slower than his other employees. Jael would take her in, and if nothing else, put her in the servant's quarters and give her tasks that she could handle. She would have far better treatment than with her own flesh and blood.

Carmi sat at the end of the long table and continued picking at the meat from a leg bone with his teeth. He looked at her over his greasy chin. "She has many pleasures. She has no need to see that thing."

"One visit. I'll help her catch up on the work she misses."

Carmi threw the bone onto his plate. "Why do you continue to try my patience? You think I don't see through your pretense? You ungrateful girl. I give you everything and you scorn my generosity. If you want to run back to Japheth, then so be it, but Beth does not leave my home."

Denah stood abruptly and let her chair crash to the floor. Carmi grabbed her arm as she passed and hissed into her face. "Once you leave my home, you're never welcome back."

Chapter Forty-three

Rustling tree limbs parted, revealing the horns of a rhinoceros as it stepped into the clearing, sniffing the air. One particular scent caught his interest above the conglomerate of odors arising from the clearing. He trotted to the defecation stack left by the female, added his own contribution then scraped his feet through the pile before joining her in the stream. He side stepped a bowl shaped nest on his way, constructed of bent foliage, where a gorilla slept soundly after somersaulting around the clearing with a pair of young baboons. A pomegranate colored ibis interrupted her preening to acknowledge the rhino then to honk at a wolf as it dashed past her on its way to roll in the new pile of feces. The wolf was smiling.

So was Japheth. He couldn't contain it. He wanted the sights and sounds to be forever ingrained in his mind. He wanted to remember each creature, to study it, to understand it. He wanted to remember their individual quirks, the nuances that made them unique. Everything, except maybe the smell.

Birds and beasts continued arriving to the trampled clearing although the pace had diminished considerably. Japheth took note as they sauntered out of the woods or soared in from the sky. Some came in pairs, male and female. Others came alone and waited for another of its kind to arrive. Only when both were present did they allow themselves to be led to a pen or carried to a cage. Young creatures arrived with mothers then fearlessly left her side as she disappeared back from where they came. Of the clean beasts, six were always in pairs with one single that was beautiful and perfect, as the sacrifices to God were meant to be.

Shem wiped the sweat off his brow with the back of his arm, then stooped to pick up a tortoise intent on making the climb up the ramp on his own power. It was going to be a three or four day journey to its cage, and they only had two. Japheth hauled its mate from a flat stone in the creek where it soaked up the sunshine. He followed his brother to the top floor where Noah and Ham were converting the empty rooms into additional living space for the newest arrivals. All of his traps were now dwellings in the ark, except for the one with the misplaced latch. It was sitting outside the ark, holding a pair of screeching chimps who figured out how to secure the enclosure from the inside so they had control of their own coming and going. Thus far they were content outside the ark, supervising everyone and everything in the near vicinity.

Japheth stopped Shem on the top of the ramp on their way out and pointed to their mother. Jael stood with her hands on her hips addressing the monkeys in the voice that the boys clearly recalled from their childhood, the voice that meant business. It short order a furry arm poked through the bars with a fluffy ball of chinchilla dangling from its grasp. Jael took the rodent and set it free before stomping away.

The brothers laughed as they scanned the clearing below, taking deep breaths as they stretched out their spines. They had long abandoned trying to keep count of the creatures they shuttled and shooed into the ark but Japheth knew they passed the ten thousand mark and were probably closer to fifteen. Still, the ark was not at capacity.

Most of the four legged creatures were small enough to carry and the myriad varieties of birds and insects found ample space among them, not even requiring cages of their own. The behemoth pair was young, barely taller than he, as were the elephants and all the great lizards that came with their mothers to be left in Noah's care.

A hundred or so kinds still waited and from the ramp, it looked like it should be an easy procedure to get the remaining ones aboard by nightfall. Shem and Japheth knew differently. There was no biting or clawing or stinging or spraying and most pairs climbed the ramp with minimal prompting. The rest had to be coerced to leave their playground, then stay put once they were on board. One young giraffe galloped up and down the ramp eight or nine times before it finally allowed itself to be led inside.

They learned the first day that it was better to let the more rambunctious ones run about and use up energy before trying to get them on board. It was easier to gain compliance when the creatures were fatigued. After the initial fuss, the youngsters settled into their spaces, relaxing quickly and without further agitation. Jael said it was no different than little boys at bed time.

Eran waved her hand at Shem from the clearing. She stood beside a young hippopotamus who nibbled at the flattened grass. Japheth scanned the clearing for Naomi who also waved and pointed to the other hippo wading in the stream. It was the routine they devised for getting the kinds together in the same space. The women spotted and the men fetched.

Japheth slapped his brother's back and they went off to gather in the curvy beasts. Each grabbed a carrot on the way. A leading rope had only been successful with the smaller animals. Most of the large ones just stood or sat when the rope was pulled. Bribery was their latest innovation.

Japheth approached the hippo and held out the carrot and was immediately bowled over as it jumped toward him and took the treat. The ground squished when landed. He fell in dung from who knew what, and with the beast standing over him, couldn't get up. Naomi got in a squat and looked under the hippo's belly, laughing, until he too had to chuckle. She gave the beast a push from behind until it stepped far enough forward to let Japheth stand. A brown smear of excrement covered his clothing on one side.

It wasn't the first time he sat in it or stepped in it the past few days, just the first time he laid in it. Part of the day's duty. He shook his head and proceeded pushing the firm, gray flesh from behind, steering it toward the ark. Over his shoulder he saw Shem running backward with a carrot, his hippo trotting after him in anticipation. Japheth saw the thick rope of python slink in his brother's direction, not in time to warn him. Shem fell over backwards and the carrot was in the air for the fastest bidder. The hippo had the benefit of momentum and took the prize. Shem, too, resorted to pushing from behind.

As the first glimmer of starlight appeared, the clearing was free of everything that flew, crawled, hopped, pronked, or just plain walked except Noah's family. Even the insects and frogs, birds and bats that normally filled the clearing were absent, frightened away from the pounding hooves and beating wings of the creatures that God sent. There was silence. Deafening silence. Japheth stood with the others and stared at the ark, now loaded with passengers. It was oddly still despite the thousands on board.

Japheth inhaled and put his hand to his head, running his fingers through his hair. It was still so overwhelming. His father's vessel housed bits of all creation that grew and dwelt on the dry land. When the waters came, the ark would preserve this remnant and they alone would survive the wrath of their Creator. Noah said little when it became obvious the rooms he intended for other people would house the beasts of the earth. The spaces he intended for mankind were filled with fur and scales, claws and beaks, wings and tails. Man, made in God's image, stayed home, refusing to hear, refusing to come, refusing to be saved. Even now, Japheth knew his father would sleep in the crocodile pen to make a place for anyone choosing survival at the last moment.

Noah and his wife, and his sons and their wives. His mind fought to keep hold of the hope that Denah would come in time. Earlier, when he searched for a place to unload a pair of sloths that clung to his legs, he discovered some of Denah's belongings in a storage bin. Someone else kept the hope alive as well.

Chapter Forty-four

The darkness was heavy. It tried to suck the strength from her resolve but Denah was keenly awake, fully dressed, and lying under her covers, waiting. Her ears listened for any indication of movement in the house. All she heard was Beth's even rhythm as she breathed. Her father had gone to bed a few hours past, after plenty of wine and a rich dinner. It was time.

She quietly made her way to Beth's bed and laid a hand on her shoulder. Beth opened her eyes and the smile was already in place. Denah smiled back and put her finger against her lips. It was fortunate the girl was too simple to understand the fear. She would trust Denah implicitly.

The game was well rehearsed. Beth popped out of bed clothed, pressing a finger against her lips to remind herself that she had to be like a fox, soundless, as she prowled in the darkness. The girl wore only a simple scrap of a tunic and the shoes she wore in the barns. It would be chilly in the night air, but they wouldn't take blankets or coats, nothing of Carmi's that would be missed. Denah waited until Beth's eyes adjusted then led her out of the room, out of the house. They were nearly to the stable when it occurred to her that her feet weren't cold. They weren't wet, not even damp.

She stopped for a moment and looked out over the landscape. The terebinth trees at the far edge of her father's property were visible, black swatches of varying heights creating a knit wall. She could see the branches where they rose from the trunk and forked, climbing ever upward to the star filled sky. The barns, the house behind her, all without the shroud of mist that came with the fall off night. Every night.

Denah shivered and hugged her arms over her heart. It pounded in its confinement. The clarity of her surroundings brought an onslaught of anxiety, like a covering had been peeled back and all was exposed. She was exposed. It was as if she was being watched, and judged, and not only her, but everything, everywhere. A flood of guilt and shame washed over her heart and mind and she was overwhelmed with the need to collapse on the earth and call to the God of Japheth, the God of Denah.

A hand tugged at her elbow. Beth smiled. Unaware. Innocent.

Denah forced her legs to remain rigid. She turned her eyes to the moon, circled in a halo of soft rings. She waited for God to speak, to act, to make himself known. He was silent, as he had been the past three days. If the Creator had no new instructions, she would follow the one he already gave. She would leave. What she heard with her heart, she would heed, despite the cost.

Beth stopped at the entrance of the stable and allowed Denah to enter first. The mare was restless in her stall and fidgeted as they rummaged for the reins that were hidden beneath the straw. It would return to its master on its own so nothing of Carmi's would be taken. No thing. Not no one. Beth couldn't remain here. Denah would see to her removal and safe placement under Jael's wing. Noah could handle the wrath of Carmi and any demands for payment. Denah would be banned from her father's home. It didn't matter. She couldn't stay here, not now. Not seeing him with eyes of truth. She didn't allow her mind dwell on the status of her own future.

"Are you going to steal that horse?"

Denah turned to the voice in the entrance of the stable. Two of her father's men stood with arms crossed blocking the doorway. A third came from an empty stall. He grabbed Beth by the arm and led her to the others. A lantern was lit and two more men arrived. "Get Carmi," one said.

◆

The curses from her fathers' lips reached the stable before he did. He pushed past his men and stood with his hands on his hips, breathing heavily. He was draped in velvety robes, and had not bothered to put on shoes. His puffy red eyes spewed fire.

"I told them to be on the alert for you," he said.

Denah said nothing. She caught her sister's eye and gave her a reassuring nod.

Carmi followed her gaze. "Stealing what's mine is worthy of death. So is running away."

"She had no idea what we were doing. I told her it was a game." Denah tried to stand still and willed her legs to hold her.

Carmi snorted. "Yes, daughter, a game. And who will win this game, hmm?" He held a hand out to one of his men who placed a knife in his grasp. He took Beth and pulled her to him, putting the blade at her throat, then nodding at another servant who did the same to Denah.

Carmi smiled. "Who wins? Who dies? I'm so tired of the two of you."

Denah flinched and felt the sharp burn in her skin and a trickle of warmth on her neck.

"One lives, one dies. You choose Denah, you who think you

are so clever."

The knife eased on her throat. "Father, don't do this."

"Choose," he said. Carmi held her eyes. Dark, unrepentant, evil pools stared at her. There was no forgiveness lurking beneath his anger.

Denah's throat was dry. "Let her go."

"This one lives then?"

Denah nodded and felt her legs give way. She was jerked back against the man who held her. One arm around her gut, the other at her throat. She closed her eyes and held her breath.

Her father laughed. Denah forced her eyes open. Carmi sneered as he pushed Beth to the ground where she lay in a crumpled heap, wrapping her arms tightly over her head and rocking in place. He raised his knife to Denah's cheek. "Get away from me. If I ever see your face again, I'll slice it to pieces."

The men stepped away from the door and let her through. Denah ran past the house and out into the street. She was alone, unarmed. She leaned against a tree for a moment and caught her breath. There was nothing she could do for Beth now.

What was she to do?

The streets of the city were under the spotlight of the moon with no misty fog to provide a cloak of obscurity. Debauchery floated on the night air in a city that stayed awake until dawn. Men were out, seeking amusement, and she would be easy prey. Her death would not come quickly at their hands.

Japheth's face centered in her mind. His hands would kill her, but with mercy. The safest way to get to him was on the path outside the city wall.

Denah peered into the sky and whispered to her God. "You told me to go and I'm going. My fate is in your hands."

◆

There was something odd about the night and Japheth got out of bed for the third time. He went to the window and looked at the ark. It stood in solemn watch under the moonlight. It was then he realized how clear everything appeared. The gentle misty air of night that gave the ark a soft finish was absent, the sharp clarity of the moon, softened by rings of dimmer light. He shivered. By the moon's position he knew morning was far off yet, but the seven days were ending.

His mind was suddenly filling with images, from his youth, from that morning, from days ago. He saw himself, like he was watching someone else, and feeling that man's emotions, thinking his thoughts. The weight pummeling his chest drove him to the floor. He lay flat with his arms out stretched. He let his mind pour out its hurts and fears, its guilt and shame along with tears that flowed unending. His mind raced over his arrogance as a young man, his pride when he defied his father, his foolish rejection of the One God. Quickly those images played out in his memory until he was left with the face of his wife, who he sent away and threatened if she ever returned.

He could not leave her behind.

He begged his God, "Please, help me find her."

◆

The gang of young men saw her slinking in the shadows. Denah dove for cover beneath the shrubbery along the wall. They were drunk and up to no good so she waited silently until she was sure they were gone, staggering up the street, yelling for her to come out and join them.

The creek gurgled into the city through the familiar stone arch. Denah plunged into the cold water and wriggled through the space. She pulled herself up on the other side and climbed the bank, leaning against the city wall long enough to know that her splashing went unnoticed.

The woods were a sharp contrast to the moonlit streets of town. Here shadows predominated with only intermittent shafts of light. Denah felt a sense of relief. The trees were a comfort and would shield her as she followed the stream to Noah's vineyard. She waited a moment longer for her eyes to adjust to the deeper darkness, the tall dark trunks surrounding her like pillars of protection.

Then one moved.

Denah was not alone.

◆

The door slammed in Japheth's face. Denah had been thrown out of her father's home in the middle of the night and the servant had no idea where she had gone.

◆

The nephilim surrounding her were armed for destruction. There were thirty at least and each had a spear and a long bladed knife. There were piles of rags soaked in oil and low burning fires hidden behind jars, ready to set the town ablaze. The growls of the muzzled dogs intensified as a large man bent down and hauled Denah to his side.

He smelled of sweat and burnt hide. Then he spoke, and she recognized another odor. She remembered. He remembered, too. "You," he said. His breath was full of garlic.

Denah forced her head up to look at his face. The sickle shaped scar was there, above his left eye.

The nephil ran a grimy finger over the shallow slice across her throat. "Did your husband miss?" he asked.

Denah bit down on her lip.

The nephil continued to eye her closely as his comrades shuffled impatiently. "A man of honor. It was a pleasure to let the fool live." It was he and his son who walked away from certain death but warring men would not share stories of humiliation. Denah saw no reason to correct him.

"Where is it you are going at this hour with the slice of death on your throat?"

Denah mumbled one word. "Home."

The nephil's eyes fixed on her face as voices rose behind him. 'Kill her and let's get moving' was the consensus among his men. The nephil squinted his eyes, drawing the sickle downward. "No," he said.

The voices murmured. He held up his meaty hand and silenced them. "She lives," he said. He stood full height, towering over Denah. "Go then, go home."

Denah took a hesitant step forward as the wall of men separated, yanking snarling dogs back. She stumbled past them, then picked up her pace, running as hard as she could. When she had to stop and ease the sharp ache in her chest, she turned back the direction she came. There was only darkness and silence.

There was no one there.

◆

Noah allowed the horse to run free as Japheth jumped off. "I couldn't find her. I searched everywhere. Everywhere."

Noah ran a hand through his beard. "I trust in my father's God, son. I trust his decisions. I don't know what else to do now."

Japheth sighed. "I know. It's not in my hands."

Noah put his arm around his son. "There's smoke in the city."

Japheth turned and looked at the dark plume streaking the pale morning sky and nodded. "Nephilim," he said.

Both turned away and faced the ark. "It's been seven days," his father said, as if Japheth wasn't keenly aware. "The others are on board." Noah faced Japheth and put his hands on his shoulders. "There is one remaining in the house," he said.

Renita. Noah sent the others to their families. She had no where to go, no one to take her in, no one to bring back to the ark of salvation. "She isn't on the ark?"

Noah frowned. "Not even Renita believes the waters will come. She has seen what God can do. With her own eyes, she witnessed the arrival of the beasts and the birds, but she has hardened her heart to the truth. She refuses to see. Refuses to believe. Refuses to be saved."

Noah paused, looking toward the house. "She may be persuaded, if that's what you want, Japheth."

Japheth shook his head. As he frantically searched the darkest corners of the city, he knew he couldn't consider any other woman. Denah was his and he wanted no one else by his side. "I don't wish that Renita be left behind, but she is not my wife. I would rather be alone."

Noah turned to his home, a wordless farewell. Japheth wrapped his arms around him and pulled him in close. Both cried as the years of trusting and rebellion, faith and doubt, diligence in the face of derision, fell over each other's shoulders. Noah broke the hold. "We have to go, son."

Japheth allowed his father to take his hand and lead him up the path toward the ark for the last time. He wouldn't have done it alone. He wanted to go back, back to the city to find her.

His family stood silently on the platform as they arrived. "Go on in," Noah said. "God will be in the ark, God will be with us. We must not be afraid."

One by one the family retreated into the interior. Japheth stood just inside the great door, and waited.

♦

The sun was above the horizon as Denah ran past the vineyards and into the clearing, heading for the house. Then she stopped. The clearing was littered with refuse. The grass was trampled flat. The usual cacophony of bird calls was absent, gone like the mist. Even the tree leaves seemed to be turning away from her, leaving her alone in the vacant space. Fear crawled up her spine.

Then she remembered the words God spoke to her heart. "Come home," he said.

Home.

Not the house where she was raised.

Not the house of Noah.

The ark.

Her eyes flew to the vessel. It sat in an odd stillness as the light of dawn pierced the air and illuminated the massive structure. It was brighter than she had ever seen it, the normal pale backdrop being eaten up by rolling gray whorls.

Denah screamed. Her eyes locked onto the darkness climbing fiercely behind the sun drenched ark until a brilliant flash of jagged light broke through and the sky itself rumbled in anger.

Denah bolted through the clearing to the ark of Noah where she knew the God of Adam waited. At the top of the ramp she stopped. Japheth stood before her.

♦

She was breathless and gasping for air. Her wide eyes looked fearful and a gash across her throat sent blood down her neck, now dried stripes that disappeared into her wet garment. Refuse from the clearing covered her legs. But it was Denah. She was here.

Japheth crossed the distance between them and wrapped her in his arms, holding her as she shook against him.

"I don't deserve this," she said.

Japheth ran his hand down her hair. "Nor do I."

Chapter Forty-five

Darkness unrolled on the sky above them like wool batting. The daggers of light ripped through the whorls and swirls with rumbles and moaning as the fury progressed toward the city, pushed by a cold, biting wind. The dust of the earth was stirred into a frenzy beneath trees that writhed and shook, great limbs cracking and falling to the ground below. Denah clung to her husband.

Noah pulled them into the ark where the others stood motionless, speechless, as they watched the familiar blue disappear under the blanket of God's wrath. Denah couldn't look at them. Jael's hands grasped hers. "I'm glad you're home," she said.

Japheth stepped to the pulleys that connected to the door. "The door, father. We have to shut the door."

Ham and Shem broke from their trance and positioned themselves near the cables, their arms already bulging with energy to heave the door in place. Noah didn't move. His voice was quiet as he spoke. "We're not strong enough alone, boys."

Japheth grabbed a cable anyway and Denah could see the frustration in his face. He pulled, then his brothers added their strength but the force of the pull was all wrong, like he knew it would be. Finally he dropped the cable, acknowledging the futility of

Blood of Adam - 325

trying to move the massive weight with only four men. The boys faced their father, understanding finally seeping through "God told you to build it this way," Japheth said.

Noah chuckled. "God never said anything about those pulleys, son. That was your plan, not his."

A resounding crack ripped through the air followed by a boom that made the deck tremble beneath them. Noah led his wife, and his sons, and his son's wives to the center of the ark, away from the portal that led to the only life they had ever known. They sat on the floor side by side, hand in hand, as the thick veil covered the sky and sealed the heavens from the earth. A low murmur rose from inside the ark and filled the corridors. Denah noticed the animals for the first time, cowering under the passing judgment.

"In the beginning," Noah started.

The hinges of the great door groaned. Denah's heart jumped and Japheth tightened his grip on her hand. The structure rose from its resting position on the ramp, evenly, easily. It snapped into place, sending vibrations along the planking, down the corridors, through her limbs. No locks held the door in place, and she knew no man could move it from its closed position. The unseen hand of God sealed them in.

Another tremor rippled across the floor and they heard the ramp crash to the earth. Denah squeezed Japheth's hand in the darkness. She could hear the ping of water dripping then felt it fall on her skin. It was coming from above, through the windows. From the sky itself.

Noah stood. "Close the shutters and light the lamps," he said.

Denah followed her husband to the windows and peered out into the wet sky. The gentle stream in the clearing exploded as she watched, a torrent of water surging from within the earth and ripping through the land. Mossy stones were propelled into the air into the blackness above, that continued to drain like a sponge being wrung out and never depleting. It made a sheet in front of her, a sheet that stretched out to the horizon, beyond the city in one direction and as far as the sea in the other. Through the veil she saw a cow stumble in the torrent as it tried to climb the knoll. It slipped and fell beneath the surface before the churning flow sent it floating beyond the ark. She fell to the floor and held her head in her hands. She didn't want to see any more. "Beth," she whispered. "Beth."

Japheth closed the remaining shutters and collapsed beside her. He put her head on his shoulder, repeating Methuselah's words. "The iniquities of the wicked heap woe on the innocent."

"I'm not innocent, Japheth."

"Nor am I," he said. He looked up at his father who paced the long rooftop corridor with his hands raised to his God. His father, who never questioned, never doubted the words of prophesy. Noah, the man of faith. "In the midst of God's wrath," Japheth said, "we're caught in a flow of mercy."

Chapter Forty-six

The hoot of an owl perched in the rafters outside the room woke Japheth with a start. He sat on the edge of the bed and listened to the answer from its mate down the hall. He shook Denah awake. "Listen," he said. Denah sat beside him as the two birds called back and forth. He could hear a rooster somewhere, and a goat, too. He could hear. The continuous drone from the driving rain was missing.

They ran to the top deck where Noah stood with Jael. The shutters were open and the ark swayed gently on the waves, not listing and lurching as it had for nearly six weeks. The heavens were blue once again, though puffs of white dotted the horizon. Japheth looked in every direction. There was water, water and more water.

It was gone. The land was gone.

Forty days of continuous deluge, forty days of the earth rendering itself in two, exploding from within with fire and fumes and the ferocity of a God-All-Powerful. Now the rain had stopped, the fury subsided. The sun sat on the edge of the water, sending a golden shaft toward them, flooding Noah's face with a radiant glow.

Japheth leaned out into the sunshine, feeling the light wind whipping his hair in all directions. He stared down at the water, a grave of immeasurable depth, burying all mankind and the beasts of the earth, far, far below. The violence of the surging waters destroyed all that he knew. Noah's land was gone. As far as he knew, the earth itself dissolved.

"We'll have to wait for the water to recede a bit," Noah said, "before we venture out again."

Japheth rolled his eyes and punched his father on the shoulder. "So much for forty days on board. God didn't tell you how long we'd float, or what we might expect now?"

"No, son. It will be a changed earth, and a new beginning for all of us. One thing will be sure. One thing, as sure and as constant as the stars, however. Our God will be with us."

Epilogue

Naomi nodded in approval at the embroidered pattern Denah showed her for inspection. Her sister-in-law was patient as she taught the stitches and found reason to praise even the worst knotted bits. Denah set the work down to stir a pot of beans, a pot that no longer sloshed with the current. The ark stood firm on solid rock.

The nausea that accompanied the rocking vessel hadn't ceased. It came every morning. Denah rubbed her hand over her belly and smiled.

For more than two months the floorboards had been still, the waters outside creeping away, bit by bit each day. The door remained closed, so they continued as before, feeding beasts and cleaning waste. It was routine now, after more than a year of practice. The chores were completed with less exhaustion, less time. Less meant more restlessness. Denah longed to feel the mud squish between her bare toes.

Noah was ready, too. He already had the stack of stones ready by the door, one stone from each grave that once stood on his land. There were many of them, enough for a fine altar. Her own child's was among them.

At the moment, her father-in-law was asleep in a hammock. Jael had him tucked in one arm, a newborn chimp nestled in the other. Ham whittled away on his latest invention, a shrill device he called a whistle. It made the wolves howl but already they knew to come to the sound to receive their food. Eran sat cross-legged on the floor beside him and played her flute, her own melodies of praise to the One God. Japheth and Shem sat with a tablet they made from salt, flour and water. Shem carved a stylus and stamped the words of the beginnings into the soft dough then baked it in the sun. He was using it to teach Japheth how to read the words of God for himself.

Denah grinned at him from across the room. She didn't deserve his forgiveness, or his friendship. He offered both. She wondered once, what she had done to deserve the life she was handed, against her desires. Now she was grateful she didn't get what she deserved. She would teach her sons and their sons and their sons about the grace of God so they would learn to hear him with an open heart.

They would know the words of the beginnings.

They would know the God of Adam, the God of Methuselah, the God of Noah.

They would know the God of Denah.

Points to Ponder and Discuss

Q: How historically accurate is this story?

A: Noah was born almost 1,000 years before Abraham. The historical information we have from this time in history is very limited, found only in the early chapters of Genesis, and all archeological data was destroyed in the flood. Many of the customs associated with Biblical times have yet to be established. There are no Hebrews, no Israelites, no pagans to conquer. There is one people, one language. The earth is one land mass and it never rains. Therefore, the customs and details in my novel are fictional, my representation of how it may have been. How do you envision the earth, its people, and customs before the flood?

Q: Who found grace?

A: The Bible tells us that Noah found grace in the eyes of the Lord (Genesis 6:8). He was blameless and walked with God (6:9). He was a great man of faith (Hebrews 11:7). What about his wife? His sons? In verse 7:1 God tells Noah to take his family onto the ark because "I have found you righteous." The 'you' is singular. Was Noah the only true believer? Did God heap grace on Noah by allowing his family to be preserved?

I took liberty in handing out faults among the characters, Noah included. He was human, after all. Did you find this contrary to scripture, or was it offensive to what you believe about this legendary family?

Q: How long did it take Noah to build the ark?

A: Were you taught in Sunday School that it took Noah 120 years to build the ark? Often the communication from God in Genesis 6:3 and 6:12 are lumped together, but Scripture doesn't actually tell us how long the construction took. If you do the math with the ages of his sons, etc. it seems like it had to be less that 120 years (see Answers in Genesis article; How long did it take Noah to build the ark?, 6/10). We don't know that Noah even knew about the 120 year judgment countdown. This may have been told by God to Moses, after the fact, when Moses was writing Genesis. I gave Noah twenty years to build his vessel, with the help of his sons and hired hands, and I felt that was a generous length of time. It may have been much longer, of course, without outside help and if there was destructive opposition.

Q: How many animals were in the ark?

A: References vary, from 2,000 to 50,000, depending on how species are divided. It seems 16,000 is a common number, each with inherent DNA that allowed for vast variation as they multiplied. Many of these were birds and bugs, not necessarily requiring cages, and large animals probably came as juveniles. The average animal size is that of a sheep, so there would be plenty of room on the ark for them and all the supplies. There are great articles on the internet with detailed theory information.

After God directs his chosen beasts to Noah's land, I didn't portray them all simply marching two by two up the ramp. I gave Noah's family more work to get them situated. I think this portrays the way God frequently works – there is His part and our part. Young David, for example, still had to walk out and confront Goliath. He still had to find those stones and fling the one that killed the giant. Noah got splinters in his hand building that ark, an ark that God could have just spoken into existence. Why do you think God does this? Can you think of examples in your own life?

Q: Why did all the children of the earth die?

A: I struggled with how to portray the death of all the earth's children in the flood. We consider them innocent, and it seems unfair. The Bible says we are all born sinners, however, and there is no promise of a long, pain free life on this earth. As difficult as it is, their deaths weren't unjust. I do believe that children, and some mentally impaired adults, are not held accountable for their sinful nature, unable to choose/reject God. I think the 'Beths' of the land go to heaven. They suffered in their deaths, yes, in the arms of the parents that refused to listen to warnings of judgment. To what extent do you believe parents are accountable for the faith demonstrated by their children?

Q: Wasn't Shem Noah's firstborn?

A: Do an internet search on the birth order of Noah's boys and you'll see justification for about any order you choose. Ham is generally regarded as the youngest because of Genesis 9:24. Shem is listed first in the sequence of names in Genesis 5:32, 7;13, and 9:18, indicating firstborn, but Moses may have put him there because of his importance as the forefather of Abraham. Genesis 10:21 indicates Japheth as the oldest in the NIV, but not all translations word this verse the same way.

I chose Japheth as the eldest and included his loss of firstborn status as we see with Jacob/Esau, Ephraim/Manassah, Joseph/Reuben, and with Shimri in 1 Chronicles 26:10: ...although not the firstborn, his father appointed him the first.

Q: Why did Noah prepare lodging for more than eight people?

A: I didn't portray Noah as having all the information, or completely understanding the information, required for his ark building task. For instance, he believes his preaching will draw hundreds of people to the ark (he doesn't want to believe his preaching is in vain), he underestimates the number of beasts he'll have on board (how many kinds can you name?), and he thinks the ark will rise on the water then settle back down in the same location forty days later (He's never seen rain. How can he visualize a world wide flood?).

Isn't this how God deals with us? We aren't given all the time-lines and details, just asked to step forward in the faith of what He provides. Can you relate to Noah's situation?

Q: Who were the Nephilim?

A: Genesis 6 refers to giants, or nephilim, and 'sons of God.' Who were they? This is another area of debate among Biblical scholars. Essentially there are three theories. The first is the Sethite View: the sons of God are Godly men in the line of Seth, son of Adam, who married ungodly daughters of Cain's lineage. The nephilim are their offspring. The Royalty View says the sons of God are kings who married commoners. The third, Fallen Angel View, believes the sons were heavenly beings that married human women. Check out the articles below for the rationale and objections for each of these, or see my blog at gracebythegallon.com for July 2012.

Bodie Hodge has a great article (Who Were the Nephilim? AnswersinGenesis.org) and so does Tim Chaffey (Battle over the Nephilim, Answersmagazine.com, Jan-Mar 2012).

Q: How old is the earth? Did the flood really happen?

A: I believe in a young earth, created completely by God six thousand years ago in six literal days. See my blog, gracebythegallon.com, Truth in the Text Series, for detailed explanation. Evidence abounds for this belief but the primary reason I accept a young earth age is because God tells us this. I choose to believe God over the theories of man.

I also believe a world wide flood completely altered the land-scape and climate of earth. Again, there is considerable evidence for this. There are hundreds of books and articles available on this topic at the Answers in Genesis website.

What do you believe?

Q: Did Denah deserve salvation?

A: She trusted the power of false gods. She made shameful choices. Her life wasn't built on faith in the One God. But, she did make the right choice eventually. She chose to believe in the God of creation, to trust in His truth. By God's grace, that was enough.

It still is. We all have the tainted blood of Adam. We are all blemished in God's eyes, unfit for His presence. But He has provided a way for us to be sin-free, a way to be holy in the eyes of our Creator. He has given us an ark of salvation, His Son, Jesus. Acknowledge your tainted soul, believe in the saving grace of Jesus, and board the ark of salvation.

Throughout history, God has warned of impending judgment for rebellion against Him. Destruction follows. He has warned us once again of His final judgment and it will occur. God waited patiently for Noah's generation, and He waits now for ours. He won't wait forever. Be ready.

Thank you for reading this book.

About the Author

Rachel S. Neal lives under the Big Sky of Missoula, Montana with her husband, cat and as many daylilies as she can fit into her garden. She believes in the accuracy of God's Word and writes to share those truths in fictional format. When her hands aren't typing, they are transforming discarded remnants into her version of art. You can find out more and visit her at gracebythegallon.com.